SORCERESS

by Ken Warner

River Torsa
Forsaken Hills
MADISON
Orchard Lake
River Mayne
VANCE
STILES
ARTHOS
UNIVERSITY
PERRIN
STROM
ROSES
ULSTER
FOSLAND
River Mayne
OXCART
HIGHGATE
STOUTWALL
Rhun Lake
YORK
SMITHTOWN
STANBRIDGE
MIDDLE MAEDA

NORTH SEA
BLACKSAND
ROCKPORT
HIDO
NORTHCOAST
River Arson
River Tonca
River Morna
River Ember
Spanbrook
River Lago
Forsaken
Hills
DORSHIRE
KONG
UNIVERSITY
Oldport
STOUTWALL
HIGHGATE
River Hale
Keepstone
MAEDA
Mystic Mountains
Bastion
Green Mountains
Great
Desert
WATCHTOWER
Northern Anthar Mountains
LONELY
SEA
BAYFAST
River Ronus
River Xago
River Xago
PYTHA
ETERNAL
SEA
OSTLAND
OKSET
Southern Anthar Mountains
SHIFAR
N
HORN
ANORIA

CONTENTS

SORCERESS

CHAPTER ONE
DEVELOPMENTS

ira sat in the library with the twins, Leda and Alanna. Though her official position was court mage, Jezebel had entrusted her daughters' education to her as well—their book learning, at least. Khaldun taught them magic, and Allison trained them in combat.

Mira could hardly believe the girls were fourteen already—only a couple of years younger than their mother had been when she ascended to the throne. They'd celebrated their birthday only a few weeks earlier. Leda resembled Allison, with her slender figure and long, flaxen locks. Mira hadn't met Allison before her transformation, but Khaldun told her that Leda's fair complexion matched the princess's as well. Alanna was the spitting image of her mother, with her stouter build and dark, curly hair.

"There are no elves in Anoria, are there?" Alanna asked.

"No," Mira confirmed. "They have not been seen here in almost nine hundred years."

"Since Nyro's downfall," Leda said.

"Yes, that's correct," Mira said with a nod. "It is said there's another continent on the other side of the world, and that's where the elves reside."

"How did they defeat Nyro?" Alanna asked. "I thought she was the most powerful mage who ever lived."

"That's true," Mira agreed. "And not much is known about that battle. As the chief mage, Nyro had helped her predecessor conquer almost all of Anoria, and as empress, she ruled with an iron fist for three centuries. But eventually, the lords of every great house united to overthrow her. History tells us only that they had help from the elves, but next to nothing is known about how that came about or the methods used to imprison Nyro and her Sacred Circle."

"But it had to be magic," Alanna said, fiddling with her wand. "Khaldun told us that all the elves are mages."

In the years since Prince Henry's demise and Nyro's liberation, Khaldun had continued Syllith's research, traveling throughout Dorshire and Maeda and scouring every princedom's libraries for information about the Pythan Empire, the elves, and the final battle with Nyro. His study of the elves, in particular, had become something of an obsession. "That's not exactly right," Mira told her. "All elves can call the four basic forces—earth, air, fire, and water."

"Without a wand or staff, right?" said Leda. "They can call magic with their bodies, just like human sorcerers."

"That's right," said Mira. "But *their* mages are the only ones who can call the magical force."

"So, most elves can't make themselves invisible, or cast illusions?" asked Leda.

"Or imbue physical objects with magical properties," said Alanna. "Or detect static spells."

"Do the elves have necromancers?" Leda asked.

"That's an excellent question," Mira said. "And we don't know one way or the other. The references we've found to elvish mages indicate only that they can wield the magical force. But whether they have sorcerers or necromancers, we can't say."

Human sorcerers were different from normal wizards and witches. They underwent a physical transformation, typically between puberty and young adulthood, that turned their skin golden and opened their channels of power, enabling them to practice magic without an instrument.

Becoming a sorcerer was not a choice. Only those who had inherited magic from both parents could become one, though most never did. It was not known what caused some people to undergo the metamorphosis, but Allure, one of the university governors—and a sorcerer—could tell if a mage had the transformation in them.

Any sorcerer could become a necromancer by binding a demon. But only a few of them possessed the spells necessary to complete the rite. It was a closely guarded secret, and since Nyro's downfall, only one sorcerer had attempted it: Myrddin. He'd been Spanbrook's chief mage prior to Princess Jezebel's ascension.

Her Highness had brought the girls to Allure several years ago, when Alanna exhibited her first signs of magic. Jezebel had gone to great lengths to ensure the princedom stayed in her family, and feared that one or both girls might become a sorcerer, making them ineligible to rule. But Allure told her they were too young. She confirmed that Alanna had inherited magic from both parents— much to Jezebel's chagrin. She'd been careful to choose mates with no known history of magic in their families. But Allure couldn't yet tell if she had the transformation in her.

Allure determined that Leda had received magic from only one parent, meaning the girls had different fathers. This was extremely rare for twins, but Jezebel had taken several different men to bed in a short time frame in her attempt to produce an heir. Leda could never become a sorcerer.

Jezebel had always wanted more children, and had tried getting pregnant many times with several different men over the years, but had never been able to conceive after the twins. Mira knew how much this worried her, but she never showed it.

"What were they like?" Alanna asked.

"The elves?" said Mira; the girl nodded. "It's tough to say for sure—no one alive today has ever seen one. And records are scant."

"Khaldun told us that the university purged the libraries of every book or scroll they could find pertaining to Nyro or necromancy," said Leda. "But I don't understand why they included historical texts."

Mira sighed. "Fear can be a powerful motivator. Nyro was the worst kind of tyrant, enslaving the masses and murdering people for sport. Her reign lasted far longer than the lives of her subjects, so Anoria's entire population had known nothing else. The governors wanted to eliminate any possibility of another mage following in Nyro's footsteps. But there's no denying they became overzealous."

"We must have *some* information about them, though," said Alanna. "Otherwise how would we know they overthrew Nyro?"

"Khaldun has found a few texts that mention them," Mira said. "One historian described them as tall and muscular, reaching seven to eight feet in height, with ebony skin, pointy ears, and green eyes. He said their beauty surpassed that of any human he'd ever seen. Another account tells us that their civilization and culture exceeded Anoria's in every way. They possessed weapons and ships far more advanced than ours, and their knowledge of mathematics and engineering eclipsed that of our greatest scholars. Their streets were said to be paved in gold, and their cities' buildings reported to reach the sky."

"The Shifari are tall and dark-skinned," Leda observed. "Are they related to the elves?"

"Another excellent question," Mira said, sitting back in her chair. "We don't know. But that is what the stories suggest."

"Stories?" Alanna asked skeptically. "Like the ones grandfather's nursemaid used to tell him?"

"Yes, exactly," Mira said with a chuckle. "Khaldun has been unable to find any historical record confirming this. But according to oral tradition, the first Shifari came here from the elven continent. They found my people occupying Pytha, so continued across the Anthars to the land we know as Shifar. It was mostly lush rainforest, and unpopulated. So they settled there, and established their kingdom."

"But they can't be elves," said Leda. "Not all of them can do magic."

"*Of course*, they're not elves," Alanna said, rolling her eyes. "They don't have pointy ears or green eyes, either, do they? Just because they're not light-skinned northerners doesn't mean they're elvish."

"Oh, they're human, there's no question about that," said Mira. "And it's unknown what their relationship to the elves might be. But the stories also say they brought magic to Anoria. The people in Pytha had established permanent settlements and developed trade and agriculture, but those living in modern-day Kong, Maeda, and Dorshire were nomadic hunters and gatherers. It is said the Shifari were responsible for introducing agriculture and modern construction techniques to those populations."

"They could have *taught* them how to farm and build cities, but not how to do magic," Leda said. "Unless they already had it in their blood."

"Quite right," Mira agreed. "But over time, many Shifari ended up mating with the natives from the other areas of the continent."

"So, does that mean that anyone with magic has Shifari blood in them?" Alanna asked.

"Yes, if the stories are true. But keep in mind, all of this must have happened thousands of years ago. By the time of the Pythan Empire, the five kingdoms had existed for as long as anyone could remember. Bloodlines have mixed so much over all those years that it would be impossible to trace specific connections at this point."

"I wish I'd been born an elf," Leda said wistfully. "Then I could do magic without a wand."

"And you wouldn't be so freakishly pale," Alanna said.

"Excuse me, ladies," a voice said from behind Mira before Leda could retort. Turning in her seat, she found Emma standing there, leaning on her staff and smiling at them. Her Highness's younger sister had moved into the castle several years ago, and taken over as steward after Oswald's untimely passing. She'd also become a witch, and been reinstated in Jezebel's line of succession once she'd come of age. "I'm afraid the lesson's over for today. Princess Jezebel has asked me to convene the privy council."

"Aw, must she always interrupt just as our discussion is getting interesting?" Leda complained.

"Our discussions are *always* interesting," Alanna said, getting to her feet. "But I still don't understand why *we're* not allowed to attend the council meetings yet. We're nearly the same age mother was when she became princess."

"Be thankful circumstances have not forced you into adulthood ahead of your time," Emma said. "Enjoy your youth while you still can."

"Yeah, yeah, I know," Alanna muttered. "Mother had to travel the continent at a young age uphill both ways in the snow to find a great sorcerer—we've heard this story a thousand times."

The girls collected their books and wands from the table, and headed out of the library toward the living quarters. Mira and Emma went the other way, crossing the atrium. This area was open all the way to the ceiling, four stories up, and hosted numerous long tables with oil lamps for nighttime study. The library's wings extended to either side, all four levels packed with bookshelves, filled from floor to ceiling with tomes both ancient and modern. The library occupied the very heart of the new castle's keep.

Princess Jezebel had long wanted to upgrade Spanbrook's defenses. Everyone here believed Nyro would return in force, and the princess had done everything in her power to prepare for that day. Her earliest efforts had involved repairing and expanding the city's outer wall to include the newer structures. She'd begun considering plans for improving the old castle's fortifications, but the city center was packed so densely that any expansion would have been difficult and expensive. It would have involved tearing down nearby buildings, and thus displacing many of the city's wealthiest, most powerful families.

In the end, though, none of this proved to be necessary. An enormous diamond deposit had been discovered in the hills outside the city, on land the princess already owned. Over the years, this had made Spanbrook one of the richest princedoms in Dorshire, and provided the funds to build a new castle.

Castle Barclay was located just south of the city, and they had modeled it after Castle Stoutwall. Its outer walls were twenty feet thick and rose over forty feet high. It sat in the center of a lake, providing a natural moat that had been dredged to a depth of more than thirty feet. The only way in from land involved crossing the bridge to a small island in the middle of the lake, and then the forty-foot drawbridge to the castle. Inside that were two sets of heavy gates, constructed of multiple layers of hardwood reinforced with iron plates. Twenty feet beyond the gates were the inner walls, also forty feet high and twenty feet thick, and another set of gates.

They kept the moat stocked with demon fish, a venomous breed with razor-sharp teeth. Its poison could kill a full-grown man within five minutes. Khaldun kept a supply of antidote in his chambers in case anyone not invading the castle suffered the misfortune of falling into the moat.

As with all castles, there were hidden escape tunnels built into the structure, but only the members of the privy council knew where to find these. And only Khaldun, Jezebel, and Allison knew about *all* of them. They connected to a network of tunnels beneath the city that ultimately led to various locations beyond the outer walls.

Construction had taken the better part of a decade. Though they'd moved into the castle a couple of years ago, it still felt brand new to Mira. The interior felt like a maze with its expanse of corridors and chambers, and she still got lost on the way to her chambers occasionally.

Though they'd been unable to confirm this, Mira believed Castle Barclay was now the largest single building in Anoria. Others were taller, some by quite a lot. But in terms of square footage, none surpassed it. Unlike some other rulers who had come to possess great wealth, Jezebel wasn't shy about flaunting it. Of course, the princedom had the military and thaumaturgic might to protect it.

"It sounds like Khaldun's obsession might be rubbing off on my nieces," Emma observed with a knowing grin.

"Oh, with the elves?" Mira said. "Yes, that may be. But their thirst for *any* knowledge rivals my own at their age, and that's saying something."

"Good. We wouldn't want any dolts in the family."

Leaving the keep, they found Allison in the courtyard, training with Imani. Badrick had passed away several years earlier, and Jezebel had promoted Imani to master-at-arms. The Shifari had arrived with the Eagle Company, but frequently clashed with its captain. *He'd* wanted to have her transferred to the dungeons, but her military acumen was too valuable to waste.

Mira and Emma stopped to watch for a few minutes. Allison had always been a natural fighter, but Imani had brought her skills to a whole new level. At just over seven feet tall, she towered over the princess, and wearing full plate, she looked like she could squash Allison in her skin-tight, black leather. But Mira knew the princess had been working spells on the material for years; it could turn a blade better than any metal. She had a matching hood and facemask, but never wore those in practice.

An iridescent sheen covered both Imani's plate and Allison's leather. This was an aftereffect of the spell Khaldun had placed on them—and the armor of every knight in their army as well as every soldier's chain mail—to protect against magic. He and Jezebel had encountered dwarves wearing armor with the same enchantment on their way through the Anthar Mountains, and he'd learned the spell soon after. It had no effect on the magical force, so it couldn't remove invisibility, or cancel an illusion. But it would protect their people from the four basic forces, and those were the ones most commonly used in battle.

As Mira watched, Imani swung at the princess with her giant two-handed sword. Allison wielded two longswords; she parried with one and sliced at her with the other. Imani darted out of range before lunging in to stab her in the chest.

Allison sidestepped. Suddenly, one of her blades disappeared, a dagger taking its place an instant later. Among her many talents, the princess had mastered void magic, enabling her to move weapons into or out of oblivion very quickly. She stepped in, pinning Imani's arms with one elbow and sticking the knife into the gap between her chest plate and helmet. "Yield!"

Imani chuckled. Freeing one arm, she pinned Allison's knife arm to her chest, pulling the dagger away from her throat. Lifting the princess off her feet with her sword arm, she hurled her away from her. Allison went horizontal, spinning in midair, her ponytail whipping around her, before landing on her feet as Imani charged with an overhead blow. She deflected her blade with her sword, stepping behind her and jumping on her back, wrapping her legs around her torso. Her sword vanished; she used that hand to pull Imani's head back, slipping the knife through the gap in her neck again. "Yield!" Allison shouted once more.

Imani struggled mightily, trying to throw Allison off of her, but the princess held on. Finally, she collapsed on her hands and knees, dropping her sword and laughing.

"Yield, you crazy bitch!" Allison yelled. "You'd be dead three times by now!"

"All right, Princess. I yield."

As the ruling monarch's wife, the title was hers, even if "princess consort" was more accurate, but Jezebel and Allison both eschewed their honorifics as much as possible. While most of the staff derived amusement from Jezebel's grimaces when addressed with them, Allison's threats of physical violence engendered only fear. Nobody called her "princess" to her face. Except Imani.

The two had had a short but torrid love affair soon after Imani's arrival. Due to the necessity of taking men to bed to make babies, Jezebel had always insisted on allowing Allison the freedom to take other lovers, too. Yet Allison had never shown any inclination to do so before Imani—or since. And despite having Jezebel's consent, Allison had felt horribly guilty afterward. While Jezebel's trysts had been borne of pragmatism, Allison's were the result of unbridled passion.

"*Do not* address me that way!" Allison said, getting off of Imani's back and trying to push her over.

Imani only chuckled, getting to her feet and removing her helmet, revealing her short, black hair. Spotting Mira and Emma, she smiled, taking Mira's breath away. Imani was the most beautiful woman she'd ever seen. She wasn't normally attracted to females, but there was something about Imani that never failed to arouse her. The effect was similar to being in Allure's presence, only not quite as strong, and Imani was no mage.

"Allison, Lord Commander," said Emma, "Her Highness has requested your presence in her council chambers."

"I wish she'd refrain from these surprise meetings," Allison said. "It would be nice to bathe first."

"Don't worry, Princess, I can smell only your perfume," Imani told her. Allison glared at her. "Boy!" she added, summoning her squire. Tomas hurried over; Mira hadn't noticed him standing by the armory. He helped her out of her armor, and handed her a change of clothes, blushing as she stripped out of her undergarments. Having no qualms about public nudity was one of the woman's many peculiarities.

Allison didn't bother changing; her leather suit was much more comfortable than Imani's plate. Mira accompanied the women into the castle. The building's front section included the great hall, throne room, and administrative offices. They climbed the stairs to the council chambers, located above the offices. Jezebel, Khaldun, Camilla, Gregor, and the delegates were already here.

Camilla's twin sister, Gemma, had gone missing many years ago, not long after Fosland's defeat. She'd gone out to the market and never returned. Khaldun had gone looking for her, but she'd vanished without a trace. Camilla hadn't been the same since. Mira hadn't known her well prior to Gemma's disappearance, but knew from others that she'd become quiet and withdrawn.

The university had assigned Gregor to Spanbrook to replace Gemma. He'd been a young wizard, having graduated only a few years earlier. Camilla had taken him under her wing during his first few years, continuing his education. His confidence had grown over the years, and he'd become an indispensable part of the princess's staff.

After the conflict with Henry, Spanbrook had formed a consortium with five of the six bordering princedoms. Only Wayland had refused to join. Initially, the group had hired the Eagle Company collectively. Spanbrook had raised a standing army of ten thousand, and each of the other member princedoms had established a military force as well, though none as large as Spanbrook's. Officers from the Eagle Company had trained them all.

But the Eagle Company didn't come cheap, and some of the other monarchs had balked at extending their contract when the time came. They had their armies, so they no longer felt the mercenary unit was necessary. That was soon after the discovery of diamonds in Spanbrook, so Jezebel had decided to rehire the company on her own. They served as the army's elite guard, and had added the best of Spanbrook's soldiers to their ranks, swelling their number to over six hundred.

A few years later, Prince Reuben's son assassinated him and claimed Wayland's throne for his own. He'd petitioned to join the consortium and apologized for his father's actions against Spanbrook. The rest of the rulers welcomed Wayland into the fold.

Not long after that, they'd received word that Keepstone, the capital of the old kingdom, had annexed a few neighboring princedoms. Fearing the rise of a new warlord, the consortium's rulers had voted unanimously to consolidate, creating a single, unified princedom, with Princess Jezebel as its ruler. With Spanbrook's three sorcerers, military might, and economic prowess, it only made sense for her to be the leader. Each of the other sovereigns retained control of their respective territories as provinces of the larger whole, and sent delegates to serve in Jezebel's court for four-year terms. The delegates and their families lived in the old castle.

The others wanted to declare Jezebel the "high princess," but after Henry's reign, the term had left a bad taste in her mouth. She'd insisted on keeping the title of "princess." And in the end, their fears had proven to be unfounded. After sending an envoy to Keepstone, they'd learned that Prince Leto had formed a union with several of his neighbors, similar to their own consortium. The envoy had found no evidence of aggression against the surrounding princedoms.

Jezebel got to her feet as Mira and the others entered the chambers. Allison strode across the room to her, embracing her and kissing her deeply. Though their comfort with public displays of affection offended some, Mira had to smile. Their passion for each other had only grown over the years.

Jezebel retook her seat at the head of the table, Allison to her right. As Spanbrook's chief mage, Khaldun always sat to her left. This also kept him across the table from Imani, which he'd told Mira was a good thing, as close proximity to her distracted him. Emma sat down next to Khaldun, and Imani left one chair empty next to Allison, taking the next one. Mira sat down next to Imani; she didn't mind the distraction. Invariably, her lovemaking sessions with Khaldun were more intense after spending some time next to this woman.

Camilla and the delegates had taken the remaining seats. Moments later, Captain Amari of the Eagle Company arrived, taking the seat Imani had left for him. Amari was short for a Shifari, rising only to a little over six feet. His head was shaved clean, he wore an eye-patch over his left eye, and there was a scar running down the right side of his face.

"Good morning, everyone," Jezebel said, smiling around at them, "and thank you for joining us on such short notice. We've had strange reports from Rockport that I wanted to bring to your attention. Emma?"

One of Jezebel's early initiatives as princess had been to improve communication between Spanbrook and the other powers in Dorshire and Maeda. There had been no sign of Nyro anywhere on the continent since her liberation, but if she were to show up, Jezebel wanted to know about it right away. Toward this aim, she had sent Khaldun to deliver mirrors to all the major cities that they could use to contact each other. Such arrangements had already been put in place with the university, Highgate, and Stoutwall. Keepstone and the Bastion had refused, their rulers distrustful of magic and unwilling to believe that Nyro had survived so many centuries in any form. Salerna had tried establishing ties with Okset and Horn in Shifar with much the same result. But most of the others had agreed. Managing these communications had become one of Emma's many duties.

Khaldun's mirror was tied in to all of the others as well, as were Allison's and Mira's. They'd discovered long ago that Mira could use a mirror to communicate, as long as her channels of power were closed. It took magic to show the other person's image in the mirror, but not to see that image. That was why non-mages could use mirrors this way, too.

Mira had worried that one of the others could use their mirror to eavesdrop on their conversations, but it didn't work that way. A mirror could be used to communicate with only one other at a time, and there was no way to override or tap into an active connection.

"Princess Jelena's steward told me that several of their people have seen unusual beings moving through the forest outside the city," Emma said. "The crew of one of their merchant ships spotted two of them from the sea, walking along the shore. And then a farmer saw one moving through his fields. He gave chase, but the being disappeared in the trees."

"What kind of 'being', exactly?" said Khaldun.

"Tall ones—at least seven feet—with ebony skin and lean, muscular bodies," Emma said with a knowing grin. "The farmer got a closer look, and he says the one he saw had green eyes and pointy ears."

"Elves?" Khaldun said, sitting up straight. "There are elves in Rockport? What are they doing there?" Mira had to stifle a giggle; she knew how eager he was to meet an elf.

"They don't know," Emma said with a shrug.

"Jelena would like us to send someone to investigate," Jezebel said. "Given our sorcerers' ability to detect magic, she figures one of them would be best suited to tracking these *beings* down, and I agree. All elves possess magic, don't they?"

"I'll go," Khaldun said. "I can leave immediately."

"I'm sending Allison," Jezebel said. Shortly after Fosland's defeat, Azure had made flying carpets for Dorshire and Maeda's remaining sorcerers. In fact, he'd made extra, so most of them had a spare they kept with them at all times, tucked into the void in case of an emergency. Allison had been reluctant to try it at first, but over time, had become as good a flyer as Khaldun.

Khaldun oozed disappointment, but didn't object.

"Your Highness, I should accompany Princess Allison," said Imani. "We have no way to know if these invaders are friendly or not."

"I'm pretty sure I can handle this myself," Allison said, producing a dagger out of thin air and cleaning her nails. "You just want to go for a carpet ride."

"I agree with Imani," said Jezebel. "No one here doubts your fighting prowess, but this could be dangerous. A prelude to an invasion, perhaps. Imani will go with you."

Allison nodded, tucking the weapon back into the void.

"Prelude to an invasion?" Khaldun repeated with a frown. "Do you truly think so? The elves were the ones who defeated Nyro before leaving Anoria in peace. We have no evidence that they've become hostile toward us."

"Nor do we have any evidence to the contrary," Imani said. "It's been centuries since we've had any contact with them. We have no way of knowing *what* their intentions might be."

"And it's been a decade and a half since Nyro's escape," Jezebel said. "What has she been doing all this time? Where has she been? She *told* you she's planning on establishing a new empire; perhaps she's enlisted the elves' help."

Mira didn't want to believe this any more than Khaldun did. But she had to admit anything was possible.

"In that case, maybe I should go, too," Khaldun suggested.

"Oh, no," Jezebel said, shaking her head. "*You're* going to Blacksand."

"Blacksand?" Mira said with a start. She'd spent half of her formative years there and inherited her father's holding before her transformation into a sorcerer. But she'd had no contact with anyone there since. Khaldun had delivered them a mirror, but spoke only to the prince's steward.

"Yes, and I'd like you to go with him," Jezebel said. "Prince Carlo's youngest daughter found something intriguing in their library. A reference to some historian who was chronicling Nyro's defeat and the fall of the Pythan Empire."

Mira had accompanied Khaldun on most of his missions to the other princedoms, especially when they were building their alliances and establishing communications. Other than Allison, Mira was the only member of Jezebel's staff who'd been raised a highborn, and Allison no longer had any patience for diplomacy. Mira had proven to have a certain knack for it, having helped persuade more than a few rulers to join them who otherwise would have demurred. She'd fallen ill right before Khaldun's trip to Blacksand, though, so hadn't gone with him that time.

"Wait—a historian who was alive at that time?" Khaldun said. Mira wasn't sure if he'd been more excited about news of the elves, or this.

"The book she was reading dates from that era," Jezebel said. "Carlo and his family are true believers. I daresay they fear Nyro's return nearly as much as we do. He's had his daughter scouring their library for any record of those days, and this is the first she's found. But they have no sorcerers."

Many times, people had concealed ancient texts by tucking them into the void. Only a sorcerer could detect such a hiding place. For this reason, Khaldun had spent much time revisiting the libraries Syllith had already searched in her day. She'd been a normal witch at the time, so he was able to find things she never could.

"We'll leave immediately," Khaldun said, pushing his chair back from the table.

"That won't be necessary," Jezebel told him. "You can depart in the morning. Tonight, we're holding a feast."

"A feast?" Mira repeated. "For what?"

Jezebel turned to Allison, taking her hand. Allison smiled.

"I'm pregnant," Jezebel announced.

CHAPTER TWO
BLACKSADD

hat evening, they held the feast in the keep's private hall. Jezebel and Allison had invited only the members of their household, the delegates, and the city's noble families. They ended up with about fifty people in attendance, filling the room to capacity. The great hall could accommodate ten times that number, but they reserved that for state functions that would include the vassals, merchants, and nearby landowners.

Jezebel and Allison always wore identical dresses, one in black and the other in white. Sometimes they chose a traditional look, but tonight, Allison had settled on something less formal, with a low neckline, bare back, and a slit running high up one leg. They also wore matching diamond necklaces, either of which was worth more than most princedoms. Alanna and Leda wore matching gowns, Mira and Khaldun wore their mage's robes, and Amari and Imani their military dress uniforms.

Once everyone had arrived, Jezebel invited them to take their seats. Mira and Khaldun joined the royal family, Emma, and the two soldiers at the head table. The staff served wine, and they drank a toast to Jezebel and her baby; Jezebel drank only water. The food arrived, and they dug in. After several courses, and a few more glasses of wine, Mira was quite full and pleasantly inebriated.

Jezebel, Imani, and Amari got up to hobnob with the guests, and Allison leaned in toward the twins, asking, "So, how do you two feel about having a new sibling?"

"I can't wait," Leda said, smiling from ear to ear. "I hope it's a boy—I've always wanted a baby brother."

"I don't mind," Alanna said with a shrug. "I'm hoping to become a sorcerer, and this will ensure there's another heir. At least this one will know who their father is."

Jezebel had done her best to obfuscate her children's paternal bloodline. She wanted to eliminate any possibility of someone outside the family having a claim to the throne. Not even Jezebel knew who the girls' fathers were. But she'd hinted that there would be no doubt this time. Mira knew Jezebel's confidence had grown along with her power, and she no longer feared her offspring being usurped, obviating the need for multiple mates.

"Eventually, perhaps," Allison said with a devious grin. "But so far, I'm the only other one who knows."

"*We* know who it is," Alanna said, rolling her eyes.

"Alanna, *no!*" Leda hissed.

"How could you?" Allison said, her eyebrows raised in surprise. "We took every precaution to keep his identity a secret!"

"Oh, yes, let's see," Alanna said dramatically, "you concealed yourselves behind an invisibility spell and sneaked up to the roof, before taking off on your carpet. Only you made quite a bit of noise, so once I'd made the two of *us* invisible, we followed you up there. It was nighttime, so you didn't bother staying invisible as you flew out to the wayfarer camp east of town."

"What?!" Khaldun said, nearly spitting out his wine. "The father is a *wayfarer*?"

The wayfarers had spent nearly three months in Spanbrook, their first visit since Mira's arrival. It had been good to see her people again. Badru had hardly aged, but that was more than Mira could say for her mother, Nareen. The woman could barely walk anymore, and Badru told her she'd nearly died from a lung infection several months before. With Jezebel's blessing, Mira had begged her to come live in the castle, but Nareen wouldn't hear of it. She'd been born among the wayfarers, and she'd die there, she'd insisted. Badru promised Mira they'd continue taking care of her.

"You couldn't possibly know which one," Allison said, her cheeks turning a darker shade of gold. Mira knew this was the sorcerer's equivalent of blushing.

"Oh yes, we do," Alanna said defiantly.

"Alanna, *shut up*," Leda hissed.

"You waited until their last night in Spanbrook, which was smart," Alanna continued. "The wayfarers' visits tend to be decades apart, so there's very little chance of any of them spreading gossip to the people of Spanbrook. And you only went to his tent that once. I'm pretty sure no one else noticed. But we saw you both flirting with him when the wayfarers performed for the castle."

"Who?" Khaldun demanded as Allison hid her face in her hands. "Which one was it?"

"Well, by the time we got there, they were both inside his tent, but we could *hear* them," Alanna said with a giggle. "And that sounded like a three-way to me—"

"Alanna!" Allison said. Mira had never seen her so mortified.

"I mean, we know *you* don't like men, but it sounded like mother quite enjoyed both of you—"

"That's enough!" Emma said, failing to stifle a giggle of her own. "You will *not* repeat a word of this to *anyone*, do you understand?" She gazed around as if to make sure no one was listening. Mira didn't think they could be; the din of conversation in the room had grown quite loud, and the musicians had started playing.

"Oh, don't worry," Alanna said, sitting back with a satisfied smile. "Your secret's safe with us."

"It's safe with *me*, anyway," Leda said, her face bright red. "We agreed we wouldn't tell them what we'd done!"

Alanna only shrugged.

"So, *who was it*?" Khaldun demanded.

"They shouldn't tell us," Mira admonished, slapping his arm.

"The brewer," Alanna said, shooting Khaldun a conspiratorial smile.

"*Riyan*?!"

"Alanna!" said Emma.

"Yes, I think that was his name. He was very cute; *I* wouldn't mind bearing him a child."

"*Alanna!*" said Allison. "You are such a brat!"

"I'm only kidding, mother," Alanna said, rolling her eyes. "I don't want children. But he *was* handsome."

"I think so, too," Mira said. "Your mothers chose well."

"What did we choose well?" Jezebel asked, returning to the table at that moment. The rest of them held their breath for a second, then broke out laughing. "What did I miss?" she asked, looking confused.

"I'll tell you later," Allison said, getting to her feet. "Right now, I want to dance."

Jezebel took her by the hand and escorted her across the room, and they started dancing. Several other couples joined them, and one of the nobles came over to their table. Emma stood up and kissed him before hurrying off to dance.

"Was that Lord Asterly's younger son?" Mira asked; Khaldun nodded. "I had no idea they were a couple."

"They've been courting for months, now," Alanna said. "He's already proposed, but Emma turned him down."

"What? Why?" asked Mira.

"He wants her to come live with him in his estate," Alanna said. "But it's outside of town, and she doesn't want to resign from her post. She likes being steward and living in the castle."

"I can hardly blame her," Mira said. "I like living here, too. But she'll want to get married eventually."

"Emma's waiting him out," Alanna said. "She's pretty sure he'll agree to come live here instead if she withholds sex long enough."

Mira gasped. "Emma did *not* tell you that!"

"Of course not," Alanna said, rolling her eyes. "We had to spy on them to find *that* out."

Mira shook her head in disbelief.

The musicians played an old folk tune, and Mira and Khaldun got up to join the rest of the couples in a group dance that involved frequently swapping partners. Mira ended up with Imani at one point, and felt ridiculously short. The physical contact with her proved to be quite arousing, and when the dance was finished, she grabbed Khaldun. They bade the princesses goodnight, and hurried up to their chambers.

Mira pushed him onto the bed, climbing on top of him and kissing him as she removed first his clothes, and then her own. They made love for hours, each of them climaxing several times. Finally spent, they lay quietly in each other's arms, and Khaldun drifted off within moments.

Mira lay there for a little while, enjoying the last of the alcohol's effects, and the cool breeze coming in through the windows. She wasn't feeling sleepy yet, though. Slipping out of bed, she donned her robe, and opened the doors to their balcony. Stepping outside, she leaned against the railing, gazing out at the courtyard. From this vantage point on the top floor, she had a view of the city over the castle walls.

Taking a few deep breaths of fresh air, she spotted Emma walking arm-in-arm with the young Lord Asterly. They moved to a quiet corner and started kissing, and Mira was about to go back inside when she heard an odd noise. It sounded like quiet giggling, somewhere directly below her. Realizing what was going on, Mira opened her channels of power, extending her null. Alanna and Leda suddenly became visible, and Alanna gasped.

Emma must have heard her, because she called out, "Alanna and Leda Barclay! Are you spying on me *again*?"

The girls hurried off, both of them giggling as they went inside the keep.

"Brats!" Emma exclaimed before returning her attention to the gentleman.

Mira closed her channels of power again, chuckling as she moved inside, dropping her robe and sliding back into bed. Her null's resting state had been small at first, but kept growing. Keeping her channels of power closed during the day was no problem. But in the beginning, she didn't know how to keep them closed while she slept—she didn't even know if it would be possible.

This had the potential to become problematic. Were there a nighttime attack, Spanbrook's mages would need their magic to help combat the enemy. And before long, her null's resting state had expanded to encompass most of the castle.

The princess owned a private villa up in the hills that had traditionally been used as a vacation home for the royal family. Mira and Khaldun had gone to live there while Mira worked on her control. It took a few months, but finally, she learned how to keep her channels closed while she slept. Now, that was her normal resting state, and she only projected her null during practice sessions with the other mages, or when foiling the twins' shenanigans.

Finally growing drowsy, Mira drifted off to sleep. Khaldun woke her with a kiss in the morning. The two of them bathed together, then donned the leather suits Allison had made for them. They could deflect weapons like the princess's, but Mira's didn't have the same enchantments as the others; being a null, she had no need for those. They wore their mage's robes over the leather, and Mira donned her sword belt over that. In addition to her longsword, she kept one dagger in the belt, and another strapped to one leg. She kept her hood and facemask tucked into the belt unless she needed them. Khaldun kept his weapons and head covering in the void, tethered to his person.

They went down to the private hall for breakfast, joining Jezebel, Allison, Emma, and the twins. Leda's eyes were red and puffy, Alanna seemed sullen, and Jezebel wore a stern expression.

"Is everything all right?" Khaldun asked with an amused grin as they took their seats.

"Yes," Jezebel said, "it is, now that we've educated our children about the importance of granting their mothers some privacy and keeping their royal noses out of other people's business."

"Ah," Mira said, stifling a giggle. She had no doubt the girls would be back at it in no time.

Once they'd finished eating, Jezebel wished Allison, Khaldun, and Mira luck, embracing them each in turn, and the sorcerers headed out to the courtyard. They met Imani, and Khaldun and Allison each removed their carpets from the void. Khaldun's had special straps built into it so that Mira could fly with him. With her channels of power closed, the spells necessary to operate the carpet could function, but no magic would work on *her*. Without the earth spells that would keep Khaldun firmly in place, Mira needed the straps to keep her from falling off.

Mira sat down behind Khaldun, strapped herself in, and held him tight around the midsection. The only trouble with flying this way was that her muscles ached terribly, requiring extra stops on long journeys to get up and stretch.

Allison sat at the front of her carpet, Imani at the rear, and she shot into the sky. Khaldun took off, giving chase. The two of them raced each other for a few minutes, flying wildly and causing Imani and Mira to scream—Imani for joy and Mira out of sheer terror. But finally, Khaldun had to turn west toward Blacksand.

They stopped once, landing in a clearing in the forest below, then took off again once Mira had had a chance to work out her stiff muscles. It was late afternoon when they reached Blacksand City. Mira had been here only once before, many years ago, but it was exactly as she remembered it. Stone walls encircled the town, but dozens of houses lay beyond them. Blacksand was unique, as far as Mira knew, in that the capital city was not the princedom's largest. Gemstone-by-the-Sea was located on the coast, where the River Arcon met the North Sea, and boasted Dorshire's second largest port after Oldport. The capital was about twenty miles up the river. They landed in the courtyard, getting to their feet and stretching. A man and a young woman hurried out to meet them. Mira spotted a wand sticking out of the bosom of the woman's dress.

"Lady Mira and Lord Khaldun, I presume?" the man asked.

"Yes," Mira replied.

The man bowed, then said, "I am Jasper, the prince's steward, and this is Princess Yolanda."

"It's a pleasure to meet you," Mira said.

"Please, come inside," the princess said.

Mira had never met Yolanda before, but her reputation preceded her. After her mother had passed away a few years earlier, she'd taken on most of the duties of a princess consort. She managed the royal household, arranged all state functions, and served as a witch to boot. The truly remarkable thing was that she'd been only fourteen years old when her mother died, yet she'd carried out her role with the dignity and aplomb one would expect of an adult. Though she looked her age now at seventeen, she certainly carried herself like someone much older.

Khaldun rolled up the carpet and tucked it into the void, then the princess led them quickly across the courtyard. Mira did her best to keep up.

"Ancient history has always fascinated me," she told them. "The rise and fall of the Pythan Empire in particular. I do hope you might find something interesting in our library."

"Your Highness," Jasper said, "It would be improper to proceed without taking our guests to meet your father first."

"He can wait," she said, undeterred, leaving the steward behind.

Mira and Khaldun followed her inside and up to the second floor. Though smaller than Spanbrook's, the library was larger than most Mira had seen. The princess took them to a table along the back wall, pointing out a book she'd left open.

"This is where I found the reference to the old historian," she told them, pointing to the top of one page. "A wizard named Ronaldo wrote this. He was Blacksand's chief mage in the first days of the princedom, right after Nyro's downfall. Earlier in the book, he says that he participated in the final battle, but gives no account of it. But here, he says that his colleague, another mage named Bernard, spent days interviewing him to record his recollections. I've checked the rest of the book, and there's no other mention of Nyro or the final battle. His only interest was the founding of Blacksand. But that's encouraging, isn't it? Bernard worked *here*, so it would make sense if he hid his work somewhere in this very room."

"Yes, it certainly would," Khaldun agreed, leaning in closer to read the text for himself. "May I take a look around?"

"Yes, please!"

Khaldun returned to the library's entrance, walking methodically up and down the aisles, holding both hands out in front of him. Mira knew he was searching for hidden magic. Finally, he found something in the rear corner of the room. "This is it," he said, tapping one of the stones that made up the floor. He held out one hand and the stone disappeared.

"It was an illusion," said Mira.

"Yes, and it had probably been in place for centuries," Khaldun said. "Look at this," he said, squatting down and smiling up at Mira.

Mira moved in to get a look, and saw a wooden chest sitting in the cavity. He removed it, setting it on the floor. Opening the lid, he revealed an ornate scroll lying inside.

The princess gasped. "May I?"

"Of course," Khaldun said, straightening up.

Yolanda lifted the scroll out of the chest and unrolled it. "I'll be damned," she muttered as she read it.

"What is it?" Khaldun asked.

Yolanda showed him. "Bernard wrote this in his old age. He says he recorded everything he could learn about Nyro's final battle, but had to keep it hidden. The university kept sending mages to find and destroy materials documenting anything related to the necromancer. He didn't believe he had much longer to live, and couldn't trust anyone else to keep his work hidden. So, he made one final voyage to take it beyond the university's reach."

"Beyond their reach?" Mira repeated. "There is no such place. They have jurisdiction over the entire continent."

"This says he took it to Ostland," Khaldun said, pointing to the scroll. "The men who accompanied him built an underground chamber, with a small structure on the surface providing access to a stairway. Look, he's included a map. Without this, no one would ever find the place."

"I don't understand," Mira said, gazing at the map. "If the university had sent a sorcerer here, they could have found this just like you did. Then they could have traveled to Ostland and destroyed whatever he left there."

"There have never been many sorcerers at the university," Khaldun pointed out. "And it's a big continent. The odds were good that only normal mages would come here. And the fact that this is still here proves the point; no witch or wizard could have found it.

"Also, Ostland is uninhabited. There are no princedoms, so technically, the university *doesn't* have jurisdiction there."

"More than that, the island is filled with dangerous beasts," the princess said. "It's one big jungle. The university would have to be crazy to send someone there. I don't understand how Bernard and his people made it out alive, but it's extremely unlikely anyone else would ever risk going there."

"That's what I always thought, but it turns out it's not true," said Khaldun. "Imani told me about this long ago. She confirmed Ostland is a jungle, but there are no dangerous animals. That's a rumor the ancient kings of Shifar started centuries ago. They wanted to preserve the island in its pristine, uninhabited condition, and they figured spreading such stories would deter people from trying to settle there."

"They were right," Mira said. "Bernard must have known the truth."

"So it would seem," Khaldun agreed. "I think we've got a long journey ahead of us. Can we take this?" he asked the princess.

"I'm sure that would be all right, but it's my father's decision," Yolanda said.

Khaldun returned the chest to its cavity and restored the illusion of the stone, then he and Mira followed Yolanda to the throne room. She introduced them to her father. He was tall and thin, his features sharp.

"Ah, Lady Mira," he said with a smile, "it's good to see you again. And a pleasure to meet you, Lord Khaldun. I am happy to learn fortune has smiled upon the two of you."

"Thank you, Your Highness," said Mira.

Prince Carlo granted them permission to take the scroll, and invited them to stay for dinner and spend the night at the castle before departing. But they had a long journey ahead of them, and Khaldun felt it would be best to get underway immediately. "I'll need to check in with Princess Jezebel, first, of course, but I have little doubt she'll approve."

"We're sorry to see you leave so soon," Carlo said. "You'll need provisions, though. I don't imagine you planned for such a long trip before leaving Spanbrook."

"That is true," Khaldun admitted.

Khaldun used his mirror to contact Jezebel. As expected, she authorized their extended mission. The prince had his steward see to their needs. He supplied them with enough food and water for several days, along with a tent and bedrolls, and packs to carry it all. Mira and Khaldun thanked him profusely, then bade him and his daughter farewell, and headed out to the courtyard. Khaldun pulled his carpet out of the void and unfurled it on the ground. They took their seats, placing the packs by the front and rear edges, and Mira strapped herself in.

But before they took off, she said, "Do you think we could make one quick stop before leaving Blacksand?"

"Sure, what do you have in mind?"

Mira hadn't thought about her ancestral home much since settling down in Spanbrook. But now that they were here, she found that she missed her people. It would be nice to see them again. She expressed her thoughts to Khaldun.

"I would enjoy visiting Graystone with you," he said.

They took off, reaching the holding a half hour later. It seemed smaller than ever after living in Castle Barclay, but the cozy familiarity of it brought tears to Mira's eyes. They landed in the courtyard, and an old witch came out to meet them.

"Belinda?" Mira said, getting to her feet. She couldn't believe how much she'd aged.

"Lady Mira?" the woman said, stopping in her tracks with an expression of disbelief. "I never thought I'd see you again."

Mira hugged her, crying freely. It felt so good to see her old mentor again.

A portly, redheaded man emerged from the keep. It took Mira a moment to recognize him; he was quite a bit larger than she remembered, and had grown a beard in her absence. "Mira?"

"Charles, it's good to see you again," she said, embracing him. "This is my husband and the chief mage of Spanbrook, Lord Khaldun."

"It's a pleasure," Khaldun said, shaking his hand.

Charles invited them inside, introducing them to his wife, Chiana, and their five young children. The old steward, Reginald, checked in, his eyes welling up when he saw Mira. They spent some time catching up, and Charles invited them to stay for dinner. Mira told them they needed to get underway, but more of the household arrived as word of Mira's return spread, and she found it difficult to get away.

In the end, they agreed to stay for dinner and spend the night. They would leave the next morning at first light. An hour later, the entire group took their seats in the great hall for their meal.

Mira and Khaldun sat with Belinda and some of the other household staff. She hadn't realized how profoundly she'd missed this woman. Belinda wanted to hear about everything Mira had done since her departure, and was particularly interested to learn about her involvement in the war against Fosland.

Mira and Khaldun were enjoying the food and the company. But midway through dinner, three men arrived, hurrying to the head table to speak with Charles. Mira could tell from his expression that something was wrong. Getting to her feet, she went to see what was going on, Khaldun right behind her. The men stopped talking as she approached.

"What is it?" Mira asked.

"Tell them," Charles said, nodding to the men.

"Sorry for interrupting your meal, my lord and lady," one of them said. "But we were out hunting, and saw something we can't explain. There were three of them, men maybe, but much taller than any man I've ever seen, with emerald green eyes and pointy ears. Armed to the teeth, too, they were, carrying swords and spears. In my sixty years hunting in these woods, I ain't never seen the likes of these folks."

"That's because they're not men," Khaldun told him, bouncing with excitement. "They're elves. We received reports of them in Rockport, too."

"Elves?" Charles said. "In Anoria? After all these centuries? What do they want?"

"We don't know yet," said Mira. "What happened when you encountered them?"

"Well, as I say, we were hunting, and we caught sight of something moving in the trees. As we drew closer, it became apparent it was something big. They stepped out from behind some trees, and we were nearly on top of them. Gave us quite the fright, not being what we expected. But they only stared at us for a moment, then disappeared—vanished into thin air, I mean to say."

"Could you take us to where you saw them?" Mira asked the hunter.

"Reckon we could," he said. "But it'll be getting dark soon, and I don't fancy running into them folks again."

"Just get us close and point us in the right direction, and we'll take it from there," Khaldun assured him.

CHAPTER THREE
PREDICTION

haldun and Mira followed the lead hunter out of the castle; the other two refused to join them. By the time they moved into the trees, the daylight had failed. Khaldun called a flame to light their way. Mira had explored these woods extensively as a girl, but didn't remember her way. Full night fell as they walked, and a light fog settled around them. A wolf howled in the distance, sending a shiver down Mira's spine.

Several more minutes passed, and finally, the hunter stopped them as they crested a hill. "That's the place, right down there," he whispered, pointing toward the bottom of the hill. "They stepped out from behind those three big trees."

Mira neither saw nor heard anything, but the hunter left them, hurrying back toward the castle.

"Let's have a look," Khaldun said. Mira followed him to the trees. Holding out one hand, he said, "Someone cast an invisibility spell here. I can feel it."

"Can you do the magic to show what happened here?"

Khaldun nodded, closing his eyes. Nothing happened for a few moments, but finally, the scene changed. It was daylight, and three enormous forms stood next to them, towering over Mira and startling her. She gasped, backing away several steps. These had to be elves. They stood at least seven feet tall, probably closer to eight, their green eyes gleaming in the sunlight. Two had long, black hair, pulled back in a braid, while the third was bald; all three had pointed ears.

Each had a sword hanging from their belt and two carried spears. After only a few seconds, they vanished, and night returned.

"That's as much as I can see," Khaldun told her. He gazed farther along the path, holding out one arm. "They must have covered their trail—I can't sense their movement."

"Unless they left the path, they must have gone that way," Mira said. "Why don't we keep going and see what we can find?"

Khaldun nodded.

They continued farther into the forest, and Khaldun kept his senses open to magical evidence of the elves' passage. He found nothing, but several minutes later, Mira spotted a twinkling light up ahead. Grabbing Khaldun by the arm, she stopped in her tracks, trying to see what it was.

"Looks like a campfire," Khaldun whispered. "Let's get in closer."

"Should you make us invisible first?" No magic worked directly on Mira, but the invisibility spell would create a barrier around them, hiding everything within from anyone on the outside, including her.

"I don't think so. We should make contact if we can, and appearing out of nowhere could give the impression of hostile intent."

"They *were* heavily armed," Mira said. "I'm afraid *their* intent could be hostile."

Khaldun pressed ahead without replying. Mira followed, her anxiety rising. As they drew closer, she could hear low voices, but couldn't tell what they were saying. Three figures became visible through the trees, silhouetted against the light of the fire. Suddenly, everything went quiet while Mira and Khaldun were still about fifty feet away.

"Hello," Khaldun called out.

The fire disappeared.

"I don't think they're interested in having visitors," Mira said, her heart hammering in her chest. "Perhaps we should go back."

"Nonsense," Khaldun said. "But be ready with your null, just in case."

Mira followed him the rest of the way to a clearing in the trees. They found the remains of a fire, but it was cold, and there was no other evidence of the elves.

"They couldn't have disappeared so quickly," Khaldun said, gazing out into the trees.

"One of them must be a mage," Mira observed.

"I've tried canceling invisibility spells, but there are none here. Try extending your null—perhaps there's some other spell in place that I can't sense."

Mira opened her channels of power, and her null burst into existence, spreading out into the forest. But there was no change in their surroundings.

"*PURSUE US AT YOUR PERIL!*" a voice boomed out, sending a shiver down Mira's back. It sounded like it was coming from all around them.

"We should get out of here," Mira said, a quaver in her voice. "They certainly don't *sound* friendly."

"Yes," Khaldun said, sounding crestfallen. "Perhaps you're right."

Mira extinguished her null in case he needed to work magic and set off along their backtrail, Khaldun lighting their way with a larger flame than he'd conjured before. A deep sense of dread overcame her, and it felt like the trees were closing in around them. She breathed deeply as she moved, trying to stave off a panic attack.

But they made it back to the castle without further incident. They found Charles waiting for them outside the gate. The two of them gave him a quick recap of what they'd found as they headed inside, and he closed and barred the heavy wooden doors behind them.

"It sounds like quite the harrowing experience," he said with a frown. "Elves in Blacksand... I never thought I'd see the day."

"We should get word to Prince Carlo right away," Mira suggested.

"Yes," Charles agreed with a frown. "It'll take a day for a messenger to get there, but I'll send someone at first light."

"You needn't bother," said Khaldun. "I can alert his steward via mirror. I should notify Jezebel as well."

"Very well," Charles said with a nod. "Would the two of you like to join me for a beer?"

"I think not," Khaldun said. "I should retire to our room and take care of the necessary communications. You're welcome to stay, though," he added to Mira.

"Are you sure?" she asked.

Khaldun nodded. "The two of you must have a lot of catching up to do."

Charles led them inside, and asked Reginald to show Khaldun up to their quarters. Mira followed him into the great hall, taking a seat at one of the smaller tables as he went off to fetch their beers. He returned a minute later, sitting across from her and setting two mugs on the table. Mira took a sip as Charles said, "What do you think the elves are doing here?"

"I'm afraid I have no idea," she said with a sigh. "Princess Jezebel fears it could be a prelude to an invasion."

"You've seen them in Spanbrook, too?"

"No. We received word of a sighting in Rockport. Jezebel sent Allison to investigate."

Charles nodded, taking a swig of his beer. "My brothers and I grew up listening to tales of the elves. I always wished I could meet them. They sounded so wise and strong."

"Yes, well, let's hope our fears are unfounded." She took another drink.

They spent a half hour chatting about developments in Graystone. Mira was eager to hear how her people were doing. *Former* people, she had to remind herself. Charles went to fetch them another round of drinks.

"I'm happy for you," he said as he retook his seat. "You and Lord Khaldun seem very happy together."

"Thank you," she said with a smile. "Yes, fate has smiled on us at last. This is not a life I ever could have imagined, but it has worked out for the best."

"I have to confess, I felt guilty sending you away," he said with a sigh. "This was *your* family's holding after all. And here I was usurping you."

"That's not how I see it. You had no more choice in the matter than I did. The university's regulations for sorcerers are quite strict. But I'm glad Graystone's people are in such good hands. They seem to be thriving."

"Yes, I think so." He took a long drink. "I truly did love you, you know. Though I know you were merely settling for *me*, I would have been happy to spend my life with you."

Mira smiled. "I think I would have found happiness as well. And for what it's worth, you were the best I could find. But you and Chiana seem quite happy, too."

"We are," he said. "She's a good woman. I couldn't ask for anything more."

Mira finished her beer and bade Charles goodnight. He offered to have Reginald show her up to the guest room, but she knew where to find it. Khaldun had already dozed off, so Mira disrobed, blew out the oil lamp, and climbed into bed next to him.

"Hmm?" he said, starting awake. "Oh, I must have fallen asleep."

Mira kissed him. "How did it go with Jezebel and Carlo?"

"Good. The prince will probably dispatch a regiment here to Graystone, just to be safe. Jezebel says that Allison was unable to find any trace of the elves in Rockport, though our encounter here has her worried."

"Maybe we should return to Spanbrook," Mira said. "If an invasion is imminent, I'm sure she'll want our defenses at full strength."

"I suggested as much myself," Khaldun said. "But she wants us to continue to Ostland. She suspects Nyro could be behind the elves' activity here, and if that's the case, we'll need whatever information we can gather regarding her defeat at their hands."

Mira fell asleep in Khaldun's arms. They woke before dawn, heading down to the great hall to see if they might find some breakfast. Much to their surprise, they found Charles and his family along with the entire household waiting for them. They'd prepared a farewell feast in their honor.

Khaldun and Mira ate and drank their fill, then Mira spent a few minutes going around to say goodbye to everyone. She was in tears as she embraced Belinda, knowing this was probably the last time she'd ever see her.

It was fully light out by the time Mira and Khaldun took off on his carpet, but still early. They flew for hours, and Mira's arm and stomach muscles were burning by the time they decided to take a break. Khaldun set them down in a meadow, and they ate some of the food from Blacksand. They stopped once more and watched the sun set over the Eternal Sea. Mira was ready to camp for the night, but Khaldun told her it wasn't much farther to Oldport. There, they'd be able to stay at an inn for the night.

So, they pressed ahead, and Mira was having trouble keeping her eyes open by the time they'd reached the city. This was the largest port in Dorshire, and it looked it from the air. Though it was fully dark, the light of oil lamps dotted the land for miles around. Khaldun set them down by the docks, and they had several inns to choose from. They found one that was still serving food in the common room, so they booked a room there and sat down for a meal before retiring for the night.

They woke at dawn, ate some food from their packs, and set out early. Oldport was even more impressive during the day. Piers extended up and down the coast as far as the eye could see, and the city sprawled over the landscape. Its size and lack of city walls reminded Mira of Arthos, but it was a proper princedom. The castle stood atop a hill a couple of miles inland. Oldport's financial might belonged to the hundreds of commercial enterprises that thrived here. The princedom's rulers had long ago decided to keep their hands out of the city's economic affairs. They kept the tax rate low, and still raised significant revenue. But the princedom was relatively weak politically and militarily, and had no sorcerers.

Khaldun wanted to make it to the Bastion before nightfall. He'd struck up a good rapport with the commandant there, and despite the man's refusal to take a mirror, he'd told them they were welcome to return anytime. It would have been faster to fly from

Blacksand to Ostland in a straight line, but much more difficult—if not impossible—to navigate. And it would have been too far to cross the sea that way.

They'd kept the coast in sight on the way to Oldport, and now Khaldun could follow the River Hale to the military academy. From there, they'd fly south to the sea and then along the coast to Bayfast, and hence to the mouth of the River Xago, the traditional boundary between Maeda and Shifar. From there, the crossing to Ostland wasn't far at all.

They wanted to avoid Keepstone, though. Leto might not be a warlord like Henry, but he hadn't been friendly the last time they'd met him, either. Instead, they stopped at a point along the Hale near the foothills of the Green Mountains. Once they'd had a chance to stretch and eat, they took off again. But as they approached Keepstone, it became apparent something was wrong.

As the former capital of the ancient kingdom of Dorshire, Keepstone was mighty and magnificent. Across the river from the Green Mountains, the city seemed to grow out of a rocky bluff, with walls more than thirty feet high built atop sheer cliff faces. Anyone attempting to sack it would have to march their army up the single road from the plain below, with its multiple switchbacks exposing them to weapons fire and thaumaturgic attacks from the castle above.

Leto always kept a heavy guard along the city walls, but today, they filled the ramparts along the entire perimeter. An entire garrison stood at arms in the courtyard, and their army had formed ranks down on the plain. It looked like they were ready for an imminent invasion, but Mira could see no opposing force anywhere nearby.

Khaldun wanted to stop and find out what was going on, and Mira agreed. They landed on top of the keep, where they found Leto's sorcerer, Legion, along with a dozen soldiers. The sorcerer walked over to them as they stood up and stretched. "Greetings, Lord Khaldun and Lady Mira." The voice was female today, and serious. Nobody knew if Legion was a man or a woman. They wore a leather suit, similar to Khaldun and Mira's armor, along with a black facemask and helmet, leaving only their red eyes visible. They dressed much like Salerna's sorcerer, Azure, in fact, except that no one had ever seen them remove their facemask. Despite the skintight clothing, their small body could have been male or female. As far as Mira knew, not even Leto had seen their face. Their voice was different every day. According to rumor, Legion had absorbed the souls of mages they'd defeated in battle over a century ago, adding their power to their own. But nobody alive today knew the truth of the matter. "We didn't expect to see you in Keepstone again so soon."

"Nor did we expect to be here," Khaldun said. "We are on our way to take care of some other business, and we noticed the city's state of military readiness. Are you expecting an invasion?"

Legion regarded them for a moment before saying, "You had better come with me. His Highness will want to see you." They turned and strode away. Khaldun rolled up his carpet, tucking it into the void along with their packs, then he and Mira followed them.

Mira had met Legion only once before, when she'd traveled here with Khaldun to try establishing communication by mirror. Others had told her they were one of the most powerful sorcerers on the continent, and Mira didn't doubt it. Leto had asked for a demonstration of her null, and she'd obliged, in the sorcerer's presence. They'd never experienced such a negation of their powers before, and asked Mira to stop. Through her null, she'd been able to sense their magic, and it was at least as strong as anyone else's she'd encountered.

Interestingly, Mira's null had had no effect on the sound of their voice, which had been male and quite low that day.

Legion led them through a small structure in the roof that housed the stairway to the rest of the keep. Down two flights, they led them into the throne room. They spoke to the guard for a moment, who announced them to the prince.

Leto had been conferring with a couple of his advisers, but they stood aside at the announcement, taking positions on either side of the throne. The guard escorted them up to the prince, and Legion followed.

The prince was of medium height with a strong build. His hair and short beard were black with flecks of gray. The visible areas of his cheekbones were covered in pockmarks. He wore a silver crown on his head.

"My lord and lady," he said, "what brings you to Keepstone?"

"We were only passing by, Your Highness," said Khaldun. "But we noticed the disposition of your forces and wished to inquire. We saw no sign of an enemy on our way from Oldport."

Leto nodded, his brow furrowed in concentration as if he were trying to make some difficult decision. Finally he rose, saying, "There's something I need to show you. Sorcerer, join us."

Leto led Legion, Khaldun, and Mira through a door in the rear corner of the throne room. Moving through a long corridor and descending several flights of stairs, they emerged into what appeared to be a cellar, with its damp stone walls. The prince led them through a passage that felt like a tunnel, only dimly lit by torches on the wall. Mira noticed a foul odor that only strengthened as they moved, until she thought it might make her sick.

Finally, they reached the end of the corridor, and Leto led them into a small chamber that had probably been used to store food at one time. Mira gasped. Lying on a table was the body of an elf. It had to be eight feet long. Its long, muscular arms and legs must have been powerful in life. Someone had cut open its torso from its chest to its groin, exposing the internal organs. Mira had to look away and take a deep breath to keep from vomiting.

"Do you know what this is?" Leto asked.

"Yes, Your Highness," Khaldun said, also looking away. "It's an elf."

"You are correct," the prince said. "Do you know what it might be doing in my princedom?"

"I'm afraid not," said Khaldun. "There have been reports of them in Rockport and Blacksand as well, though. Princess Jezebel fears an invasion."

"My thought exactly," Leto muttered. "Two of our guards stumbled upon this one and two others while on regular patrol through the foothills of the Green Mountains. They gave chase, but the elves vanished.

"I sent Legion with four more soldiers to capture and interrogate one of them. That proved impossible." He nodded to his sorcerer.

"It took an entire day to find them," Legion said. "They left no trail, magical or otherwise. But flying a low search pattern over the foothills, I detected an invisibility spell. Canceling that exposed the three of them. There were two warriors and one mage; this was one of the warriors. The mage tried to cancel the spells keeping the carpet aloft, so I had no choice but to retaliate. When I did, the warriors fired on us with their bows.

"We landed, and the elves killed all four of our soldiers in seconds. I managed to fell this one before the other two fled. The wound shouldn't have been fatal, but their mage killed him before disappearing."

"*Their* mage did this?" Khaldun asked. "Why?"

"I can only guess that they didn't want to be slowed down by his injuries," Legion said.

"Why did you cut him open like this?" Mira asked.

"We wanted to determine if they were indeed elves, and if so, how they are different from us," Leto explained. "Besides the pointed ears and green eyes."

"It became apparent during the battle that their bodies are resistant to magic," Legion said.

"Do they have nulls like Mira?" Khaldun asked, sounding alarmed.

"I said 'resistant,' not 'impervious,'" Legion replied. "My spells did affect him, but it took much more power than our people could withstand. Their skin is tougher than ours, too. It was difficult to pierce. And their bones are stronger—I dulled three saw blades trying to cut open this one's breastbone. Otherwise, they're not much different from us. Red blood flows through their veins, and though their internal organs are arranged a little differently, they're just as fragile as ours."

"If you can get through their skin and bones," Leto said. "An army of elves will be extraordinarily difficult to defeat in battle. Neither our weapons nor our magic will affect them nearly as much as theirs will us."

"But we have no reason to believe they've come here with armies," said Khaldun. "So far, we've seen only a few of them in three different princedoms."

"What do *you* think they're doing here?" Leto demanded, fixing Khaldun with his gaze. "I hardly think this is a social call. The ones we've seen must be scouts, sent here to probe our defenses."

Khaldun could provide no answer.

"I have called upon the Bastion to honor our ancient treaty," Leto continued. "The commandant has agreed to send his army here. The elves will have to travel to Anoria by ship, so I would suggest advising the coastal princedoms to establish perpetual watches along their shores."

"They'd be coming across the Lonely Sea, though," said Mira. "Their forces would have to land in Pytha and Kong."

"Pytha is a wasteland, and Kong is in shambles," the prince replied. "Anoria's riches lie in Dorshire, Maeda, and particularly Shifar. Sailing around the continent and landing on our shores would be far easier for them than marching overland. Once they've overrun Oldport, they can sail up the Hale and attack Keepstone. That's why the Bastion's forces are coming here."

"You think they're coming here to rob us?" Khaldun asked.

"They're coming to kill us, Lord Khaldun. Once we're all dead, they can take whatever they want."

CHAPTER FOUR
OBSET

haldun and Mira bade the prince farewell, and Legion escorted them back to the keep's roof. As Khaldun removed his carpet from the void, Legion produced a small mirror. "I honored my prince's wishes when last you visited, but I can do so no longer. The entire continent will need to work together if we're to have any chance of victory."

Khaldun nodded. Taking the mirror and pulling out his own, he undertook the complex spell work that would link Legion's to the rest. Linking two mirrors was fairly straightforward, but connecting one to multiple others, especially when only one was present, was a little more complicated. When he was done, he handed Legion his mirror.

"Thank you, and Godspeed," they said.

Mira sat down on the carpet and started strapping herself in. Once Khaldun had placed their packs along the front and rear edges, he used his mirror to apprise Jezebel of what they'd learned here. After that, they took off, following the mountains toward the Bastion.

"Do you think Leto's right about the invasion?" Mira said in Khaldun's ear, her arms around his midsection.

"I don't *want* to believe it," he said. "But I fear he may be correct. The elves we encountered certainly didn't seem friendly. And I cannot imagine why else they might be here, sneaking around like this."

"That's true," said Mira. "If their intentions were diplomatic, surely they would have visited the castles to make formal introductions."

They flew in silence, and dread filled Mira's soul.

A little before sunset, they reached the Bastion, nestled between two mountain peaks. It was smaller than Keepstone. From afar, it looked like one giant, circular building. In truth, there were dozens of buildings, all abutting each other, though the academy took up over half the total space. The rest of the town existed to serve the school.

Mira spotted a line of people leaving the Bastion, and many more far below setting up camp by the river. Khaldun landed on the academy's roof. One of the guards approached them; Mira recognized him from their last visit, though she couldn't recall his name. The Bastion had a cadre of mages who helped simulate the thaumaturgic conditions soldiers could expect to encounter in battle during their training exercises. But they had no sorcerers.

Khaldun rolled up the carpet, tucked it and their packs into the void, and then the two of them followed the guard inside. He escorted them to Commandant Bishop's office. The door was closed, and the commandant was yelling at someone, but stopped when the guard knocked on the door.

"Come in!" he yelled. "What?" he added when the guard opened the door. Mira couldn't see inside from her position in the corridor.

"Sir, Lord Khaldun and Lady Mira from Spanbrook are here."

"Well, don't just stand there, send them in! And you," he added to whoever else was inside, "get out of my face."

A red-faced man emerged, hurrying up the corridor. Khaldun and Mira moved into the room, and the guard closed the door behind them.

"I know I told you two you were welcome here anytime," the commandant said, getting to his feet to shake their hands. "But I have to be honest, this is *not* a good time."

"So we've heard," Khaldun said with a grin. "You're getting ready to depart for Keepstone, I presume?"

"How'd you know? Did you stop there on your way here?" Khaldun nodded. "Leto and his damn treaty. The man's a raving lunatic if you ask me."

"Do you think he's wrong about the elves?" Mira asked.

"No, unfortunately, he's probably right about that. But he expects us to drop everything and come to his aid. What about the Bastion?"

"Is he wrong about the treaty?" Khaldun asked.

"No, he's right about that, too. But that godforsaken thing was written when the Bastion was still part of his princedom. We've been independent for nearly two hundred years, now. But my damn advisers say we should go anyway, if we hope to preserve peaceful relations with Keepstone in the future.

"Anyway, what the hell do you two want?"

"Lodging for the night, nothing more," Khaldun said.

"You're welcome to stay, but you'll need to leave at dawn. We're marching at first light, and locking this place up tight before we go."

"We can do that," Khaldun said. "Thank you."

Khaldun and Mira joined the commandant for dinner in the Bastion's hall. The food was simple, but good. Bishop drank heavily, and insisted that they do so as well. Mira wanted to abstain; they still had far to travel, and she would be miserable if she were hungover. But the man wouldn't take "no" for an answer. His drink of choice was whiskey, which Mira abhorred, so she and Khaldun agreed to wine instead. The commandant didn't eat much, instead producing a pipe and smoking while they finished their meal, regaling them with stories of battles he'd won in his youth, fighting for his home princedom of Bayfast.

After dinner, one of the guards showed them to the guest quarters. Mira's head was spinning from the wine, and that along with Bishop's stories about glorious victories had given her some relief from her sense of impending doom. She made love to Khaldun, then fell into a deep sleep.

Rising early, Khaldun and Mira ate some of the food they'd packed, then met the commandant in the great hall. They left the academy with the last of his people and bade him farewell and good luck before boarding their carpet and flying away.

They flew over the Green Mountains, crossing into Maeda, and stopped to rest an hour later. Resuming their journey, they reached Bayfast before sunset.

Bayfast was the most powerful princedom in southern Maeda. The castle overlooked the bay leading to the River Rona. Khaldun landed on the keep roof. As he and Mira got to their feet and stretched, she spotted an enormous tiger lying by the entrance to the building. It stood on its hind legs and transformed into a man—a naked one. He picked up a bundle from the ground, which turned out to be his robes. Once he'd donned those, he walked over to meet them.

"Hello again, Beast," Khaldun said with a grin.

Beast was Bayfast's sorcerer. He stood nearly six feet tall, with a mane of straw-colored hair and a long beard. A shapeshifter like Semblant, he could transform only into a tiger. And unlike Semblant, his shifting abilities did not include objects he might be carrying or wearing, so he could only transform naked.

"Greetings, my lord and lady," he said with a grin, giving them each a tight hug and patting them on the back. "You didn't contact us by mirror, so I assume this is a social call?"

"Just passing through on our way to Ostland," Khaldun said. "We were hoping to spend the night here, if it's all right with Princess Miranda."

"The princess is away on a hunt," he told them. "I'm in charge while she's away, and it's quite all right with me. Have you eaten yet?"

Beast preferred to take most of his meals out in the city. So he led them through the castle, and they exited through the front gates. He took them to one of his favorite haunts, a tavern overlooking the bay. Khaldun and Mira had accompanied him here on their last visit, too. They sat down at a table on the outdoor patio, and someone hurried over with bowls of fish stew and mugs of ale moments later.

"How are you doing with your transformations?" Beast asked as they started on the stew.

"No progress," Khaldun said with a frown. "I can change the color of my eyes, hair, and skin at will, as well as those of others, but that continues to be the extent of it."

"Aye, well shifting is different for everyone, I'm told," Beast said. "That may well be as much as you'll ever be able to do."

"It's not terribly useful, I'm afraid," Khaldun said with a sigh.

"I'm not so sure about that," Mira replied. "It's come in useful when you've wanted to hide the fact that you were a sorcerer."

"True," he conceded.

"So, what takes you two to Ostland?" Beast asked. "That's quite the trek from Spanbrook."

Khaldun and Mira took turns telling him about the old historian in Blacksand, and the elves that had turned up in some of the princedoms.

"I think Leto and the commandant are probably overreacting," Beast said, finishing his ale and ordering another. "It's in their nature to be suspicious of everyone and everything, isn't it? With all their military training, that's what they do."

"That's true of the commandant, perhaps," said Mira. "But not Leto."

"He trained at the Bastion as a young man," Beast said, "before inheriting the princedom."

"Oh, I didn't know that," she said. "The elves we encountered hardly seemed friendly, though."

"It is said they're arrogant, I'll grant you that," Beast said, taking a swig of ale. "But from what you've said, they haven't acted aggressively, have they?"

"They slaughtered Leto's soldiers," Khaldun said incredulously.

"I would, too, if they tried capturing *me*," Beast said with a hearty chuckle. "And it would serve them right."

"You haven't seen any elves in Bayfast, then?" Mira asked.

"No. And I do prowl the woods at night in tiger form, so I probably would have smelled them, at least, if there were any here."

"Why would they suddenly show up in Anoria after all this time, if it *weren't* an invasion?" Khaldun asked.

"Obviously, I don't know. But the idea that they'd cross an ocean just to kill us and plunder our riches is absurd," Beast replied, laughing again. "The stories tell us the elves are wealthy beyond our imagination. Streets paved in gold and all of that. What need would they have for anything of ours, hmm?"

"I hope you're right," Mira said.

They spent a couple more hours catching up over drinks. Mira wished she could adopt Beast's carefree outlook on things, but the elves' presence in Anoria worried her. She couldn't get Leto's predictions out of her head.

The next morning, they continued their southward journey. There was still some daylight left by the time they'd reached the River Xago, but not enough time to make the crossing to Ostland before nightfall, and they didn't want to cross into Shifar. A small village sat on this side of the river, but it had no inn. So, they made camp out in the forest, eating from their provisions.

They woke at first light the next day, and flew across the water to Ostland. This made Mira a little nervous, given the lack of a place to land in case of an emergency. But the flight was uneventful.

They reached the island, Khaldun landed on the beach, and they rested for a little while before continuing. According to the map they'd found in Blacksand, the historian had buried his text by the northern end of the bay on the island's southeast shore. They reached the bay a little before sunset, but found a settlement near the shore. It was a walled village, and two of the guards in the watchtower by the gates had spotted them, waving as they circled overhead.

"So much for Ostland being uninhabited," Khaldun said.

"We don't need to stop here, do we?" asked Mira. This place gave her an uneasy feeling.

"I think we should," Khaldun said. "With the dense foliage, it'll be tough to spot our destination from the air. And according to the map, it's not too far inland. They've seen us already, so they're sure to send people after us if we don't stop first. It'll be all right. Hell, they might even be able to help us find the place."

Khaldun landed out in front of the gates. The doors opened, and three guards emerged to meet them.

"Welcome, my lord and lady," their leader said, bowing slightly. "What brings you to our village this fine afternoon?"

"I am Lady Mira from Spanbrook, and this is my husband, Lord Khaldun," she said. "We're looking for an ancient structure here on the island. The last we knew, the island was uninhabited, so we were a little surprised to find your village here."

"His Highness, Prince Kamari, has claimed Ostland for Okset," the guard told them with a smile. "And I assure you, there are no structures here beyond our settlement. The island *had* always been uninhabited prior to our arrival."

"I'm sure you wouldn't mind if we have a look for ourselves?" Khaldun said. "We have it on good authority that there is a small building here. It may be hidden."

"The decision is not mine to make," the man said apologetically. "You will need the prince's permission."

"That will take some time," Khaldun said. "We've traveled far, and it will take two more days to make it to Okset and back."

"There should be no need to travel there, my lord," the guard said. "We can reach the castle by mirror."

"That's terrific," Mira said, breathing a sigh of relief. She wasn't looking forward to two extra water crossings.

"If you'll come with me, we keep the mirror inside the guard tower."

Khaldun rolled up the carpet and tucked it into the void. They followed the guard into the settlement, and climbed the steps to the tower's upper level. He retrieved a mirror from a cabinet, staring into it and saying, "My lady, do you have a moment?"

It took a few moments before a female voice replied, "Yes, go ahead."

The guard explained the situation, then handed his mirror to Mira. Gazing into it, she found a sorceress with flaming red hair staring back at her. Khaldun stood right next to her, and the woman said, "Mira and Khaldun. We've heard about the two of you. Why do you seek this mysterious structure of yours?"

"My lady, we discovered a message from an ancient historian in the princedom of Blacksand," Mira explained. "He chronicled the events surrounding Nyro's downfall, but in his old age, didn't feel it was safe to keep his work there."

"I should think not," the woman said. "The governors at the time were quite thorough in their purge of such things. I'd be very curious to learn what you discover."

"We have your permission to search for this building, then?" Mira asked.

"It's not *my* permission you need," she said with a chuckle. "I'll need to consult with His Highness. This might take a little while; he's quite busy. If you don't mind waiting there at our settlement, I'll make contact again as soon as I have an answer."

Mira sighed; she should have known it wouldn't be so easy. But they had little choice. Now that they'd made contact, they'd only create conflict between Okset and Spanbrook if they tried to proceed without awaiting the prince's decision. She wished they could have avoided being seen and found the historian's hiding place on their own, but it was too late for that now.

The guard told them they'd been about to sit down for dinner, and invited Khaldun and Mira to join them. They agreed. He escorted them to a hall in the middle of the settlement, where they found a couple of dozen people sitting down to eat. Most of them were soldiers, but Mira noted a few plainclothes men as well.

The quality of the food surprised Mira for what seemed like a temporary settlement. They served venison that had been prepared in a rich sauce, along with the most delicious wine she'd ever tasted.

"What is it your people are doing here?" Khaldun asked their host.

"We are surveying this area of the island," the guard replied. "His Highness wishes to build a new city here, so our job is to find the best location for it."

After dinner, they returned to the guard tower. They got to talking with the guard, whose name they learned was Idir, and he proved very curious about the goings-on in the northern princedoms. He'd never seen a carpet before, and told them he'd always wished he could fly like a bird, so Khaldun ended up giving him a ride on the carpet.

The hour grew late, and Mira found herself getting drowsy. But finally, the prince's sorcerer reached out to them again.

"His Highness would like to meet the two of you in person before making his decision," she told them. "It is late, so you are welcome to spend the night in our village. If you leave at dawn, you should make it here at a reasonable hour."

This was frustrating. Though she appreciated the offer of lodging, Mira had hoped they could be on their way to their destination in the morning. This would add two full days to their journey.

Idir escorted them to the living quarters. The entire village slept in the same building, and there were only bunk beds. So Khaldun and Mira lay down on an empty bunk, and Mira fell asleep almost immediately.

They rose first thing in the morning, ate a quick breakfast in the hall, bade Idir farewell, and took off for Okset. This crossing took quite a bit longer than the previous day's, and Mira's muscles were aching by the time they'd reached the city.

Okset City was unlike anyplace Mira had visited before. It stretched as far as the eye could see, much like Arthos, but unlike the free city, the buildings all seemed to be constructed of stone or brick instead of wood. The castle was easy to locate, sitting atop its hill near both the sea and the river, gleaming white in the morning sunshine, with many bulbous domes and tall towers. Mira was pretty sure Castle Barclay was larger, but that was a fortress, while this looked more like a palace. But she could tell its appearance was deceiving. It still had thick, high walls around its perimeter, and the surrounding terrain was steep. Only one road led to its gates, with multiple switchbacks.

As instructed, Khaldun flew over the ramparts and landed in the courtyard. The sorcerer from the mirror hurried over to meet them as Khaldun and Mira got to their feet.

"Welcome to Okset," she said. "I'm Siren, His Highness's chief mage. Please come with me; he's eager to meet you." Khaldun rolled up the carpet and tucked it into the void along with the rest of their gear. "You two should be aware, the Shifari like to bargain," she said as she led them toward the keep. "His Highness in particular. Between you and me, I suspect he'll grant you what you want, but he'll expect something in return."

"Like what?" Mira asked suspiciously.

"I'm afraid I have no idea," Siren replied. "What do you have to offer?"

Mira could think of nothing the prince would see as an equitable trade.

"You're not from Shifar," Khaldun observed.

"No, honey," she replied. "I grew up in Rockport. But I transformed on my sixteenth birthday, and after a few years training at the university, I've spent my entire adult life here. His Highness is the fourth ruler of Okset I've served. He ascended to the throne only a year ago. But all three of his predecessors reigned for decades."

"You look much too young to have been here that long," Mira said.

"I like you," Siren said with a grin.

They entered the keep, and Siren guided them to the throne room. It reminded Mira of the one in Highgate, with the marble columns running up the middle, only it was bigger. Prince Kamari sat on his throne, a scepter in his hand, and a golden crown upon his head. He wore royal robes, and a diamond necklace. Mira thought he looked more like a king of old than a prince, only much younger. She doubted he'd reached his twentieth birthday.

"Your Highness, may I present Lady Mira and Lord Khaldun from Spanbrook," Siren said with a bow, before taking her place by the prince's side.

"Welcome," Kamari said with a nod, his smile friendly. "My sorcerer tells me you are searching for the hidden works of an ancient historian. Please, tell me more about this."

Khaldun and Mira explained what they'd found in Blacksand, and Khaldun's ongoing search for information about Nyro's downfall and the elves.

"My father believed that the people of Shifar were descended from the elves," Kamari said pensively when they were done. "He told my siblings and me that we came to Anoria from the elven continent many thousands of years ago. And that we were the first humans to wield magic, having inherited it from our elvish forebears." The prince took a deep breath. "I think it's all nonsense," he said, cracking a smile. "Never have I seen an elf, but it is my understanding that they are as different from humans as a dolphin is from a shark. It makes no sense to me that we could be related."

"I would have to agree, Your Highness," said Mira. "Elves have been spotted in some of the northern princedoms. Prince Leto's sorcerer in Keepstone had a confrontation with a few of them, and managed to capture one. They do look similar to us, but not entirely the same."

"Is it true they have green eyes and pointy ears?" the prince asked with a smile.

"Yes, it is," Mira said. "And their skin and bones are much tougher than ours, and it seems they have a natural resistance to magic."

"How would you know that about their bones?" he asked, narrowing his eyes.

"Oh, well the elf they captured was dead. He'd been injured in the battle, and his people sacrificed him rather than allow him to slow them down," Mira said. "Leto's sorcerer, ah… cut him open."

"Ah," Kamari said with a nod.

"Your Highness, Leto is afraid the scouts we've seen mean an invasion is imminent," said Khaldun. "And Princess Jezebel fears Nyro could be involved. We need to find the historian's chronicles of her downfall to see if it contains any information that might be helpful, should war with the elves come to pass."

The prince regarded him placidly for a few moments before chuckling softly. "Nyro died centuries ago. I find it difficult to believe she has survived in any form. Reports to the contrary are nothing but ghost stories, like those we tell each other around our fires at night. And the elves are supposed to possess riches even greater than Okset's. I cannot imagine why they'd have any interest in Anoria."

Mira opened her mouth to reply, but Kamari continued before she could say anything. "I have no interest in your historian's chronicles. It is all ancient history, and I look toward Okset's future, not its past. You may explore our island of Ostland to your heart's content and retrieve whatever documents you might find there."

"Thank you, Your Highness," Khaldun said with a bow, and Mira sighed in relief.

"I would ask only for a little something in return," the prince said with a smile.

"We have brought only the supplies we required for our journey," Khaldun said, "but we would be happy to have our princess send whatever payment you would request."

"The flying carpet you arrived on," Kamari said. "Would you be willing to part with that?"

Mira's heart leaped into her throat. "Your Highness, without that, it would take months for us to return home."

Khaldun looked confused.

"You find that a strange request?" the prince asked him.

"It was my impression that Your Highness was distrustful of magic," he said. "The carpet can be flown only using air and earth spells."

"Distrustful of magic?" the prince repeated. "Not at all. Siren has been my family's most trusted adviser for generations; we depend upon her and our other mages. What gave you this impression?"

"My apologies, Your Highness," said Khaldun. "We heard that you'd turned away Highgate's envoys, and I thought it was the mirror—"

Kamari waved his hand dismissively. "We use mirrors all the time. It was the alliance with Highgate I rejected. We have no need to maintain communications with Salerna or any of the other northern rulers. Okset and our neighbors possess sufficient military might to repel any invader."

"I don't doubt it, Your Highness," Khaldun said. "We will need our carpet to return home; however, it is Salerna's chief mage, Azure, who creates them, and I have no doubt he would be willing to supply you with one for Siren to use. My mirror is connected to his, so I can confirm it with him, if you wish."

"That would be acceptable," the prince said with a nod.

"Ah, forgive me, Your Highness," Siren said, looking alarmed. "Perhaps one of the others would be better suited—"

"Can normal wizards or witches control a flying carpet?" the prince asked Khaldun. "Lady Siren is afraid of heights."

"Yes, Your Highness. However, doing so requires their full concentration, making it difficult, if not impossible, for them to cast other spells while in flight. Sorcerers have no such trouble, and can travel much faster, to boot."

Kamari nodded. "You will take Siren with you. Once you have completed your mission in Ostland, she will fly with you to Highgate. As long as Salerna's mage honors our agreement, you will then be free to return home with whatever you have found on our island, and Siren can return here on her own carpet."

Siren turned a lighter shade of gold, and Mira had to stifle a chuckle. If she was afraid of heights, she was in for a miserable time.

CHAPTER FIVE
CHRONICLES

haldun used his mirror to update Jezebel on their progress, and she approved their detour to Highgate. Azure told him he did have a couple of extra carpets ready to go, and Princess Salerna agreed to let Okset take one.

There was not enough time that day for the return flight to Ostland, so Prince Kamari invited Khaldun and Mira to spend the night in Okset. He had his steward show them to guest quarters on the top floor of the keep.

The accommodations stunned Mira. The room included a giant four-poster bed, a writing desk, and their own washroom with running water. They were no larger than Spanbrook's guest rooms, but much nicer, with gilded mirrors, plush carpets, and tapestries hanging on the walls. Their balcony had a beautiful view of the sea.

They joined the prince and his advisers for dinner in the private dining room. Mira was surprised to learn that Prince Kamari was nearly thirty, but still unmarried. He had three younger siblings, so there was no worry about keeping the princedom in the family. And Siren hinted that he was enjoying his position as the city's most eligible bachelor too much to settle down with one woman just yet.

Mira enjoyed the meal and the wine very much. After dinner, the prince invited them to join him for a concert in the great hall. Mira and Khaldun had brought no other clothing, only their leather suits, so the prince arranged for their master of wardrobe to provide them with matching gold mage's robes.

Okset's nobility and wealthiest merchants all turned up for the concert. Mira and Khaldun sat with the prince and his closest advisers as his honored guests. After the performance, they thanked the prince for his hospitality, and wished him a good night before retiring to their chambers.

The next morning, Mira and Khaldun met the prince for breakfast, then headed up to the roof with Siren. She blanched as Khaldun unfurled the carpet.

"Are you sure this thing is safe?" she asked, backing away from it.

"I've never lost a passenger," he assured her.

Mira sat down in the middle and strapped herself in. Khaldun positioned Siren by the rear edge, then took a seat at the front. This arrangement was necessary to keep the weight balanced, but Mira hated not being able to hold onto Khaldun in the air. The straps kept her secure, and the shield Khaldun cast around them eliminated the wind, but Mira felt much less safe this way.

As they lifted off and shot into the sky, Siren screamed. Her voice sounded ordinary, making Mira wonder about her name.

They flew for hours, finally reaching Ostland in the middle of the afternoon. Khaldun set them down on the beach, and Siren stumbled to her feet and vomited. Mira grimaced.

Siren led them into the village, where they met Idir. They sat down to eat in the hall, and Khaldun asked the guard to take a look at their map. He seemed pretty confident he could find the old historian's hiding place, so after their meal, he led the three sorcerers into the forest.

After an hour or so, Idir stopped by the edge of a meadow, saying, "This should be the place."

Mira gazed around the area, but saw no buildings of any kind. "Do you sense anything?" she asked Khaldun. "Maybe he tucked the stairway access into the void."

"My thought exactly," Khaldun said. Holding out one arm, he turned in a slow circle, finally adding, "There's something over there." He led them into the meadow. Halfway across, he stopped, waving his hand from side to side. A small brick building appeared out of nowhere with a popping sound.

"I'll be damned," Idir said, touching the wall. "Was this invisible?"

"No, it was tucked into oblivion," Khaldun explained. "It was here, in this location, but in a different plane of existence. You could have walked right through the space it occupies now and felt nothing."

"I'll never understand magic," he muttered.

There was a metal door, but they couldn't find a handle or lock.

"It appears to be sealed magically," Khaldun observed.

Mira extended her null just wide enough to encompass the structure, and the door popped open. She closed her channels of power again.

Khaldun stepped inside, calling a small flame to light their way. A narrow set of steps led into the ground. He led the way down, followed by Siren and Idir, with Mira bringing up the rear. At the bottom, they found a chamber barely big enough for the four of them. It appeared to be empty. But Khaldun held out his hand, and a cavity appeared in one wall. Inside, Mira could see a wooden chest.

Removing the chest, Khaldun placed it on the ground and opened it. Inside was a leather-bound book. Mira picked it up and opened it, scanning several pages, but it was written in a language she didn't recognize. She showed it to Khaldun.

"The writing isn't familiar to me, either. We'll have to see if any of Salerna's people recognize it."

The four of them returned to the surface and hiked back to the village. It was still early, so Khaldun and Mira decided it would be best to get underway. They had another long journey ahead of them. Bidding Idir farewell, the three sorcerers took their seats on the carpet, Mira clutching the book, and they flew away.

As sunset approached, Khaldun set them down near the northeasternmost tip of the island. They made camp and started a fire. Idir had replenished their food supply, and included a jug of wine. So they sat around the fire and shared a meal and passed the jug around. It was strong, and Mira found herself feeling a good buzz before too long. Siren drank more than the other two combined. "Needed this after all that flying today," she explained.

"So, why do they call you Siren?" Khaldun asked.

Siren giggled. "You sure you want to know?"

Khaldun nodded. "Why not?"

Siren focused for a moment, then opened her mouth wide. At first, nothing happened. But then Mira noticed a beautiful voice singing a high note, the sound coming from all around them at once.

Khaldun's expression went blank. He rose to his feet and stripped out of his clothing.

"Khaldun!" Mira said with a gasp. Visibly aroused, he started pleasuring himself. "*What* are you doing?" she demanded, failing to stifle a giggle.

The enchanted voice stopped, and Siren said, "He'll snap out of it in a moment."

Sure enough, Khaldun froze, his eyes going wide as he stared down at himself. He hurriedly put his clothes back on. "Making someone masturbate against their will," he muttered angrily. "What an interesting talent you have."

Siren chuckled. "I'm sorry; that was inappropriate. All this wine has gone to my head. But it's not only that. Watch." She opened her mouth, and the otherworldly voice returned. Suddenly, Khaldun stood up again, and started dancing circles around the other two. The voice faded and he stopped.

"It's so strange," he observed. "I'm conscious of what you make me do, but powerless to stop it. You can force someone to do anything you want?"

"More or less," she said. "As a sorcerer, you should be able to stop it now that you realize what's happening. Try it."

"Whoa, hold on," he said, holding out his hands as if to say "Stop!" "Only the dancing this time, all right?"

"Yes, yes, I promise." Siren opened her mouth a third time. The voice returned, and Khaldun resumed his dancing. But moments later he stopped, even though the voice continued.

"You're right. I could sense your magic and cancel it."

"No regular mage has ever been able to do that," she said.

"I'd like to try canceling it, too," said Mira. "No magic will work on me, though. Could you enchant Khaldun again?"

"Of course," said Siren. She cast her spell once more, and Khaldun started dancing again. Mira had no trouble canceling the magic.

"It's similar to the spell Dredmort used to bend Allison to his will," Khaldun said to Mira.

"There's more to it, though," Siren said. "I can use it to deflect magic and projectiles, too."

"Like a shield spell?" Mira asked.

"Yes, but it works across a much larger area," Siren explained. "I used it to protect the entire castle from trebuchets when a neighboring prince attacked during Kamari's grandfather's time."

"You'd be good to have in a battle," Khaldun observed, retaking his seat.

"Honey, you'd better believe I am."

The three of them laid out their bedrolls and slept under the stars. The next morning, they ate a light meal and broke camp. As they took their seats on the carpet, Khaldun asked Siren if she'd be willing to assist by calling air. "We'll get there much faster this way," he explained.

With Siren's help, they made it to Highgate after only two more days. Landing on the keep roof, they found one of Salerna's wizards waiting for them. Khaldun tucked their things into the void, and the man escorted them inside the building to the princess's throne room. They found Salerna waiting for them, Azure by her side.

"Welcome back, Lord Khaldun and Lady Mira," Salerna said with a smile. "And this must be Lady Siren?"

"Yes, Your Highness," the sorcerer said with a bow. "It's a pleasure to finally meet you."

"The pleasure is all mine, I'm sure."

"Could I take a look at this book of yours?" Azure asked.

"Yes, of course," Mira said, moving up to the dais and handing it to him.

Azure opened the cover and flipped through the first few pages. "This is written in the script of the ancient tongue of Dorshire."

"Can you read it?" Khaldun asked.

"I cannot. But we have scholars here who can," he said.

"We owe Nyro credit for the spread of the common tongue to every corner of the continent," Salerna said.

"I wasn't aware of that," Mira said. "I thought the common tongue predated her reign by several centuries."

"Yes, it did," Salerna said. "However, its use was not too widespread outside of northern Maeda and eastern Dorshire. She made it the official language of her empire, and all its citizens were required to learn it."

"Then it's a little surprising that a historian from the later days of the Pythan Empire would have used the ancient tongue," said Khaldun.

"There were many who passed on the old languages as an act of resistance," Azure said. "Particularly in the outskirts of the empire. The penalty for speaking the old tongues was death, so closer to the capital, fewer were willing to chance it."

"It's difficult to imagine Nyro ruling from this very chamber," Mira said, gazing around the room as a chill ran down her spine.

"I thought the Pythan capital was the seat of the imperial government," Khaldun said.

"It was in the beginning," Salerna said. "But Nyro moved it here once she'd taken over. Azure will take the book to our scholars. A full translation will take some time, of course, but we can have them give it a read first to glean any pertinent information it might contain, if you'd like."

"Yes, that would be wonderful, thank you," said Mira.

"This isn't terribly long," said Azure. "If they start right away, I would think they should be able to provide a summary by the end of the day tomorrow. But it will take a few weeks for them to produce a duplicate in the common tongue."

"I'm sure you'll want to return to Spanbrook before that," said Salerna. "But you are welcome to stay here with us until they have prepared their synopsis."

"We would like that very much," said Mira.

Azure hurried off to deliver the book to the scholars, while Mira, Khaldun, and Siren followed the princess to the private dining room. Her lover, Jennifer, was there already, and Azure arrived a few minutes later.

They made small talk until the meal arrived, but once they'd finished eating, Salerna asked about the elves.

"Has the looking glass shown you anything about them?" Khaldun asked after he and Mira finished recounting their encounter with them, along with the reports from Rockport and Keepstone.

"It has shown me scouts creeping through forests, nothing more," Salerna said. "I can identify neither the place nor the time of those visions. Unfortunately, the looking glass has shown me very little these last fifteen years."

"Since my arrival at the university?" Mira asked.

"Yes," Salerna confirmed. "Even the destruction of this city is invisible to me, now. It had shown me that many times before, but not once since then."

"We suspect Mira's involvement in those events was not a certainty until she transformed," Azure explained.

"So, you believe I will be here when Highgate falls?" Mira asked, dread filling her soul at the thought.

"I can think of no other reason for the looking glass's lack of revelation," said Salerna.

"Lady Mira's null hides things from your looking glass?" Siren asked.

"We believe that to be the case," Mira said, "along with sorcerous prophecy. But it should only be my *null* that does it, I would think. Were I present somewhere with my channels of power closed, then those events should be visible."

"That is our belief," Azure said.

"Of course, I have no magic beyond my null," said Mira. "So, if I were here for any historically significant event like a battle, I would probably be using it."

"Mira's presence in Highgate for such dire events might prevent you from seeing what happens *here*," said Khaldun. "But she cannot be in more than one place at once. Surely, if Leto's predictions are correct, there would have to be massive elvish invasions in Maeda and Dorshire's port cities, wouldn't there? Has the looking glass shown you nothing of that sort?"

"It has not," Salerna said. "Which may mean that the decisions that would lead to such developments have yet to occur."

"Whoever's in charge of the elvish forces might be awaiting the reports from their scouts," Mira said.

"Time will tell," said Salerna.

After dinner, one of Salerna's people showed Siren, Khaldun, and Mira up to their chambers; Siren was staying right across the hall from them. Khaldun and Mira availed themselves of a bath before going to bed.

The next morning, Azure took Siren down to the plain for her first flying lesson. Khaldun and Mira joined them, and in no time, the sorcerer was swooping around the city on her new carpet.

"It's not as bad as I thought it would be," she said when they were done. "Being in control is much less nerve-wracking, though. I did *not* like being a passenger!"

Mira spent the day exploring the city with Khaldun. She'd spent some time here after the battle fifteen years earlier, but only on the battlefield and inside the castle. They visited several museums and ate at a tavern on the city's first level.

That evening, Salerna summoned Khaldun and Mira to her conference room. They arrived to find the princess and Azure sitting at the table.

"Our scholars have finished their review of your book," Salerna told them as they sat down, nodding to Azure. He put the spells in place to protect the room from observation, magical or mundane.

"The text explains that for most of Nyro's rule, her people thrived," Azure said. "The historian doesn't spend much time on those years, but references several other historical treatises that are unknown to us."

"They must have been destroyed in the purge," said Mira. "Are the stories we've heard about Nyro's tyranny false, then?"

"Not false, but confined to the final decades," Azure replied. "Saliman was brutal, but for much of Nyro's reign, Anoria prospered.

But apparently, she then had a prophetic vision of the elves coming to destroy her empire. After that, everything changed. She declared martial law, conscripting hundreds of thousands of citizens into the imperial military, and requisitioning all available resources to build more weapons and ships.

"Resistance cells developed all over the continent. They started sabotaging imperial production facilities. Nyro crushed all the ones she could find. Some survived, and their leaders sent a delegation to the elvish continent to ask for aid. They refused. The elvish leaders had no interest in human affairs.

"Eventually, the resistance received word that Nyro was preparing to invade the elvish lands. Once again, they sent a party to warn the elves, hoping that such news might finally prompt them to take action here. But they laughed at the warning, not believing humans would pose any threat.

"Only then, Nyro did invade. Her forces slaughtered tens of thousands of elves before they were driven back to their ships. They returned in defeat, but Nyro became more brutal than ever as she prepared a force ten times larger to make another attempt. But finally, the elves came to Anoria before she could attack again."

"How did the historian find out about Nyro's prophetic vision?" asked Mira. "And for that matter, how did the resistance learn about her plans for the invasion? Surely, Nyro would treat such matters with the utmost secrecy."

"There was a traitor," said Azure. "The historian doesn't identify them, but it was someone very high up in the imperial administration."

"It must have been a general, if not a member of the Sacred Circle," said Mira. "I can't imagine anyone of a station much lower than that would have been privy to such information."

"Indeed," said Azure. "The historian made the same guess, but he didn't know, either. The elves sent a thousand ships, carrying a force of half a million soldiers, along with hundreds of mages. They started in Dorshire and Shifar, driving the imperial armies inland, ultimately confining them to Middle Maeda. After a final battle outside of Highgate, they forced Nyro, her Sacred Circle, and their surviving forces to flee to Pytha.

"Only that was a trap. Their mages had taken positions throughout the Anthar and Mystic Mountains, preparing powerful spells. Surrounded by the mountains and the sea, Pytha made the perfect prison. Once the elvish military had driven Nyro and her inner circle all the way to the capital, their mages unleashed their magic, erecting the barrier around the entire kingdom. They sent one hundred warrior mages who together managed to nullify Nyro's magic, then they slaughtered her and the Sacred Circle—their bodies anyway—releasing their souls as demons.

"The elvish magic drew upon the life force of the surviving Pythans, killing them all when the barrier went live. Only Nyro and her necromancers survived that. Thousands of Pythan citizens had started fleeing the kingdom when the war came to their land, but very few managed to escape. They became the wayfarers."

"We knew the elves used the Pythans' life force to create the barrier," said Khaldun, "but I had no idea the elves sacrificed themselves in such great numbers."

"They didn't," Azure said. "The spells they used had no effect on the elves, and the barrier allowed them to pass. Once they were done, they left Pytha. Their people erected the watchtowers, and left instructions with the surviving human mages for the barrier's maintenance.

"The historian also recorded information about elvish magic that could prove useful. He confirmed that all elves can call the four basic forces, but only the mages have command of the magical force. There are no elvish sorcerers or necromancers. He also explained that elves walk in our world and the spectral plane at the same time. Demons have no effect on them—they cannot be possessed, for example—nor do they fear them. But they also have no way to control them."

"So, the elves couldn't use necromancy against Nyro, but neither could she use it against them," Mira said.

"That would seem to be correct," said Azure. "With the exception of ghouls. They are physical beings, and Nyro was able to use them quite effectively against the elves."

Mira shivered, recalling the ghouls Allison had summoned in the battle here.

"What happened to Nyro's conjurnor?" Khaldun asked. "I assume they must have been a descendant of King Saliman."

"Yes, the historian says that Nyro took very good care of Saliman's progeny," said Azure. "He reports that he was captured in Highgate when Nyro was driven into Pytha. He confirms he was the conjurnor for all of Nyro's necromancers, but doesn't mention what might have become of him after that."

"The death of Nyro and her necromancers would have freed him from those bonds, though, right?" asked Mira.

"Yes, that's correct," Azure said. "Their deaths would have severed any connection he had to them. He would have returned to being a normal man."

Mira was still processing all this new information, but could think of no other questions. "Please, thank your scholars for their analysis. This could be very helpful should the elves invade again now."

"I will," Azure said with a nod. "And we'll let you know once they've finished their full translation."

CHAPTER SIX
UNEXPECTED VISITORS

haldun and Mira retired to their chambers. Once she'd drawn a bath, they stripped out of their clothes and climbed into the tub together. Mira lay back against him, and he wrapped his arms around her.

"That was a lot to take in," Mira said with a sigh. "I'm curious who the traitor might have been. For some reason, I have trouble imagining Nyro revealing her prophetic visions to *anyone*."

"I'm not so sure," Khaldun said. "She talked about things she'd seen in the scroll she left in Spanbrook."

"That was different. She did that because she'd foreseen someone finding it and needed to manipulate them. And she knew it wouldn't be read until long after her downfall. I'd imagine in life, she was much more secretive."

"Perhaps. I'm more curious about her conjurnor. I always just assumed he probably died in the battle."

"I doubt he survived very long," said Mira. "The historian said Nyro took good care of him. I'm sure people would have regarded him as a traitor—his entire family, for that matter. They were Saliman's descendants after all. And *he* was the one responsible for starting it all."

"That's true. He was the one who conquered the rest of the continent and established the empire, not Nyro."

After their bath, Khaldun and Mira dried off and went to bed. They made love but wanted to get an early start for home the next morning, so didn't stay up too late. As Mira started drifting off, though, there was a knock at the door. Slipping out of bed and donning her robe, she went to answer it.

"I'm sorry to disturb you," said Siren, "you were sleeping. I can come back in the morning."

"No, no, it's all right. We only just turned in for the night. Please, come in."

"Oh, hello," Khaldun said, sitting up in bed and rubbing his eyes. With a wave of his hand, he lit the room's oil lamps.

"I'll be flying back to Okset in the morning," she said, "assuming I don't get lost along the way. As you've seen, Prince Kamari concerns himself only with the affairs of Shifar, ignoring the rest of the continent. But I grew up in the north, and it sure has been good getting some real news from you two these last few days. Would you be willing to stay in touch by mirror?"

"Yes, that would be lovely," Mira said. "Will you get in trouble with the prince for this?"

"I don't think so. He has no interest in establishing communication with the rest of the continent, but I doubt he'd mind my contacting the two of you now and then."

"I'd be happy to set this up for you," said Khaldun, "but I'm afraid we don't have any spare mirrors."

"I brought one," she said, removing it from her robes. She walked over to the bed and handed it to Khaldun.

"I can connect it to several of the other princedoms' mirrors as well, if you'd like," he said.

"No, just yours," said Siren. "The prince might object if I were talking to the whole continent. And besides, I haven't met any of the others, so I'd feel a little shy contacting them out of the blue."

"Understood," he said with a chuckle. Mira fetched his mirror for him, and Khaldun performed the spells to connect it to Siren's.

"Thank you so much," she said, taking her mirror from him. "I'll let you two lovebirds get back to, ah, sleeping," she added with a sly grin on the way out the door.

Khaldun and Mira rose early and met Salerna, Azure, and Siren in the private dining room for breakfast. After that, they bade the princess farewell, and followed Azure up to the roof. Khaldun and Siren removed their carpets from the void, unfurling them on the ground. They said goodbye to Azure, thanking him for everything, then took their seats on their carpets. Mira strapped herself in as Siren lifted off, flying a slow circle around them.

"I'm not sure about this," she said, fear in her eyes. "It's a *long* way back to Okset."

"You can do it, Siren!" said Mira. "We believe in you!"

"All right. Here it goes…"

Siren shot off to the south, her scream fading into the distance. Mira chuckled as Khaldun lifted off, setting out to the northwest. Around midday, they landed by the banks of the River Torsa to stretch and eat.

"You made it from Highgate to Spanbrook and back in the same night when you kidnapped Henry, didn't you?" Mira asked.

"Yes, but I had Battleaxe with me then," Khaldun reminded her. "Having a second sorcerer calling air makes an enormous difference. I'm not nearly as fast on my own."

Mira nodded. She often found herself wishing she could *do* magic. Being a null was extremely useful in battle, but with her husband and the entire royal family all being mages, she sometimes felt left out. And always being a passenger when Khaldun and Allison could travel far and wide under their own power was humbling, too. Though she'd probably scream like Siren, just once, Mira wished she could fly a carpet on her own.

They resumed their journey and made it to Spanbrook before sunset. Heading inside, they found Allison and Jezebel in the private dining room with their daughters, just starting their meal.

"Welcome home," Jezebel said, getting to her feet and embracing them each in turn. "Sit down, you must be starving."

Mira and Khaldun took their usual seats at the table. Alanna and Leda demanded an immediate recounting of their journey, so they took turns telling the tale as they ate. They stopped short of discussing the historian's chronicles and Keepstone's dead elf, though. It would be best to contain some of that information, and the girls couldn't be trusted to keep a secret.

After dinner, Jezebel invited Mira and Khaldun to the princesses' chambers for a nightcap. Alanna and Leda complained about being left out, but only halfheartedly.

Five minutes later, Mira and Khaldun joined Jezebel and Allison in the fourth-floor master suite. They each took a seat at Jezebel's private work table, and she poured them each a brandy. Once Allison had put the usual protective spells in place, Jezebel said, "Tell us about the historian's book." Mira and Khaldun spent the next several minutes recounting everything Azure had told them.

"Necromancy doesn't work on the elves?" Allison said when they were done. "I'd imagine that must have been a nasty surprise for Nyro. Take that away, and she's no stronger than Khaldun or me."

"No stronger than *you*, maybe," Khaldun muttered.

"Except for ghouls," Jezebel said pensively. "Those could be useful if it comes to an invasion."

"This changes our plan of last resort," Khaldun said.

"Having you and Allison bind demons to become necromancers, you mean?" Jezebel said.

"Yes, us, or the university's sorcerers."

"That's fine with me," Mira said, taking a sip of her drink. "I would prefer never to see either one of you take that step."

Allison had taught Khaldun how to summon a ghoul many years ago. Though he lacked the princess's affinity with the spirit realm, and disliked using that type of magic, he was proficient enough to use the monsters in battle.

And although the university's new governors had adopted a more pragmatic stance regarding necromancy, it was still best to keep information about its potential use a closely guarded secret. If some of the other princedoms were to learn that Spanbrook's sorcerers possessed the spells necessary to become necromancers, it could bring trouble.

They discussed the ramifications of their new information for a little while. But Mira and Khaldun were tired from their journey, and they'd be rehashing it all in the privy council meeting first thing in the morning anyway. So, the two of them wished the princesses a good night and retired to their own chambers.

The next morning, Khaldun and Mira met the princesses, Captain Amari, Imani, Camilla, Gregor, Emma, and the provincial delegates in the privy council chambers. Jezebel called the meeting to order, and asked Mira and Khaldun to recount their journey. They took turns, focusing primarily on the elves in Blacksand and Keepstone, and the historian's chronicles.

"Your Highness, I believe Prince Leto's predictions will prove true," Amari said when they were done. "I can see no other reason for the elves' presence in Anoria. An invasion must be imminent."

"Salerna has seen nothing in her looking glass," Khaldun reminded them.

"You do not want to believe that the elves would attack us," said Imani, "but you cannot allow your infatuation with them to color your judgment. Maybe they will invade, maybe not. Either way, it cannot hurt to prepare."

"We *are* prepared," Amari said. "Your armies stand ready to defend the princedom, Your Highness."

Jezebel nodded. "We should have ample warning if they do land troops on the continent. We have mirrors in Northcoast, Rockport, and Blacksand, and any force heading here would have to come ashore at one of those princedoms."

"Not necessarily," said Imani. "Surely there are places along the shore where they could land unobserved from any of the port cities. And then we would have no warning."

"It would make no sense for them to bypass the ports," Amari retorted. "Any invasion force would need to establish a supply line before heading inland. And where else would they acquire those supplies? Anything they could possibly need passes through those ports."

"Unless they had some reason to target Spanbrook specifically," said Mira. Jezebel's eyes snapped to hers at those words, and Mira could have sworn she saw fear there. But it passed after only a moment.

"If that were the case, there would be no reason to send scouts to Keepstone," said Amari. "There is no quick overland route from there to here. I believe their aim will be to conquer all of Dorshire and use that as a launchpad to take the entire continent."

"We could send someone to one of the watchtowers," Khaldun suggested. "Using the seeing stone, we could scan the waters off the coast of Dorshire for an elvish fleet."

"That's not a bad idea," Jezebel said pensively. "But there's no telling how long it would take to complete such a search. The kingdom's coastline extends for thousands of miles, and there's no way to know how far off shore they would be."

"Only Princess Allison or Khaldun could make such a journey in a reasonable amount of time," said Imani. Allison shot her a withering look, and Mira failed to stifle a smile. "And with the discovery of elves in three different places now, it would be best to keep them here. Heaven knows we'll need them if the elves *do* invade."

They discussed the situation for another half hour, but ultimately decided there was nothing more to do but remain watchful. Jezebel would consider the idea of sending someone to the watchtower. She adjourned the meeting, but asked Allison, Khaldun, and Mira to stay behind. Once the others had departed, she put the protective spells in place, then retook her seat, but said nothing.

"What is it?" Allison asked, concern in her voice.

Jezebel took a deep breath. "When Khaldun summoned Nyro in his tower, right after we found the artifact hidden in the old castle, she *recognized* me."

"I remember," said Khaldun.

"The sight of me enraged her. Yet the only way she could have known me—"

"Was through prophecy," Allison finished for her.

"What if there *is* something significant about Spanbrook—or me?" said Jezebel. "Could Nyro be leading an elvish invasion force here just to destroy our princedom in an effort to alter some future outcome she foresaw?"

"There *is* something significant about Spanbrook," Khaldun said. "Nyro grew up here. And we already know she saw someone here as a potential avenue to freedom. But that's done, now."

"And Amari's right," said Mira. "If Spanbrook alone were the target, there would be no reason to send scouts to Keepstone."

Jezebel sighed. "You're probably right. But I still don't—"

At that moment there were screams outside. The four of them got up and hurried to the windows. Down in the courtyard, people were shouting and running toward the castle entries. Gazing up at Khaldun's tower, Mira spotted the cause of the alarm.

"*DRAGON!*" she said.

One of the beasts had landed on the tower roof. It raised its snout to the sky and roared.

"What in the hell is *that* doing here?" Jezebel demanded, hurrying out of the council chamber.

Allison, Khaldun, and Mira followed her. As the four of them emerged from the castle, the dragon leaped into the air. Mira was ready to expand her null around them at the first sign of flames. The beast circled the courtyard once before landing in its center, roaring at the sky again. Mira had spotted a rider on its back, and now, he clambered off the animal as it lowered its head to the ground.

"Hold it right there," Khaldun said as the man approached them. "Who are you and what do you want?"

"I apologize for causing alarm," the man said, holding his ground and raising both hands in a gesture of peace. "Our chieftain sent me here to deliver a message."

"Go ahead," said Khaldun. "We're listening."

"I was directed to deliver my message only to the Lady Mira."

"I'm here," Mira said, moving up to stand next to Khaldun.

"My instructions are to speak with you and no one else," he said apologetically.

Mira turned to Jezebel; she nodded. Opening her channels of power and extending her null only far enough to protect herself, Mira approached the man. "What is your message?"

"Perhaps there is somewhere more private we could go," he suggested, gazing around at their surroundings.

Mira spotted people looking out many of the windows.

"My office," Jezebel said.

"Right this way," Mira said to the man.

He turned to his dragon for a moment. The beast roared, then turned, taking several steps before extending his wings and taking off. He landed on the tower again.

Mira led the man into Jezebel's office. "Well, let's hear it," she said, sitting against the front edge of the desk.

"Lady Mira, I am Kashi of the dragon lords. Our chieftain, Lavinia, has sent me here to find you."

"Lavinia?" Mira said suspiciously. "Vano is the chieftain."

"Vano has passed away. Lavinia is his daughter."

Salerna had sent Azure to contact the dragon lords not long after Fosland's defeat. But when he approached their lands, they tried shooting him out of the sky with dragon fire. He'd barely escaped with his life.

Knowing how effective the dragons had been in the battle, Jezebel decided it was worth another attempt. She'd sent Khaldun and Mira to try making contact. Not wanting to suffer the same fate as Azure, they'd taken his carpet only as far as the highlands north of the Forsaken Hills, then made the crossing through the Anthars on foot.

Vano's people found them as they approached their aeries on the eastern side of the mountains. They'd tried incinerating them with dragon fire, but Mira had used her null to protect them—dragon fire was magical. Mira and Khaldun had allowed themselves to be captured and interrogated, knowing that was likely the only way they'd ever meet the leader. Their captors told them that the chieftain *never* met with outsiders. But that very night, Vano had come to see them. Old and stooped, leaning on his wizard's staff for balance, he took one look at Mira before inviting the two of them to dine with him.

Once inside his hall, he'd ordered the rest of his people to leave. And with only Khaldun and Mira present, his appearance had transformed. He straightened and his skin turned golden.

"You're a sorcerer," Khaldun had said with a gasp. "But your eyes—"

"Aye, my eyes are normal," he'd said, taking his seat at the head of the table, still moving like an old man. "Our people belong to no princedom, so the university has no jurisdiction here—though they must think they do. My parents hid me away after I transformed. And since my father's passing over two centuries ago, I have reigned as chieftain."

Before Khaldun or Mira could broach the topic of an alliance, Vano explained that Henry had sent Dredmort and a red-haired witch to kidnap his son. They'd threatened to kill him unless Vano agreed to send dragons to support them in their war against the other princedoms. Vano had always kept his people—and his dragons—out of the princedoms' affairs. But he explained that his children were his weakness. He'd agreed to send one rider with four dragons in exchange for his son's life.

In the end, Vano's son never returned. Salerna had sent people to the Darkhold to determine what had become of him. They'd discovered that Henry had ordered him executed the same night that his people infiltrated the university.

Mira and Khaldun had explained to Vano what happened with Nyro, and asked if he'd be willing to join their alliance. He'd demurred, saying that "until the end of the world," he would never allow his dragons to participate in another war. They'd taken his answer back to Princess Jezebel, but kept the fact of his being a sorcerer a secret, even from her.

"Chieftain Vano was a good man," Mira said to Kashi. "I'm terribly sorry for your loss."

"Lady Mira, Chieftain Lavinia has requested that you come to visit her. She wanted me to tell you that 'the end of the world might be upon us.' She said you would know what that means."

Mira gasped, recalling the old chieftain's words. "I would very much like to visit again. But Princess Jezebel would have to approve, of course."

"Could we ask her now? Darkwing will need to rest—we've flown almost nonstop these last two days. But you and I could depart first thing in the morning. The chieftain is very eager to meet you."

Mira led him back out to the courtyard. They found Princess Jezebel conferring with Emma, Khaldun, and Allison. Mira asked her if they could speak in private for a moment. Leaving Kashi with the others, Mira followed the princess back into her office. Jezebel took a seat behind her desk, and Mira sat across from her, telling her about the chieftain's request.

"Intriguing," Jezebel said. "Do you think this means she's ready to commit to an alliance?"

"I never met Lavinia, so it's hard to say. But the wording of her message certainly makes me think so."

"If we *are* facing an invasion, I would very much like to have the dragons on our side. I think you should go. But I don't want to send you alone with this messenger. Khaldun should go with you again."

"Yes, I would prefer that as well," Mira said.

Mira went to get Allison and Khaldun. Once inside Jezebel's office, they explained the situation to them. The two of them agreed that this opportunity was too great to pass up, so they returned to the courtyard to give Kashi the news.

"Terrific," he said. "Darkwing and I will be happy to fly with you. And the chieftain will be pleased with your decision."

"Will you join us for dinner this evening?" Jezebel asked.

"I think not," he replied apologetically. "Darkwing would become anxious in my absence; I have brought enough food for a few more days. She needs to hunt, so I will take her into the wild north of here to make sure she doesn't eat any of your people's livestock. We will return here at dawn."

"Where will you sleep?" Allison asked. "We do have guest accommodations you could use."

"Thank you, but I will sleep under the stars with Darkwing."

Kashi turned, holding up one arm. The dragon roared, leaping into the sky, swooping once around the courtyard, and landing only feet away. The man bade them farewell as the beast lowered her head to the ground. He climbed up to his perch on her shoulders, and she took off once more, disappearing beyond the castle walls.

"Well, my lord and lady," Emma said with a grin. "It looks like you'll be traveling again. I'll prepare your food and supplies." She hurried off.

Mira and Khaldun spent the next couple of hours training with Allison. Princess Jezebel insisted that they all keep their combat skills sharp, herself included. So she and the mages all scheduled time with Allison every week. Mira had learned to wield a longsword in her youth, but had no natural talent for combat. But given her inability to perform magic, the training was particularly useful for her.

Today, however, she was not at her best. She couldn't stop thinking about going to see the dragon lords again, and her lack of concentration showed. Were it not for her leather suit, Khaldun would have skewered her repeatedly.

Mira and Khaldun returned to their chambers when they were done. They bathed together, then Mira got dressed and went to meet Leda and Alanna in the library for their lesson. That evening, she gathered with Khaldun, Emma, and the royal family for dinner in the keep. The meal was delicious as always, and the wine was making her sleepy. She was ready to turn in early before their journey the next morning.

But as they were preparing to head upstairs, there was a commotion outside. Mira and Khaldun followed Jezebel and Allison out to the courtyard to see what was going on. She spotted a man on horseback trying to get past the guards. But as they moved closer, she realized who it was.

"Father!" said Jezebel, running over to him. Mira was surprised to see him; she knew Robert avoided the castle as much as possible. "What are you doing here?"

"Your Highness," he said, removing his hat and nodding to her. "I came as quickly as I could. We found them lurking about the homestead. You'd better send someone."

"Found whom?"

"The elves, Jezebel!"

CHAPTER SEVEN
THE DRAGON LORDS

ow many elves?" Jezebel demanded. "And where exactly did you see them?"

"I saw three," said Robert. "Creeping around the barn. They disappeared when they saw me. I hurried into the house to alert your mother, then came straight here."

"You left mother there?" Jezebel said.

"She barred the door; she'll be all right." Jezebel frowned at him, and he added, "You know Vivien. I never could have gotten her to come with me."

"You're right, of course," she said, nodding. She told one of the guards to lower the gates and raise the drawbridge.

"Hold on," said Robert. "Let me get out of here before you button the place up."

"You'll be safer here," Jezebel said.

"It's my home, Jez. That's where I belong."

She agreed reluctantly, and he rode off, heading out of the castle. "Go," she said to Allison, Khaldun, and Mira. "Do whatever you can to capture one of them alive. It's time to get some answers."

The three of them hurried up to their chambers to change into their armor. Mira donned her sword belt, grabbed her daggers, and ran up to the roof with Khaldun, right behind Allison. They pulled their carpets out of the void, unfurled them, and took their seats. Allison took off while Mira was still strapping herself in, then Khaldun shot off behind her.

Though it was growing dark already, the sorcerers knew the terrain well, Allison in particular. They reached the Barclay farm in no time, setting down by the barn. Khaldun started by the door, holding out his hands to detect any magic.

"Someone cast an invisibility spell here recently, but I sense no trail."

Allison held out both arms, her hands glowing. The earth around them trembled, and a shadow rose from the ground, taking human shape, and engulfing Allison. Mira hated it when she summoned demons. She'd witnessed it more times than she could count, but it still sent a chill down her spine every time. The shadow disappeared and Allison closed her eyes. Moments later, she opened them, saying, "There are three elves out at Rockhedge. Let's go!"

They retook their seats on their carpets and took off, flying over the Devil's Wood and staying close to the treetops. Reaching the standing stones in their clearing, they circled the area once, but Mira couldn't see anyone. Suddenly, Allison's carpet dropped—she called air to cushion her landing. Khaldun set down, and he and Allison tucked their carpets into the void, pulling out their weapons.

Three jets of fire shot at them from across the clearing; Mira canceled them. Then she canceled the invisibility spell hiding the elves. There were three—two with weapons and one without, presumably two warriors and a mage. The warriors charged.

"Expand your null," Khaldun told her. "We don't want their mage interfering."

Mira opened her channels of power, allowing her null to engulf the entire site. She could sense the three elves by their magic. Their power felt more ethereal than that of human mages, as if it were woven into their surroundings. Much like a demon's, in fact. The mage stood out simply by virtue of being stronger.

Allison engaged the warriors, her swords moving like a whirlwind. In seconds, one elf was lying dead on the ground, and she'd disarmed the second. She had him face down in the dirt, pinning him with one knee.

Their mage ran, faster than any human, disappearing among the trees. Khaldun and Mira gave chase, but they'd lost sight of him in the dark. Khaldun could find no trail, and even with her null at its maximum size, Mira had lost him. They returned to the clearing to find Allison's elf lying unconscious on her carpet.

"Let's get this one back to the castle," she said.

They flew back to Castle Barclay, landing in the courtyard. Amari had mustered the troops, and they'd formed ranks, establishing a defensive perimeter around the castle. Allison and Khaldun tucked their carpets into oblivion, and Allison called air to move the prisoner inside the castle and down to the dungeons. Mira had told one of the guards to alert Princess Jezebel to their return, and she joined them moments later.

Once Allison had moved the elf into a cell, she closed the door, producing a key to lock it. She canceled her knockout spell to revive him, then Mira extended her null to make sure he couldn't use magic against them.

The elf got to his feet, taking in his new surroundings for a moment, then regarded them with a defiant expression. The sight of him took Mira's breath away; this was her first good look at him. His perfect skin, toned body, and piercing eyes alone set him apart from any human she'd ever seen. But more than that, he projected a vibrant energy, as if he were more alive than any Anorian she'd ever met. The physical attraction she felt rivaled what she'd experienced around Allure.

"What are your people doing in Anoria?" Allison demanded.

The elf clenched his jaw and stared beyond them.

"Do you understand me?" she asked.

"We speak your putrid tongue," he said.

"Tell me why you're here."

"You brought me here. You tell me."

Allison sighed. Turning to Mira, she said, "I need magic."

Mira closed her channels of power, extinguishing her null.

Holding out one hand, Allison cast a spell. The elf's expression went blank.

"Why are your people in Anoria?" Allison asked again.

"The supreme leader commands it."

"Who is the supreme leader?"

"Estrid the Conqueror."

Allison shot Jezebel an inquisitive look, but she only shrugged.

"Who is Estrid?" Allison asked the elf.

"Our supreme leader."

"Yes, so I've come to understand. But where did she come from?"

"Drengrvollr."

"Which is where?"

"The westernmost kingdom."

"Estrid is an elf?"

"Yes, of course."

"And why did he send you here?"

"The supreme leader is female."

Allison sighed. "All right, why did *she* send you here?"

"To gather information."

"About what?"

"The powers that govern your lands."

"And what information specifically?"

"Your military and thaumaturgic capabilities."

"Are your people going to invade Anoria?"

"Yes."

"When?"

"I do not know."

"What is the purpose of the invasion? Is your supreme leader planning to conquer us?"

"No. She wants to exterminate you."

Allison fixed Jezebel with a gaze, her eyes wide.

"When did Estrid come to power?" Jezebel asked him.

"She became our supreme leader four years ago."

"And what does that title mean, exactly? Supreme leader?"

"She rules over all the elven kingdoms."

"But she came from Drengrvollr?"

"Yes."

"When did she come to power there?"

"Fourteen years ago."

"And then she conquered the rest of your continent?"

"Yes."

Jezebel took a deep breath. "I think we're done here," she said to Allison.

With a wave of her hand, Allison enclosed the cell in glowing, golden energy. She canceled the spell making the elf susceptible to suggestion.

The elf's eyes went wide, and he looked back and forth between Allison and Jezebel for a moment. "Our people will slaughter every last one of you! Your kingdoms will burn!"

Jezebel ignored him, ushering the rest of them back upstairs. "We'll keep him under heavy guard," she told them once they reached the main level. "Allison's spell will ensure no one else's magic can penetrate his cell, inward or outward."

"Why would their supreme leader want to exterminate our people?" Mira asked.

"I don't know," Jezebel said, shaking her head. "But her initial rise to power took place soon after Nyro's liberation. I find it difficult to believe that's a coincidence."

"I would have to agree," said Allison. "I believe the three we encountered tonight must be scouts, like the ones that have turned up elsewhere. But I should fly a patrol around our borders to make sure there are no additional forces headed this way."

"I'll go with you," said Khaldun.

"No," said Jezebel. "You need your rest before the two of you fly east tomorrow. But I'll have Emma check in with Rockport and make sure no armies have come ashore."

Khaldun and Mira headed up to their chambers, disrobed, and went to bed. He drifted off right away, but Mira couldn't sleep. She couldn't understand the hatred she'd seen in the prisoner's eyes. He *wanted* all of their people dead. But why? They hadn't had contact with the elves in centuries. What reason could they have for seeking their extermination?

Nyro had to be behind it. But how? Could Estrid the Conqueror be Nyro? She'd possessed Syllith before passing through the portal she'd created. Could she have gone to Drengrvollr, used an illusion spell to make herself look like an elf, then proceeded to conquer their entire continent?

This all sounded so unlikely. Nyro would have been starting with *nothing*. Syllith was *naked* when she moved through the portal, for heaven's sake. How could Nyro have conquered an entire continent—using Syllith's body the whole time—without even having any clothes on her back? And if she'd been possessing Syllith all this time, using an illusion spell to masquerade as an elf, wouldn't someone detect the ruse? Most of the elves couldn't detect static magic, but the mages would. Could Nyro have avoided every elvish mage for fifteen years?

Mira had a feeling Nyro must have found some other way to pull this off. She couldn't imagine what it might be, but felt certain she had to be behind this invasion somehow.

Khaldun roused her before dawn. She didn't remember dozing off, but didn't feel like she'd slept more than a few hours. They met Jezebel, Allison, and Emma in the dining room for a quick breakfast. Rockport hadn't reported anything amiss, and Allison had found no armies on her patrol of their lands. Jezebel was planning to hold an emergency privy council meeting later that morning, but it didn't seem they were under attack just yet.

Heading out to the courtyard with Khaldun, Mira spotted Darkwing flying in from the west. She circled once before landing only yards away from them. After shaking her head like a dog, she lowered it toward them, sniffing them.

"Don't be afraid," Kashi called down to them. "I've let her know that you're friends and you'll be flying with us today."

Mira trembled with fear as the dragon nudged her with her snout. She'd never been so close to one of these beasts, but this one almost seemed like she wanted to play.

The dragon reared suddenly, lifting her head to the sky and roaring. Mira backed away in surprise, nearly falling over.

"She's eager to get underway," Kashi told them.

"We're ready," Khaldun replied.

He removed the carpet from the void, laying it out on the ground. The two of them took their seats, and Mira strapped herself in as Khaldun tucked their packs into the void. After that, they lifted off, shooting into the sky. The dragon followed, catching them with ease.

They flew for several hours before touching down in a field somewhere in eastern Newberry to take a rest. Mira stretched for a minute, then they ate lunch with Kashi. The dragon gamboled around the field, chasing the occasional bird, before dropping onto her back and rolling around, reminding Mira of nothing more than a cat.

"She seems so playful," she said. "Nothing like the ones we encountered during the Battle of Highgate."

"Darkwing's one of our younger dragons," Kashi said. "But the ones you met enjoy playing, too. Of course, you probably didn't see that side of them then."

"Hardly," Mira muttered.

"It's my understanding that a dragon is fiercely loyal to its rider, and will allow no one else to fly them," Khaldun said. "Is that true?"

"Aye, it is," Kashi said. "Most dragons never take any rider. But the ones who do form a bond with only one human that lasts a lifetime. In some instances, a dragon will bond with a new human if their rider passes away, but it's almost always with someone in the same family. A spouse or offspring."

"You're not a mage, though," said Mira. "For some reason, I thought riders controlled their dragons through magic."

Kashi chuckled. "I don't think *anyone* controls a dragon. They're pretty independent-minded. But no, it's not magic. At least, it's not human magic. When a dragon bonds with a human, they touch your mind."

"You *communicate* with her?" Mira asked, surprised that such a thing was possible.

"Not in words," Kashi said. "It's more like feelings, or images. When I took her to hunt last night, I showed her a picture of the forest in my mind, and imagined her making a kill."

"She can see your thoughts, then?" Khaldun asked.

"Aye, and I can see hers. Not all the time, though. Only when she's got something she wants to tell me. And I'm pretty sure that's how it works both ways."

"The rider who participated in the Battle of Highgate was a mage, though," said Mira.

"He was one of our few," Kashi said. "Chieftain Vano only sent him because he knew he'd encounter magic in the battle. It was a shame to lose him. Ephraim was a good friend."

Learning his name saddened Mira. He'd always been some faceless, nameless rider in her memory. But knowing his name and that he'd only fought them because Henry's people had blackmailed their chieftain into helping his war effort made him human in her memory.

They took off again, crossing the River Mayne just before sunset. They landed again, making camp in a meadow far from any settlements. It was cold here, and Mira was glad Emma had packed their furs; she hadn't given the weather much thought. Khaldun got a fire going while Mira set up their tent.

The three of them sat up for a few hours, eating and sharing tales by the fire. Darkwing had curled up nearby. Mira and Khaldun went to sleep in their tent, but Kashi chose a spot near his dragon, lying down in the grass. As Mira was about to close the flaps, she saw the beast move one wing to cover her rider.

Early the next morning, they got underway again. After a short rest in the highlands north of the Forsaken Hills, they reached the Anthars. Kashi led the way across the mountains, and a little before sunset, his people's aeries came into view as they passed over the eastern slopes. Most of them were little more than caverns, some naturally-occurring, with others dug out of the rock long ago. But there was one structure built upon a rocky outcrop. It looked like the ruins of an ancient castle, and that was where the chieftains of the dragon lords had made their home for many lives of men. Far below the castle, Mira spotted a basin in the mountainside, as if someone had carved a bowl out of the rock. She knew from her last visit that they used that area as a corral to train new dragons. But new mothers also kept their hatchlings there, as it provided some shelter from the wind.

Kashi landed Darkwing in the building's courtyard and clambered off his mount. Khaldun touched down nearby, and he and Mira got to their feet and stretched.

"Wait here for a moment," Kashi told them, "and I'll let Chieftain Lavinia know we've arrived."

He hurried into the building, and Darkwing took off, probably going to hunt. Khaldun rolled up their carpet, tucking it into the void.

Kashi returned a few minutes later. "The chieftain will see you now. Please, come with me."

He led them into the castle, to a room that had probably been the great hall. There were long wooden tables here, but this section of the building had no roof. Kashi led them to the far end of one table, where there was a pitcher of wine and three glasses.

"Please, have a seat, and she will be here shortly."

Kashi left the room, and Khaldun and Mira each took a seat. Only moments later, a woman with wild blond hair walked in. She wore furs and thick boots. Khaldun and Mira got to their feet, but she walked past them, sitting at the head of the table.

"Wine?" she asked, pouring herself a glass.

"Sure," Khaldun said with a shrug. Mira nodded.

The woman poured them each a glass, drank hers, and then refilled it. Sitting back in her chair, she said, "It was my father's dying wish that I invite you here, Lady Mira. Many years ago, long before that Foslander son of a bitch ascended to his throne, he had a dream about a wayfarer woman coming to our aeries. And when you visited the first time, he knew you were the woman from his vision."

"He was a sorcerer," Khaldun said. "It's not uncommon for our kind to have prophetic dreams."

"Aye. Well, as you know, we typically kill trespassers. I only decided to let you live when I realized you were a null. My father had never told me about his dream, so I didn't know he'd want to meet you."

"Why did that change your mind?" Khaldun asked.

"Nulls aren't exactly common, are they? I was curious."

"But either one of us could have canceled the dragon fire the normal way," Mira said. "How could you have known I was a null?"

"Because *I* tried to incinerate you, too," she said, pulling a wand from her furs and laying it on the table. "And that didn't work, either, even though neither one of you cast a counter-spell."

"You're a witch," Khaldun said, pointing out the obvious.

"Yes, I am. And it's a good thing my spell failed that day. In that first vision, my father saw *you* becoming a dragon rider... and the leader of our people."

"*What*?" said Mira, startled by this revelation.

"My reaction exactly," Lavinia said, taking a long drink. "Members of my family have led the dragon lords since the beginning. My brother should have taken the mantle next, but as fate would have it, it's fallen to me. And I'm not willing to give it up."

"Then I don't understand," said Mira. "Why did you invite me here now?"

The chieftain took a deep breath. "Because my father had a second vision that he never told me about until his final days. It was a dream of Anoria burning, all of its princedoms falling. Now, we don't care much for the affairs of the rest of the continent. But he saw our people dying, too. All of us."

"The end of the world," Mira muttered.

"Yes. He believed he'd live to see it. But only a few nights before he passed, he had those two dreams again. My father knew he was dying, and he believed the end of days would be coming soon. He made me promise to bring you here."

"What did he want me to do now that I'm here?" Mira asked.

Lavinia said nothing for a moment, finishing her wine. "I think he wanted me to meet you. To evaluate you, perhaps, as a potential leader. And I'll be honest, I was curious. What was it about you that made him believe you'd be a better chieftain than I?"

"I assure you, I have no desire to supplant you," Mira said. "I don't know the first thing about dragons, and I don't belong here. I am not one of your people, and I have a home that I do not wish to leave. But… your father might be right about it being the end of the world."

Mira and Khaldun spent a few minutes telling her about the elves.

"Nyro," she said when they were done. "The ancient demon, rising out of legend. These are ill tidings, indeed. Perhaps my father's visions were true, after all. But I'm not sure how you fit into them."

"I am no dragon lord," said Mira. "But we would like to establish an alliance between our people and yours. If an invasion is imminent, and it does seem like this is what your father foresaw, Anoria could use the dragon lords' help."

Lavinia sat back in her chair, taking a deep breath, and steepled her fingers together. "I will have to consider this. This may be what my father intended. But I am chieftain now, and Anoria does not yet burn."

"Perhaps we could agree to stay in communication," Khaldun said, pulling a small mirror out of the void and placing it on the table. "I've connected this to my own. If the elves do attack, we could use this to contact you. Then, perhaps, you would consider coming to our aid."

Lavinia nodded, taking the mirror and examining it. "That is acceptable." She got to her feet. "The hour is growing late. You are welcome to dine with us and spend the night in our aeries. Our newest hatchlings will be going to sleep by now, but in the morning, I will take you to see them before you depart."

"I would enjoy that very much," Mira said, standing up with Khaldun. "Thank you, Chieftain Lavinia."

The clans arrived, sitting down around the tables, and thirty minutes later, their feast was served. Mira learned that the clans took turns hunting and cooking. The food was delicious, and the wine plentiful. Mira grew full and drunk, and worried that she might fall as Kashi led them up to the caverns later that night. He explained that most of them were connected by a tunnel system that crisscrossed the interior of the mountain.

Mira and Khaldun had a cave to themselves. It was chilly, but Khaldun lit a fire, and they had their tent and their furs to keep them warm. The noise of the wind moving through the passage produced an eerie whistling sound, as if an invisible giant were playing an enormous flute.

"It's interesting that Vano had a prophetic dream about me," Mira said as they lay in their tent. "This proves it's possible."

"Yes," Khaldun agreed. "Now that they know us, there'd be no reason for you to use your null here, unless the aeries were under attack. Vano must have foreseen an event when your channels of power would be closed."

Mira slept well, dreaming that she was a dragon lord, riding her mount high above the mountains. The next morning, Khaldun and Mira ate with the clans, then Lavinia led them out of the castle. Gazing skyward, Mira gasped. There were *dozens* of dragons flying above the aeries, swooping and diving.

"Magnificent, aren't they?" the chieftain said, following her gaze.

"Yes, they are," Mira agreed. Suddenly, she spotted an enormous dragon moving into view above the highest peak, dwarfing the others. "That one is huge!"

"That's Magna. He's the sire of our crash, and he was my father's."

"I'm sorry, your *crash*?" Mira asked.

"It's the term for a group of dragons. Although this is the last one in Anoria. Many centuries ago, it is said they filled the skies from Horn to Hido. But they are a dying breed."

"Will Magna take another rider?" Khaldun asked.

"Probably not," Lavinia said sadly. "My father bonded with him when he was only a boy. It would be unusual for a dragon to accept anyone else after so many years."

"But your father was over two hundred years old," said Mira.

"Aye. So is Magna. They were born on the same day, in fact."

"I had no idea dragons were so long-lived," said Khaldun.

"Most live over a century," Lavinia replied. "Few make it to two hundred. Magna is the oldest dragon we've had in a thousand years, if the stories have it right."

She led them down a steep and winding path to the corral. A low, stone wall formed a perimeter around the area's upper rim. Gazing into the basin below, Mira spotted half a dozen hatchlings lying in what looked like giant bird's nests. A full-sized dragon stood nearby, next to a woman Mira recognized from the meals they'd shared with the dragon lords.

"Would you like to meet one of the hatchlings?" Lavinia asked.

"Yes, I would love to," said Mira.

"You'd better wait up here," the woman added to Khaldun. "The mother will be extremely protective. They usually allow women to come close, but not men."

"Yes, I think I'd better stay here," Khaldun said.

Lavinia led Mira down a narrow flight of steps to the floor of the corral. As they crossed the basin, she held up one hand, giving the other dragon lord a signal. The woman led the mother dragon away from the hatchlings. "Malina is her rider," she explained. "She should be able to keep her calm while we visit the hatchlings."

Mira's pulse quickened as they approached the nests, and she kept one eye on the mother. The dragon roared, but didn't make any aggressive movements. As they reached the hatchlings, Mira realized they had feathers.

"Only the babies have them," Lavinia said when Mira asked. "They lose them by the time they make their first flight."

The hatchlings seemed timid; most had backed away to the other side of the nests. But one remained close, gazing at them curiously. Mira stepped closer, holding out one hand. The dragon waddled cautiously forward, sniffing her. But then it rubbed its head against her hand. Mira stroked him, giggling nervously. "I never thought I'd get to pet a dragon."

"He likes you," Lavinia observed.

Mira heard a rattling noise coming from his throat. "What is that sound?"

"He's purring."

"Like a cat?" Mira asked, shocked that such a fearsome animal would do this.

Lavinia nodded. "The adults do it sometimes, too. But only when they're very relaxed. Usually right before going to sleep."

Suddenly, the mother roared, startling Mira. She backed away from the hatchling, and it squawked at her.

"It's all right," said Lavinia. "She's just letting you know the hatchling is hers."

But the dragon reared, roaring again, and then charged toward them. Mira backed farther away from the nests, Lavinia with her, and would have bolted, but the woman said, "Don't run."

They'd put a good amount of distance between them and the hatchlings, but the dragon pursued them. It shot a jet of fire at them, but Mira canceled it before it could hit them.

"Mira!" Khaldun yelled. "Get out of there!"

"Come on," Lavinia said, grabbing Mira by the arm and pulling her toward the steps.

It was too late. The dragon lunged, its jaws wide open, several rows of teeth gleaming in the morning sunlight. Mira covered her head with her arms, certain she was about to die.

But suddenly, there was an ear-piercing roar, and a second, much larger dragon landed on the first, flattening her head against the ground. Mira screamed, ignoring Lavinia's warning and running for the steps.

Lavinia hadn't moved. "Magna! Get off of her!"

The dragon sire stepped away from the mother, and she hurried over to her hatchlings. He roared, then turned to Mira. She was about to dash up the steps, but Magna held her gaze. Mira froze as he strode toward her. He stopped only a few feet away from her, lowering his head as if he were bowing.

Lavinia hurried over, staring at the dragon in awe. At that moment, he lifted his head and roared, before running several steps and taking to the air.

"I'll be damned," Lavinia muttered. "Did he communicate with you?"

"What? No..."

Lavinia nodded, but said nothing more. They hurried up the steps, and Khaldun held her tight.

"I thought I was about to lose you," he said.

Mira returned his embrace, unable to stop shaking. Once she'd calmed down, the chieftain led them back up to the castle. She thanked them for coming, and promised she would consider providing assistance in the event of an invasion. Khaldun and Mira bade her farewell, and took off on their carpet.

CHAPTER EIGHT
OLD FRIENDS

t feels like taking me down there to meet the hatchling was some sort of test," Mira told Khaldun as they flew. "A test that I failed."

"Maybe she wanted to see if the dragon would bond with you. Her father foresaw you becoming their leader, so that probably *was* a test."

"She asked me if the sire communicated with me."

"Did he?"

"No. But how could he? I'm a null—*no* magic works on me."

"I'm not sure that qualifies as magic," Khaldun said. "They're dragons, not people. Only people can do magic."

"Their fire works magically, though," Mira said. "Isn't that what you told me?"

"Yes, I'd forgotten about that. When Henry's forces attacked the university, the dragons' fire weakened Cyclone's shield spell. That wouldn't happen with normal fire."

"See? Dragons *can* work magic. I'd never be able to communicate with one."

They rode in silence for a few minutes, then Khaldun said, "Why don't we stop at the university? We can get a good meal, spend the night in a feather bed, and ask the governors about dragon magic. One of them is bound to have our answer."

It was a two-day journey back to Spanbrook, so they'd have to stay *somewhere* that night. But their flight path would not take them near the university. "We can't. We need to get back to Spanbrook as quickly as possible—the elves could attack any time now."

"It's not very far out of the way," Khaldun said. "It might add an hour or two to our journey tomorrow, no more."

Mira agreed. The nights were cold, and she would enjoy a hot meal and a feather bed. They could always communicate with the university by mirror, but it would be good to see their old friends again, too.

A few hours later, they stopped to rest and eat on the top of a mesa in the Forsaken Hills. Taking off again, they reached the university before sunset. When they reached the protective dome, Khaldun cast the spell to open a portal, closing it again once they'd flown through. They landed in front of the administrative buildings to find Allure teaching a young sorcerer. This was no one Mira recognized. She had long, black hair, and stood no taller than Allure.

Allure waved, but kept working with her student. They were practicing illusions, and as Khaldun and Mira watched, the sorcerer cast a spell creating an entire herd of sheep milling about the grounds. They finished the lesson a few minutes later.

"What brings you two back to the nest?" Allure asked, embracing them each in turn. Mira's heart skipped a beat, and her breath caught in her throat when she touched her.

"We were on our way home from the dragon lords' aeries, and figured we'd stop in to visit," Khaldun said. "And we had a question for you."

"Oh? What about?"

Mira told her about her experience with the dragons. "I was wondering if it would be possible for me to communicate with a dragon, given the existence of my null."

"That's a great question," Allure said with a frown. "I'm afraid I don't know much about dragons. We should ask Sage. If anyone knows, it would be her. Why don't you two come home with me, and I'll invite the others over for dinner?"

"That sounds wonderful," Mira said with a smile.

They headed off toward the governors' mansions. The university had rebuilt after Fosland's attack all those years ago. The new mansions were all made of brick or stone, and they'd imbued the roofs with spells that repelled fire. They'd used those same spells to protect the library's contents years earlier, which was the only reason their enormous collection had survived.

"Who's the new sorcerer?" Khaldun asked.

"Her name is Fang," Allure said.

"She's a little young for a name change, isn't she?" he said. "I haven't even taken one yet."

"No, that's her given name," Allure said. "She's from a village in Kong."

"You haven't had many new sorcerers in recent years, have you?" asked Mira.

"She's the first since Henry's downfall."

"Isn't that strange?" Khaldun asked. "That's a long time to go without any new ones."

"Not really," said Allure. "These things tend to go in spurts. We'll get quite a few all at once, and then none for a long time."

"Who's her conjurnor?" Khaldun asked.

"I don't know. It's part of the new security measures we've put in place to make sure no one can do what Dredmort did to Allison. Fang doesn't even know who her conjurnor is. Only Sage knows—she's the one who performed her rite of binding."

"Everyone still knows who the governors' conjurnors are, though," said Mira. "That's easy, because they're governors, too."

"Not necessarily, anymore," Allure said. "More than half of our conjurnors have passed away since the attack here. Steps were taken to reassign their heirs, and those people's identities were kept from the rest of us. The conjurnors are no longer serving as governors; we've replaced them with the most senior non-sorcerer mages."

"So, you don't know who your conjurnor is anymore?" Khaldun asked.

"I do not."

"Well, this should make it *much* tougher for someone to do what Dredmort did," Mira observed. "It had become common knowledge that Dana was Allison's conjurnor."

They reached Allure's house, and found Semblant inside, sitting at the dining room table, reading a book, and drinking wine from an enormous glass. He barely acknowledged Khaldun and Mira, but got up to embrace Allure.

She used her mirror to invite the other sorcerers to join them, and had her staff get to work preparing a feast. Khaldun and Mira sat down at the table, and Allure poured them each a glass of wine. Battleaxe and Mist showed up a few minutes later, greeting Khaldun and Mira much more amiably than Semblant had. Cyclone showed up soon after, and finally, Sage arrived. Semblant got up to greet her, and Mira was surprised to see that Sage was actually a little taller—not nearly as massive, though.

They all joined them at the table, and Allure made sure everyone's wine glass was full. Then she told Sage about Mira's question about the dragons.

Sage sat back in her chair, taking a long drink of her wine. "I don't know. But I can make an educated guess."

"Yes, please do," said Mira.

"It's important to point out that while your null eliminates any magic that comes in contact with it, it would be incorrect to say that you cannot have *any* interaction with magic."

"Invisibility spells work as long as I contain my null inside of them, for example," Mira said. "Same with shield spells. And I can use a mirror to communicate, as long as my channels of power are closed."

"Yes, exactly. And if someone casts an illusion outside of your null, you can see it," Sage said. "And of course, you can fly on Khaldun's carpet, as long as you keep your null extinguished."

"Because the magic doesn't have to interact with *me*. His spells affect only the carpet, and from there, the usual forces of nature act on me."

"Correct," said Sage.

"But to communicate with a dragon, that magic would have to interact with me."

"*If* that is magic," Sage said. "We don't know if it is or not. But I suspect that it is."

"So, I'd never be able to communicate with one," Mira said, feeling crestfallen.

"I didn't say that," said Sage, holding up one finger. "There are two fundamental types of magic. Thaumaturgic and sympathetic. Nearly all the spells with which you're familiar qualify as thaumaturgy. Those are the ones that use the five magical forces.

"But sympathetic magic is different. I assume, for example, that you sense the same feelings around Allure as the rest of us?"

"*Everyone* does," Allure said with a smile.

"Yes, I do," Mira said with a giggle. "But that's not *magic*, is it?"

"It is," said Sage.

"But I feel the same thing around our master-at-arms, Imani," said Mira. "Not as strong, perhaps, but she's not even a mage."

"The term 'mage' applies only to those who practice thaumaturgy," said Sage. "It's unusual, but it is possible for non-mages to perform sympathetic magic. Such is almost certainly the case with your master-at-arms.

"But Allure's ability to read people also qualifies as sympathetic magic. She's not using any of the magical forces when she does that."

"That might explain how Nyro was able to communicate with us through the artifact," said Khaldun. "Her magic shouldn't have been able to penetrate the elvish barrier."

"I am nearly certain that she used sympathetic magic to do that," Sage said.

"So, if I'd been present for that, *I* would have seen and heard Nyro, too?" Mira asked. "It wasn't an illusion spell?"

"Definitely not illusion, and yes, I do believe you *would* have seen the same thing as the others."

"Well, we can put this theory to the test," Allure said, getting to her feet and walking over to Mira.

"How?"

"If I can read you despite your null, then we know sympathetic magic works on you," she said, taking Mira's head in her hands and closing her eyes. Mira felt nothing, but Allure said, "You are fiercely loyal to your husband, Princess Jezebel, and her family. If necessary, you would die to protect them, and everything you've helped build for the last fifteen years. I sense no personal ambition in you—you have no desire for power or riches of your own." Allure opened her eyes, gazing into Mira's and keeping her hands on her for a moment longer. She caressed her face as she removed them. "Your people are lucky to have you, Lady Mira."

Allure retook her seat.

"You read all of that in me?" Mira asked. Allure nodded. "So sympathetic magic *does* work on me."

"And that means you most likely *can* communicate with a dragon," Sage concluded.

"I didn't, though. Which means Magna probably didn't try to bond with me."

"We've speculated that Nyro gained control of Syllith somehow when she hit her with that bolt of energy at the Temple of the Goddess," said Khaldun. "And I've always wondered how Nyro could have done that through the elvish barrier. Could that have been sympathetic magic?"

"No, I do not believe so," said Sage. "I've thought about this many times over the years. My research into the matter has proven fruitless because, of course, nearly every text about necromancy was destroyed during the purge. But the monks at the temple must have weakened the barrier there enough for Nyro to squeeze a small fragment of her soul through it in the form of that energy bolt."

"So, essentially, she possessed Syllith?" Mira asked.

"Yes, but it couldn't have been a full possession, of course," said Sage. "It would have been only a splinter of Nyro's essence embedded in the recesses of Syllith's mind. I doubt she was even aware of it; she seemed to be in control whenever we saw her. Nyro would have exerted her power only when necessary, to force the events she needed to happen."

"Like killing Warhammer and Enigma," Allure said sadly.

"Yes, exactly," Sage said. "Even a partial possession qualifies as necromancy, though, and *that* is a form of thaumaturgy."

"It's a shame Syllith's going to go down in history as a traitor," said Khaldun.

"Not here, she won't," said Sage. "I've made sure the governors and all of our other mages know the truth."

"What about me?" Mist said. "Is what I do sympathetic magic?"

"Sugar, I don't have the *slightest* idea," Sage said, prompting laughter from the others. "There is *no* record of any other sorcerer doing what you do. Trust me, I've looked.

"But in all seriousness, what you do is shapeshifting. When you get right down to it, it's not all that different from Semblant's ability. No one's ever transformed into a thick fog before, but that's thaumaturgy. You're using the magical force to do it."

"But they're only using the magic for the transformation itself," said Mira. "Once they've changed, there's no active spell, so my null doesn't turn them back."

"Exactly," Sage said with a nod. "But it *would* prevent them from transforming."

"How about prophecy?" asked Khaldun. "That must be thaumaturgy, right?"

Sage heaved a sigh. "I'm not entirely convinced prophecy is legitimate."

"Only because *you've* never had a vision," Allure said.

"No, because all the examples I know about turned out to be self-fulfilling in nature," Sage retorted. "Nyro left the artifact in Spanbrook because she foresaw someone from Spanbrook liberating her one day. But someone was able to liberate her only *because* she left that artifact. Her actions made that possible, not her dream.

"That being said, I have spent quite a bit of time studying the phenomenon."

"She's writing a book about it," Allure said in a stage whisper.

"Yes, I am," Sage replied. "Sadly, there is nothing in our library about prophecy, so I intend to change that. There's no way to know for sure, given the nature of prophetic visions, but I believe thaumaturgic magic resonates in time the same way it does in space."

"You're talking about the spell that can reveal magic that's been performed in a given place," Khaldun said.

"Yes, exactly," Sage replied. "It leaves an echo in the space where it was performed. And if I'm right, it reverberates in time as well, making it possible for powerful mages to see those events before they happen."

"It's pure thaumaturgy, then," Cyclone said.

"The effect is, yes," said Sage. "But our perception of it must be sympathetic. Think about it—when you have a prophetic vision, you aren't *doing* magic. You're merely sensing the reverberations in time. Salerna's looking glass should be the same."

"So *I* would be able to see visions in the looking glass?" Mira asked.

"Yes, I believe so," said Sage. "The water in that bowl is tuned to the vibrations of thaumaturgic magic taking place in the future—or in the present or the past. But it's sympathetic magic that allows you to see those visions."

"Salerna has noticed that the looking glass won't show her events where I'm present," said Mira. "She wasn't able to foresee the battle with Fosland fifteen years ago, for example. We've assumed that's because of my null. Do you think that's right?"

"Certainly," said Sage. "Your null shuts down thaumaturgic magic. So of course, it would also eliminate its reverberations through time, making the events around you invisible to prophetic visions as well as the looking glass."

"But what if my channels of power are closed?" asked Mira. "If I were to show up somewhere without my null extended, could someone see *that* event in a prophetic dream?"

"I don't see why not," said Sage. "But most things that would be sufficiently significant to cause a prophetic dream would probably entail your use of your null. Like the Battle of Highgate. Mundane events that are historically insignificant don't generally cause prophetic visions."

"That's exactly what we were thinking," Khaldun said with a nod.

"But *you* would still be invisible," Sage continued. "Only the events unfolding around you could be seen in prophecy."

Mira frowned. "Chieftain Vano of the dragon lords told his daughter he had a dream of me coming to their aeries."

"That shouldn't be possible," said Sage. "He saw you specifically?"

"No, Lavinia said only that it was a wayfarer woman," Mira said.

"It must have been a normal dream," Sage said, "and only a coincidence."

"Another self-fulfilling prophecy," Khaldun said. "Lavinia only summoned you because of her father's dream."

Mira nodded, but didn't find that explanation entirely satisfying.

Dinner arrived a few minutes later, and they all talked and laughed as they ate. Mira felt at home here. It was the only place outside of Spanbrook that gave her that feeling. They weren't family like the Barclays, perhaps, but these were her people. If circumstances ever forced her to leave Spanbrook, she knew she could be happy here.

Once they'd finished their meal, Cyclone asked, "What's going on with the elves? We've been hearing about their scouts showing up in various princedoms in Dorshire."

Khaldun and Mira spent a few minutes apprising them of the recent developments.

"Drengrvollr," Allure said when they were done. "That name sounds familiar, but I can't place it."

Sage opened her mouth to reply, but Khaldun said, "It's the westernmost of the five elvish kingdoms. And historically, the most warlike."

"Apparently I'm not the only scholar at the table," said Sage. "Do you know the names of the other four?"

"Mestrland is the largest," said Khaldun, "and the most populous. It occupies the south-central region of their continent. The kingdom possesses the greatest riches, and has advanced elvish culture more than any of the others. Their greatest musicians, artists, and mathematicians have all come from Mestrland. Ellrivollr lies to the east of that, and is said to be the oldest kingdom, where the very first elves resided in the forgotten years. Askaheimr occupies the northwest of the continent, where volcanoes fill much of the land. And Snaerverold lies to the east of that. Most of that kingdom is covered in perpetual snow, and the majority of its people live along the southern border. At least, those were the kingdoms around the time of Nyro's fall, according to the texts I've read."

"Very good," Sage said, nodding appreciatively. "I'm impressed. You and I might be the only two people in Anoria who could name all five. But you're right, we have no idea if the geopolitical situation on their continent still looks the same today."

"It sounds to me like someone's a little infatuated with the elves," Battleaxe said with a knowing grin. "We've all heard the stories. Are they as beautiful as they say?"

"More," said Mira. "We've seen only one living one up close, but the experience took my breath away. The most physically attractive person I've ever met."

"Uh-oh, Khaldun has some competition," Battleaxe said.

"No, never," Mira said, taking her husband's hand and leaning over to kiss him on the cheek. "Perhaps if I were unmarried, though…"

The others chuckled.

"It's a tragedy, though," said Khaldun. "For years, I've wished I could meet the elves. Learn from them, and experience their culture. But now it seems we'll only face them across a battlefield. I don't understand it. They were the ones who helped Anoria defeat Nyro. Why do they attack us now?"

"Nyro must be behind it somehow," said Sage. "They've shown no interest in this continent or our people in centuries. I can imagine no other explanation."

"Well, beautiful or not, if they do invade, you can count on the university to help," said Battleaxe. "We will not stand by and allow Nyro to conquer Anoria again."

The others voiced their agreement, and they drank a toast to victory.

Khaldun and Mira stayed up late, sitting by the fireplace with Battleaxe and Mist, drinking mead and chatting about recent events. Although the threat of invasion filled Mira with dread, Battleaxe seemed eager to meet the elves in battle. "Combat is my thing," she said with a shrug when Mira asked her about this. "The elves are supposed to have the greatest warriors the world has ever seen. I'm keen to test my mettle against them."

That night, Mira and Khaldun stayed in Allure's guest room. The next morning they rose early, sitting down for breakfast with their host. Semblant wasn't present, so they bade Allure farewell, and returned to Spanbrook. They flew all day, stopping a couple of times to rest, and reached Castle Barclay late that night. Khaldun didn't normally like risking a nighttime flight, but he knew the terrain around their princedom very well.

The following morning, they sat down for a meeting with Jezebel, Allison, and the rest of the privy council. They reported what they'd learned from the dragon lords, and told them that the university was ready to assist in the coming battles.

"Excellent," said Jezebel when they were done. "Their aid will undoubtedly prove invaluable."

"Have we heard any more news about the invasion?" Khaldun asked.

"We have not," Jezebel said with a sigh. "But I'm afraid we do have some bad news to report."

Emma pulled out her mirror, gazed into it for a moment, then excused herself and hurried from the room.

"Our prisoner took his life last night," said Allison. "He'd tried to escape a couple of times when I opened his cell for the staff to provide him food and water, but I was able to stop him. So, last night, he used strips he tore from his clothing to hang himself."

"Were you able to get any more useful information out of him?" asked Mira.

"No, I think he told us everything he knew that first night," said Allison. "He was a foot soldier, unaware of his leaders' plans."

Emma returned, her expression horrified as all eyes turned to her. "Your Highness, Rockport is under attack. The steward reports that their lookouts spotted enormous ships with black sails approaching their coast. Princess Jelena mobilized her troops. The invading elves have come ashore, and Rockport's forces have engaged them, but their numbers are sure to overwhelm them. The steward estimates at least ten thousand warriors have disembarked from the ships."

"We have to send aid," Jezebel said.

"I'll go," said Allison, pushing back from the table.

"No, we need you here," said Jezebel, taking her hand. "The elves are sure to march here next, and may have a force already underway. Khaldun and Mira, I would like the two of you to go to Rockport. Render what assistance you can, but do not take any unnecessary risks. We will not sacrifice you to save a foreign princedom."

"Learn as much as you can about the enemy," said Amari. "The number and strength of their mages, and what tactics they use against Rockport."

"And try to ascertain who commands them," said Jezebel. "I'm sure Nyro wouldn't lead an individual campaign herself, but it could be one of her Sacred Circle."

"We'll get underway immediately, Your Highness," said Khaldun, as he and Mira got to their feet.

They left the council chamber, hurrying back to their chambers. Once they'd donned their leather armor under their mage's robes, and Mira her sword belt, they returned to the courtyard. Khaldun removed his carpet from the void, unfurling it on the ground. Moments later, they soared high above Spanbrook, heading north.

CHAPTER NINE
FLASHBACK

yllith leaned over the railing, retching noisily, but she'd emptied her stomach's contents hours ago. She held on for dear life as the ship rose and fell like nothing more than a cork in the massive waves, heaving unproductively once more. Finally, she collapsed on the deck, shivering in the cold, her soaked robes providing no warmth. The captain's mage had told her they'd managed to avoid the worst of the storm, but she couldn't imagine a sea rougher than this. Or didn't want to, at least.

They'd been at sea for weeks already, and thankfully, this was the first storm they'd encountered. Though she'd never spent much time on the water, Syllith's stomach had been fine until this.

After a few more hours, the waves diminished, the rain became a light drizzle, and the wind subsided. Syllith's stomach calmed along with the weather, so she made her way back to her quarters. Someone had left her dinner, which she ate hungrily. Because she was a mere human, the elves didn't consider her fit to join them at table, but she was thankful they provided her food at all. She'd gone without for days at a time on many occasions since leaving Anoria.

Stripping out of her drenched clothing, Syllith stared down at her body; she could hardly believe the change. After years of captivity, she'd looked like no more than skin and bone. The fleshy parts of her had diminished to nothing, including her breasts, which had grown flat. She'd never spared much thought for her physical appearance, but many had told her she was beautiful. After her imprisonment, she'd doubted anyone would offer her such praise.

But after only a few weeks on this godforsaken boat, her body was recovering. Her figure looked more feminine, and her breasts were growing. Not that their food was all that plentiful, or tasty, but it was more than she'd eaten in many long years.

Years of starvation had done nothing to her scars. The way they overlapped, she'd never been able to tell how many there were. At least five or six, each from a knife wound to her chest. She shuddered with the memory of that experience, foggy though it was.

Syllith lay down in her bed, pulling the blankets over her, trying to eliminate her chill. In the past, she would have cast an air spell to dry her robes and warm herself up, but now, she lacked the skill. She chuckled derisively at the thought: a mage who could do no magic.

Since starting this hellish voyage, she'd tried to rekindle her abilities. Normally, the power would be transferred from a mage's wand or staff after their transformation into a sorcerer. But Syllith's staff had been left behind in Anoria. And Nyro had shown no interest in helping her regain her magic. In fact, she suspected she'd taken steps to prevent it from coming back. But she'd made some small progress since boarding the ship. Only a spark of flame here and there. And once, she'd been able to create a little whirlpool in her tea.

After fifteen years, her magic *should* have returned, even without the spell that would relinquish the power from her staff. Normally, this would take weeks or months. Nyro *must* have done something to inhibit the process. But Syllith feared another possibility. The demon had triggered her transformation unnaturally. She never would have become a sorcerer on her own. What if undergoing the metamorphosis this way meant that her powers would *never* return?

No, that couldn't be the case. If it were, even the tiny results she'd achieved these last few weeks would have been impossible. She wouldn't let herself lose faith.

As she lay there, memories of that fateful night came flooding back, as they did so often. At first, she tried to block them out of her mind, but it was futile. There was no escape. Sobs racked her to the core as she recalled uttering Enigma's true name. That had been Nyro's doing, not hers, but she'd used her lips, her tongue, and her voice to speak the spell's words. Syllith had no choice but to watch in horror through her own eyes as the love of her life utterly ceased to exist. Not even as a demon could he come back.

The pain was too much to bear, and since gaining her freedom, Syllith had often thought of ending her life to escape it. But strangely, it had also started to give her strength. The memory of the atrocities Nyro had forced her to commit fueled her desire for revenge. She'd spent her entire adult life doing everything in her power to prevent that monster from returning. Now that she'd failed in that endeavor, she'd pour her entire soul into thwarting her.

She had hoped to get warning to those in power in Anoria before the invasion could begin. But this journey was taking too long. How much time would Nyro need to launch the operation? Surely the elvish fleet would make the ocean crossing far more swiftly than this little transport could.

But there were still ways she could help. Alerting her people that Nyro was behind the invasion, for one thing. If she was right, they'd have no idea. This invasion would seem inexplicable to them after so many centuries without any contact from the elves whatsoever.

And if some of her other notions were correct, she could help the humans take away some of Nyro's power, too. So much of what she'd done was unprecedented that Syllith couldn't be certain. Nobody could until they tried what she had in mind. But if she *was* right—and she was pretty sure she was—it would be worth it.

Thinking back to all the things Nyro had forced her to do, she wanted to see her burn in hell. To avenge Enigma, most of all. But Syllith didn't possess the power or the knowledge to do to Nyro what she'd done to him. Her best hope, the desire to which she clung with her entire being, was to weaken Nyro enough that others would be able to destroy her.

Nyro had possessed Syllith's body right after triggering her metamorphosis. She'd never forget the power coursing through her when Nyro used her body to perform magic. This, more than anything else, was the reason she believed she could regain her abilities. Her channels of power had worked just fine for Nyro, so there was no reason they shouldn't work for her.

The first thing Nyro had done was to use the pyramid to open a portal to somewhere else. They stepped through it to a grassy slope overlooking the sea. Syllith had had no clue where she was, but she could see buildings in the distance. Nyro had started walking toward them, and Syllith felt embarrassed by her nakedness. But Nyro had cast an illusion spell, and Syllith's body had transformed. She'd grown much taller and more muscular, and her skin had turned ebony. Moments later, another illusion spell had provided clothing.

Syllith had read enough about the elves to realize then where they must be. Nyro had used the artifact to transport them across continents. Syllith had never imagined such a thing was possible. But as they approached the village, she spotted elves walking up and down the road, and there could be no doubt.

They strolled into town, and Nyro stopped across from a place that looked like a tavern. She leaned against a wall, watching people come and go for a while, and Syllith had no idea what she was waiting for.

"Nine hundred years, and the elvish tongue hasn't changed much," she heard herself mutter. Was that what Nyro had been doing? Listening in on conversations to make sure she could still speak the language?

Finally, a male elf emerged from the tavern and they approached him. Nyro used her mouth to speak to him. She could feel and hear herself uttering the words, but couldn't comprehend what she was saying.

The elf smiled, taking them by the hand. They walked to the other end of the village, and he opened a door for them, following them inside a two-story house. The elf said something to them that Syllith didn't understand. Nyro smiled, uttering a reply that made the elf chuckle. He led them upstairs to a bedroom.

Syllith panicked as she realized what was going on here, but there was nothing she could do to stop it. The elf disrobed. He was much larger than any man she'd ever seen, and all the proportions were the same. Even the idea of taking him inside of her was painful; she couldn't believe Nyro was going to try this. But she removed the illusion of her clothing, pushed the elf into the bed, and climbed on top of him.

Instead of making love to him, she produced a knife and slit his throat. Syllith hadn't seen where the knife had come from—her attention had been on other things. But it was no illusion. The elf died, blood spurting out of his neck.

Discarding the knife, they rifled through his belongings, finding a money purse. It was heavy in her hand. Opening the strings, she gazed inside, and felt herself smile. This would be more than enough. For what, Syllith didn't know.

They left the house and returned to the tavern. Nyro made her take a seat at a table in the rear corner. The server bustled over, and Nyro spoke to him. Minutes later, he returned with a mug of dark liquid. Nyro brought it to their lips, and they drank the entire mug. Syllith didn't understand how Nyro had made their mouth line up with the illusion's—they weren't nearly the same height—but she tasted the alcohol going down like fire.

The food arrived, and they ate hungrily. Syllith couldn't tell what kind of meat it was, but it tasted delicious. Once they'd finished, Nyro paid for the meal, and had a second mug of alcohol, drinking this one more slowly. They sat there late into the night, watching people come and go. Syllith didn't understand what they were doing.

Finally, they got up and followed a female elf out of the tavern. She led them across the village and out to the countryside. Nyro had kept her distance, but made them invisible as they left town. They walked for a while until finally, the elf turned onto a lane leading to a farmhouse. Nyro sped up then, reaching the front door right behind her. She cast a spell, and the elf opened the door for them, standing aside to let them go inside. The elf moved in behind them, closing the door behind her.

With a thought, Nyro lit the room's oil lamps. Then she canceled her illusion spell, retaking Syllith's true, naked appearance. The elf led them upstairs to the bedroom and disrobed. Syllith knew Nyro still had her under her spell, but was powerless to do anything to stop her. Nyro lay down on the bed, and the elf spent the next hour pleasuring her with her tongue and fingers. They climaxed repeatedly.

Finally, Nyro rose from the bed, and made the elf lie down. She cast a spell to stop the elf's heart, then waited a few moments to make sure she was dead. Nyro placed one hand on the body, and it started glowing where she touched the flesh. Syllith didn't know what she was doing, but felt the magic flowing through her. This was much more powerful than anything she'd done so far.

Suddenly, Syllith's body collapsed, hitting the floor. It took her a moment to realize what had happened: Nyro had left her body. Getting to her feet, she gazed around the room frantically, trying to locate the demon. She was nowhere to be seen. Syllith bolted toward the door—this could be her opportunity to escape. But the door slammed shut.

"Leaving so soon?" a voice said from behind her.

Syllith nearly jumped out of her skin. Turning, she saw the dead elf sitting up, grinning at her.

"It's—it's you?"

"Yes, it is I," she said, holding both arms out to her sides. "Don't you *love* this body?"

"You killed her… how can you be possessing her?"

"I'm not. *This* is my body now."

"*What*?" This defied any concept of magic Syllith had ever known.

"I'd foreseen my downfall long before the elves' arrival in Anoria," Nyro said, lying back on the bed and running her hands up and down her new body. "I used the portal to come here and capture a few of them. If I had to fight them, I needed to learn about their abilities. And it turned out necromancy has no effect on them. Apparently, they walk in our world as well as the spirit realm. They cannot be possessed, but neither can they become demons. When they die, their souls dissolve. But if you preserve the flow of energy through their channels of power at the moment of death, they can be *reanimated*."

"Reanimated?" Syllith repeated. "But how? If their soul dissolves—"

"Not with their own soul. With mine. Or any demon's. I tried it with one of the ones I'd bound. He took the elf's body as if he'd been born in it. Of course, then I killed him again; I had no use for an elf back then. But now, I do. Oh, what great purpose I have in mind for this body. A mage's body—that was key. Only then could I channel the magical force through it."

"This elf was a mage?"

"Yes. Now come here and make love to me."

Syllith refused, but Nyro cast a spell, forcing her to do whatever she wanted late into the night. But finally, she grew tired. Syllith thought this might be her chance to get away, but it was no use. Nyro knocked her out.

The next morning, Nyro slapped her to wake her up. She had dressed in the elf's clothes. Syllith tried calling fire to incinerate her, but nothing happened. Nyro laughed. "Get up and make us breakfast," she said before leaving the room.

Syllith sat up in bed, swinging her legs over the edge. She tried again to call fire, but couldn't. None of the forces would respond to her command. Rifling through the chest of drawers, she tried to find something to wear, but the elf's clothes were all far too large for her. Finally, she draped the bed sheet around herself and made her way downstairs.

Nyro was staring out the front window. With a wave of her hand, she incinerated Syllith's sheet. Syllith screamed in frustration, but Nyro didn't react. She went to the kitchen and made breakfast.

"Do you know the five elven kingdoms?" Nyro asked as they sat down to eat. Syllith named them. "Yes, so they existed nine hundred years ago. Today we will find out if that is still the case. Do you know where we are right now?" Syllith shook her head. "We are in the kingdom of Drengrvollr, not far from the capital city of Krokr. I chose this place for its proximity. Of course, we'll have to confirm that's still the capital before we go there.

"We'll need to spend some more time at the tavern to gather the information I need. But the question is what to do with you while I'm gone."

"I'm surprised you've let me live this long."

"Oh, don't worry. I *need* you. You can look forward to a very long life, my love. But keeping you here alone leaves too much to chance. No, for now, I don't think I can let you out of my sight. So you'll have to accompany me. You'll be my deaf, dumb cousin from Mestrland, I think. Yes. Of course, you can't go naked, or look human." With a wave of her hand, she cast an illusion making Syllith appear to be an elf again. One more spell, and she was wearing a simple elvish dress.

After breakfast, they left the house, walking back into the village and returning to the same tavern, taking the same table in the back corner of the room. When the server came over to them, Syllith tried to ask her for help, but found she couldn't speak. Her mouth wouldn't open, her tongue was stuck to the roof of her mouth, and her voice refused to work.

The server returned with two mugs of the same black liquid as before, and Nyro told her to drink. Syllith didn't move, but suddenly found herself drinking against her will.

They spent a few hours at the tavern. Nyro seemed to be listening in on the conversations around them. She went to sit at the bar for a little while, and struck up a conversation with one of the others. Syllith tried to get up and leave, but found her legs wouldn't work.

Finally, Nyro returned, and told her it was time to go. They left the tavern, and set out on the road. "Fate has smiled on us today. Drengrvollr's military might has only increased since my last visit here. And Krokr is still its capital. This will allow our plans to unfold more easily than I had dared to hope."

Leaving the village, they passed the farmhouse where they'd stayed the previous night, and kept walking. After a few hours, they crested a hill, and Syllith gasped. Far below sat an enormous city on a bay. It was unlike anything she'd seen in Anoria, with its marble buildings and gilded domes.

"Remember this day, sorcerer," Nyro said. "And this place. This is where my new reign will begin."

Dread filled Syllith's soul as they descended toward the city.

It was almost evening by the time they'd reached Krokr. Nyro led them to a boardinghouse on the city's outskirts. She paid for a month, ordered food to be delivered to them, and took Syllith up to their room. Of course, Nyro had chosen the penthouse. It spanned the entire upper level, with an open patio on the front overlooking the bay.

Nyro stripped out of her clothes, and canceled Syllith's illusion spells, leaving her naked, too. Once they'd eaten, Nyro lay down in the bed and forced Syllith to pleasure her. Syllith tried to resist, but Nyro's control was complete. Once she was sated, she knocked her out.

Syllith woke the next morning to find Nyro out on the patio, regally dressed, gazing into the distance. She tried leaving, but their door was magically sealed, and Syllith was still unable to work any magic to remove the spell.

"You're finally awake," Nyro said, walking inside. "We'll be attending the senate's proceedings today. Drengrvollr is a kingdom in name only; the true power here resides in the senate. You'll need to accompany me, of course."

"Your deaf and dumb cousin from Mestrland, again?"

"Yes, the role suits you," Nyro said with a chuckle. She waved her hand, casting the illusions to transform and clothe Syllith. Today, she wore robes to match Nyro's.

They left the boardinghouse, walking along the cobblestone streets to the city center. It was busy here, with hundreds of elves going about their business, oblivious to the demon walking among them. Syllith tried leaving her side several times, but it was no use. Nyro's spells kept her in line.

The senate occupied an enormous marble building, domed in gold, with ornate columns supporting the roof. Once inside, they passed through the atrium and up the stairs to the balcony overlooking the main chamber. Down on the floor, dozens of elves sat at benches and tables arranged in a semicircle around a central dais. A male elf was speaking, his booming voice filling the space. Syllith didn't understand a word. But the other senators booed or cheered loudly at times, depending upon which section of the room they occupied.

Once the elf had finished his speech, he bowed, and went to take his seat. A female elf moved to the podium next, and the room quieted as she started speaking. She wore golden robes with a diamond brooch at her neck. Syllith noted a scar running from her left eye to her neck. Her voice was not as loud as the previous speaker's, but she spoke dramatically, holding her audience in thrall.

One speaker after another took the podium, and Syllith found herself dozing off. She didn't know elvish, so there was nothing here to hold her attention. Finally, Nyro poked her in the ribs to wake her up, indicating that it was time to leave. Syllith realized that the senators had adjourned.

They returned to the boardinghouse, ordered food, and went up to their penthouse. Nyro removed her clothes the moment they arrived, canceling Syllith's illusions at the same time. She didn't understand her preference for nudity, and wished there were something she could do about it.

"What do you think, sorcerer?" Nyro said, taking a seat at the table and digging into their food. "Which of the senators should I replace?"

"How could I possibly have any opinion? Without knowing the language, I have no idea what any of them said."

"The meaning of their words is irrelevant. There were three who held the greatest sway. The male who was speaking when we arrived, the female who followed him, and the second-to-last male."

"I must have fallen asleep by the end, but I agree the first two were powerful speakers."

"The first male isn't a mage, so it's down to the female and the last male."

"I'm sure either one would do."

"Yes, quite. However, I don't think I'd like to have a cock swinging between my legs for the next several years. We'll take the female. They've adjourned for their siesta, but we'll return before the end of their afternoon session. We'll follow Senator Estrid home and take her there."

CHAPTER TEN
ROCKPORT

ira held on tight as Khaldun flew them north at top speed. Rockport was a thriving port city, though it was smaller than Northcoast, Blacksand, or Oldport. Its power had always been economic, not military. At Jezebel's urging, Princess Jelena had established a standing army, but it numbered only a few thousand troops. Mira doubted they could repel the invaders.

Khaldun made them invisible as they approached the city. The castle stood atop a hill on the western side of the river. Mira spotted several regiments of elvish troops on the ground, equally split between the two sides of the river. Only a quarter of their force was engaged in battle with the Rockporters. Jelena's troops had established a position at the bottom of the hill, blocking the road to the castle. But if Mira's estimate was right, only about a thousand of them remained.

This attack meant their worst fears had come true: the elves were invading Anoria. Their troops were organized and disciplined, operating as if guided by a single will. Rockport's forces looked like a rabble in comparison, lacking even common uniforms. Dozens upon dozens of human corpses littered the battlefield, but Mira couldn't spot a single dead elf.

Flying over the elvish force, Khaldun unleashed his magic, sending a fire tornado through their ranks. They canceled it before it could do much damage. He made several passes above them, hurling lightning bolts, turning the ground beneath their feet to quicksand, and evacuating the air they needed to breathe. But the elves canceled his every spell within moments. With *all* their people able to do magic, they didn't need a mage to counter his efforts.

Finally, Khaldun called an illusion of an enormous dragon swooping toward them. But someone canceled that, too, proving they had at least one mage present. Most elves couldn't work with the magical force.

Khaldun took them to the castle, landing on the keep roof, where they found Princess Jelena with her steward and wizard. Mira had met them before, but couldn't recall their names. The wizard was older with a big pot belly.

Unstrapping herself, Mira got to her feet, and Khaldun rolled up the carpet, tucking it into the void. She followed him over to the princess.

"Your Highness," Khaldun said with a bow.

"Welcome, Lord Khaldun and Lady Mira," she said. "You know my steward, Jefferson, and my mage, Roman."

They both greeted Khaldun and Mira.

"Despite my best efforts, I was unable to weaken the attackers," said Khaldun. "Every one of their soldiers can call the basic forces, and they've got at least one mage with them. You should order your remaining forces to retreat and prepare for a siege."

"I fear for the people of Anoria," Jelena said, gazing out at the battle. "They are cutting down our men like wheat. Who among our people can stand up to such an enemy?"

"Princess Jelena, please, heed his advice," the wizard said. "Recall our army while we still have one."

Jelena nodded. "Do it."

Roman held out his staff, calling air, and generated the sound of several trumpet blasts, amplified tenfold. The Rockporter army began its retreat, and the castle gates opened.

"We should help," Khaldun said to Mira.

He removed the carpet from the void, along with their hoods and facemasks. Mira donned hers; they left only her eyes, nose, and mouth exposed. They flew over to the barbican directly above the gates. Khaldun dropped Mira off there before taking off again. Opening her channels of power, Mira expanded her null.

Khaldun went invisible as he flew off. But moments later, a wall of fire appeared, separating the retreating Rockporters from their attackers. Someone canceled it moments later, but Khaldun restored it, creating three more beyond it. Jelena's forces reached the castle, pouring into the courtyard.

Mira could sense the elvish mage trying to negate her null, but it was no use. It worked as well against his spells as it did any human mage's.

The elves started shooting arrows at the Rockporters, felling several more of them. But minutes later, the last of the army made it inside, and they closed the gates.

Mira closed her channels of power, eliminating her null as Khaldun approached on his carpet. He landed on the barbican; Mira climbed on, and he flew them back to the keep.

Rockport's soldiers lined the ramparts and took their positions in the courtyard, ready to defend the castle. The elves formed ranks, but kept their distance. Their archers launched a volley of flaming arrows over the walls. Khaldun called a giant shield spell to protect the castle; the arrows bounced off harmlessly, landing outside the walls.

"Their mage is trying to cancel my shield," Khaldun told them, "but he lacks the power."

After several minutes, the elvish archers fired another volley. This time, their arrows stuck to Khaldun's shield spell, their flames burning bright green.

"I've never seen anything like this," he said. "The arrows are burning holes in my spell. I can't hold it—the shield is about to collapse."

"Be ready to cast a new one," said Mira. Khaldun nodded. Mira expanded her null, canceling the arrows' flames along with the shield. The projectiles fell to the ground, and Khaldun restored his shield spell.

Several minutes went by, and an eerie quiet fell on the castle. Mira's nerves frayed as she waited to see what the elves would do next. She hadn't seen any siege engines, but surely they'd make some attempt to infiltrate the castle.

Suddenly, one of the soldiers in the courtyard shouted, "The walls! They're melting the walls!"

Looking where he was pointing, Mira spotted a giant section of the stone wall that was starting to glow. A thin plume of smoke was rising from the same area. "He's right!" she said, opening her channels of power. She could sense dozens of fire spells hitting the castle as her null canceled them.

But it was too late. The wall collapsed, forming a giant pile of rubble. The elvish soldiers began climbing over it, pouring into the courtyard.

"Princess Jelena, it's time to evacuate," said Khaldun. "The castle is lost. We need to get you, your family, and as many of your people out of here as we can."

"I agree, Your Highness," said Roman. "With the wall compromised, we cannot hope to repel them."

The princess sighed, a tear slipping down her cheek. "So be it."

Roman and Jefferson led the way into the keep, Jelena right behind them. Khaldun and Mira brought up the rear. The princess collected her children—a girl of fourteen or fifteen, and her brother who looked several years younger. They hurried down the steps to the main level.

"We have an escape tunnel that leads out to the forest," Roman told them. "There is a hidden entrance in the undercroft's south wall."

"Take the princess and her family immediately," Khaldun told him. "Gather as many of your people as you can and get them out of here," he added to Jefferson. "Mira and I will hold off the elves as long as we can, then we'll follow, and collapse the tunnel behind us."

Jefferson hurried off, and Roman led the royal family away. Khaldun and Mira ran back up to the roof. The elves were decimating Rockport's remaining soldiers. Mira didn't think more than a few hundred remained. Khaldun went to work, calling fire to incinerate individual elves. This took more power than it would have against a human, but still proved effective. He focused on the ones closest to the keep's entrance to give their people their best chance of escape. Within minutes, the castle's forces had dwindled to no more than a hundred troops.

"It's time to go," Khaldun told her.

Mira followed him back inside. Down on the main level, Khaldun cast spells to seal the keep's entrance, then they hurried down to the cellar. They found Jefferson ushering the last of their people into the tunnel. Khaldun and Mira followed him inside, and Khaldun sealed the door behind them.

Once they'd made it beyond the castle's walls, Khaldun turned, calling earth and collapsing the tunnel at several points behind them. The passage became utterly dark, so he called a flame to light their way.

Several minutes later, they reached the tunnel's end, emerging in a small cave. Making their way out of that, they found the princess and her people waiting for them in the forest.

"Now what?" Khaldun asked the wizard.

"We have a small, underground fortification up in the hills. It provides a view of the city and the harbor, so we should be able to see the elves' activities from there."

"Lead the way," Khaldun said with a nod.

Roman set out through the trees. Princess Jelena and her children followed him, surrounded by her castle guard. The remaining members of their staff went next, and Khaldun and Mira brought up the rear.

Mira expanded her null both to protect them from any thaumaturgic attack and to alert them to any pursuit. She could detect magic users this way, which included all the elves.

For an hour they marched into the hills, finally reaching a rocky bluff. Roman led them into a cave, calling a flame to illuminate their way once Mira had closed her channels of power. At the rear of the cavern, he canceled an illusion spell, revealing a metal door embedded in the rock. Opening it, he moved inside.

Khaldun and Mira entered last, and he sealed the door magically. They climbed a winding stairway, emerging into a cavernous space. It had brick walls, but Mira had seen no structure from the outside. Roman explained that the princess's ancestors had had the natural cavern fortified, providing an emergency shelter for the royal family.

Steps led up to a ledge where Mira could see a set of narrow, horizontal windows. Climbing up, Khaldun and the wizard right behind her, she gazed out one of the openings. She could see the path they'd taken to get here, and sure enough, it also provided a clear view of the city and its harbor.

The elves had collapsed the rest of the castle, leaving only a pile of rubble. They were making camp in the fields near the river.

"It doesn't look like they're marching to Spanbrook," said Mira.

"Not today, at least," Khaldun replied.

"I didn't see these openings from the ground," said Mira.

"Illusion spells mask them, my lady," Roman said.

"One of their mages might detect them if he's looking for magic," said Khaldun. "But I see no signs of pursuit."

"They probably don't care about the royal family," said Mira. "Rockport's army is destroyed, and now that they hold the port, they can confiscate every incoming ship's cargo and supply their troops indefinitely."

The three of them descended the steps, and Khaldun approached the princess.

"Your Highness, please allow us to evacuate you and your family to Spanbrook," said Khaldun.

"No, I will not leave my people. But I would be grateful if you would take my children with you."

"Very well," Khaldun said with a nod.

"How soon will you depart? I would like a few moments with them… to explain everything."

"Take your time, Your Highness. We still need to go take a look at the enemy camp."

The princess went off to talk to her children. Khaldun and Mira let Roman know they were leaving for a little while on a scouting mission, then headed out. Once outside, Khaldun removed his carpet from the void, and they took off. He made them invisible, and flew to the elvish camp.

The soldiers were setting up their tents in perfectly straight rows. At the southern end of the fields, they were erecting barracks buildings. Mira assumed these would be for their commanders.

"Take us down over there," Mira said, pointing toward the construction area.

Khaldun landed by the river near the building project, but far enough away to avoid detection. Getting to her feet, Mira closed her eyes, opening her channels of power and expanding her null. She let it grow to its fullest size, yet it still wasn't large enough to encompass the entire camp.

She sensed thousands of elves, their magic so similar to a demon's. Peppered throughout the camp were their mages, identifiable by their greater power. Focusing on the construction area, she gasped.

"What is it?" Khaldun asked.

"I'm not sure… there's someone immensely powerful by the buildings."

"One of their mages?"

"Yes, but his magic is not like the others. Khaldun, he feels human."

"*Human?*"

"Only his power exceeds that of any sorcerer I've ever met."

"It could be one of the Sacred Circle. We should try to get a closer look."

Mira nodded. She closed her channels of power, and they took off on the carpet. Khaldun made them invisible and flew them closer to the barracks. Mira spotted a group of elves in golden plate armor. Standing among them, facing the others, was the tallest elf she'd seen so far. He was bare-chested, exposing bulging muscles. Even without her null, she could feel waves of power emanating from him.

"I think it's the half-naked one," she whispered to Khaldun. "But it's impossible to say for sure without my null."

"I can set us down over there in the trees," he suggested. "We should have a clear view of them from there."

Mira agreed, and he flew them into the woods. They touched down, but stayed on the carpet in case they needed a quick getaway. Extending her null, Mira sensed the group of officers. Sure enough, the shirtless one was the one who felt different.

The elf turned, seeming to sense her null, and for a moment, Mira was sure he was staring right at her. "Make us invisible," she hissed as she closed her channels of power, her heart leaping into her throat.

"Done," Khaldun said a moment later, but the elf had returned his attention to the others.

"Let's get out of here," she suggested.

"Yes. Good idea."

They flew back to Jelena's refuge, moving inside and sealing the door behind them. Inside, they found the princess huddled with Roman and Jefferson.

"My children are ready to depart," she told them.

"Your Highness, with your permission, I think we would like to spend the night here with you and your people," said Khaldun. "We will leave tomorrow instead."

"You are welcome here, of course," she said, looking confused. "Has something changed?"

"No," he replied, taking a deep breath. "We'd like to see if there's any change in the elves' activities come morning."

Khaldun and Mira moved off to a quiet corner, sitting down on the floor. He produced his mirror and contacted Princess Jezebel to update her on the developments in Rockport. The two of them ate dinner with Jelena and her people.

She introduced her children, Susan and James, to Khaldun and Mira; there hadn't been time earlier. At sixteen years of age, Susan possessed a quiet confidence, much like her mother. But James seemed terrified, more so than the situation warranted. Mira was surprised to learn he was fourteen—he seemed much younger than Jezebel's children.

The princess had already sent a couple of her guards to the top of the hill to keep watch. But Khaldun and Mira feared they'd be defenseless against any thaumaturgic threat that might arise, so they decided to join them. They set up their tent, and Mira took the first watch while Khaldun went inside to get some sleep.

The night was quiet and peaceful, without any sign that an invasion was underway. Mira kept her null expanded to its fullest size, but sensed no one approaching. Far below, she could see hundreds of little fires in the enemy camp. But one by one, they winked out as the night grew darker, until only a few dozen remained.

A little after midnight, Mira slipped into the tent, lying down next to Khaldun, and kissing him to wake him up. She told him the night had been uneventful so far. He kissed her, then left the tent to take the second watch. Mira closed her channels of power and drifted off to sleep.

Waking at dawn, she emerged from the tent, and found Khaldun chatting with Jelena's wizard. She could see activity in the elvish camp, but nothing had changed. Khaldun reported that his shift had been as quiet as hers.

They took down their tent and headed back inside. Princess Jelena was up and about but her children were still asleep. Once she'd woken them, she bade them farewell, hugging them tight.

Khaldun and Mira led them outside, and he pulled the carpet out of the void, rolling it out on the ground. Mira sat down and strapped herself in as Khaldun situated Susan and James on the front two corners. Then he took his seat at the rear and they took off. James screamed as they streaked across the sky to the south.

They reached Spanbrook a little after noon. The army had set up their camp in the fields north of town. Their numbers matched the elvish force, but Mira wondered if it would be enough.

Landing in the courtyard, they met Emma with Leda and Alanna in tow. Mira introduced Susan and James to them, and Emma ushered them all inside. Khaldun and Mira went to see Jezebel. She wasn't in her office, but then Mira spotted her standing atop the mage's tower with Allison and Captain Amari. It was Castle Barclay's tallest structure, providing a view of the entire city and the surrounding farmland.

Khaldun and Mira went inside and hurried up the steps. Moving through Khaldun's office, they headed up to the roof. They spent a few minutes giving the three of them a more detailed account of events in Rockport.

"You're sure this elvish commander wasn't a human using an illusion spell?" Jezebel asked when they were done.

"Certain," said Mira. "He still appeared elvish inside my null."

"He could be a human shapeshifter," Allison suggested. "Your null wouldn't change his shape because he's not using any active spell to maintain it."

"That could be," Mira said.

"Semblant and Beast are the only shapeshifters we know about, and we just saw them at the university and Bayfast," said Khaldun.

"Tell me again why you believe his magic is human," said Jezebel. "I'm not sure I understand that."

"It's difficult to explain," said Mira, collecting her thoughts. "Wizards and witches are the hardest for me to sense, and sometimes, I miss them. Their magic is like the beam of a lighthouse, focused in only one direction. It's easiest to detect them when they're actively casting spells—or trying to do so inside of my null. That's when their light shines the brightest.

"Sorcerers, on the other hand, are like lighthouses with beams that project in all directions at once. They're much easier to sense, whether they're using magic at the time or not.

"The elves are different. Their light is always there, like a sorcerer, but there is no structure containing it. To extend the analogy, their magic is like an open flame, from a bonfire, perhaps, instead of a lighthouse. It's part of the environment, instead of being walled off from it. That's how demons feel, too."

"But this elf felt like a lighthouse?" Jezebel asked.

"The largest, brightest one I've ever sensed," said Mira. "Only Princess Allison comes close."

"My instinct tells me it must be one of the Sacred Circle," said Allison. "But I don't understand how that could be. They are all demons now. And elves cannot be possessed."

"And there was no sign of them coming this way?" Jezebel asked.

"None that we could see," said Khaldun. "They were building barracks, which would make it seem like they're planning for a long-term occupation of Rockport."

"They'll come here eventually," Amari said. "It's only a question of timing."

Jezebel nodded. "We should send a regiment to our northern border. They can take a mirror and send warning if the elves send a force this way." Franconia, now Spanbrook's northern province, used to be a separate princedom, and shared a border with Rockport to the north. "The northern army has already taken position outside of Franconia City. We're sending an additional five thousand troops, with the Eagle Company in the lead. That will bring our force there up to a full ten thousand."

"And leave us with only five thousand to protect Spanbrook," said Khaldun.

"Rockport is the nearest port city," said Amari. "Any force invading Spanbrook will most likely come from there. But the provincial armies are maintaining patrols in the other territories as well, so we'll have advance warning regardless of which way they come. The Eagle Company can fall back to Spanbrook with the rest of our army if necessary. But I'm hoping to defeat the enemy in Franconia."

"The elves flattened Rockport's forces with only a quarter of their army," said Khaldun. "It might make sense to move our southern armies into Franconia, too."

"Our people are far better trained and better equipped," said Allison. Mira knew only the knights wore plate armor, but even the chainmail worn by the infantry was imbued with spells to repel magic. Most of the elves couldn't remove those spells—doing so required use of the magical force, which only an elvish mage could wield. And even then they'd have to do it one soldier at a time.

"Khaldun's right," said Mira. "I didn't see a single dead elf. Their warriors are larger, stronger, and faster than our people. We have mirrors in all the neighboring princedoms, so we'll have plenty of warning if the elves send an army from somewhere else. But right now, the one in Rockport is the only one on the field. We should reinforce our northern flank as much as we can."

Jezebel nodded. "Captain?"

"The enemy is least likely to attack from the south. We could send half of our forces from Ashland and Monroe."

"That would bring our force in Franconia up to fifteen thousand," said Jezebel. "Let's do it."

"Right away, Your Highness," Amari said with a bow before hurrying off.

"I'll continue patrolling our borders from the air," Allison said, taking Jezebel's hand. "It's impossible to hide an entire army on the move, even with invisibility spells. They kick up too much dirt and make too much noise. Don't worry. No matter which way they come, we'll have plenty of warning."

"Yes," Jezebel said, heaving a sigh. "It's only… We've spent fifteen years preparing for something like this. And now I worry it's not enough."

"It will be," Allison told her. "Our people are ready."

Mira heard footsteps pounding up the steps. She turned to see Emma hurrying onto the roof.

"I've just heard from Jelena's steward," she said, trying to catch her breath. "They've spotted more ships offshore. Hundreds of them, with black sails, headed west."

"*Hundreds*?" Khaldun repeated.

"They must be heading for Blacksand," Jezebel said. "Send word to Carlo, right away. I'm afraid I must ask the two of you to make another journey," she added to Khaldun and Mira. "Blacksand is far better prepared for an attack. Their army is larger than Rockport's and better trained. I'm eager to see how they fare against the elves. Hopefully with your assistance, they'll be able to emerge victorious."

"We'll leave immediately," said Mira.

CHAPTER ELEVEN
NECROMANCER

yllith and Nyro returned to the senate in the afternoon, both of them wearing illusions of clothing, and Syllith disguised as an elf. They sat in the balcony near the stairs. When the senators adjourned, Nyro led Syllith downstairs, and they followed them out to the street.

Many of the senators set out on foot, but the wealthy ones had carriages waiting for them. Estrid was among them. She climbed into her carriage, and it set out into the city. Nyro and Syllith followed on foot, a good distance behind. The carriage headed up to the manor houses high up on the hill. Once they'd moved out of the city proper, Nyro made them invisible.

The carriage stopped in front of an enormous mansion, with marble columns holding up the roof. A butler emerged from the house to open the door for the senator. The carriage left as Estrid followed the butler inside.

Nyro led Syllith around to the back of the structure, and they slipped inside through a rear entrance in the cellar. Moving up the steps to the main level, they emerged into the kitchen. Two chefs were hard at work preparing the senator's dinner. Nyro knocked them both out with a wave of her hand. They ran into the butler on their way out of the kitchen, and she rendered him unconscious, too. Moving through the house, they encountered three more servants, and Nyro put them all under.

Finally, they moved into the hall, and found Estrid sitting at the head of the table, drinking a glass of wine. Nyro strode over to her, taking a seat at the table, and forced Syllith to do the same. Estrid said something that Syllith was sure translated to "Who the hell are you?"

Nyro answered her in elvish as she poured herself a glass of wine, taking a long drink. The senator got to her feet, but Nyro forced her back into her seat with a gesture. Nyro spoke to her for a few minutes, and Estrid's expression grew steadily more terrified. Finally, Nyro knocked her out.

"I'm afraid my power is inadequate for our next step," Nyro said, rising from her chair, and forcing Syllith to stand up.

"If *your* power is inadequate, then I'm afraid there's no mage alive who's up to the task," Syllith said.

"You flatter me. But that is wrong. Many mages can do things I cannot in this form. I'll need you to kill me before we continue."

"*What?*"

"Don't worry. Only this body will die," she replied with a smile. She used her magic to force Syllith to stop her heart. The elvish body collapsed.

Moments later, Syllith felt Nyro's demon possessing her body and taking over completely. She reached out with one hand, pulling the pyramid out of the void. Syllith had lost track of it, and wondered where it had gone. Pouring her power into the artifact, Nyro created a portal, walking through it and closing it behind her.

Taking in her new surroundings, Syllith had to shield her eyes. It was morning here. She spotted a castle in the distance and knew immediately where they were. Though she couldn't act on it, her impulse was to cover her nakedness. They were in the middle of a dirt road, and no one else was in sight, but she knew it would only be a matter of time before they ran into someone.

Nyro cast an illusion, turning Syllith into a male farmhand, wearing the appropriate garb. They set off up the road, reaching Spanbrook Town twenty minutes later. Nyro took them into the market outside the castle walls. They strolled about for a bit, pretending to be interested in various shopkeepers' wares. Until they ran into a familiar face.

"Hello, Gemma," Nyro said to the witch.

Gemma regarded her for a moment before saying, "Hello," but there was no light of recognition in her eyes. "I'm sorry, do I know you?"

"Yes, you certainly do," Nyro said with a grin, casting her spell.

Gemma's expression went blank as she followed them out of town. They walked for fifteen minutes, then, once out of sight of any onlookers, Nyro produced her pyramid and created another portal. She led Gemma through it, closing it behind them, and tucking the artifact back into the void.

They'd returned to Estrid's hall. Nyro released Gemma from her spell, and removed her illusion. Syllith stood naked before the witch.

"You," Gemma said, backing away from her. She lifted her wand, calling fire in an attempt to incinerate her.

Nyro canceled her spell. "That wasn't nice." Waving her hand, she called fire, too, incinerating Gemma's clothes.

The witch started in surprise, pointing her wand for another spell. Nyro incinerated that, too. "What do you want?"

"I have a bit of a problem," Nyro said, sitting at the table and pouring herself more wine. "I'm going to kill this elf," she said, nodding to Estrid, still slumped over in her chair, "and reanimate her body with my soul. Then, I'll need to bind our friend Syllith to her."

"You *are* Syllith," Gemma said, looking at her as if she'd gone mad.

"Try to keep up, dear," Nyro said, taking a long drink of wine. "I am Nyro, currently using this frail human body for my purposes." Gemma's eyes went wide, and she backed away a little farther. "And my problem is that elves cannot perform necromancy, nor does it work on them. I can't very well perform the rite of binding on Syllith from inside her body. Once I reanimate the elvish body, of course, I'd be able to perform the first part of the rite. But I would not be able to create the bond or force Syllith's soul back into her body. And I need her *alive*. So, that's where you come in. You will be performing the rite for me."

Gemma stared at her incredulously for a moment, then laughed. "I don't know the spells. And even if I did, you just destroyed my wand."

"Neither of those things will be an issue," Nyro told her. Getting to her feet, she held out one hand toward the witch, and Syllith could feel the power flowing through her.

Gemma screamed. Falling flat on her back, she writhed and foamed at the mouth as her skin turned golden. Nyro had triggered her metamorphosis into a sorcerer.

Nyro sat down and drank more wine as Gemma completed her transformation. Once it was done, she sat up, staring down at her body. "No… This is madness," she said, getting to her feet. "If necromancy doesn't work on elves, then you *can't* bind Syllith to this one."

"It turns out that I can," Nyro said with a smile. "You see, elves walk in our world *and* the spectral plane at the same time. They are like a cross between a human and a demon, in that way. They cannot bind a demon or become a necromancer because their living souls cannot be *merged* with those of a demon.

"However, binding a sorcerer does *not* require an elf's soul to be merged—only tethered. And from the experiments I conducted before I was killed, I believe *that* can be done. I've modified the spells for you already, although there will be some trial and error involved. But I remain confident it will work in the end."

Horror bubbled up in Syllith's stomach and she wanted to scream. What possible reason could Nyro have for binding her? Her spells already gave her complete control of Syllith's every move. She was surprised she didn't just kill her at this point—she could reanimate Estrid's body and use that for everything else she had planned. The rite called for seven days of fasting, but Syllith knew Nyro wouldn't bother with that.

"I-I won't do it," Gemma stammered, backing even farther away. She held out one hand, trying to use magic against Nyro, but nothing happened. Gemma turned to run, but Nyro stopped her with a wave of her hand, forcing her to come back to the table. Syllith recognized the blank expression on her face and knew Nyro had taken total control. She made her take a seat at the table.

Nyro got to her feet. Calling air, she moved the senator to the floor, laying her flat. Calling fire, she burned away her clothing. Taking a knee, she used the spell to stop Estrid's heart. Once she was sure she was dead, she placed one hand on her chest. The elf's skin began to glow as the power flowed through Syllith's body.

Syllith collapsed, feeling disoriented for a moment as Nyro left her body. Getting to her feet, she gazed frantically around the room. She could escape now, but she'd have to act fast. Gemma was on her feet, too—Nyro's spell must have died when she left Syllith's body. "Gemma—come with me," she said.

"Syllith?" she said, horror in her eyes.

"Yes, but let's go!"

Syllith ran toward the door, Gemma right behind her. But it slammed shut before they reached it.

"The party is only starting," a voice said from behind them.

Skidding to a stop, Syllith turned to find Estrid standing at the head of the table, smiling at them. Holding out one hand, she forced Syllith and Gemma to return to her. She made Syllith lie down on the floor, and tree roots grew out of the floor, pinning her arms and legs. She struggled against her bonds, then blacked out.

For a time, Syllith faded in and out of consciousness. At one point, green flames engulfed her, though she felt no pain and didn't burn. Another time, she opened her eyes in time to see Gemma plunge a dagger into her chest. She tried to scream, but passed out again.

Syllith found herself floating up near the ceiling, staring down at her body on the floor. Gemma uttered words she didn't recognize, and for a moment, Nyro stared up at her and smiled. She tried to leave. Her spirit was free to travel the spectral plane, and if she could escape, it would foil Nyro's plans for her. She'd be dead, but her life had become a living hell, and she had no desire to continue living it.

But when the time came, Gemma's spell slammed her soul back into her body, like a slab of iron to a lodestone. Syllith opened her eyes to find Nyro staring down at her. She had no idea how much time had passed, but it was dark outside the windows.

"I'm afraid it didn't work," Nyro told her. "We'll have to try again once I decide how to modify the spells."

Gemma stood nearby, staring across the room, her expression vacant. Syllith tried to get up, but her bonds were still in place. Her chest ached where Gemma had stabbed her, and her head was pounding.

Several minutes later, Nyro forced Gemma to try again. Like last time, Syllith tried to flee in spirit form, but it was no use. Though she was channeling her power through Gemma, Nyro was too strong. Syllith returned to her body only to learn that the rite had failed again.

Over and over again, Nyro modified her spells, and forced Gemma to perform the rite. Syllith lost track of how many times she died only to be resurrected again. But finally, as she opened her eyes after returning to her body one last time, Nyro smiled down at her. "I know your true name, sorcerer."

Syllith's bonds withdrew into the floor and disappeared. Icy claws of dread clutched her heart. She sat up but quickly realized she was too weak to stand. Turning onto her side, she vomited.

"Lie down," Nyro told her, and Syllith complied. She had little choice. "I think we both need some rest before we proceed. And for my part, a little celebration may be in order. You have served your purpose admirably," she added to Gemma.

Turning her head, Syllith saw Gemma stumble as Nyro released her hold.

Gemma turned to run, but Nyro pointed a finger, incinerating her from within. Gemma screamed, but the sound was cut off as fire consumed her body.

As ill and horrified as she felt, Syllith fell asleep. She woke to find herself still on the floor. Sitting up, she discovered her strength had returned. Delicious aromas filled her nose as she got to her feet.

"It's about time," Nyro said. She was sitting at the head of the table, sipping from a glass of wine. A feast fit for a queen filled the table. "Sit down and eat. You must be starving."

Only one other place had been set, right next to Nyro. Syllith sat down and filled her plate, scarfing down her food. She noticed that it was dark outside. "How long was I out?" she asked as she filled her plate again.

"It's been a few days. Not surprising after being killed so many times."

Nyro explained that she'd disposed of the bodies of Gemma and the spare elf, and the staff had no idea she was anyone but Senator Estrid. "They were, of course, curious about the naked human sleeping on the floor, but I've taken measures to ensure they don't talk about you. They can't leave the house, either, so that helps."

"Why not?"

"Shield spell. We'll dispose of them when the time comes, but for now, they're useful."

A shiver ran down Syllith's spine. "Why did you bother binding me? For that matter, why are you keeping me alive?"

Nyro regarded her for a moment in silence. "Unlike the servants, you will have a purpose to serve for a *very* long time to come."

After dinner, Syllith felt sleepy again. Nyro led her upstairs to the senator's bedroom, and forced her to lie in bed with her. Syllith nodded off almost immediately.

The next morning, Nyro cast her illusion to make Syllith appear as an elf, and the two of them took a carriage into the city. When they reached the senate building, Nyro used her magic to force Syllith to move up to the balcony and sit down. Nyro walked into the main chamber, chatting with some of the other senators. None of them seemed to notice that Estrid wasn't herself.

Syllith struggled to stay awake during the session. She still hadn't recovered her full strength, and listening to endless debates in a language she didn't understand did nothing to hold her attention. Nyro only listened today, without making any contribution to the discourse.

They took their midday meal at a nearby tavern during the siesta, then returned to the senate. That evening, Nyro remained behind to chat with one of the other senators. He was tall even for an elf, with bulging muscles visible through his tunic.

Nyro forced Syllith to make her way down the stairs as she left the building with the other senator. The three of them climbed into a carriage, and Nyro chatted with him as they made their way across the city.

But they didn't go to Estrid's manor. The carriage stopped, and they disembarked in front of an even larger mansion, farther up the hill. The unknown senator held the door open for them, and Syllith followed Nyro inside. He led them into his hall, and they sat at his table. Once one of the servants had poured wine for them and left the room, Nyro used her magic to knock out the senator. He slumped onto the table. Syllith followed Nyro through the house as she rendered the rest of the staff unconscious, then they returned to the hall.

"The time has come to reveal your great purpose, sorcerer," Nyro said, retaking her seat at the table. "As an elf, *I* cannot bind a demon. But as a human, *you* can."

"What? No…" Syllith said, realizing what was about to happen.

"Tonight, we'll be starting with Gnasher," Nyro told her. "You will bind him, and then he will take this elf's body. As you are bound to me, I will control him through you."

"Gnasher was one of your Sacred Circle," Syllith said, terror and dread threatening to overwhelm her. "You're going to resurrect all of them."

"Assuming this works as I expect, yes."

Nyro forced Syllith to summon Gnasher's demon. The shadow rose through the floor, filling half the hall. Syllith performed the rite to bind the demon, and it howled in rage. The moment she'd completed it, she felt Gnasher possess her.

"Your Majesty," she said, grinning ear to ear. "Though I confess I despaired, you have delivered on your promise. I am eager to take my place by your side and help you establish your eternal reign."

"Welcome back, my most faithful lieutenant," Nyro said with a smile. "I have procured this body for you. I hope it is to your liking."

"It will do nicely," Gnasher said through Syllith's mouth, examining the elf slumped across the table.

The demon used Syllith's body to call air, moving the senator onto the floor. She knelt next to him, casting the spell to stop his heart. Once the elf was dead, she incinerated his clothes, and placed a hand on his chest. The area began to glow, and moments later, Syllith collapsed as Gnasher left her body. She scuttled away, knowing what would happen next.

The elf opened his eyes, sat up, and smiled. Getting to his feet, he said, "Oh, yes. This body will do *very* nicely."

Nyro stood up and embraced the elf, plunging her tongue into his mouth. She lifted him onto the table, climbed on top, and made love to him. Nyro forced Syllith to take a seat and watch. It went on for hours, the two of them climaxing over and over again.

Finally sated, they got off the table. Nyro revived the staff, and they served them dinner. After the meal, Syllith went to the gilt-framed mirror on the wall, staring at her reflection. She'd grown accustomed to her golden skin, but her eyes caused her to gasp. The irises were white now, with only a ring of black around their edges. Syllith was a necromancer.

They slept in Gnasher's manor that night, all three of them in the senator's bed. The next morning, they returned to the senate, without any of the others suspecting that anything was amiss.

That night, Nyro and Syllith went home with another male senator. This time, Nyro forced Syllith to bind the demon who had been known as Xythor in life. They killed the senator, and Xythor took his body.

They attended the senate the next day, and went home to Estrid's house without any of the others. But over the next three weeks, Nyro repeated the process, forcing Syllith to bind the rest of her Sacred Circle, and giving them each the body of an elvish mage to reanimate. There were only a handful of mages in the senate, so once they'd taken them, Nyro had to cast a wider net to include the rest of the city. She made love to every one of them once their rite was complete, the females as well as the males, and forced Syllith to watch every time.

Syllith felt every demon overpower her utterly when they possessed her. She wasn't nearly strong enough to control any of them. But through her bond with Nyro, she could feel *her* commanding them. Syllith was nothing but a conduit for Nyro's power. And this was the sole reason she was keeping her alive. Nyro had explained that while every member of her Sacred Circle could—and would—function completely autonomously, her connection would allow her to take complete control at any time, from any distance, just as if they were still demons.

After the eleventh time, Nyro and Syllith went home to Estrid's manor. They sat down to eat, and Nyro said, "It is complete. My Sacred Circle has been reborn. Now we can proceed with the next stage of my plan."

"You've only resurrected eleven," Syllith said. "What about Blaze?"

Nyro sat in perfect stillness for a moment. She drank her entire glass of wine, then placed it on the table and got to her feet. Grabbing Syllith by the throat, she lifted her out of her chair, knocking it to the floor. She walked a few paces, Syllith struggling to free herself the entire time, then brought her face close to her and said, "You will never speak of her in my presence again. Do you understand?"

Syllith didn't understand what was going on. She tried to say, "Yes," but her voice refused to work. She nodded furiously instead.

"Good," Nyro said, throwing her to the floor. She returned to her seat, resuming her meal as if nothing had happened.

CHAPTER TWELVE
THE BATTLE OF BLACKSAND

haldun and Mira flew west, stopping just before sunset to rest and eat. Though neither of them liked flying after dark, their circumstances were dire, so they pressed ahead. It was the dead of night by the time they'd reached Blacksand, and Mira expected a member of the staff would greet them. But it was Princess Yolanda who was waiting for them when they landed in the courtyard.

"Welcome back, my lord and lady," she said, embracing them each in turn, and kissing them on the cheek. "We never expected to see you both again so soon. I only wish it could be under better circumstances."

"Thank you, Your Highness," said Mira. "We are happy to render assistance in your time of need."

"My father and the rest of his advisers have already relocated to Gemstone-by-the-Sea," she said as they walked across the courtyard. "That's where any invading force is sure to attack. We'll stay here tonight, then we can ride out in the morning."

"I can take us on our carpet," Khaldun suggested. "It'll be faster."

The princess led them inside to the great hall, where her people had a hot meal ready and waiting for them. "Princess Jezebel's steward advised us to expect your arrival at this late hour, so I made sure we were ready."

"Thank you," Khaldun said, as they dug into their meal.

Yolanda sat with them while they ate, discussing the preparations they'd been making for the coming battle. Once they'd finished eating, she escorted them upstairs to the guest chambers. "Father will be convening our privy council at Gemstone in the morning, and of course, he has requested your presence. I am sorry that not much remains of the night, but I hope you will get some sleep, at least."

Mira did sleep well, though she felt like it had been only a few minutes when the first light of dawn woke her through the windows. She kissed Khaldun, and he started awake. They headed down to the great hall for breakfast, where they met Yolanda again. After their meal, she escorted them to the keep roof. Khaldun unfurled his carpet, positioning Yolanda on the front edge before taking his seat at the rear. Once Mira had strapped herself in, they took off for the short trip to Gemstone.

Only minutes later, they landed on the roof of the castle's keep. The building sat atop a bluff at the tip of a peninsula, with the North Sea on two sides, and the River Arcon on the third. Looking down from the rear of the keep, Mira could see the sheer cliff face below the castle walls. She estimated the water to be about a hundred feet down.

The front of the castle faced Gemstone City. The area closest to the castle was the oldest, fully enclosed behind a thirty-foot wall. But over the years, the city had spilled over its original boundary, and those areas had no wall.

The river formed a natural harbor, hosting the city's docks and piers. Mira suspected that's where the elves would come ashore. Black sand beaches stretched for miles to the city's southwest, with massive waves crashing on the shore. Beyond the city, farmland extended as far as the eye could see. Mira spotted Blacksand's army camped along the river beyond the harbor.

Any invading force would have to come ashore in the harbor—the sea was too rough for such a landing. They'd have to contend with Blacksand's troops the moment they landed. And the only approach to the castle was through the city, and up a single road with many switchbacks.

Yolanda escorted them inside, and they found Lord Eldrick with the prince's advisers in the lord's council chambers. Mira recognized the steward, Jasper, and Yolanda introduced them to their wizard, a tall, thin man named Lester, their master-at-arms, a shorter, stoutly built man named Horace, and their general, a woman of average build named Gwendolyn.

"Please call me Gwen," the general said, shaking their hands.

They all took their seats again, and Khaldun and Mira sat down in the two chairs they'd left open next to the princess. Prince Carlo arrived a minute later, and they all stood until he took his seat at the head of the table.

"Thank you for joining us on such short notice," he said to Khaldun and Mira. "We understand you were present for the attack on Rockport. Perhaps you could apprise us of how the battle unfolded there?"

Khaldun and Mira took turns recounting the events.

"Remarkable," Eldrick said, sitting back in his chair. "You say the elves accomplished this with only a quarter of their total force?"

"That's correct, my lord," replied Khaldun.

"We have twelve thousand men and women in our army, ready to defend the princedom," the prince said. "In addition, we have called in the levies, and expect another five or six thousand to arrive in the coming days. Though, how many will arrive in time remains to be seen."

"We can expect my lord and lady to assist our mages in the battle?" Gwen asked.

"Yes, that's why we're here," Khaldun said. "But I must warn you that *all* of the elves can use magic. Only their mages can call the magical force, but we witnessed a dozen or so elves melt one of the castle walls in Rockport, causing it to collapse. They did it without the help of any of their mages."

"It would be best for this battle to position me on the ramparts for the duration of the attack," Mira suggested. "I should be able to protect the building from such spells."

"Our troops all have the enchanted armor, thanks to Lord Khaldun," said Yolanda, "which should help neutralize the elves' thaumaturgic advantage."

"The elves must realize we're better prepared than Rockport," said Gwen. "They did send scouts. So, their commanders will be aware of the size and disposition of our army. They'll know the landscape, and the location of the harbor, and my understanding is that their scouting parties have all included mages, so they will be ready for our enchanted armor."

"Meaning they'll find some way around our defenses," said Yolanda.

"Yes," Gwen replied. "It's unlikely that they'll come ashore in the harbor, for example."

"Where else could they land?" asked Mira.

"There are a number of smaller ports along the coast to our southeast," said Eldrick. "Their soldiers could offload there and march here over land."

"It might be wise to move half of our regiments to that region," Yolanda suggested, "in case they do come that way."

"With all due respect, Your Highness, I disagree," said Gwen. "Reducing our force around the city could prove disastrous if they do decide to make landfall in the harbor. Regardless of where they land, it'll be Gemstone City itself they want, so let them come to us. We should position our entire army to protect the city. Once we know where they're coming ashore, we can send a few regiments to hinder that process."

"We should have ample warning," said Khaldun. "Our ships would take five days to make it here from Rockport. We know elvish vessels are more advanced and probably faster. They could make it here in four, perhaps three days, which would put them here two days from now at the earliest. Your people should spot them from land as they approach, and I can fly patrol as well."

"Won't their mages make their ships invisible?" asked Yolanda.

"Perhaps," said Khaldun. "They didn't in Rockport. And it might not help, especially with that many vessels. We'd still see their wakes in the water."

"As much as it pains me to suggest this, we might also consider destroying the piers and docks in the harbor," said Eldrick. "This will make it harder for them to land there, and leaving the debris in the water will prevent them from getting too close to shore."

"An excellent idea, my lord," said Gwen. "You might consider doing the same thing at the ports down the coast as well."

"Very well," said the prince. "We will keep the bulk of the army close to the city perimeter to ensure our defenses are at their full strength, regardless of which way the attack comes. And we will make their landing as difficult for them as we can."

"In addition, I would suggest evacuating our people from the ports to the southeast of here," said Jasper. "And the citizens of this city, for that matter. We have time. They should find safety in some of our interior holdings."

"Yes, I agree," Carlo said. "Please take care of the arrangements."

After the meeting, Mira spent an hour discussing their thaumaturgic response to the impending attack with Khaldun, Lester, and Yolanda. Mira would stay on the ramparts, using her null to protect the structure and the people inside from magical attack. They'd need the castle in case a defeat on the battlefield forced them to fall back.

Yolanda and Lester would take positions on the city walls, and do as much damage to the elvish army as they could. Khaldun would provide support from the air, assisting Blacksand's army wherever they needed it the most.

Eldrick's staff spent the rest of that day and all of the following day evacuating the city. They sent messengers to alert the nearby coastal holdings to do the same. Gwen moved several garrisons inside the city, into positions where they could harass the enemy on their way to the castle. Several more garrisons moved into the castle. An entire regiment moved through the harbor area, destroying the piers and docks.

Khaldun spent much of his time flying patrol, and Mira found she didn't have much to do. She spent most of her time with Yolanda, assisting her as she helped prepare the castle for battle. The evening of their second full day in Gemstone, Khaldun and Mira ate dinner in the great hall with the rest of the castle's inhabitants, then Yolanda invited them up to her chambers. They sat up late drinking wine and chatting.

"I don't know how the two of you hold it together so well in the face of this invasion," Yolanda said, taking a long drink of wine. "It's all I can do to keep myself from running around the courtyard screaming my head off. Who ever thought we'd live to see the elves attacking Anoria?"

"We've been thinking of little else for fifteen years, I'm afraid," said Mira. "Ever since the Battle of Highgate, and Nyro's escape, we've feared something like this. I guess we've had more time to get used to the idea. But truthfully, I'm scared, too."

"So am I," Khaldun said. "But it helps to have something to do. When you can focus on your work, it keeps the fear at bay."

"True enough," Yolanda said. "I'm glad I'm not alone, though. You two seem so brave, yet knowing you're as afraid as I am makes this a little easier."

Khaldun and Mira returned to their chambers and went to bed. But a banging on their door woke them up in the middle of the night. Mira sat up, rubbing the sleep from her eyes. "What's going on? It's still dark out," she said as she got up to answer the door. It was Yolanda.

"The elves attack," she said, and Mira could see the fear in her eyes. "My father has ordered everyone to take their positions."

Khaldun and Mira dressed in their leather armor, donning their robes on top of that. They followed Yolanda up to the keep roof, awash in moonlight. The prince was there, along with Lord Eldrick, Lester, and Jasper, all staring off into the distance. Following their gaze, Mira spotted the elvish ships with a gasp. They'd run aground on the beaches to the southwest of the castle, dozens and dozens of them. Elvish warriors were pouring over their sides, landing in the sand and running to higher ground.

"So it begins," said the prince. "Everyone to your stations!"

Mira, Yolanda, and Lester joined Khaldun on his carpet, and he lifted off, landing on the ramparts near the barbican. Mira got to her feet, bending over to kiss him, then he took off again with the other two mages. She watched him drop them off on the city wall, then he shot into the sky.

Mira opened her channels of power, expanding her null to include the entire castle. The Blacksand troops to the city's south and southwest had already formed ranks, ready to meet the elvish onslaught. Those regiments camped to the southeast were on the move, heading to positions to back up the rest of their troops. The levies had arrived from the nearest holdings over the past couple of days, swelling the army's total number to more than fifteen thousand.

A giant waterspout formed off the coast; Mira couldn't see Khaldun, but knew this had to be his doing. The twister hit one of the elvish ships that had just landed. It destroyed the vessel, sending timber flying everywhere, but someone canceled it before it could hit the next ship. Another formed, blasting apart a ship coming aground closer to the castle, but someone canceled that one, too. Khaldun hurled a few more, each one destroying one vessel, but no more ships arrived; the elves had finished disembarking from the others.

The elvish army was forming ranks faster than Mira would have thought possible, again giving her the impression that a single will guided them. Khaldun refocused his attention on the troops, sending numerous cyclones through their lines. Each one hurled dozens of soldiers high into the air. But someone canceled his next round of tornadoes almost the moment they'd formed.

Horns sounded, and the elvish army charged. They crashed into Blacksand's army like a tidal wave, but their lines held. The sounds of metal clashing with metal drifted up to Mira, along with the screams and battle cries.

Mira spotted individual elves going up in flames, but didn't know who was casting the spells. Khaldun was still out there somewhere, and Yolanda and Lester would be on the southwest section of the city wall by now. There was no evidence of the elves using magic against the Blacksanders, but that might only be because of their enchanted armor.

It looked like the elvish army had about ten thousand troops on the field. The Blacksanders outnumbered them by roughly fifty percent. And while they fared much better than the Rockporters had, their numbers still dwindled as the battle raged on. By dawn, Mira guessed that the two armies were equal in size.

Mira wished she could move to the city wall and assist with the battle. But there wasn't much she'd be able to do. If the elves were using magic, it was having no effect against the enchantments on their troops' armor. So far, Mira had felt no thaumaturgic assault impact her null, either.

Suddenly, Mira noticed a low rumbling sensation—she could feel it in the rampart's stones as well as hear it. She noticed several structures in the city's outskirts collapsing, but couldn't see what was causing it. The rumbling grew stronger, and finally she spotted its source. A giant fissure had opened in the earth, swallowing entire companies of Blacksand's troops. Their screams reached her ears, as the remaining troops began a lateral movement, trying to escape their comrades' fate.

Their discipline impressed her. Caught between the enemy army and an enormous pit in the ground, they stayed organized. But the elves followed them, keeping up their constant onslaught. Though they'd suffered casualties, they outnumbered the Blacksanders by a wide margin now. Mira didn't know how much longer they could hold out.

A second rumbling sensation started, stronger than the first, and Mira spotted a new fissure forming out beyond the city, where the Blacksanders had moved. Troops screamed as they tumbled into the earth. Mira wished she could have stopped it, but the spell was beyond the range of her null.

Blacksand's army began a tactical withdrawal, moving into the city. The elves did not pursue them. Mira wondered what they were up to, but they formed ranks and stood their ground. She estimated their number at less than eight thousand.

The gates in the city wall opened, and Blacksand's remaining troops moved inside. Mira guessed only about five thousand remained, putting their losses around ten thousand. The gates closed again after the final companies had moved inside.

Moments later, Mira spotted Khaldun's carpet flying toward her, and she closed her channels of power. As Khaldun drew closer, she realized he was carrying Gwen, Yolanda, and Lester as passengers.

Lester's hair had been singed off, and he had burns on his head and neck. "We're regrouping at the keep," Khaldun told her as he brought the carpet in low. Mira climbed on board for the short trip across the courtyard. Landing on the roof, they got up from the carpet and met Prince Carlo, Lord Eldrick, and Jasper. Mira opened her channels of power, unleashing her null.

"Your Highness, our troops fought bravely, but the elvish forces overwhelmed us," said Gwen. "Their people are much faster and stronger than ours. We can defend the city walls for a while, perhaps, but at this point, I believe we will need to retreat to the castle and prepare for a siege. The garrisons we have embedded in the city can harass the elves on their way by, reducing their numbers as much as possible before we begin the next phase of this battle."

"I agree, Your Highness," said Khaldun. "Yolanda, Lester, and I can keep up our thaumaturgic onslaught from the ramparts, and Mira can continue protecting the keep with her null. We may yet claim victory."

Carlo gazed across the city, his expression grave. "Why did the elves break off their pursuit, I wonder."

"They'll be regrouping, preparing to assault the city wall," Eldrick said. "Lady Gwen is right, Your Highness. We must prepare for a siege."

Carlo nodded. "Very well, please proceed."

At that moment, Mira felt an incredible surge of power slam into her null. "Someone's trying to attack the castle. It felt like an earth spell, but it had more energy than I've ever felt before."

"They've got a powerful mage with them, and unlike the one in Rockport, he's participating in the battle," said Khaldun. "We saw Nomad open a fissure in the ground many years ago, but these two were far bigger. Whoever it is must have an affinity for earth spells."

"Can he break through your null?" Carlo asked.

"No, Your Highness," said Mira. "It's at its full size, which takes it halfway to the city walls. The mage won't be able to get a spell through it." Another blast of power hit her null as she spoke. "He just tried again, but his magic died."

"You'll have to retract your null somewhat if we're going to work magic from the ramparts," Khaldun said. "But it would be best to keep it at its full size until then."

Mira started to reply, but at that moment, the ground shook beneath their feet.

"What was that?" Carlo said, fear in his eyes.

"An earthquake?" Eldrick said. "I've never heard of one in these parts."

"It's magic, I think," Mira said as another tremor struck. "The mage can't get through my null, so he's hitting the bedrock far below the castle instead, beyond the reach of my power."

"The castle will fall if this keeps up," said Eldrick. "You can't stop the shaking?"

"I'm afraid not, my lord," Mira said apologetically. "My null only works against magic. And his spells aren't hitting the castle directly."

"We've got to evacuate," said Khaldun. "Your Highness, I can fly you, the princess, and Lord Eldrick to safety."

"And what happens to our people?" Carlo demanded. "We throw them to the wolves? I will not abandon them."

"They can escape through the tunnels," said Yolanda. "The one that starts in the kitchens comes out in a barn south of the city. But there are other entry points in the city that the soldiers can use."

Carlo sighed. "And where shall we go? If Gemstone can't withstand this onslaught, we possess no holding that can."

"Go to Spanbrook," Khaldun suggested. "They will attack there too, eventually, but combining your remaining force with ours could help us prevail."

"Your Highness, I have to agree," said Eldrick. "We've lost. But we may yet live to fight another day."

"How safe will the tunnels be during an earthquake?" Carlo asked. "If they collapse, our people will die here."

"I'll go with them," said Mira. "My null will stop them from hitting the castle or tunnel system directly until we're clear."

"I agree," said Khaldun. "It will take some time for these quakes to take out the castle. But we must hurry. I will fly you, your daughter,

Lord Eldrick, and Lester to safety, and we can regroup with the others at the tunnel's end."

The prince agreed. Mira embraced Khaldun, kissing him and wishing him luck, then he flew off with Carlo, Yolanda, Eldrick, and Lester. Mira followed Jasper and Gwen into the castle. Gwen hurried out to the city to organize the army's evacuation. Jasper alerted the castle's occupants. Minutes later, Mira followed him to the kitchens, where he pushed a stone near the ovens, revealing a hidden tunnel entrance as a section of the wall moved into a recess.

Mira kept her null extended to its full size as they moved into the tunnel. Jasper had lit an oil lamp to illuminate their way. The ground shook over and over again as they led the castle's occupants through the passage, causing streams of dirt and dust to fall on their heads. Despite what they'd said earlier, she feared the castle and tunnel would collapse around them.

They reached an intersection in the tunnels, and found Gwen's people approaching from the connecting passage. It took almost an hour, but finally, they reached a large chamber, with a stairway leading up. Jasper climbed the steps, pushing a trapdoor open over his head. Some hay and dust fell through the opening, as daylight flooded the passage.

Mira followed him up the steps, emerging inside a barn. They found Khaldun waiting outside with his passengers. "It's going to be a long walk to Spanbrook," she said, hugging her husband.

"You and I aren't going to Spanbrook," he told her with a grim smile. "I contacted Jezebel to apprise her of our situation here. She heard from Salerna. The princess has seen hundreds of ships with black sails rounding the western end of Dorshire, south of Blacksand. We believe they must be headed for Oldport."

"If that's where we're going, I wonder how Salerna was able to see anything," said Mira. "Surely, I'll be using my null."

"She couldn't see Oldport itself, only the ships at sea."

"If they take that city, there's nothing to stop them from reaching Keepstone next," said Mira. "Oldport doesn't have a strong military; they don't stand a chance."

"Yes, exactly. Jezebel wants us to inflict as much damage on the elvish army as we can. The university is sending Mist, Battleaxe, and Cyclone to assist."

"It'll take them days to get there," said Mira.

"Flying together on the same carpet, with three of them calling air, they could make the journey in a day. The elves will take longer than that. We should accompany Carlo and his people as far as we can today. I can fly patrol and make sure we've escaped any pursuit. Then you and I can depart for Oldport at first light."

Once the rest of the Blacksanders had emerged from the barn, Mira closed her channels of power, eliminating her null. Seconds later, the ground shook beneath them. Yolanda screamed, pointing back toward the city. Turning, Mira saw Castle Gemstone collapsing, large chunks of it falling into the sea.

CHAPTER THIRTEEN
EMPIRE

he night after Syllith brought up Blaze, the twelfth and missing member of the Sacred Circle, Nyro hosted a party at Estrid's house for her reborn demon-elves. The household staff prepared a magnificent feast, serving enough food for an army, and an endless supply of wine and liquor to go with it. Syllith had never seen anyone eat or drink as much as Nyro's inner circle did that night. And when they were done, the party turned into an orgy, the elves having sex in groups of two or three, in every possible combination of male and female. It went on for hours, and Syllith could not believe the depth of their hunger. Although she knew demons yearned for the pleasures of the flesh, and these had existed without corporeal form for centuries, it still seemed excessive.

One of the males approached Syllith at one point—she'd been sitting in the rear corner of the room, trying to fade into the walls— asking her if she would like to participate. But Nyro gripped his arm, saying, "No, Reaper. She's off limits."

Syllith breathed a sigh of relief. The elves were much too big for her, and the mere thought of one of them penetrating her was painful.

It took the entire night for Nyro's people to sate themselves, and finally, as the sky outside grew light, the guests departed. Nyro took Syllith up to bed, and Syllith passed out the moment her head hit the pillow. She woke only a few hours later, and the staff served them breakfast in the hall.

"The time for celebration is behind us," Nyro told her. "Today, we get to work. We will restore Drengrvollr to its former glory."

"What former glory?"

"In ancient times, the Drengrvollri kings conquered most of the elvish continent. Only Snaerverold remained independent. The warriors of the southern kingdoms couldn't withstand their winters. In time, the others rose from the ashes and drove the Drengrvollri back to their own kingdom. They slaughtered the king, dismantled their army and navy, and forced them to adopt a democratic government.

"But the people have never forgotten their former greatness. They believe they are superior to the rest of their kind, and deserve to rule the entire continent. The pacifists have managed to hold onto power in the senate for centuries. But we will change that."

"How? If the senators are democratically elected, it would take a coup to overthrow them. And if you do that, their people will stop you. They're all magic users, and you have no army to back you up."

"Not yet, I don't. That will come in time. But there will be no coup. We need the people on our side. It will take time, but we will appeal to their grudges. Their distrust of the other kingdoms. And their pride. It may take a year or two, but we will establish a majority and defeat the pacifists in the senate.

"From there, we will rebuild the kingdom's military might. And we will conquer the rest of the elvish kingdoms. This continent will be mine."

Syllith was shocked. She never would have imagined that Nyro desired an *elvish* empire. Was it revenge that motivated her? The elves were the ones who came to Anoria's aid and incarcerated her and her Sacred Circle. That was fine with her. As long as Nyro was occupied here, she wouldn't bother with the humans.

Estrid had represented Krokr in the senate, so there was no need for Nyro to go anywhere else. But she dispatched her circle to their home districts to stir up support for the militarists in the neighboring territories.

Syllith didn't understand why Nyro kept updating her on her progress, and asked her about this one day. Nyro told her that she wanted Syllith to document her rise to power. She wanted an accurate record of it. So, she produced parchment and writing implements, and forced her to start chronicling her progress.

Months went by. Nyro never let Syllith out of her sight. She dragged her to every senate session, forcing her to remain in her balcony seat the entire time. As she traveled her district, giving speeches and raising money, Syllith was always by her side. They ate every meal together, and slept in the same bed at night. When Nyro took one or more of her circle to bed with her, Syllith was there, forced to watch.

Everything went according to Nyro's plan. It took her two years to oust the pacifists in the senate. At the very next session, she advanced a proposal to raise an army and build a navy, and it passed. Construction on the warships started a few weeks later. Six months after that, the first vessels set sail, docking in the bay.

The other kingdoms must have had spies in Krokr. An armada from Mestrland showed up one morning the following year and attempted to destroy the shipyards. The Drengrvollri navy demolished them; their ships were faster and stronger than those from Mestrland, many of them equipped with metal-reinforced rams below the waterline. The Drengrvollri rammed some of the enemy vessels, causing them to sink. They moved in close to the others, using grappling hooks to lash the enemy vessel to their own, allowing their soldiers to board the Mestrlander ship and fight at close quarters. They brought the Mestrlander commander to Nyro, and she beheaded him herself. After two more years, Drengrvollr had raised an army over a hundred thousand strong, and built an entire fleet of warships, numbering in the hundreds.

One morning, Syllith arrived at the senate building with Nyro to find a massive crowd cheering her as they stepped out of their carriage. She had no idea what was going on. Inside, they found giant banners with the ancient Drengrvollri coat of arms emblazoned on them hanging from the balconies. The session started, and the senator

Syllith recognized only as Gnasher gave an impassioned speech. Syllith had picked up a little elvish over the years, and understood some of what they were saying, but not enough to comprehend what was happening. But when Gnasher was done, the chamber broke out in cheers and applause as Nyro approached the podium. Gnasher placed a golden crown upon her head.

Syllith learned later that they'd voted unanimously to restore the monarchy and name Nyro—or Estrid, as they knew her—the queen.

Nyro's public appearances increased tenfold after that. She spoke often to crowds numbering in the thousands. Banners with the royal coat of arms started showing up all over the city, and they conducted military parades through the streets.

One morning, Nyro took Syllith to the docks. They boarded a ferry, where she realized Reaper was waiting for them. As they set out across the bay, Syllith said, "What the hell is this? Where are you taking me?"

Nyro made no reply. They reached an island not far from shore, but far enough from the capital that Syllith had never seen it before. It was small, hosting nothing but an ancient-looking castle. They docked, and Reaper led them up to the structure. Inside, Syllith found an entire staff waiting for them.

Leaving Reaper behind, Nyro led Syllith upstairs to one of the bedrooms. It included a luxurious four-poster bed, an enormous fireplace, and a desk with enough writing supplies to last a year.

"We are invading Mestrland today. This will be the first step in establishing my new empire. From there, we will take Ellrivollr, and then Askaheimr. We will leave Snaerverold for last. I must make sure we are at our full strength before we attempt that. It is their winter, not their people, that will be our greatest enemy.

"I expect this to take many years. Once we have conquered a kingdom, we will have to spend time fortifying it militarily and winning over the hearts and minds of its people before proceeding to the next.

"It will no longer be feasible to keep you with me night and day. So here you shall remain, and Reaper will look after you."

"Why him?" Syllith demanded. "Choose any of the others, I beg you." Reaper was the craziest of the bunch. His mind had deteriorated the most during their incarceration, and despite his vast power, he was the most animalistic, more like a typical demon. Nyro had had to replace him in the senate, and hide him from public view lest his peculiar behavior alert the populace to their true identities. And he'd developed an obsession with Syllith. Many times he'd tried to take her sexually when he didn't think Nyro was paying attention. She'd stopped him every time, but Syllith feared what he would do to her in her absence.

"Reaper's usefulness to me has waned. In life, his special power was necromancy. He bound more than a hundred demons. In death, it seems he lost himself to them. Our long captivity was not kind to him.

"He needs to rest. This place will serve as a refuge for him. The staff will cater to his every need. Fear not, I have included servants who will sate his every sexual desire. But he will also take care of you. Keep you alive and make sure your needs are met as well. I will keep him apprised of our progress, and he will relay my messages to you, so you can keep up your writing."

And with that, she departed. It was the last time Syllith had seen her.

For the first couple of years, everything went as Nyro had promised. Though she was a prisoner, Syllith lived a life of luxury. She ate and drank as much as she pleased, slept as late as she wanted, swam in the bay during the warmer months, and kept herself busy writing. Reaper gave her periodic updates on Nyro's progress, and Syllith kept up her chronicles. He was so well behaved, Syllith felt certain Nyro must have put him under her spell to prevent him from harming her.

Nyro's forces had conquered Mestrland, and she'd abolished their senate, declaring herself empress. Mestrland was the richest kingdom on the continent, though the wealth was concentrated with the society's elite. Nyro had put the kingdom's resources to work, expanding her army and navy. She had her circle traveling the land, meeting with the kingdom's citizens, and rooting out local corruption. Her new empire started every manner of public works project, improving the lives of Mestrland's common people.

Reaper's chambers were at the other end of the castle, but Syllith could hear him. Every night, he took at least a couple of other elves to bed. Usually females, but sometimes males, too. It went on for hours.

And more and more, Syllith noticed him leering at her. He'd show up while she was bathing, pretending it had been accidental, but his eyes always lingered on her. And he started finding excuses to touch her, whether clasping her shoulder in greeting, or patting her thigh when he was done giving her an update from Nyro. It made Syllith's skin crawl.

One night, after becoming particularly drunk at dinner, Reaper invited Syllith to join him and his servants in bed. Syllith refused. She hurried up to her own chambers, but Reaper followed her. He dragged her kicking and screaming to his bedroom. None of the others were there. He used his magic to stop her from resisting, then tore her clothes off and raped her.

Syllith had never experienced such pain, physically or emotionally. She'd bled from the genitals and anus for days. For hours, she'd sit in her chambers, trying to revive her magic. But Reaper must have been keeping up whatever spells Nyro had been using to prevent her power from returning.

Reaper avoided her for the first few days after that first incident. But then it happened again. Before long, it became a regular thing. Syllith wanted to kill herself, but Reaper kept her under his constant control. After Syllith hid a knife from the dinner table and tried to murder him, he threw her in the dungeons, without any clothes.

Syllith's existence had gone from pampered to tortured. Reaper would starve her for days, then show up with a platter of food, piping hot, and eat it in front of her. He gave her enough to keep her alive, but only barely.

And he used her to sate himself sexually almost every day. Inside, Syllith was screaming the entire time. But Reaper's spells kept her silent and compliant. She tried desperately to kill herself, but there was no way to do it. Her magic had never returned, Reaper never gave her utensils to eat, and there was no clothing she could use as a noose. Even if she had the tools to do it, she lacked the control. He kept her as a prisoner not only in the dungeon, but in her own body. Though he kept the cell locked at all times, it was hardly necessary. His magic ensured she couldn't get up and walk out even if he left the door wide open.

Reaper still updated Syllith on Nyro's progress, though there was no point anymore. She had no way to record anything.

Nyro had spent years enriching Mestrland's populace, and they loved her for it. She'd taken down the elite class, executing many of them, and imprisoning the rest. When she was ready, she invaded Ellrivollr. Militarily, this was easier than Mestrland's conquest had been. Ellrivollr had led the rest of the continent in opposing Drengrvollr's rule all those centuries ago, and they were also the ones who'd forced democracy and pacifism on them. The kingdom was reputed to be the cradle of elvish civilization, and its people were proud. It wasn't as rich as Mestrland, but its wealth was already distributed equally across the entire population. As a result, it took Nyro much longer to win over the people.

Syllith knew years had gone by, but in her despair, she'd lost track of time. Every day was a living hell, and there was no reason to count the days. There was no way to escape, and she could only hope for an early death.

Eventually, Reaper told her that Nyro had finally moved on to Askaheimr. Conquering them had been easy. And winning them over was simple. She'd only had to allow them to share in the bounty of her empire, and they were hers. Askaheimr's people had always been envious of the other kingdoms' wealth, but unable to reproduce it because of its desolate landscape.

And in time, Nyro decided to brave the Snaerverolder snows to take the final kingdom. Its people had long ago mastered the area's harsh conditions, and Nyro had sent scouts to embed themselves in their villages and learn their ways. They came back and taught her armies. So when she was ready, her people accomplished what ancient Drengrvollr had never been able to achieve: uniting the entire continent.

And then one day, Reaper came to tell Syllith about Nyro's next big campaign: the invasion of Anoria.

"*What?*" she'd said, her voice cracking after so many years without use. "Why? The humans pose no threat to her. She has already established the greatest empire the world has ever seen. What could she possibly stand to gain in Anoria?"

"Her Majesty has meted out her revenge against the elves for incarcerating us for all those centuries," Reaper told her. "Now, she will have her vengeance against the humans for calling for their aid in the first place."

"Conquering Anoria will cost far more than she stands to gain. Its riches are nothing compared to the empire's."

"It's not conquest she's interested in," Reaper said with a crazed laugh. "It's *extermination.*"

This news had ignited a new spark in Syllith's bosom. She had to find a way out of her prison so she could warn her people. It seemed like an impossible task, but the idea consumed her, and she spent every waking hour trying to devise some means of accomplishing it. There had to be something she'd overlooked, some tool she could use to provide herself an escape.

Seven days after Reaper's dire news, a crashing noise woke Syllith in the middle of the night. She sat up, listening for any more noises. And then the stone floor shook as if from an earthquake. There was another crashing noise, and someone screamed.

She heard something tumbling down the steps to the dungeon. And moments later, Reaper moved into view, lying flat on his back.

Syllith gasped. What the hell was going on? Had he gotten so drunk he'd passed out and fallen down the stairway?

But then she heard footsteps descending the steps. Syllith held her breath. She spotted the light of an oil lamp approaching, and then a tall figure with white hair and a long beard stepped over Reaper.

Staring at the ancient elf, she said, "Who the hell are you?"

CHAPTER FOURTEEN
OLDPORT

ira marched eastward toward Spanbrook with Prince Carlo and his people. They stuck to the forest, in case the road was being watched. Mira walked with Yolanda for much of the time, but the princess was quiet. She knew in part how she must be feeling, having been forced to leave her own home more than once.

Khaldun had left to fly patrol. He returned to them a few hours later. Mira joined him as he gave his report to the prince. "I've found no sign of pursuit, and I do not believe they are watching the road. Since destroying the castle, the elves have left the city alone. They've got their troops rebuilding the harbor's piers and docks."

"They had no desire to take the castle, or to kill or capture me," Carlo said. "Not the usual behavior of conquerors."

"Your Highness, we believe they are interested in the port cities only to establish supply lines for their armies as they march inland," Khaldun said. "They intend to conquer the entire continent, so individual princedoms do not concern them beyond the resources they can provide."

The prince nodded, but said no more. Khaldun and Mira took their leave, and stood aside to let the rest of the line pass. They'd accompany the rear-guard for a while.

"I think I spotted their mage," Khaldun said. "He was tall, even for an elf, and walked naked among the others. I could feel his power even from the air."

"He possesses a deep affinity for earth spells, whoever he is," said Mira. "I've never seen anything like that."

"No, neither have I. When Nomad opened the fissure in Oxcart that time, it took everything he had. He needed a few minutes to recover. But this mage opened a larger opening, and then a second one in no time. Not to mention the earthquakes. Those would have been well beyond Nomad's abilities."

Khaldun said nothing more, but Mira could tell he had something on his mind. "What are you thinking?"

He heaved a sigh. "I don't understand how it could be possible, but I wonder if this was Xythor."

"From Nyro's Sacred Circle?" Khaldun nodded. "He's a demon now, and the text we found says elves can't be possessed."

"I know. But I can't help but wonder if Nyro found some way around that. It would make sense that she'd send her top lieutenants here to conduct this invasion. The mage we saw in Rockport could be Gnasher. According to the stories, he possessed the strength of ten men, and could rip people limb from limb with his bare hands."

"Yes, and it was also said he had jaws like a crocodile, and used them to tear people apart," Mira said. "The mage in Rockport didn't have a particularly large mouth."

"No, but he had the muscles. If it is the Sacred Circle, who knows how they acquired bodies? They're elvish now, not human, so surely they wouldn't match their original forms precisely."

Mira didn't know what to think. They knew for sure Nyro had freed her champions from their incarceration in Pytha. But they had no idea where they'd gone from there, or what they'd done. Maybe these elvish mages *were* the Sacred Circle reborn somehow. It would explain why the mage she'd sensed in Rockport had felt human, despite his elvish body. Whoever they were, their power eclipsed that of any human sorcerer.

As the sun set, the Blacksanders made camp in a field not far from the road. Khaldun had flown patrol a few more times, and continued to find no evidence of pursuit. It seemed like the elves didn't care what became of them.

With the army and remaining staff from Gemstone Castle, they had over five thousand people, too many for Khaldun to enclose in an invisibility spell. But they stationed guards around the perimeter of the field, and Mira kept her null extended to protect them from thaumaturgic attack. She could keep her channels of power open while she slept, and anyone attempting to cast any kind of spell inside her null would awaken her immediately.

Khaldun and Mira had set up their tent next to Yolanda's. Khaldun built them a fire, and the three of them sat around it late into the evening, sharing a bottle of hard liquor the princess had managed to procure from one of the soldiers.

"I never imagined we'd lose Castle Gemstone," Yolanda said, taking a swig of alcohol and handing the bottle to Mira. "Seeing it fall into the sea like that… Who could possess the power to do such a thing?"

"No human mage, certainly," Khaldun said. He told her about their thoughts regarding Nyro's Sacred Circle.

"Xythor?" she repeated when he was done. "There were twelve of them total?"

"Yes," Khaldun confirmed. "And he was the only one who refused to take a different name."

"Why was he naked?" Yolanda said, failing to stifle a giggle. "Is that an elvish thing? Walking into battle with your cock exposed for the world to see?"

"I don't think so," Khaldun said with a grin. "It's more of a Nyro thing, I believe. The few representations of her I've seen all show her nude. And according to one text, she refused to wear clothing, and wouldn't allow anyone in her presence to do so, either. I have no idea why, though."

"And you think the one in Rockport was Gnasher?" Yolanda said. "Who were some of the others?"

"We don't *know* that these mages are members of the Sacred Circle," Mira told her, taking a drink from the bottle and passing it to Khaldun. "This is pure speculation at this point."

"True," said Khaldun. "And I don't know all of them. Syllith did, I think. Other than Gnasher and Xythor, I know of Typhoon, Artifice, Reaper, and Howler—oh, and Blaze."

"I'm going to guess Blaze and Typhoon were known for fire and weather spells, respectively?" said Yolanda. "What about the others?"

"Yes, that's right. But like Xythor, their command of their particular forms of magic far exceeded anything today's sorcerers can achieve," said Khaldun. "Legend says Blaze surrounded the entire university with fire when they attacked there. And it is said Typhoon sent a hurricane to flatten the entire city of Northcoast.

"Artifice was known for illusions," Khaldun continued. "In the battle to take Keepstone, he made the entire city and its army see the surrounding plain turn into a field of lava. Howler was a shapeshifter known for changing into a giant wolf. He would infiltrate enemy camps at night in that form and maul the troops. And Reaper was the most powerful necromancer among them. It is said he bound more than a hundred demons, and could send them all at once to possess enemy soldiers and turn them against their comrades."

Mira shivered at the thought. "It is terrifying to think they could be walking among us again."

"Were they all male, then?" Yolanda asked.

"No," Khaldun replied. "Typhoon and Blaze were female. And I know Gnasher, Xythor, and Artifice were male. There are no clear records about Reaper or Howler, but it is said her necromancers were split evenly between males and females."

"I do hope you are wrong about this," Yolanda said with a dark chuckle, taking the bottle from him and drinking. "Yet I fear you are probably correct. Nyro returned to life, so it stands to reason that she would find a way for her Sacred Circle to do the same."

"She *possessed* Syllith," Khaldun said. "Whatever she's done with the Sacred Circle is something different."

Khaldun and Mira had agreed that the two of them would keep watch all night, so he went into the tent to get some sleep, while Mira stayed up. Yolanda remained a little longer before retiring to her own tent. Mira walked the camp, keeping her null extended to its full size, but sensed no intrusions. After a few hours, she crawled into the tent beside Khaldun and woke him with a kiss.

Khaldun returned to wake her at dawn. He'd spent most of his watch airborne, without detecting any sign of pursuit. The two of them sat down to eat breakfast, then went to confer with Prince Carlo. Mira was nervous about leaving the Blacksanders, but as the prince pointed out, if the elves did attack, there would be little the two sorcerers could do to save them from slaughter.

"We will proceed to Spanbrook as planned," he told them. "Hopefully there, we can stand together with Princess Jezebel and find a way to defeat these invaders."

If they pushed it, they could make it from Blacksand to Spanbrook in fifteen or sixteen days, but it could take longer. Mira hoped they would make it there before the elves attacked. But just in case, Khaldun gave Yolanda a mirror he'd connected to his. He told her to check in with him once they reached Spanbrook's border to find out if it was safe to proceed to Castle Barclay.

Khaldun and Mira broke camp, bade Princess Yolanda farewell, then flew away on Khaldun's carpet. They stopped at midday to rest and eat, and then again at sunset. Mira was tired, and her muscles cramped, but they didn't want to delay. They kept flying until they reached Oldport.

Khaldun had been in contact with Battleaxe by mirror. She'd arrived with Mist and Cyclone the previous afternoon, and they'd taken rooms in an inn up in the hills near the castle, affording them a view of the entire city. Khaldun and Mira landed outside the inn, and found the three sorcerers in the common room waiting for them. The two of them took a seat at their table, and a young man hurried over to serve them food and ale. They spent a few minutes telling the others about the developments in Blacksand.

"Adding five thousand more troops to Spanbrook's army should help tremendously," said Battleaxe. "If the army from Rockport attacks there, and Princess Jezebel recalls some of her forces from her outlying territories, they'll outnumber the elves two to one."

"It'll depend on how soon the elves attack," said Khaldun. "It's at least fifteen days' hard march from Blacksand to Spanbrook. Probably more."

"We'll need more mages, too," said Mira. "Will the three of you join us there when the time comes?"

"Unless we can stop them here, we'll be continuing to Keepstone," said Cyclone. "But Allure, Semblant, and Sage will be going to Spanbrook."

"Have you had any luck with Prince Frederick?" Khaldun asked.

"*Bad* luck," said Mist, rolling her eyes. "Bastard refused to grant us an audience."

"Why?" asked Mira. They were university governors—it was exceptionally uncommon for a governor to visit any princedom, and they were usually welcomed like royalty.

"He's sore that we refused to assign a sorcerer to his princedom," Battleaxe explained.

"Ah, that would do it," Khaldun said.

"We can try in the morning," said Mira. "As emissaries of Spanbrook, we might have more success."

They stayed up late, catching up over several more rounds of ale, then they headed upstairs. Battleaxe had already reserved a room for Khaldun and Mira. Early the next morning, the two of them headed over to the castle on foot; it was only a few blocks away from the inn. But the guards at the gate refused to admit them.

Khaldun pulled his carpet out of the void, and they flew up to the keep. Landing on the roof, they encountered several more guards hurrying out to meet them. Mira introduced Khaldun and herself, and explained the reason for their visit. But their leader refused to allow them inside, and insisted that they leave.

Khaldun enclosed Mira and himself inside a shield spell, and pushed past them. The guards tried to apprehend them, but couldn't penetrate his magic. Inside, they moved down to the main level, finding the prince in the great hall.

"What the hell is this?" the man demanded. He was sitting at the head table, his breakfast laid out before him on several large platters. "I thought I told you to reject all foreigners!"

"Apologies, Your Highness," the leader of the group from the roof said with a bow. "We tried to stop them, but, sir… they're sorcerers!"

"Bah! Worthless fools," he muttered. To Mira and Khaldun, he added, "Well, you're here now. You may approach."

They walked up to his table.

"Prince Frederick, I am Lady Mira from Spanbrook, and this is my husband, Lord Khaldun. We are here to warn you of an impending elvish invasion. Their ships were seen rounding the western edge of Dorshire the day before yesterday. They could arrive here any day now."

"Elves?" he said with a derisive chuckle. "What in God's name would the elves want with us? They haven't been seen in Anoria since ancient times."

"Your Highness, they are here, we can assure you," said Khaldun. "We've seen them for ourselves. They've already taken Rockport and Blacksand in preparation to conquer the rest of Dorshire, and they're coming here next."

"Bullshit. Unlike me, boy, Blacksand has an army. A damn large one, at that. And Gemstone Castle is impregnable—no army has ever taken it, and none ever will."

"Your Highness, Gemstone Castle is *gone*," Mira told him. "One of their mages hit it with earthquakes, and most of it toppled into the sea."

The prince stared at her for a moment, worry and confusion on his face. "That's impossible… How could anyone…"

"Sir, you must prepare for their arrival," said Khaldun. "Lady Mira and I are here with three other sorcerers from the university. Alert your troops and—"

"*Troops*?" he said, spittle flying from his mouth. "I've just told you we have no army. Only the City Guard, and they'd be no match for elves. This is a commercial city, for fuck's sake!"

"Then order them to help your people evacuate," said Mira. "If they do here what we've seen elsewhere, they'll be content to take the harbor. We believe they're taking the ports to establish supply lines for their forces as they proceed inland."

"But they have destroyed the other castles, so we can expect them to do the same here," Khaldun added. "Evacuate now, Your Highness, before it's too late."

Frederick stared at him in shock for a moment, saying nothing.

"Your Highness!" said Mira, startling him out of a daze.

"Never did I think we would face this day. Half the continent relies on the goods moving in and out of Oldport. Why would anyone ever attack? Destroying this city would cripple the trade—"

"Sir, the elves don't care about any of that," said Khaldun. "They're here to annihilate us. If you're going to evacuate, you must do it *now*."

"Yes, yes, of course," he said, finally getting to his feet. He summoned his steward and master-at-arms, and gave the order to commence the evacuation.

Khaldun and Mira left the hall. They waited in the courtyard for a few minutes, watching as the castle came to life. Its occupants started emerging, some heading to the stables, and all of them leaving either on horseback or on foot. The prince's steward dispatched a dozen heralds to spread the word throughout Oldport, and the city's bells started ringing.

Khaldun and Mira returned to the inn, catching up with Battleaxe, Cyclone, and Mist in the common room. As they finished breakfast, a herald rushed inside to announce the evacuation, then ran out again.

The other patrons started talking, expressing disbelief that an invasion could be imminent. Mira got to her feet, addressing the room, and assuring them it was real. The innkeeper emerged from the kitchen, asking what the ruckus was about. Mira explained the situation and told him he and his staff needed to leave immediately.

Khaldun and Mira left the inn with the other three sorcerers. People were hustling about, and Mira heard several people talking about their plans to leave the city.

They decided to take to the sky and see if they could locate the incoming fleet. Battleaxe, Cyclone, and Mist had flown to Oldport together on Battleaxe's carpet, but the other two had brought their own. Khaldun and Mira soared into the sky on his carpet, the other three right behind them.

Only normal traffic was coming and going in and out of the harbor. Flying out to sea, they headed north. They spotted a few ships, but they were Anorian merchant vessels. After an hour, there had been no sign of the elvish fleet. Mira was starting to wonder if they'd decided to bypass Oldport. She supposed it would be possible to land somewhere farther south, but then they'd have to cross the Green Mountains to reach Keepstone.

But finally, she spotted black sails on the horizon, and pointed them out to Khaldun. The sorcerers moved in closer to the fleet. Mira estimated there were at least a hundred ships. Khaldun tried calling fire to incinerate one of them, but nothing happened.

"They must have spells in place to prevent fires," he said.

Cyclone went to work. The skies to their west grew dark, and Mira spotted a dozen waterspouts forming, headed directly for the fleet. But as the twisters grew closer, they disappeared. Someone powerful on one of the ships must have canceled them.

The thunderheads moved in, and heavy hail pelted the ships. A barrage of lightning hit, striking multiple vessels. Mira could feel the energy in the air, but the bolts had no discernible effect.

Suddenly, Mist screamed. Her carpet buckled in the middle, and she dropped like a stone. Someone had canceled the air providing her lift. Khaldun dove, racing past her. He positioned their carpet directly beneath her, and Mira reached out, helping the sorcerer make a safe landing on their carpet. But moments later, Battleaxe tumbled out of the sky. Cyclone saved her, and they decided to head back to land. They reached Oldport and landed by the lighthouse.

"They've got someone powerful with them," Cyclone told the others. "No one's ever been able to cancel my twisters so easily."

"We believe Nyro might have found a way to restore members of her Sacred Circle to life," Khaldun told them. "We saw an elf in Blacksand we think was Xythor. Another in Rockport could have been Gnasher. If Typhoon is with this fleet, she'd have no trouble canceling your magic."

Cyclone shook her head. "The Sacred Circle reborn. This is worse than any nightmare."

"We've got a few hours before they get here," said Battleaxe. "Let's head back to the inn. We should have a clear view of their arrival from the roof. Once their troops are on dry land, without the protection of their ships, we should have better luck against them."

They took off again, landing out in front of the inn. The streets were clear now; Oldport looked and sounded like a ghost town. Making their way into the building, they climbed the steps to the top, opened the trapdoor, and used the folding ladder to get to the roof.

Mira couldn't believe how quiet the city had become. She could hear the gulls crying down by the harbor. Looking to the south, she could still see people streaming out of the city. They'd probably seek refuge in some of the princedom's smaller holdings.

Sure enough, almost three hours later, the enemy fleet's black sails moved into view. The first ships sailed into the harbor, unloading their passengers before moving out again. They decided to wait until the elves had established their camp before striking again. So, Mira kept watch while the others went inside to eat.

The elvish ships kept cycling through the harbor, offloading their troops before heading back out to sea. One regiment after another formed ranks and marched eastward. In the distance, Mira could see them making camp in the fields beyond the city's outskirts.

Khaldun returned with the others; he'd brought her a plate of food. Mira hadn't realized how hungry she was, and scarfed it down. When she was done, she spotted a couple of enemy regiments headed into the city.

"They're probably going to the castle," Khaldun said. "But we should be ready to fly, just in case."

The troops continued in their general direction. But as they drew closer, it became apparent that he was right. They reached the castle, forming ranks in the square right in front of it. Horns sounded, but it didn't look like they were doing anything.

"Look at the castle walls!" Mist said.

It took a second, but then Mira realized the walls were glowing. The elves were using their magic to melt the stone. A minute later, the castle collapsed in a cloud of dust. When the air cleared, only a giant pile of rubble remained. The enemy troops marched back to the harbor.

Getting all of the ships unloaded ended up taking the elves a few more hours. But finally, the last of them dropped off their passengers and headed out of the harbor.

"All right," Battleaxe said. "Let's go see what kind of damage we can inflict."

The five of them got onto their carpets and took off, heading east. Khaldun cast the spells that would allow them to see each other while invisible. Mist rode with Cyclone this time, keeping her own carpet tucked into the void. As they approached the enemy camp, they all went invisible.

Khaldun circled the area once. As they'd seen before, the camp was organized into perfectly straight rows. Mist had transformed, and Mira saw her descending earthward in cloud form. She engulfed the entire camp, making it impossible to see anything within. Suddenly, lightning bolts started striking inside the fog, dozens in rapid succession, over and over again. Screams filled the air, sending a chill down Mira's spine. It was the sound of elves dying a painful death.

But then a howling noise drowned out the screams, coming from somewhere downriver. A gale swept through the camp, moving Mist eastward. Mira lost sight of her through the trees. The carpets had to move higher to escape the blast, and before long, the fog surged up, swallowing their formation, then vanished. Mist had retaken her human form on Cyclone's carpet.

As Khaldun moved in closer to the camp again, Mira got a view of dozens of elvish corpses littering the ground. It was the most she'd seen anywhere so far.

Khaldun called fire, creating an enormous wall of flame by the western end of the camp. It swept through the area, burning everything it touched. More elves died, but others canceled the flames before they'd moved very far.

The four of them started incinerating individual elves. But before they'd killed more than a few dozen this way, someone canceled the air beneath their carpets, and they plummeted earthward.

Mira screamed. Khaldun grabbed her in a bearhug, calling air at the same time to cushion their landing. They still hit the ground hard, rolling several feet before finally coming to a stop. Mira got to her feet, unstrapping herself from the carpet and dusting herself off. "How did they find us while we were invisible?"

"Their mage must have sensed our spells," Battleaxe said. They'd landed in an open field, south of the camp. "We'd better get out of here."

But as she spoke, Mira spotted a giant, naked elf approaching them. Standing at least eight feet tall, she was the most beautiful being Mira had ever seen. Sharply delineated muscles rippled beneath smooth, ebony skin. She pierced Mira's soul with her emerald green eyes, and a mane of sleek, black hair fell to her shoulders. In one hand she held a gleaming sword with a tiger head on its hilt. The blade was longer than any Mira had ever seen.

The elf smiled. Before Mira could react, Battleaxe pulled her weapons out of the void, striding across the field to meet this foe.

"Battleaxe, *no!*" Khaldun cried.

But it was too late. The sorcerer charged, engaging the elf in a blindingly fast whirlwind of steel. They both moved too quickly for Mira to track what was happening. She could only see a blur of metal, occasionally catching a brief view of an axe or sword as it changed direction. Battleaxe wore her usual skin-tight, black leather, the visible areas of her golden skin contrasting against the elf's dark body.

Battleaxe screamed as a jet of blood spurted across the grass. Mira's heart jumped into her throat. But a second later, the elf howled in pain as a red gash opened across her left breast. The battle continued, neither able to dominate the other, and Mira noticed a group of elves emerging from the camp to watch.

Mira screamed when one of Battleaxe's weapons went flying, landing near Khaldun. He picked it up and held onto it, watching these two warriors with rapt attention.

The fight continued, and moments later, the elf's sword went spinning into the field. Battleaxe moved in, swinging her remaining weapon. But the elf caught the axe's handle in both hands, and the two of them stood there battling for control. Finally, the elf kicked Battleaxe in the ribs, knocking her through the air and ripping the weapon from her hands. Battleaxe landed flat on her back with a grunt as the elf leaped, raising the axe over her head for a death blow.

"NO!" Mira screamed.

Battleaxe turned onto her stomach, desperately trying to scamper away. But an instant before the elf reached her, she vanished. Her enemy landed, embedding the axe in the ground. Rising to her full height, she scanned the field, looking for Battleaxe, but she was nowhere to be seen.

The elf stared at Mira, Khaldun, Mist, and Cyclone, and smiled. Her beauty was so intense it was painful to behold, and Mira had to look away.

"Which of you possesses the courage to face me next?" the elf called out.

Before any of them could react, a massive fire tornado formed around them, wind and flames circling them faster than the eye could see. It roared like some kind of monster, the noise filling Mira's ears. The wind whipped her hair around, blowing it across her face. She pulled it away to see the elf advancing on them.

There was no escape. Mira could cancel the tornado, but none of them could hope to defeat the elf in single combat.

Suddenly, Mist transformed, engulfing the elvish mage and hitting her with lightning bolts, over and over again. The tornado disappeared. Khaldun tucked Battleaxe's weapons and carpet into the void as Cyclone unfurled her carpet and took off. Mira got onto Khaldun's and strapped herself in, and they shot into the sky right behind her.

"You tucked Battleaxe into oblivion, I assume?" Mira asked.

"Yes. I'll free her as soon as we land."

The elf's screams faded into the distance as they moved into the outskirts of the city. Khaldun and Cyclone landed, and he freed Battleaxe from the void.

"You just saved my ass," she said as he returned her belongings to her. "Thanks for that."

"Any time," he said with a grin.

"What's it like in the void?" Mira asked.

Battleaxe considered this for a moment. "Like floating in endless darkness. I felt no ground beneath me, and it was utterly silent."

"Were you aware of time passing?" Mira asked.

"Why, how long was I in there? It wasn't days or weeks, was it?"

"No," Mira said with a chuckle. "Ten or fifteen minutes, perhaps."

"That sounds about right," Battleaxe said with a nod.

Mist's fog rolled over them. She retook her normal form and said, "Holy hell, that mage is strong. She blew me away again like it was child's play."

"Strong fighter, too," Battleaxe said, admiration in her voice. "I've been beaten before, but never so easily."

"Who else has beaten you?" Khaldun asked her suspiciously.

"Warhammer a few times when we used to train together," she replied. "And there was a classmate at the Bastion, a Shifari woman. She was a couple of years behind me. We were a pretty even match. But half the time I only lost because I was distracted. She's got that same sexual energy as Allure."

"Was her name Imani, by any chance?" Mira asked with a knowing smile.

"You've met her?"

"Of course, I have. She came to Spanbrook with the Eagle Company. She's our master-at-arms now."

"I'll be damned," Battleaxe said. "I didn't know she joined them. Shouldn't surprise me, though. She always did have a problem following orders. Wouldn't have lasted long in any of the princedoms' armies."

"The elvish mage must be Typhoon," said Cyclone. "No one else could have called that fire tornado she used to trap us. I'm not sure *I* could have created something that fierce."

"We'd better get to Keepstone and warn them what's coming," said Battleaxe. "The idiot refused to take a mirror, so we have to alert them in person."

"Not true," Khaldun said with a grin. "Legion let me link mine to theirs right before we left."

"Perfect," said Mist. "Because it's almost dark, and I despise flying at night."

"Yeah, and I could use a meal, several drinks, and a good night's sleep after that fight," Battleaxe said. "Come on. Let's get back to the inn."

CHAPTER FIFTEEN
ADORIA

he old elf stared at Syllith in surprise. "I could ask the same of you. What is a human doing in Drengrvollr?"

"You speak the common tongue."

"The *human* tongue. It is far from common among my people. But yes."

"So, who the hell are you?" she repeated.

He regarded her in silence for a few moments, looking her up and down, making Syllith self-conscious. She wanted to hide her nakedness from him, but had no way to do so. "My name is Asmund. From Ellrivollr, the southeast kingdom of this continent. I have traveled far to come here."

"And *why* are you here?" she asked suspiciously.

"You first. Tell me your name, human."

"I am Syllith."

"And how did you come to be here?"

"It's your turn."

Asmund chuckled. "Very well. Years ago, word of Estrid's rise to power came to my people. News that she had been crowned queen, and that Drengrvollr had voted to cast democracy aside. Though this was disturbing, it was hardly surprising. The rest of the continent forced representative government on this kingdom, and it was never a natural fit.

"However, Estrid's invasion of Mestrland was shocking. The kingdoms had kept the peace for centuries. When she took Ellrivollr,

I watched in horror. And I started to suspect that all was not right with our supreme leader."

"Your people *allowed* her to take over. Reaper told me she gained the support of the populace after the initial invasion."

"Yes, and I couldn't understand it at first," Asmund said with a nod. "Her rule goes against everything my people stand for. Ours was the oldest democracy in the world. We have never known any other way. But I realized that those who voiced dissent quickly disappeared from public view.

"Digging deeper, I discovered that Estrid was silencing them. Some she subdued with magic—mostly those who were indispensable to the operation of the bureaucracy in some way. They were no longer themselves, and after subduing one of them myself, I realized they were under a spell limiting their behavior.

"Most dissenters simply vanished. I uncovered evidence that some had been murdered. Others had been thrown into makeshift jails, and Estrid used them to blackmail other officials.

"It took me many years to learn the truth. And by the time I did, Estrid had conquered the entire continent. I helped establish a resistance movement. We've got operatives in all five kingdoms, but progress has been difficult and dangerous. Estrid has her spies everywhere, and when one of us is outed, they are killed.

"Over time, my concerns regarding the supreme leader took a different turn. And when she announced her plans to mount an invasion of Anoria, it removed any lingering doubt I might have felt: Estrid was not the person we believed her to be."

Syllith chuckled derisively. "You're right about that. But how did that announcement finally open your eyes? And how did you find this place?"

"Invading Anoria serves no purpose. Our people stand to gain nothing from such a campaign. Yet it will cost us dearly in lives and resources. I decided to investigate Estrid's origins to figure out what was going on.

"Estrid spent most of her life representing Krokr in the Drengrvollri senate, so it made sense to come here. According to neighbors, her manor on the hill had been vacant since her departure for Mestrland. However, I was able to track down a few members of her household. They were terrified of me, and refused to talk at first. I had to use magic to get the truth out of them. But then, they reported witnessing a radical change in her behavior roughly fifteen years ago. They told me stories about wild parties and orgies. And a human woman living with Estrid, going everywhere with her, disguised as an elf.

"There had been no reports about any such companion in the other kingdoms. So, I figured she must either be dead, or still living in Krokr somewhere. After a visit to the city's hall of records, I discovered that Estrid purchased this island shortly before her invasion of Mestrland. And so, here I am."

"You're a mage, then," said Syllith. Asmund nodded. "Senator Estrid died fifteen years ago. Nyro killed her before reanimating her body."

"*Nyro*?" Asmund said, gasping in surprise. "The ancient empress of Anoria? The human necromancer?"

"The one and only," Syllith said.

"That's impossible. I remember when my people sent a force of arms to Anoria to take her down. They killed Nyro and her Sacred Circle."

"You *remember*?" Syllith repeated incredulously. "That was nearly a millennium ago. How can—"

"I am that old," Asmund said with a chuckle. "I was only a boy then, but I watched the ships set sail. Like your people's sorcerers, our mages are long-lived. Though my longevity is extreme even among my people. But please explain to me how Nyro could be the one behind all of this."

Syllith took a deep breath. She spent the next hour telling him everything, starting with her discovery that Nyro and her Sacred Circle had survived in demon form inside the barrier surrounding Pytha. She described the events leading to Nyro's liberation, and everything she'd done since coming to the elvish continent.

"These are grave tidings indeed," Asmund said when she was done. "I must warn my people back home. If we can get the word out—expose her true identity—we may be able to topple her and put an end to this madness."

"What about me?" Syllith said. "What about my people? I've got to get out of here and warn them. Will you release me?"

"Yes, of course," he said. With a wave of his hand, her cell door unlocked.

Syllith moved into the corridor. She stared down at Reaper's body for a moment, then dropped to her knees, straddling him and trying to choke the life out of him.

"No!" Asmund said, pulling her away from him. "What are you doing?" he demanded as she fell onto her back.

"You have no idea what he's done to me here," she said, tears streaking down her cheeks. A dam had burst inside of her the moment she'd stepped out of that cell, and the pent-up rage of the last decade and a half was pouring out of her. "I *will* kill him."

"If what you have told me is true, he will return to his demonic form when this body dies," Asmund said, standing between Syllith and her tormentor. "Then he will go to Nyro and alert her to your escape."

Deep inside of her, a kernel of reason recognized the truth in his words, tempering her rage. "What do you propose, then? If he regains consciousness, he's sure to alert her anyway."

"I will perform the magic necessary to lock him away inside his own mind," said Asmund. "It will leave him able to eat, sleep, and drink, but little else. Using the same spells Nyro used to control you, I will ensure the remaining staff will take care of him and keep him alive. This will give me the time I need to rally my people, and you the ability to travel to Anoria unhindered and warn yours."

"That won't work," said Syllith. "Nyro's been checking in with him, updating him on her progress. If he fails to respond, she'll know something's wrong."

Asmund nodded, taking a deep breath. "In that case, I will cast the same spells to control Reaper *and* the staff. Reaper will believe that you are still here, in your cell, and will continue responding to

Nyro as if nothing has changed. And I will ensure he has no memory of my presence here."

Syllith agreed.

Asmund called air to move Reaper up to the castle's main level, laying him on the floor. Syllith spotted the servants lying unconscious. Asmund spent the next several minutes casting the spells to control Reaper. When he was done, he took care of the staff one at a time, casting the spells to lock them into perpetual service taking care of Reaper, and never leaving the island. Syllith knew Nyro had made arrangements for regular supply deliveries, so as long as those continued, this arrangement should work indefinitely.

"It is done," Asmund said. "They will wake up after we have left, and continue with their lives as if nothing has happened."

Next, he cast an illusion to disguise Syllith as an elf child, wearing typical elvish garb. He made himself appear as a young magistrate. They left the house, making their way down to the dock by the light of the twin moons. A small boat was tied up there. The two of them boarded, and Asmund rowed them across the bay. They went ashore on a secluded beach outside of the city. Once he'd hidden the boat in the weeds, they made their way on foot, reaching Krokr as the sun cracked the horizon.

Asmund took her to the central market. Most of the stalls weren't open yet, but they found an open one selling clothing. He purchased a set of robes and a pair of sandals for her, then they made their way to the harbor. At the end of one of the piers, they reached a small, ocean-going vessel. Asmund called out to an elf on the deck. He nodded, disappearing inside and returning a minute later with a second elf. That one disembarked, eyeing Asmund skeptically as they exchanged muttered words. Then he cracked a smile, embracing the old mage and patting him on the back.

The sailor led them on board, and they moved below-deck to a chamber at the rear of the vessel. The two elves conversed in their native tongue for several minutes. Syllith didn't need to speak the language to understand that the sailor was reluctant to help. Finally, Asmund produced a purse, placing half a dozen gold coins on the table. The sailor seemed to start coming around, judging from his tone and body language, but they continued talking for several more minutes. Asmund placed a dozen more gold coins on the table. At last, the sailor nodded, shaking his hand before collecting his payment and leaving the cabin.

"Captain Einar has agreed to transport you to Anoria," Asmund told her in hushed tones. "He didn't want to take the job, but I explained the situation, and offered a king's ransom in gold, and he finally agreed."

"You told him the truth about Nyro? And about me?" she asked, her heart hammering in her chest. "How do we know we can trust him?"

"Relax, human. He's a member of the resistance. I've known him for many years, and his father for decades before that. He knows you're human, so once you've lost sight of land, there will be no need for you to maintain your disguise."

"Why are you willing to help me like this? That was no small payment."

"We must do everything in our power to stop Nyro. I will do what I can here to forestall this invasion, but I fear it may already be too late. If you can get a warning to your people—if they're prepared— they may be able to prevent her from carrying out her plans. Find a way to end her."

Syllith nodded. "Thank you."

Asmund gripped her shoulder. "Good luck, human."

It had taken Einar a few hours to recall his crew. But then they'd set sail right away, leaving the bay and moving into the open ocean. Syllith had changed into her robes and tried canceling the illusion making her look like an elf child, but her magic refused to work. But one of Einar's crew was a mage, so he removed the spell for her.

"You speak the common tongue," Syllith said in surprise.

"Only a little. We trade with Horn in Shifar sometimes. Learned it there."

That had been weeks ago. Syllith had exchanged few words with him since then. It was a lonely journey, but she was alive, they provided food and water, and she was going *home*. She could only hope it wasn't already too late.

The good weather held for the next three weeks. Syllith spent most of her time in her cabin. Nightmares disrupted her sleep most nights, infused with memories of her time in captivity with Reaper, so Syllith caught up on her sleep during the day. But she did spend some time on the deck each day, relishing the sunlight and ocean breeze.

Finally, early one morning, the crew spotted land. The captain took them in close, but his mage explained that they were near northern Pytha, and there was nowhere to land. They'd been making for Kong, but the wind hadn't cooperated, and the captain was eager to get to Horn. Syllith had explained Anoria's geopolitical situation to Asmund, and he'd tried to talk Einar into taking her to Northcoast, but he'd refused. The elves didn't have any dealings with the northern princedoms, and landing in Horn would have added weeks, if not months to her journey. She needed to get to Highgate, or the university, or somewhere with people she knew. Einar had agreed to take her to a port in southern Kong, insisting that was the best he could do.

But there were no ports in Pytha. And the coast was too rocky for them to get any closer. They could send her with a rowboat and enough food for a few days, but their supplies were low until they could restock in Horn. Syllith had little choice. So she thanked them and bade them farewell, then took the sack they'd given her, and climbed into the rowboat. Lowering the paddles into the water, she rowed herself to shore, watching the ship fade away in the distance.

It took her about an hour, and her muscles ached by the time she was done, but she made it to land. A big wave pushed her the final distance onto a rocky beach. Climbing out of the boat, she pulled it farther inland. She doubted Nyro's forces would come anywhere near the Pythan coast; the former kingdom was a wasteland. They'd probably sail around Kong and land in northern Maeda and Dorshire. Or else go south and start in Shifar to make their way north. But just in case, Syllith hid the boat behind a rocky outcropping, where it wouldn't be visible from the sea.

Gazing inland, she could see the Mystic Mountains in the distance. Her food wouldn't last more than a few days, and she had no knowledge of hunting. Nor did she possess the necessary equipment. Nor was there likely to be any game in this area. But if she could make it up the pass to the watchtower, she might still find supplies there. Enigma had kept the place stocked, and the dried and salted foods he stored there could last for years. And she could get a look in the seeing stone to apprise herself of developments across the continent. If Nyro's invasion had already commenced, she'd need to adjust her plans accordingly.

Taking a deep breath, and hoisting her sack over her shoulder, Syllith set out, heading generally westward. As long as she kept the mountain range's foothills to her right, she should have no trouble finding the route to the watchtower.

Hours went by, and Syllith focused on putting one foot in front of the other. The straps of her sandals were chafing against her ankles, and her entire body ached. This was the most physical activity she'd had in years. But she pressed ahead.

She stopped a couple of times to rest and eat. But she'd have to keep herself on rations to make the food and water last as long as possible. Finally, as the sun set, she decided to rest for the night. There was nowhere to shelter, and nothing but rocky desert as far as the eye could see. But with the lack of life here, she didn't think she'd have to worry about predators. She lay down on the ground, drifting off to sleep in no time.

Something woke her in the middle of the night, and she found herself in a windstorm. The air was thick with dust, and the wind gusts whipped her hair around. She slept only fitfully after that. At dawn, she got up and kept going.

Syllith marched for two more days, and the distant mountains hardly seemed to get any closer. Finally, as sunset approached on her third day in Pytha, she spotted buildings in the distance. Drawing closer, she could see they were the remains of an ancient village. Centuries of erosion had worn away much of the brick and stone surfaces, but this would still provide some respite from the wind.

Taking shelter inside one of the structures, she ate some of her food, and lay down to sleep. She was dozing off when a noise in the distance startled her awake.

Syllith sat up, holding her breath and listening intently. There it was again—it sounded like something squeaking. She heard it a couple more times, and decided it must be a trick of the wind. But then she heard voices.

Scurrying to the opposite wall, she gazed through an opening that had probably been a window. She spotted a flickering light in the distance. Who the hell could this be? She waited with bated breath as they approached. There were at least three distinct voices, two male and one female. Finally, she spotted a wagon moving into view, with two horses pulling it. A man and a woman rode on the front of the wagon, and two more men walked alongside it, one bearing a torch, and the other a staff. The mage had cast a flame to light their way. The wagon stopped right outside her building.

"I don't think we'll find much here," the man in the wagon said, as he and the woman stepped out of it. "But let's check the buildings before we turn in."

"Shit," Syllith muttered, moving away from the window as one of the men approached. She had no way of knowing who these people were or if they posed any danger to her. And she didn't want to find out the hard way. Muttering the spell to make herself invisible, she tried desperately to call upon her magic. But nothing happened.

Light spilled across the floor from the adjacent chamber. Syllith thought about climbing out the window, but it was too late. A young man moved into the room, starting and yelling in surprise at the sight of her.

"Who are you?" he asked, stepping closer. But then his eyes went wide, and he backed away, holding his staff a little tighter. "You're a sorcerer?"

Syllith's golden skin was a dead giveaway, though in truth she *wasn't* a sorcerer anymore. But he didn't seem to know the difference between a sorcerer and a necromancer, and she didn't want to enlighten him. "I am. But I mean you no harm. I was sheltering here for the night, but I'll be on my way."

"No, no—we didn't mean to disturb you. We didn't know you were here. It's not very often we encounter anyone else in the wasteland, especially not a sorcerer."

"Who the hell are you talking to?" a voice called from the other room. The man with the torch moved into view, shouting in surprise when he saw her, nearly dropping his torch. "Apologies, my lady," he said, holding one hand on his chest. "Never expected to find anyone else out here."

"We should let her be," the wizard said, nudging his comrade out of the room. "She was sheltering here. We can move on."

"Nonsense," he said, refusing to move. "This ain't no shelter—you haven't even got a bedroll. Sleeping on the hard ground can't be all that comfortable. Why don't you join us? We've got food, and a spare tent you're welcome to borrow."

"I wouldn't want to be a burden," she said, reluctant to put her trust in these people without knowing anything about them. "You can stay here; I'll leave."

"Won't be any burden at all," the man said. "These lands are lonely and inhospitable. Come on. Sulee's cooking us a stew tonight, and trust me, you don't want to miss that. Anyway, she's gonna insist that you join us. So you might as well surrender now."

"Who are you people?" Syllith demanded. "What are you doing in this wasteland?"

"We're antique dealers," the wizard said. "Well, they are, anyway. I'm the hired help."

"*Antique dealers*?" she repeated. "No one's lived here in a thousand years. What the hell could possibly bring you to this land?"

"That's exactly the point," the wizard explained. "Ever since the barrier came down, and people started exploring this land, ancient Pythan artifacts have become a hot commodity in Kong. Rich folks will pay an arm and a leg for pottery and earthenware from this area."

"And especially for jewelry," the other man said. "The stuff has become hard to find, though. There wasn't much to begin with—

seems like the magic covering this land must have worn a lot of it away over the centuries. And after the barrier came down, there was something of a rush, and those early scavengers picked the bones nearly clean. But we still find enough to keep us going."

Syllith was exhausted, and doubted she'd make it much farther on foot tonight. And a hot meal was too tempting to refuse. These people seemed harmless enough, so she agreed to join them.

The wizard introduced himself as Farid. The man was Yuze. His brother was the man driving the wagon; his name was Bolin, and his wife was Sulee. Syllith emerged from the building with Farid and Yuze, and they introduced her to the other two. Sure enough, Sulee insisted that she join them. Bolin got a fire going, and Sulee started preparing their meal.

Syllith, Farid, and Yuze sat around the fire, and Yuze produced a bottle of liquor, offering it to her first. Syllith took a long swig. She hadn't tasted alcohol in years, and it burned going down.

"If you don't mind my asking, what brought you to Pytha?" Farid asked.

"It's a long story," she said. "Has anything, ah, unusual been going on in Kong lately?"

"Unusual, how?" Yuze asked.

"Militarily."

"*Militarily*? Nah, no one in Kong has a military. Just all the gang leaders jockeying for territory, but that's nothing new."

"No one from the outside?" Syllith asked.

"What, you mean from Maeda?" Yuze said. "Not a chance. They don't want nothing to do with our land. At least, I haven't heard of any of them coming over. What about you?" he asked his brother.

Bolin shrugged and shook his head.

Syllith breathed a sigh of relief. Maybe Nyro's invasion hadn't started yet.

Sulee served them piping hot stew in ceramic bowls, and Syllith wolfed it down. She burned her mouth a bit, but it was worth it. The stew was delicious. Sulee refilled her bowl, and she downed that, too.

"You are too skinny," the woman observed. "It doesn't look like you've eaten well in a year."

Syllith snorted. "It's been a bit longer than that, I'm afraid. Thank you for the meal—this is very good."

Sulee insisted she have a third bowl. Syllith couldn't refuse, and felt stuffed by the time she'd finished it.

They set up their tents after that. Sulee and Bolin retired for the night, and Yuze climbed into his tent a few minutes later. But Syllith sat up with Farid, drinking and talking.

"Farid's not a Kongese name," she observed. "And your features are darker. You could almost pass for a wayfarer."

"My father was one," he said. "He left the troupe when he came of age, and ended up in Hido. My mother named me after him."

"That explains it," she said. He was attractive. Syllith suspected he was probably popular with the ladies. But he had to be half her age.

"Where are you from?" Farid asked, eyeing her suspiciously. "I thought I could identify all the sorcerers in the northern princedoms, but you don't match any of the descriptions."

Syllith chuckled. "I've, ah, been away for a while."

"You must have studied at the university. They wouldn't admit me because of my heritage."

"I was a governor," she confessed. "But that was actually before I transformed."

"You were a *governor*?" he asked, awe in his voice. "Why did you leave?"

"Not by choice," she muttered. "I'd rather not talk about it, though."

"Oh, of course," he said. "I'm sorry, I didn't mean to intrude. It's just that… well, I've always been fascinated with the sorcerers. Allure and Semblant, most of all. I would love to meet them someday."

"They are powerful," Syllith said with a nod. "I served with them."

"I always wished I could transform, but I'm a little too old for that now."

"How old are you?"

"Thirty in a few months. What about you?" he added with a grin.

Syllith took a swig of alcohol. "Older than thirty," she said, rolling her eyes, and handing him the bottle. He took it from her, his fingers lingering on hers.

"You don't look much older than me," he said with a smile, holding her gaze. "I've heard sorcerers make the best lovers." Syllith chuckled, averting her eyes. When she looked up, he was sitting right next to her. "Is it true?"

"I'll let you be the judge of that," she said, embracing him and plunging her tongue into his mouth.

CHAPTER SIXTEEN
BRACING FOR THE STORM

haldun and Mira returned to the inn with Battleaxe, Mist, and Cyclone. It was strange seeing the city so empty, and the inn completely vacant. Battleaxe and Mist went to the kitchen to start cooking, while Khaldun used his mirror to contact Legion. Cyclone brought them each a bottle of mead. Mira was pretty sure she'd consumed more alcohol in the past few weeks than she had in the previous year.

Legion sounded like a playful young woman today. Mira would never get used to hearing a different voice every time they spoke to the sorcerer. Khaldun let them know they'd evacuated Oldport, effectively surrendering it to the elves. And he told them about the mage they suspected was Typhoon. Legion was intrigued to learn that the Sacred Circle might have found a way to take elvish bodies. They reported that the combined armies of Keepstone and the Bastion were ready for the onslaught. Khaldun told them that Battleaxe, Cyclone, and Mist would be flying to them first thing the next morning.

Khaldun contacted Jezebel next, and apprised her of the situation as well.

"Jelena says the army in Rockport hasn't shown any signs of moving out," she told him. "But I suspect they'll start marching inland soon, now that they've landed in Oldport. Spanbrook and Keepstone are sure to be their two primary targets. You and Mira had better return here. Allure, Semblant, and Sage are heading here from the university tomorrow."

"Understood. We'll get underway at first light, so we should make it there late tomorrow night," said Khaldun. "Battleaxe, Mist, and Cyclone will be flying to Keepstone."

It was almost an hour later by the time Battleaxe and Mist served dinner, but it was delicious, and well worth the wait. They sat up late drinking and chatting after that.

"You're telling me that Imani can't beat Allison?" Battleaxe said incredulously after Mira told her about the princess's training sessions with the master-at-arms. "That must be because she uses magic, right?"

"She doesn't cast spells against her, but she does move weapons into and out of the void," Mira explained. "She'll start with two swords, then swap one for a dagger, for example. But it's been a few years since Imani could defeat her."

Battleaxe shook her head in disbelief, chugging the rest of her mead.

"It's true," said Khaldun. "She took out the two elves we found at Rockhedge without taking so much as a scratch. It's something else. Other than Imani, you're the only person I've seen fight the way she does. It's like she goes into some sort of trance."

"Well, I'll be glad to have her fighting on our side, then," Battleaxe said. "But I never would have imagined her possessing such skill after seeing her at the university."

"She might have been slow to learn magic at first, but she was already a formidable fighter before she left Spanbrook," said Mira. "Don't forget, she was the heir to a princedom. Her father made sure she learned combat from a very young age."

"And her magic has grown at a frightening pace since those days as well," Khaldun said. "When Allure started teaching her, she said it was like a dam burst inside of her. And trust me, that flow has only increased over the years."

Mira nodded. "I can sense her power through my null, and she's nearly as strong as Typhoon, and the mage we encountered in Rockport. Gnasher, I guess."

"That's impressive," Cyclone said. "Allure did say she possessed the potential to rival Nyro one day. It would seem she's living up to that prediction."

"Good thing," said Battleaxe, taking a long drink of her mead. "Because that old bitch is going to show up here any day now. And the rest of us sure as hell can't take her."

"The rest of us can't even take the Sacred Circle," muttered Cyclone.

"Probably not," said Mist. "Well, the end of the world could be upon us. But for tonight, we've got an entire inn to ourselves, and all the alcohol we could want."

"I'll drink to that," said Battleaxe, and they all clinked their glasses together.

Cyclone volunteered to take the first watch that night. She headed up to the roof as the others retired to their rooms. Mira lay down with Khaldun and fell asleep almost immediately.

They returned to the common room in the morning and sat down for breakfast with the others. Battleaxe had taken the second watch, and reported no developments overnight. The army was still camped by the river, and didn't look like it was moving out anytime soon.

Once they'd finished eating, they left the inn. Bidding each other farewell, they got onto their carpets and departed. Battleaxe, Mist, and Cyclone rode together, heading southeast, while Khaldun and Mira set out to the northeast.

The two of them stopped at midday in a clearing in the forest to stretch their legs and eat some of the provisions they'd taken from the inn. They stopped again just before sunset, then kept flying. It was fully dark by the time they'd reached Castle Barclay. Khaldun landed in the courtyard, then they headed inside once he'd tucked his carpet into the void.

They found Jezebel and Allison in the private hall with Allure and Sage. The four of them got up to greet them, embracing them both in turn.

"You must be exhausted from your journey," said Jezebel. "Sit down, I'll have the kitchen prepare you a meal."

Mira and Khaldun sat down with the others as she hurried off. Allison poured them each a glass of wine.

"Where's Semblant?" Mira asked, taking a sip.

"He went for a walk," Allure said, "as a giant bear. Said he wants to familiarize himself with the landscape before the battle."

"As a bear?" Khaldun repeated with a grin.

"That's been his recent obsession," Allure said. "Before this, it was tigers."

"Either way, he should have no trouble slaughtering elves," Sage said.

"Could he transform into a dragon?" Mira asked.

"That's a good question," Allure said with a shrug. "I don't see why not. I'll ask him when he returns."

"Speaking of dragons," said Khaldun, "we should check in with Lavinia. This might be a good time for her to join the fight."

"Yes, definitely," Mira agreed.

"I'm sorry, but who's Lavinia?" Sage asked.

"The dragon lord chieftain," said Mira. "I'll contact her in the morning."

Jezebel returned, and several minutes later, the staff served Mira and Khaldun their meals. The group retired for the night after that.

Early the next morning, Khaldun and Mira joined the princesses, Emma, Amari and Imani, Camilla and Gregor, Allure and Sage, and the provincial delegates for a privy council meeting. "Semblant won't be joining us," Allure told the others. "He eschews formal gatherings at all costs these days."

"I don't blame him," Jezebel said. "So would I, if I thought I could get away with it." The others chuckled. "Now that the elves have landed their third army in Oldport, we believe their attack here is imminent. Spanbrook and Keepstone are the most powerful princedoms in Dorshire, so we expect the armies from Rockport and Oldport to march inland in an attempt to sack our castles."

"What about the force in Blacksand?" asked Mira. "Will they come here, too?"

"It's hard to say, my lady," said Amari. "They may send those troops into central Dorshire, though there is no concentration of power in any of those princedoms the way we have here and in Keepstone."

"We must assume they will come here," said Imani. "Which means we will face a two-pronged assault. We have had no news of any elvish forces landing to our east. Your Highness, we should send our remaining territorial forces from Newberry, Monroe, and Ashland to reinforce our troops in Wayland. That will give us fifteen thousand soldiers there, as well as in Franconia."

"And leave those territories defenseless?" said Emma.

"We still have five thousand troops in Hadley who could move into Ashland very quickly should we see an attack from the south," said Allison. "But the only enemy force in that direction is the army heading to Keepstone. They'd have to march across half the continent to get here, which would give us plenty of warning."

"General? What do you think?" Jezebel asked Amari.

He mulled it over for a minute. Mira suspected he was reluctant to agree with any proposal of Imani's on general principle. But finally, he said, "I must agree, Your Highness. The only likely landing point to our east is Northcoast, and so far, there have been no reports of elvish ships in that area. We would have plenty of warning were they to show up there."

"And any army landing in Northcoast would most likely be heading to Stoutwall or Highgate," said Allison. "I agree with Imani. We'll hear from Jelena the moment the army in Rockport moves out. And we can send carpets to patrol the lands west of here to give us advance warning of any movement by the army in Blacksand. The initial battles will take place in Franconia and Wayland."

"Very well," said Jezebel, taking a deep breath. "As we've discussed, you'll lead our forces in Franconia," she said to Amari. "And we'll send Imani to take command in Wayland."

"What about the remaining troops from Blacksand's army?" said Sage. "They're headed here, aren't they?"

"Yes, but still many days out," said Jezebel. "They'll arrive ahead of the enemy, though."

"I wouldn't be so sure," said Khaldun. "The elves are larger and stronger. Their longer stride alone will give them a speed advantage. I fear they will overrun Carlo and his troops."

"We could transport the Blacksanders here by carpet," Allure suggested.

"Five thousand of them?" said Amari. "We have five carpets. Even with eight passengers per carpet, it would take over a hundred round trips to get them all here."

"Semblant can take twenty people per trip," said Allure. "Maybe a few more."

"What? How?" asked Khaldun.

"He can transform his carpet into a much larger one," Sage explained. "It's something he's been working on."

"That gets us down to fifty trips," said Allure.

Khaldun frowned. "I'm afraid the math doesn't work out. It took about seven hours for Mira and I to fly to Blacksand from here. Their armies have been on the march for five days, so it would take perhaps four hours to reach their current location. Round trip, that's eight hours per trip. Fifty trips will take us… sixteen days."

"It won't, though," said Mira. "The others will keep marching as you do this, so every flight will be shorter than the last. It should work out to eight days total."

"They'd be here almost as fast if we let them walk," said Allison.

"We can tuck additional people into the void on every trip," said Sage. "Each of us should be able to take another hundred or so that way. I doubt we'd be able to move many more than that into the void at once. But that gets us down to nine trips."

"The faster we do this, the less distance the people on the ground will cover," said Allure. "We're probably looking at close to three days' work, flying around the clock." Sorcerers could go several days without sleep, but Mira knew this would still be exhausting work. "A small price to add five thousand more troops, I should think."

"Yes, I agree," said Jezebel. "But what about their armor? It's enchanted to repel magic, so you can't tuck it into the void, can you?"

"It works only against the four basic forces," Khaldun reminded her. "It has no effect on the magical force, so tucking it into the void won't be a problem."

"Very well," said Jezebel. "Let's do it. We should bring the prince and his advisers here, but the troops can go directly to Franconia. Moving Hadley's troops to Wayland will give us twenty thousand soldiers for both battles."

"I'll contact Princess Yolanda and let her know to expect us," said Emma.

"What about our mages?" said Amari. "Who goes where?"

"Allison, Khaldun, and Mira make a good team," said Jezebel. "We'll send you three north to Franconia along with Camilla and Gregor. Our sorcerer friends from the university are also accustomed to working together, so we will ask you to fly to Wayland when the time comes, as well as the other mages you've brought here."

"Your Highness, we should evacuate the children and your parents as soon as possible," said Imani. "As well as Princess Jelena's children. To one of the outlying territories for now—either Newberry or Monroe." The former princedom of Newberry was now Spanbrook's easternmost province, while Monroe was its southeasternmost one.

Jezebel took a deep breath. "Yes, of course. The girls aren't going to like it, but it's for their own good. I'm not sure how much luck we'll have convincing my mother and father to leave, though."

"*Someone's* going to need to keep an eye on our devils," Allison said with a grin. "I'll take care of Robert and Vivien."

Jezebel nodded. "Take them to our castle in Monroe. We will do everything in our power to defeat these invaders here and in Keepstone. However, should we fail, we do have a contingency plan in place. I have been in touch with Princes Leto and Augustine, and we will fall back to Stoutwall if we lose here. That's likely where the elves would go next—it would give them a foothold in Maeda. And if Stoutwall falls, we will make our last stand in Highgate."

"You sound like you've already lost hope," Khaldun observed.

"Of course not," Jezebel said, sitting up straight. "You know me better than that. I'm simply being pragmatic. Our forces will outnumber the elves more than two to one. And we will be fielding six of the continent's most powerful sorcerers. But we must not take anything for granted. This will be the toughest fight of our lives. And if we are to prevail, we must be fully committed to victory *here*."

"What about the dragon lords?" said Sage. "Have we heard from them?"

"Not yet," Mira said with a frown. "I did try reaching Lavinia this morning, but have had no luck so far. I will keep trying."

The meeting adjourned, and Mira headed out to the courtyard with the rest of the sorcerers. Semblant was waiting for them in bear form. He stood up on his hind legs and roared when he spotted Allure, and Mira guessed his height at nine or ten feet. Allison asked Mira if she'd like to accompany her to Monroe, and Mira agreed, so the princess swapped carpets with Khaldun, then hurried off to fetch the children.

Semblant shifted back to his human shape, and Allure told him about their plan. He pulled his carpet out of the void, unfurling it on the ground. Then he stood upon it, transforming it to three times its original size. Mira kissed Khaldun, wishing him luck, then he took off along with Semblant, Allure, and Sage, heading west.

Allison returned to the courtyard moments later, Leda and Alanna in tow, Susan and James right behind them. Allison positioned the other four on the carpet as Mira strapped herself in. Alanna was next to James, and Mira spotted her taking his hand. She smiled, but Alanna turned, saying, "Don't get any ideas, my lady. He's terrified of flying, so I'm merely offering him comfort."

"Of course, Your Highness," Mira replied, stifling a giggle.

They took off for the Barclay farm. Landing out front, they found Robert on the porch, drinking his morning coffee.

"Well, well," he said, getting to his feet to hug his granddaughters. "To what do we owe the pleasure?" Allison told him the plan. "Oh, no. You can forget about it, Your Highness. We'll take our chances here."

"You of all people know not to address me that way, Uncle," she said, glaring at him.

"Allison. I'm sorry—"

"Jezebel needs to focus on the battle. She cannot do that if she's worried about you. Please, you and Vivien must come with me to Monroe."

"This is my home, Allison. The only one I've known for my entire adult life. Do not ask this of me."

"Grandfather, we *need* you," said Alanna. "You know I can't help myself. A new castle to explore, lots of squires running around, who knows what kind of trouble I'll find my way into?"

"She's right," Leda agreed. "*Someone's* got to keep her in line."

"You're just as bad as I am," Alanna said, looking affronted.

"Am not!"

"Enough!" Robert said, giving them a stern look.

Allison chuckled and he turned his gaze to her without softening his expression. "Jezebel has authorized me to knock you out if necessary, but I do hope you won't force me to do that."

He heaved a heavy sigh. Without saying anything, he went inside, and Mira heard him say, "Vivien, it's time to go."

Five minutes later, they were in the air again, with two additional passengers. Allison took them to the castle in Monroe. It was a little smaller than Spanbrook's old castle, but had a moat. She landed in the courtyard, and they found the steward waiting for them. Emma had sent word to expect their arrival.

They rose from the carpet, and Allison admonished the girls to be on their best behavior.

"Don't worry," Robert said, "we won't let them out of our sight."

Allison hugged them tight, then she and Mira got back on the carpet and took off, heading back to Castle Barclay. Allison dropped Mira off, then continued on her way westward.

Khaldun arrived that afternoon with his first group of Blacksanders, including Prince Carlo, Princess Yolanda, and their advisers. Emma greeted them and showed them to their quarters. The other sorcerers had ferried their passengers directly to Franconia. Khaldun took off again to take the rest of his group there.

Mira joined Emma atop the mage's tower after that, staring out at the city. She wanted to stick close to the steward, because she knew she'd be the one to receive any reports from the other princedoms—or Khaldun.

"We've always thought this day would come," Mira said with a sigh. "But it's hard to believe it's here."

"Yes," Emma agreed. "Although, I never imagined it would be *elves*. Now we'll see if the war machine my sister has built is up to the task."

Mira nodded. "I have to believe it will be. No northern princedom is stronger. If we can't stop them here…"

They stood in silence for a minute.

"I wonder if Nyro will show up," Emma said. "She did grow up here."

"Let's hope not," Mira said. "That might be the one thing we can't withstand. After everything I've seen, I believe in Allure's prophecy about Allison. But I don't think she's there yet."

Mira tried contacting Lavinia a few more times, but couldn't reach her. Mirrors had worked for her before, as long as she kept her channels of power closed. She suspected the chieftain must have been ignoring her, but she couldn't understand why. They didn't have any word from Khaldun or the other princedoms, either, and Mira had to assume that no news was good news.

That night, Jezebel held a feast in the great hall in honor of Prince Carlo and Princess Yolanda. The two royals joined them at the head table. The room was full, yet somehow it felt empty without Khaldun, Allison, Alanna, and Leda.

Mira went to bed alone for the first time in recent memory. Sleep eluded her. She thought back to all the twists and turns in her life that had brought her here with Khaldun. And about the years they'd spent building up the princedom. And she couldn't help but wonder if they were on the verge of losing it all.

The sorcerers kept up the transport operation around the clock for the next two days. Early in the morning, three days after they'd started, Khaldun, Allison, Sage, Allure, and Semblant dropped off the last of the troops in Franconia before returning to Spanbrook. Mira ran out to the courtyard to meet them. Khaldun embraced her, lifting her off her feet and spinning her around. Jezebel and Emma were there, too, and Allison hugged and kissed Jezebel.

"Have you seen any sign of the elvish army from Blacksand?" Jezebel asked.

"None," Allison replied.

Jezebel took a deep breath. "The five of you need to rest. But it would be best to send one of you to Blacksand to see if they've left yet and monitor their progress. We heard from Jelena this morning, and she reports no changes with the army in Rockport. But it will take longer for those in Blacksand to get here."

"I'll go now," said Khaldun.

"No, you haven't slept in days," said Mira. "It's not safe."

"We need to know when to expect this attack. I'll be all right, I promise."

"Let me go with you, then. At least if you start dozing off midflight, I can prod you awake," she said, poking him in the ribs.

"Fair enough," he said with a tired grin, holding her tight.

They went inside for breakfast, then the two of them took off, heading west along the road the elves would have to take to Wayland. Only a few hours later, Mira spotted their army far ahead.

"They don't seem to be in much of a hurry," Khaldun said. "They could make Wayland in five days at this pace. Four if they speed up." Khaldun made them invisible and took them in closer. The army's lines snaked along the road, extending into the distance. They found its end moving through a village, the buildings aflame and the inhabitants' corpses scattered across the ground.

Mira spotted the elvish mages bringing up the rear and a shiver ran down her spine. "Let's get back to Spanbrook."

They reached the castle and landed in the courtyard. Emma came running out to greet them—she'd been looking out for them from the top of the mage's tower. Khaldun gave her their report.

"I'll let Her Highness know immediately," said Emma. "Thank you."

"Go get some sleep," Mira told Khaldun, kissing him. "I'll join you shortly."

Khaldun headed toward the keep, and Mira accompanied Emma to Jezebel's office. They found her with Imani and Amari going over the plans for the castle's defense should the fighting fall back to Spanbrook. Emma gave her the news.

"Thank you," Jezebel said with a sigh. "I'd expect their force in Rockport to set out in the morning—please check in with Jelena then."

The next morning, Emma heard from Princess Jelena. Sure enough, she told them the army in Rockport was breaking camp. A couple of hours later, she let them know the elves were marching for Spanbrook.

The next few days went by in a blur. They evacuated the territorial rulers from Franconia and Wayland along with their families and the delegates and the nobility from Spanbrook, flying them to Castle Monroe. Most of the city's residents relocated to the countryside, either staying with relatives or camping in the wild. After that, there was nothing more to do but wait. Their armies were in position, and Castle Barclay was ready for war. The sorcerers from the university flew out to Wayland, taking Imani with them, and Mira accompanied Allison and Khaldun to Franconia. She still hadn't made contact with Lavinia. Khaldun tried, too, with no luck. They would be entering the battle without dragons.

Allison and Khaldun took turns flying patrol the rest of that day. A little before sunset, Allison found the elvish army making camp just beyond the line with Rockport. She ordered the regiment they'd stationed on the border to fall back to Castle Franconia.

After dinner, Mira and Khaldun retired to their quarters, but Mira found it impossible to sleep. Allison was keeping up the aerial patrol for the first part of the night, and Khaldun would relieve her for the second watch, just in case the elves decided to attack at night like they had in Blacksand. By the next morning at the latest, the battle would be joined.

CHAPTER SEVENTEEN
PROPOSITION

yllith pulled Farid into his tent. Once she'd taken off her robes, she went to work removing his clothing. She pleasured him with her mouth, and he moaned softly. After a minute, she climbed on top of him and made love to him.

Her thoughts drifted back to the last time she'd done this with Enigma. The love of her life. She'd known only hell since that night, her body being used by others without her having any say in the matter. *This* was her choice. After all the abuse, she felt a profound need to reassert control of her own body. Though she hardly knew Farid, this was an act of love, unlike anything she'd experienced since Enigma.

Syllith climaxed, then let Farid roll her onto her back. She kissed him desperately, wishing this could go on forever. Finally, they climaxed together, then she lay in his arms and sobbed.

"What's wrong?" he asked, worry and tenderness in his voice.

"It's nothing," she said with a sniffle. "It… it's just been a long time, that's all."

They drifted off to sleep. Syllith woke to an empty tent. Poking her head outside, she spotted the others sitting around a fire. She pulled on her robes and went out to join them. Sulee had prepared breakfast and coffee. Taking a seat next to Farid, Syllith accepted a plate and a mug from her and ate hungrily.

"I'm sorry, my lady," Yuze said with a grin. "We should have warned you Farid was a lecher."

Bolin sniggered, and Sulee smacked him in the arm.

"It's all right," Syllith said, leaning against Farid. "I'm the one who seduced him this time."

They ate in silence for a few minutes, then Farid said, "We'll be continuing north today, on our way to Hido. You're welcome to travel with us."

"I'd love to, but I can't," she said. "I need to get to the university, or Highgate, at least."

"How do you think you're going to get there?" Yuze said.

"I'll keep going west. Take the pass up to the watchtower."

"Oh, yes?" Yuze said. "And then what? Walk across the desert, and then the Forsaken Hills?"

Syllith hadn't given much thought to anything beyond the watchtower. "That's the most direct route," she said with a shrug. "And my need for haste is urgent."

"That might be the quickest way for a dragon rider," Yuze said. "But you'll never make it on foot. The lack of water alone will kill you. You'd be better served to come with us to Hido, then take a ship to Northcoast. Might be able to get passage on a barge from there as far as Arthos."

He was probably right, Syllith decided. After so many years traveling by carpet, her instinct was to think about aerial routes. It would take weeks to reach the university this way, but at least she'd get there alive. She agreed to travel with them.

They broke camp and headed out. Bolin and Sulee drove the wagon, and Syllith walked with Yuze and Farid. For the next couple of weeks, they hugged the coast to avoid crossing the Mystic Mountains. Syllith took her meals with them, and slept with Farid in his tent every night, making love to him before they drifted off to sleep.

Once they'd cleared the mountains, they headed northwest, making for the River Ling. They'd be able to follow that the rest of the way to Hido. The land grew more hospitable, and before long, they were traveling through lush forests. They met other travelers on the road, and passed through a few small villages. The people kept to themselves, but seemed friendly enough, greeting them as they passed.

Syllith finally started to feel human again, for the first time in fifteen years. Her time with Nyro had made her feel like some sort of beast, as if she'd been kept as a pet. Getting to know these traders and settling into a familiar rapport with them, Farid especially, made her feel alive. And along with that grew her rage for everything she'd endured. She had to make it to the university. By the time she got there, the invasion would probably be underway, so it would be too late to warn them.

But Syllith could still get revenge. It would require her to make the ultimate sacrifice, but she could hurt Nyro badly in the process. This thought drove her. She came to believe that this course of action was her noble purpose. She'd been born to do this, and it would make all her suffering worth it in the end.

This line of thinking made her want to enjoy whatever time she had left to the fullest. She sat up late eating and drinking with the others, and making passionate love to Farid every night.

The night after they'd reached the Ling, Syllith started awake in the middle of the night. Farid wasn't in the tent. Someone screamed, and she heard unfamiliar voices. Sitting up, she pushed the flap aside. It was dark out, with only the moonlight to see by, but one of the men had a torch. There were four men she didn't recognize, one of them brandishing a wand. Farid, Yuze, Bolin, and Sulee were on their knees with their hands on their heads, facing away from the men. Sulee was sobbing. Syllith spotted Farid's staff lying in the dirt by the other mage's feet.

"We should kill 'em now and get it over with," one of the men said. "Ain't no room for them in the wagon."

"No," the mage replied. "We take the wizard to Krigo. You know he wants mages. Kill the other three if you want."

One of the others stepped forward, stabbing Bolin in the back. He toppled over, and Sulee screamed, falling on top of him and sobbing. The man stabbed her next.

Farid lunged toward the man, ripping the sword out of his hands and stabbing him in the throat. He dropped, and Farid turned his attention to the mage. He charged, swinging the blade, but the mage called fire, incinerating him from within. Farid's charred corpse hit the dirt.

"*NO!*" Syllith screamed.

"I thought you said we had them all," the mage shouted, rushing over and reaching through the flaps. Syllith backed away, but he grabbed her by the hair and hauled her out of the tent. She struggled to get her feet underneath her, but it was no use.

"Oh shit—she's a *sorcerer!*" one of the others yelled.

The mage dropped her, and she scrambled to her feet, remembering only now that she was naked, her golden skin gleaming in the torchlight. The wizard backed away, fear in his eyes, pointing his wand at her. He cast a spell, and a glowing blue sheet of energy formed above her head, falling over her like a blanket. It bound Syllith's arms to her sides, and held her legs together. She fell, the impact hurting her right shoulder and hip.

Syllith tried to cancel the spell, but it was no use. Her magic had shown faint signs of returning in recent weeks, but it wasn't nearly strong enough to get her out of this. She spotted Yuze getting to his feet to make a run for it, but the man with the sword gave chase, stabbing him in the back before he'd taken more than ten steps.

"I'll be damned," one of the others said. "We captured a sorcerer! Krigo's gonna triple our pay for this. Maybe quadruple it. Hell, he might even forgive you for killing the wizard."

"No choice," the mage said. "He was trying to kill me. But why isn't this one resisting? You should be able to get out of this, sweetheart," he added, squatting down to get a better look at her, but keeping his distance, and pointing his wand at her. "Why haven't you canceled my spell?"

Syllith glared at him, but said nothing.

"Who cares?" one of the others said. "Throw her in the wagon, and let's get some sleep while we still can. It's only a few more hours till dawn."

"Are you a new sorcerer?" the mage asked her, ignoring the other man. "On your way to the university, perhaps?"

"What difference does it make?" the other one demanded.

"She could be faking it," the wizard said, standing up and advancing on him, poking him in the chest with his wand. "Maybe she realizes she can't take all four of us, so she's thinking she'll wait till we're asleep, then kill us one at a time."

The one with the torch walked over to Syllith, taking a knee right next to her. Looking her up and down, he said, "She sure is beautiful. We might as well have a little fun with her while we can. I've always wanted to fuck a sorcerer. You'll have to knock her out though—she can't spread her legs with this magic blanket on her."

"No!" the mage yelled, grabbing the man by the arm and pulling him away from her. "You won't touch her—any of you. We'll take her to Krigo and let him decide what to do with her."

"All right, take it easy," the man with the torch said. "You're wasting a golden opportunity, though. He's gonna charge an arm and a leg for this one. We'll never be able to afford it once *he's* got her."

"I don't care," the wizard said. "Touch her and I'll kill you, understand?"

"Yeah, sure," he said, shaking his head in disgust.

The wizard returned his attention to Syllith. "Why aren't you canceling my spell?" She said nothing. He called a flame, moving it close to her face. She could feel the heat and tried to turn her head away from it. It singed some of her hair.

"What the hell are you doing?" one of the other men demanded. "You just said we can't touch her, and now you're gonna burn that pretty face?"

"It's hot, isn't it?" the wizard said to Syllith. "I think you'd cancel it if you could." He moved it even closer, and a flame licked her cheek. Syllith screamed. He extinguished his spell, turning to the others. "She's got no magic. Might be a new sorcerer, otherwise, I can't explain it. But we should set a watch, just to be sure. She does so much as wiggle a finger, wake me immediately."

The one with the torch sat down next to her while the others went inside the tents Syllith's friends had been using. She was exhausted, but there was no way she could sleep now. After a few minutes, the man started muttering to her, describing all the things he wanted to do to her. Syllith was thankful for the mage's spell—there was no way he could touch her through that.

In the morning, they tossed her in the back of Bolin and Sulee's wagon with the artifacts they'd collected in Pytha. The mage walked next to the wagon, but she couldn't see the others. All day they continued, stopping a couple of times to rest and eat. They left Syllith in the wagon, and the mage kept his spell intact.

Syllith couldn't stop thinking about Farid, Yuze, Sulee, and Bolin—Farid in particular. She cried as she kept recalling their deaths over and over again. They'd shown her nothing but kindness, and these people had murdered them in cold blood. For a wagon-load of trinkets.

She worried, too, about how long it would be before Nyro came looking for her. As long as Reaper didn't realize she'd escaped, she should be all right. But she didn't know if that would last indefinitely, and it had already been many weeks since she'd left Drengrvollr. Surely, the invasion had started by now, but she had no way to find out for sure.

Finally, when they stopped to make camp for the night, the mage called air to remove her from the wagon. One of the others stood behind her, holding the point of his sword to her back, and the mage removed his spell. A third man tossed her robes to her, and she put them on, relieved to be hiding her body from them. The fourth man gave her some food and water. Once she'd eaten, the mage renewed his spell and they left her lying on the ground.

Syllith lay awake for a long time. The wizard took the first watch, sitting against a tree trunk and not taking his eyes off of her. She must have dozed off, because she started awake to find one of the others watching her. When she woke again, it was dawn.

They continued for three weeks, only freeing her once a day as they made camp to let her eat and drink. Syllith bounced around in the back of the wagon all day, and slept on the ground every night. The land grew more populous, and they passed through many sprawling villages. A few passersby spotted her lying in the wagon, and she tried calling for help. But they ignored her, and the wizard punched her in the head, threatening to knock her unconscious for the rest of the trip if she didn't keep her mouth shut.

One night, she woke to find the man watching her screaming as flames consumed him from within. He fell over, dead. The other three emerged from their tents, gazing around them frantically, trying to locate whoever had killed their comrade. Suddenly, one of the others started screaming as fire consumed his body, too.

The wizard started firing off spells in every direction to cancel invisibility. An unseen woman started laughing, and the third man went up in flames.

"Who's there?" the wizard demanded, fear in his voice. "Show yourself!"

The woman stepped out of the shadows, wielding a staff. The wizard called fire, trying to incinerate her, but she was too strong. She called fire, and flames engulfed his wand. He dropped it, crying in surprise.

"Krigo's going to kill you, Ming!"

The woman laughed again. "Krigo's never going to know anything about this." She called air, launching the wizard into the trees. He slammed into a trunk, his head hitting it with a loud cracking sound, and he landed face-first in the dirt. The witch called fire, and his body went up in flames. Finally, she turned her attention to Syllith. "I'll be damned," she said, moving close to get a better look at her. "I know who you are." She canceled the spell binding her, and Syllith scampered away, getting to her feet. "Why didn't you free yourself? That piece of shit, lowlife wizard shouldn't have been able to capture *you*."

"You can't possibly know who I am," Syllith said, moving to the corner of the wagon. It might provide her some protection if this witch tried hitting her with a spell.

"You're Governor Syllith from the university. *Former* governor, I should say. Oh, don't look so surprised. There aren't many sorcerers floating around, are there? And none assigned to Kong, so that means you must be from the university. Classic beauty, perfect body, raven hair, none of the others match that description. Maybe Cyclone, but she's Kongese, and you're certainly not. You're supposed to be a sorcerer, though, not a necromancer."

Syllith was stunned. She'd told Farid and the others her name, but they had no idea who she was.

"I'm Ming, by the way. And I know what happened to you," the witch continued. "One of our greatest champions, but Nyro managed to subvert you. Planted a kernel of herself inside your mind somehow. Made you do her bidding. Killed your own lover, took her to the temple where she was able to eliminate the barrier. Then opened a portal to somewhere else, and haven't been seen in Anoria since. Until now, that is."

"I didn't think any of that was exactly common knowledge," she said, completely shocked.

"Oh, it's not. Most people don't give a shit what goes on in the world. They're just trying to survive. Provide food and shelter for themselves and their family. Hardly matters to them who's ruling any part of Anoria. But I'm not most people. I'm trying to get by like everyone else, but *I know* about Nyro. And I get it. My business would die if she came back."

"How do you know what happened to me?"

"A wizard from Arthos who comes by now and then. I conduct trade with some people in Maeda, he transports the goods. A friend of his is a professor at the university, and *he* heard about the whole affair from Allure."

Syllith took a deep breath. "And how did you find me?"

"My people keep track of Krigo's goons as they come and go from the city. Let me know if they've got any interesting, ah, cargo. Now, tell me why you didn't free yourself."

Syllith was reluctant to disclose anything to this woman. But she already knew who she was, and she'd freed her anyway. "Nyro did something to prevent my magic from coming back."

"Then how the hell did you become a necromancer? You had to bind a demon to do that, didn't you?"

"That's not common knowledge, either," said Syllith.

Ming shrugged. "Doesn't make it untrue."

"Nyro forced me to do it, using a spell."

They spent the next hour talking, and Syllith told her the whole story, from the moment she'd left Anoria, until her capture by the bandits.

"Holy mother of God," Ming muttered when she was done. "You need to get to the university for sure."

"Have you heard any word of the invasion starting yet?"

"I haven't. But the mage from Arthos is about my only source of news from outside of Kong, and he hasn't come around in a few months.

"I'm on my way back to Hido, and you're welcome to accompany me. You can drive the wagon for me. I could tether my horse, but he wouldn't like that much. He's a little attached to me, so it'd be better if I ride him."

"And if I refuse?" Syllith asked skeptically.

"I'm not going to force you. You're free to come and go as you please. But without magic, or a weapon, at least, you'll have a hard time of it going alone. These parts are rotten with bandits. Like as not, you'll get yourself captured again, and then they'll take you—"

"To Krigo," Syllith finished for her with a scowl. "Who is he, anyway?"

"Gang leader. He's not the only one, but he's the worst, and one of the biggest. They're traders and business people like me, but *I* don't force people to do things against their will. Anyone of Krigo's ilk would be happy to get their hands on *you*. But they'd end up owning you. You'd do all the work, and they'd make all the money."

"I'd be a prostitute."

"You'd be a *slave*. Yes, you'd fuck for money, but you wouldn't see any of it."

"And you don't do that?"

"Sure I do. But my girls work for me by choice. They get half the money, and I keep them safe."

"I could see you're a powerful mage," Syllith said. "If you'd gone to the university, they would have assigned you to a princedom somewhere."

"Honey, I *did* go to the university. And they assigned me to Northcoast. But that life's not for me. Being someone else's servant for the rest of my days? I don't think so. I live by my own rules. And I've got a few other mages serving *me*, helping keep the big guys like Krigo off my back."

Syllith nodded. "And if I do accompany you to Hido, what do you want in exchange for your protection?"

"Nothing," Ming said with a shrug. "But I might have a business proposition for you once we get there."

"I knew there had to be a catch," Syllith said with a knowing grin. "What sort of proposition?"

"You got any money on you?" she asked, ignoring her question.

"Nothing but the robes on my back. And a wagonload of junk, unless you're taking that. I suppose it isn't really mine to begin with."

Ming gazed at the wagon's contents and shrugged. "You can have it. That's a start, I guess. But only a drop in the bucket compared to the amount you'll need for passage to Northcoast. The merchant ship captains all claim they don't take passengers. But they do if you pay them enough. You're going to need a small fortune."

"Let me guess. You want to hire me as a prostitute."

Ming looked her up and down appraisingly. "I sure do. Even after my cut, you'd make enough for your passage to Northcoast in a week. Maybe less."

"No. It's out of the question. Thank you for the offer, but I'll find another way."

"Suit yourself," Ming said with a shrug. "You could work as a mage for hire. If you land a good contract, it would probably only take you a year or so to earn enough for your voyage. But, of course, you've already said you lost your magic."

"A *year*?" Syllith repeated suspiciously. "Prostitutes are that much more expensive than mages?"

"No, mages make about the same as prostitutes, on average. But you'd be no ordinary prostitute."

"You're telling me I'd make more because I'm a necromancer?"

Ming shook her head. "You mustn't tell *anyone* about that. It would scare them shitless, and they wouldn't go near you. Say you're a sorcerer. I'm probably the only one in five hundred miles who knows the difference. So you could use their ignorance against them."

"Fine. You're telling me I'd make more because I'm a *sorcerer*?"

"You bet your sweet ass you would. So would I. Most people go their whole lives without ever laying eyes on a sorcerer, never mind fucking one. In these parts, anyway. And you know what they say about sorcerers. I don't know if it's true or not, but they're supposed to be the best lovers on the whole continent."

Syllith chuckled. "I'm sorry. That's just not going to happen. There must be some other way. I'll figure something else out."

Ming looked disappointed, but only shrugged.

"I'm going to guess the offer for protection on the way to Hido is rescinded?"

"Not at all," Ming said. "In fact, I insist. You'll never make it on your own. It'll take a week or so to get there, though."

"And you're going to keep trying to convince me to take your offer the whole way, aren't you?"

"It's a wise investment," she said with a grin. "I have nothing to lose—I'm going that way anyway. And I have *so* much to gain."

Syllith shook her head. "All right."

"We might as well get going," Ming said, gazing at the sky. "It's already getting light out."

Syllith climbed onto the front of the wagon. Ming went to get her horse, and returned a minute later. Together, they set out for Hido.

CHAPTER EIGHTEEN
THE BATTLE OF SPANBROOK

ira stood atop Castle Franconia's battlements, gazing out at what would soon become a battlefield. The sun would crack the horizon any minute now. The castle stood atop a hill by a giant loop in the north road, where it actually ran east to west. The castle was separate from the town. It was about the same size as Spanbrook's old castle, with no moat.

Their northern army had already formed ranks, extending far across the fields below. General Amari sat astride his giant mare wearing his golden plate armor, a long plume atop his helmet. The Eagle Company waited around him, the core of their defenses. Mira spotted Khaldun flying high overhead, and Allison stood next to her, carpet at the ready.

"Any minute now," Allison muttered.

Mira's stomach clenched. What they did here today could well affect the fate of the entire continent for generations to come. Any decision they made—Mira's or anyone else's—might prove to have dire ramifications. She took a deep breath, trying to calm her nerves.

Suddenly, Khaldun sent a jet of red sparks into the air before going invisible.

"This is it," said Allison.

Moments later, Mira spotted the first elves moving out of the trees, taking position in the field. More and more of them filed into view, forming their perfect lines like some giant machine. Spanbrook's forces outnumbered them two to one, yet each elf looked like some sort of god, so much bigger and stronger than any of their people. And every one of them wielded basic magic.

The last of the elvish army took their positions. Three stood apart, atop a knoll near the trees. The tallest one was bare-chested, with bulging muscles—Gnasher. Mira recognized him from Rockport. Next to him stood a female, tall and slender, wearing a sheer, green gown. Hardly typical attire for a battlefield. The third was male, shorter than his companions, and completely naked. He was also hairy for an elf, the growth resembling fur all over his chest, stomach, and legs.

"If you extend your null, will you be able to tell if those three are all Sacred Circle?" Allison asked.

"Yes, I think so."

Allison nodded. Mira opened her channels of power, extending her null across the battlefield, and engulfing the three elves in question. The one with the gown cocked her head, staring directly at Mira.

"Yes, they feel like human sorcerers," she told the princess. "Tremendously powerful ones. The one wearing pants is Gnasher. I don't know who the other two might be."

"I have a feeling we'll find out soon enough. Thank you."

"Be safe out there," Mira said, clasping her hand as she closed her channels of power.

"You too," Allison replied, giving her an encouraging smile. Standing on her carpet, she took off, flying high above the enemy troops before going invisible.

A horn sounded, and the elvish army advanced. Mira opened her channels of power again, expanding her null to protect the castle and their entire army. The elves reached their troops, and the battle was joined. Battle cries and the clanging of weapons floated up to the battlements. Spanbrook's lines held.

Walls of fire erupted among the elvish warriors, separating an entire company from the rest. The walls closed in, and the elves screamed as the flames consumed them. But someone canceled the spell moments later.

A fiery orb appeared near the other end of the field, at least thirty feet across. When it faded, Mira could see that it had turned everything inside it to ash, including many elves, leaving a crater in the ground. That had to be Allison—Khaldun had tried this spell many times, but lacked the power.

A group of elves just outside Mira's null screamed, and she spotted a dozen of them disappearing from view. They'd fallen into a pit, where fire consumed them. Khaldun had used a similar spell against Henry's wraiths many years ago, and had been working on it ever since.

The elvish mages tried unleashing their magic on Spanbrook's troops; Mira shuddered when she felt their power hit her null. She'd never experienced anything so strong, but the spells failed.

The elvish warriors were fierce and tireless. They made gains against their human opponents, but the Spanbrookers held their own. Allison kept up her barrage of fire orbs, and Khaldun took out many more elves with his hell pits.

Mira started to think they might actually win here. Then she heard a blood-curdling howl coming from the rear of the elvish lines. It was the naked mage, his head thrown back as he screamed at the sky. He leaped off the hillock, changing shape mid-jump. By the time he landed, he'd transformed into a giant wolf. Running through the elvish forces, he hit the humans and went wild, grabbing soldiers in his jaws and tossing their mangled bodies into the air.

Khaldun opened a fiery chasm below him, but the wolf leaped out of it and continued its trail of carnage. Allison hit it with one of her fire orbs. The wolf howled in agony, but it survived, its fur aflame as it cut its way through Spanbrook's lines.

A roaring noise distracted Mira from the wolf's progress. Turning, she spotted the elves' female mage holding her hands out to her sides. Out of nowhere, a wave of water several feet high burst onto the battlefield, slamming into Spanbrook's army. Mira's null had no effect on it. With a gasp, she realized there was no active magic here—the mage had diverted the River Ember. Mira could hardly believe her eyes; she couldn't fathom the amount of power it must have taken to do this. Pouring all of her power into her null, she expanded it to include the water mage. The woman screamed in fury as the wave subsided.

The water had washed half of Spanbrook's army across the field, leaving the route to the castle open, and most of the battlefield flooded. An unseen force blasted a crater in the earth beyond Mira's null, where the wave had first come into view, and most of the water receded into that, creating an artificial lake.

Mira reduced her null to allow their sorcerers to work magic against the elves. But at that moment, she spotted Khaldun flying over the battlefield, his carpet aflame. Mira's blood froze as she watched him hit the ground and go rolling across the field. The elves swarmed around him as Khaldun cast a shield spell, creating a sphere of protection around himself.

An alleyway opened through the elvish troops, leading from their mages to Khaldun. And Mira spotted Gnasher marching along it, pulling a massive longsword out of the void as he moved. Mira screamed. Khaldun turned to face the elf, pulling his own blade out of the void. But she knew he was no match for this monster. He looked tiny next to him, his power inconsequential. Gnasher raised his sword, shouting a battle cry as he advanced, and Mira felt a part of herself die.

Sage flew high above the battlefield in Wayland as the elvish forces formed their lines. They knew Xythor was coming with this group, so they'd evacuated Castle Wayland the day before. Without Mira's null, there was nothing to stop the mage from destroying it. Imani was in charge here, riding back and forth on her horse in front of Spanbrook and Blacksand's armies, her golden armor gleaming in the morning sunshine, and the rose-colored plume streaming from her helmet. Sage didn't know much about the woman, but from the little she'd seen, it was clear she was a natural leader.

Allure shot past Sage, flying the other way. They had both gone invisible, but enchanted their carpets to shine a red beacon that only they could see. She wasn't sure where Semblant had gone, though. He'd been different ever since his quasi-resurrection fifteen years earlier. Though technically he'd died, Allure had taken steps to preserve his brain, and that had been enough to bring him back to life. But he'd grown more surly and reclusive than ever.

Always good to have in a fight, though.

Sage was one step away from being useless in physical combat. She'd trained with sword and spear from a young age, but had no natural talent whatsoever. And though she was the university's preeminent scholar on Anoria's military history, battle tactics were lost on her. Hurling magic at an enemy force she could handle, though.

Out behind the army, Sage spotted three elves standing apart. One of the males was tall even for an elf, towering over the other two figures. And he was nude. A naked woman stood next to him, with multiple piercings through both ears, one through each nipple, another through her navel, and judging by the occasional flash of metal coming from her groin, one through her genitalia. Sage shivered at the thought of how painful *that* process must have been. The third elf mage was male, wearing skin-tight, black leather pants and no shirt. The first one had to be Xythor; Sage had no idea who the other two might be.

The human troops outnumbered their elvish counterparts more than two to one. In any normal battle, Spanbrook would have no trouble dominating the enemy with these numbers. Yet this would be unlike any battle Anoria had seen in almost nine hundred years.

Trumpets sounded, and the elves advanced. Sage got to her feet, swooping directly above the elvish army as they clashed with the humans. Holding her arms out to her sides, she called fire, creating a fire orb in the enemy's midst. Everything inside it turned to dust.

Across the battlefield, she spotted a giant shadow erupting from the earth and taking human form. The ghoul stomped through the elvish ranks, kicking warriors through the air. Allure's doing, for sure.

Far below, screams erupted from Spanbrook's army. Turning, Sage gasped. Their side of the battlefield had turned into an infernal hellscape, straight out of a demon's nightmare. Fields of lava surrounded them, and a giant fissure opened behind them. The sky had turned black, and a distant volcano hurled fire and ash high into the air.

Sage knew this was nothing but illusion. It was on a scale she'd only read about, and one no human mage alive could recreate. But it wasn't real. One of the other elf mages had to be Artifice, probably the male. Only he among the Sacred Circle could cast something like this. Sage flew in lower behind their troops, canceling that part of the spell. There was nothing she could do about the black sky, but at least they'd realize the fissure had been illusion. She managed to cancel some of the lava fields, too, and hoped their people might ignore the rest.

Someone banished Allure's ghoul, but at that moment, a giant bear charged out of the woods, running into the elvish formations. Semblant had arrived. Even on all-fours, he towered over the warriors. Grabbing one in his jaws, he shook him back and forth before throwing him high across the battlefield. He mauled two more with his paws before savaging another with his teeth.

Sage threw two more fire orbs into the enemy ranks, then spotted the female elf mage. Her body had turned protean, growing in size and sprouting six more arms that turned into tentacles, along with an elongated jaw. This one had to be Metamorph. Resembling a cross between an alligator and an octopus, she raced into the fray, entangling Semblant in her limbs.

Semblant roared, trying to escape her grasp, but it was no use; Metamorph was stronger. Semblant started changing, and Sage spotted wings. He'd tried transforming into a dragon the night before, and while he'd managed to take its shape, he couldn't fly or breathe fire. But this time, he turned into an eagle, flying out of Metamorph's tentacles and landing on her head. He started pecking at her eyes with his beak.

Metamorph screamed, blood gushing out of an empty eye socket. But then she managed to grab onto Semblant with her tentacles again, pulling him away from her remaining eye. Semblant changed again, this time into some kind of slime creature. He encased Metamorph's head, suffocating her. She kept grabbing at him with her tentacles, but it didn't help—it was like trying to grab water.

Metamorph transformed into a giant saber-toothed tiger, her fangs piercing Semblant's slimy form. He adjusted to cover her teeth, too, and kept blocking her airway. Metamorph transformed into a dragon next, belching a jet of fire that burned through Semblant's body, finally allowing her to breathe. Spreading her wings, she charged across the field and took to the air, shaking Semblant off of her. Semblant hit the ground, retaking his bear shape, and went back to mauling elvish soldiers.

Metamorph swooped over the human lines, breathing a jet of fire. Sage canceled the air beneath her, and she roared, crashing into the trees beyond the battlefield.

The battle raged, without either side giving any ground. The human soldiers were good, but the elves were better. Both sides suffered huge losses, but there were more dead humans on the ground than there were elves.

Sage spotted Imani leading a charge into the very heart of the elvish forces. The woman wielded her sword like a whirlwind, meting out death everywhere she struck. She reminded Sage of Battleaxe when she went into her fighting trance. Her people followed her, and before long, the entire elvish army was retreating. An ear-splitting battle cry went up from the human forces.

But then Xythor went to work. There was an almighty rumbling noise, and then the earth split open, creating an enormous fissure between the elvish and human armies. This time, it was no illusion. Dozens of human soldiers toppled into the breach before Imani ordered a retreat.

Another fissure opened behind them. This was going to turn into a rout unless they could find a way to take out Xythor. Sage hit him with a fire orb, but he emerged unscathed. Allure sent a ghoul after him. It lifted the mage by his feet and slammed him into the ground. But then the ghoul turned into smoke and disappeared.

Something roared, and Sage turned to see a giant ape charging toward Xythor. It was Semblant. He grabbed Xythor in both hands, ripping off his legs. The elf screamed, and then Semblant tore his head off, tossing the pieces aside and pounding his chest.

A shadow rose from the earth where Semblant had thrown Xythor's head. It grew forty feet high, wreathed in flame. People screamed as it threw a jet of fire at the human armies.

But suddenly a sphere appeared in the middle of the fire, blocking the jet. It was Allure with a shield spell protecting her and her carpet. She held out both arms, both hands glowing bright, and the demon screamed. The next instant, it turned to smoke, blowing away in the breeze.

Imani led her people out from between the fissures, and they reformed their lines. The elves advanced, and the battle raged on. Sage didn't know if they'd seen the end of Xythor or not, but he didn't make another appearance that day. Metamorph had gone missing, too. She wondered if Semblant had injured her more than they'd realized. Artifice kept causing trouble with his landscape illusions, but Sage was able to cancel parts of them, and their soldiers fought through them.

As dusk settled across the battlefield, the armies disengaged. Sage guessed that the humans had lost about four thousand troops, the elves maybe half of that. They were going to have to adjust their tactics the next day.

Allison came out of nowhere, landing her carpet right next to Khaldun, and pulling her swords out of the void. Mira held her breath as the two of them exchanged words. It looked like Allison was shouting at him, and finally, Khaldun got on her carpet and flew away.

Allison was facing Gnasher alone.

Mira's first instinct was to extend her null around them to make sure none of the elves could interfere using magic. The spells Allison had used to toughen her armor had physically transformed the leather, so Mira's null would have no effect on it. But on second thought, she realized she had no idea what Allison might be planning here. Perhaps she'd need her magic. Mira decided it would be best not to interfere for now, but she was ready to cancel any spells coming from the surrounding elves.

The entire battle came to a stop as soldiers on both sides jockeyed for positions to witness this fight. Allison wore her hood and helmet, leaving only her eyes and mouth visible. She looked like a child next to Gnasher, her ponytail hanging down her back.

Gnasher swung his blade toward Allison's neck. She parried with one sword, slicing with the other. Gnasher howled as a bloody gash opened across his chest. He lunged again and again, stabbing and slicing at Allison, but she evaded his every attack. Her blades moved too fast for the eye to see, but left evidence of their passage with the gory wounds they created on his body.

Gnasher howled and screamed every time Allison cut him, but she was unable to land a fatal blow. He was dripping blood, swinging his blade with enough power to cut her in half, but failed to touch her once. Allison was like a hornet buzzing around her much larger opponent.

Finally, Gnasher lunged in with a mighty overhand blow. Allison sidestepped, leaping onto his back. One blade had vanished, a dagger taking its place. She cut his throat from ear to ear, so violently that she'd nearly decapitated him. The princess landed on her feet, the longer blade replacing the dagger again, and circled her enemy.

Gnasher's expression registered surprise for a moment as he dropped to his knees, then he toppled over and died. A cheer erupted from Spanbrook's soldiers, but faded an instant later as a giant shadow exploded out of the ground. The demon grew to six times Allison's height, bearing down on her. Her swords vanished as she held out both arms, her hands glowing blindingly bright. The demon howled in agony, turning to smoke, but then it reformed, lifting one of the elvish soldiers off the ground.

The elf screamed, but the sound cut off as he died and hit the ground. The demon vanished. But then the dead elf got to his feet, smiling as his uniform went up in flames. His appearance changed, and Mira realized this was Gnasher reborn. Allison leaped into the air, her spare carpet appearing beneath her feet as she shot into the sky and disappeared.

Mira lost track of Gnasher as the armies reformed their lines and the battle resumed. The fighting continued until the elves withdrew from the field at dusk. If Mira's estimates were correct, they'd lost twice as many people as the enemy.

The army returned to their camp in an adjacent field. Mira met Amari and his top lieutenants in the great hall. Allison had gone out to see where the elves were making camp. Khaldun strode into the room a few minutes later, and Mira embraced him, holding him tight and crying into his chest.

"I th-thought I'd l-lost you," she stammered between sobs.

"It's all right," he said, returning her embrace and rubbing her back. "I'm uninjured. Everything is all right."

Mira took a deep calming breath, but held him a little longer.

Allison arrived a few minutes later. "The elves have made camp about a mile north of here. I didn't see the mages anywhere, but I'm sure they're out there."

"We should take turns flying patrol tonight," said Khaldun. "Make sure they don't surprise us with a night attack."

"Definitely," Allison agreed. "Have you apprised Jezebel of today's developments?"

"Yes," he said, taking a deep breath. "She's happy with the outcome, of course, but she wants to talk to you."

Allison sighed. "I'm sure she's *not* particularly happy about my fight with Gnasher."

"*Not happy* doesn't begin to describe it, I'm afraid."

"I'll contact her after dinner. In private."

Khaldun returned Allison's carpet to her. He still had the spare Azure had made for him.

They'd evacuated the castle staff before the battle, so a couple of soldiers prepared dinner for the sorcerers and officers. They sat down to eat an hour later.

"It seems we were right about the Sacred Circle," said Mira, taking a drink of her wine. "After you killed Gnasher, his demon left that body, and reanimated another."

"Yes, meaning there's no way to kill them permanently," said Allison. "I banished him, but he reformed almost instantly."

"There's no way to destroy a demon?" Mira asked.

"Only if you know its true name," said Khaldun. "And we don't know theirs."

After dinner, Allison left to fly patrol. She'd wake Khaldun later so he could take the second watch. Mira wasn't tired yet, so she went up to the ramparts with Khaldun.

"It's hard to believe how peaceful it is now," she said, gazing out at the moonlit landscape and starry sky. It was a clear night with a pleasant breeze—blowing the stench of battle away from the castle. Khaldun stood behind her, encircling her with his arms. She leaned into him and sighed. "Do you have any idea who those other two elf mages were today?"

"The one who transformed into a wolf must be Howler."

"He's a shapeshifter like Semblant?"

"Not like Semblant. If the stories are true, he can only change into a wolf."

"What about the other one?"

"I have no idea. She was clearly a water mage, but I haven't encountered any stories about anyone like that in the Sacred Circle."

"She diverted the Ember," Mira said with a shiver. "I've never heard of a mage with that much power over water."

Mira spotted a carpet racing toward them. Allison landed on the ramparts moments later.

"They're gone," she said, fear in her eyes. "The elves. I can't find them anywhere."

CHAPTER NINETEEN
HIDO

yllith drove the wagon all day, Ming riding beside her on her horse. They chatted about the goings-on in Hido, and Syllith spent some time trying to restore her magic. The area became much denser in terms of population, with one village overlapping the next, making it impossible to tell where one ended and another began. Many people seemed to know Ming, and walked with them for a while to chat with her. But they spoke in Kongese—one of the few languages outside the common tongue that had survived Nyro's reign.

Everywhere they went, people spotted Syllith's golden skin, and their eyes went wide. Some tried to get a closer look, while others looked scared, giving them a wide berth.

They reached Hido after three days, but it took four more to cross the city to the coast. It kept going and going, covering an area vastly larger than any city Syllith had ever seen in Maeda or Dorshire. Most of the structures in the outlying areas were mud or straw huts. Single-story wood or concrete buildings dominated the landscape after that. The coastal area featured three- and four-story brick and stone construction, with tile roofs and brightly colored walls.

Row upon row of small houseboats hugged both banks of the Ling across most of the city. But these dropped off closer to the coast, where the river formed a natural harbor. Dozens and dozens of piers and docks hosted ships of all shapes and sizes. Giant wharves filled the coastline on the North Sea as far as the eye could see in either direction, broken up only by swaths of beach. The roads near the coast were congested with all the foot and wagon traffic.

Ming owned a four-story brick building across the main road from the shore. It had a green tile roof with white, yellow, and pink paint on the walls. The witch guided Syllith through an alley to a fenced area behind the building.

"You're welcome to try selling your wares on your own, of course," Ming said as she jumped off her horse, indicating the wagon's contents. "Or I can unload it on one of the dealers I work with, for a commission, of course."

"How much of a commission?" Syllith asked suspiciously, climbing off the wagon.

"My usual rate is fifty percent, but you need the money for this more than I do, so I'll do it for twenty."

"Deal," Syllith said without hesitation. "I wouldn't have the slightest idea where to go to sell this stuff."

"Fair enough," Ming said. "I'll have my people take care of it. You should have your payment tomorrow."

A couple of stable boys hurried over to take care of the horses, and Ming led Syllith inside the building.

"This place functions primarily as an inn," she told her as they moved toward the front. "But it serves as the base of operations for my other businesses as well." A common room occupied most of this level, dimly lit and richly decorated. It was much fancier-looking than any inn Syllith had ever seen. There was a sizable crowd here, especially for the early afternoon. About half the clientele appeared to be local men and women, richly dressed. The other half looked like traders or ship captains from Dorshire or Maeda. Things must have changed in recent times—the last Syllith knew, pirates along Kong's coast made it too dangerous for ships from the other kingdoms to travel here. Scantily clad women and men sat at many of the tables, conversing with the patrons. Ming explained that her offices were in the back.

"You have male prostitutes, too?" Syllith asked in surprise. This was not something she'd seen before.

"Of course, I do. Women have needs, too, don't they? And some of my male patrons prefer them, too. No judgment here; I don't discriminate."

Ming showed Syllith to a table in the rear corner. "Have a seat, and eat and drink as much as you want. It's on the house. As are the rest of our services. I have some business to attend to, but I'll return shortly."

Ming hurried off, and a server came over a minute later, leaving a platter of food and a flagon of wine. Syllith dug in. It was a seafood dish of some kind; she didn't recognize it, but it was delicious.

Every few minutes, one of Ming's prostitutes would come over and sit next to her, offering their services. Men and women. They spoke to her in Kongese at first, but switched to the common tongue when it became clear she didn't understand. Syllith turned them all down.

Ming returned and escorted her upstairs. "This room is yours for as long as you want it," she said, opening a door on the second floor. There was an enormous four-poster bed, tapestries hanging from the walls, a carpeted floor, and a view of the ocean through the windows. "No charge, of course. If you decide to venture out into the city, please come and find me first, and I'll send someone with you."

"Thank you, but that won't be necessary. I can find my way around on my own."

"I'm sure you can. But you saw the attention you attracted on the way here. It wouldn't be safe. You can count on Krigo to have his people on the lookout for you."

Syllith agreed, and Ming left, closing the door behind her. She gazed out the window, feeling overwhelmed by the sheer size of the city. Though she was exhausted from her journey, and the bed proved to be extremely comfortable, she figured it would be best to start seeking passage to Northcoast right away.

Returning to the ground floor, she found Ming in one of the back rooms. She sent a young wizard to accompany her.

"I'm Haitao," he said as they headed toward the front of the building.

"It's a pleasure to meet you," said Syllith, shaking his hand. "My name is Syllith."

"Oh, yes, I know," he said with a chuckle. "Everyone's been talking about you since your arrival."

Syllith nodded, uncomfortable with all the attention she was getting. They went outside, and she explained what she was looking for. Haitao led her up the main street toward the river. It was slow going with the press of people and horses coming and going in both directions, but they made it to the harbor in about a half hour. Haitao led her to one of the docks where an enormous merchant vessel was moored. They found a Kongese man standing guard at the bottom of the gangplank. Haitao spoke to him for a moment, and the man shook his head, saying only a few words in reply.

"He says they don't take passengers for any price," Haitao told Syllith.

They visited three more ships with the same results before finding one that was accepting passengers. But the guard told them it would take a gold coin just to speak to the captain.

"I haven't got any money yet," Syllith said.

The guard turned them away.

Finally, Haitao suggested trying one of the foreign ships. "The captains from Maeda and Dorshire don't usually take passengers either, but when they do, it typically costs less."

They tried three ships before finally finding one that might work. The sailor standing guard led them on board to see the captain. It was a smaller vessel, with only two masts. They found the man in his quarters; the guard introduced them before heading back to his station.

"So, looking for passage to Northcoast, eh?" he said. Syllith nodded. "I guess we could do that. It'll cost ya, though."

"How much?"

He hemmed and hawed for a moment, then finally shrugged and said, "Fifty gold coins."

"*Fifty*?" Syllith repeated. "I don't have any way to come up with that much. But you need to listen to me. I'm sure you've heard about

Nyro and her Sacred Circle escaping from Pytha, right? Fifteen years ago?"

"Heard something about ancient demons, but we haven't heard anything more from them since then, have we?"

"You haven't had word about an elvish invasion in Dorshire or Maeda?"

"Elves?" he said, his eyes going wide. He shook his head and chuckled. "Elves ain't real. And I don't know nothing about any invasion. Of course, I've been moving port to port in Kong these last few years."

"An invasion is imminent," Syllith told him, "if it hasn't already begun. Nyro is planning on exterminating the entire continent. I have to get to the university so I can warn them."

The captain shrugged. "See, thing is, I wasn't planning on going to Northcoast. The money out here is way better. I could take a shipment of artifacts from Pytha, and turn a pretty good profit, but not as much as I can here. But fifty gold coins would make it worth my while."

"If Nyro succeeds, you'll be dead, along with all your clients, and money will hardly matter anymore. Please. I have to get word to the university."

He scratched his head, and squirmed in his chair for a moment, then said, "I guess I could do it for forty-five."

Syllith shook her head, storming out of his quarters. Haitao followed her back up to the deck, and they left the ship.

They tried twenty more ships, but only six were willing to take a passenger at all, and all of those asked for even more than the first one. None believed elves were real, only one had heard of Nyro, and he only laughed when Syllith told him about the coming invasion.

Syllith returned to Ming's inn feeling hopeless and dejected. She took some food and a bottle of wine up to her room. After finishing off the food and the entire bottle, she went to bed, her head spinning from the alcohol.

She spent the next few days returning to the docks with Haitao, trying to find a ship willing to take her to Northcoast for a reasonable fee, but had no luck whatsoever. Every night, she spent a couple of hours trying to rekindle her magic, but found no more success with this. Without her powers, she had no marketable skills. Manual labor was always a possibility, but she could work the rest of her life doing that and never make enough to get to Northcoast. Her payment from the Pythan artifacts came to two gold pieces, which was something, but nowhere near enough to get her to Northcoast.

Going on foot was still a possibility, but based on what she'd experienced so far, she'd need protection for such a journey, and Ming wasn't willing to provide it beyond the city limits. Not to mention crossing the Anthars so far north might be impossible. Part of her wished she'd stuck to her initial plan and tried to make it to the watchtower upon arriving in Pytha. But the journey to Highgate from there might have killed her.

And time was a huge factor. No news had arrived in Hido about any kind of invasion in Dorshire or Maeda. But that didn't mean it wasn't already underway. Syllith couldn't afford to waste any more time.

Selling her body might be the only solution. It was something she *never* would have considered were she not so desperate. But her need was urgent.

Early in the morning on her sixth day in Hido, she went to see Ming in her office. A wizard standing outside the door pointed his wand at her for a moment, and she felt his magic wash over her. He admitted her, and she found Ming sitting behind her desk. She told her that she was ready to accept her offer. Ming's eyes lit up with greed.

"Please tell me I don't need to parade around your common room wearing next to nothing," Syllith said, her stomach churning at the idea.

"Oh, no," Ming said, shaking her head. "No, no, no. That wouldn't do at all. We'll need to be very discreet with this. If word gets out, there's no telling what Krigo might try. No, honey. I'll only be telling my very best clients about you. They'll want to get a look at you first, of course, make sure you're real before they make their payment. But

I'll have you meet them here with me, then we can escort them up to your room when the time comes. Leave everything to me, darling. We'll have you on a ship to Northcoast in no time."

Later that same morning, Syllith returned to Ming's office to meet her first client. He was an older Kongese man with a big belly, a good foot shorter than Syllith. She stood there, fully clothed, while the man walked around her to examine her. He swiped a finger across her cheek to make sure her skin color was real, not just makeup. Then he paid Ming ten gold pieces.

Syllith waited in her room that evening. She had no appetite, so she'd skipped dinner, but drank most of a bottle of wine, so her head was swimming. Ming showed up a few minutes later, ushering the man inside. He only spoke Kongese, so there wasn't any conversation. The man undressed and lay in the bed, already aroused. Syllith grimaced as she disrobed, then climbed on top of him and had sex with him, feeling repulsed the entire time.

Luckily, he finished quickly, then went to sleep. Syllith fought back tears, and slept on the floor. She had nightmares about the client turning into Reaper and tying her down to rape her. In the morning, the man wanted sex again, so she got it over with as quickly as possible. He left, and Syllith went to see Ming.

She'd thought about changing her mind, but despite racking her brain, she could think of no other way to raise the necessary funds for her voyage to Northcoast. Ming introduced the next client.

After three more nights, Ming had collected forty gold coins, half of which were Syllith's. She asked her if she'd be willing to take a female client, and Syllith refused. Doing this with the men was bad enough. But Ming came to see her in the afternoon, explaining that her female client was extremely insistent and willing to pay *one hundred* gold coins for a night with her.

"One more client, and you'll have enough to book passage on a ship," she said. "Don't worry, she's attractive. Her name is Zhi, and she's one of the wealthiest traders in the city. She's been a client here for ages. If you refuse, you'll need to sleep with at least six more men."

Syllith heaved a sigh. She'd never been attracted to women, and the idea of having sex with one was revolting. But it would be one night, and then she could put this miserable chapter of her life behind her. "All right. But this is it. One last client."

The woman hadn't even asked to see Syllith first. So that night, she waited in her room, and Ming brought her the client. She was a little older, but slim and attractive. And she spoke the common tongue.

"I've very much been looking forward to this," the woman said with a smile. "Now, take off your clothes, and let me see the goods."

Syllith undressed, and she looked her up and down, licking her lips. "Very nice. Please, lie down on the bed." Syllith complied. The woman pulled a wand out of her shirt, pointing it at her and saying, "Krigo will be very pleased." Syllith tried to clamber out of the bed, but the witch hit her with a spell, and everything went black.

Syllith opened her eyes, taking in her surroundings. She was tied to a chair, still naked. Her arms were bound behind her back, her legs to the chair legs, and a gag in her mouth. She was in what looked like a warehouse, with wooden crates piled up all around her. Sunlight was streaming in through a small window, so it had to be daytime. She tried rocking back and forth, thinking that if she could tip the chair over, then maybe she could wriggle herself free, but the chair was tied to a post.

"I'm glad to see you're finally awake," a voice said from behind her. A tall Kongese man wearing fancy clothes moved into view, her female client right next to him. This had to be Krigo. He pulled the gag out of her mouth. "I worried that perhaps Yulong might have been a little overzealous with his sleep spell."

Who the hell was Yulong? The witch waved her wand, and her illusion spell slipped away, revealing her to be a wizard.

"So there was no *Zhi*," Syllith said.

"Oh, there is," Krigo replied. "But a phony message about a family emergency got her out of the city for a few days. You are exquisite, though. Well worth the hundred gold coins I paid to make this possible." He stroked her breast, pinching her nipple. Syllith spat in his face. Krigo backed away, wiping the spittle from his cheek. "Feisty, I see. That's good." He turned to say something to Yulong, then the two of them left.

Syllith screamed in rage, trying again to free herself. But it was no use. She was stuck here. Someone showed up later to spoon-feed her some soup. Syllith was inclined to spit in the man's face, but she needed the nourishment to keep up her strength. At some point, Krigo would make a mistake, and she'd find a way out of this.

The day wore on, and the sunlight faded from the window. The same man showed up again to feed her. When he was done, Yulong arrived. He said nothing, but gagged her again, then left.

Syllith started dozing off as it grew fully dark. But then she started awake at the sound of voices. Yulong moved into view, a small flame emanating from his wand. He walked around the space, lighting several oil lamps. Moments later, Krigo showed up, leading another dozen people, mostly men and a few women. Judging from their attire, they were all wealthy.

Krigo spoke to them, and they took turns moving in close to get a better look at her. Some of them touched her, fondling her breasts or rubbing her thigh. Syllith had no idea what was going on here. But then they all left with Krigo again.

Yulong stayed, but said nothing. Several minutes later, Krigo returned. "I faced something of a conundrum when Ming took you from my people. She was keeping you very well protected. And I couldn't afford to start a war to get you back. But when she finally decided to make you available to her best clients, I finally had my opportunity.

"But now, the trouble is that I can't afford to keep you. Undoubtedly you'd bring in more money than all my other girls put together. But it would be too difficult to prevent someone else from doing to me what I did to Ming. So instead, I decided to sell you."

Syllith's eyes went wide, and she tried to scream at him, but the gag prevented it.

"You're going to live a lavish lifestyle," Krigo continued. "The winner of my little auction is one of the richest merchants in Kong, and paid quite a fortune in gold to acquire you as her sex slave. She's a mage, of course; otherwise, I'm not sure she'd be able to control you. You'll be departing for southern Kong at first light tomorrow. And I just wanted to express my appreciation," he added with a grin. "Thanks to you, I just made more from a single transaction than I typically see in an entire year. I wish you all the best."

Krigo left the room. Yulong extinguished the oil lamps with a wave of his wand and followed him out, leaving Syllith in darkness.

CHAPTER TWENTY
CASTLE BARCLAY

hat do you mean, 'gone'?" Khaldun asked. "How can an entire army disappear?"

"I have no idea, but it did," Allison said. "I checked the ground where they made camp, and there's no trail leading out of that area, magical or otherwise. And I flew all around the surrounding fields, but found no invisibility spells, or anything tucked into the void."

"I'd like to go take a look for myself," said Khaldun. "No offense intended, of course."

"None taken," she said. "I'm worried I might be losing my mind. At least if you find the same nothing I did, I'll know I'm sane."

They took off from the ramparts, Allison leading the way on her carpet, Mira and Khaldun following on his. She took them to the field where the elves had made camp. Even in the moonlight, Mira could see the army had trampled the grass. But Allison was right: the only visible trail was the one leading back to the castle.

Khaldun flew low over the surrounding area, Allison close by, trying to sense any hidden spells, but came up empty. He also found no magical trace of anyone leaving the field.

"We'd better inform Jezebel," he said. "They could be moving both of their armies to Castle Barclay as we speak."

The three of them returned to the castle. Allison used her mirror to update Jezebel. The princess recalled all of their forces to Castle Barclay. She ordered a night march, and asked Allison to fly patrol over their army coming from Franconia. Sage would escort the army returning from Wayland, and the rest of the sorcerers would fly directly to Castle Barclay immediately and regroup there.

Khaldun and Mira both embraced Allison, wishing her luck, then took off on his carpet heading south. Khaldun flew low the whole way, trying to sense any hidden spells. No single mage could hide an entire army with an invisibility spell, but working together, the elvish ones certainly could. But they made it to Spanbrook City without finding anything.

Reaching Castle Barclay, they found most of the troops Jezebel had stationed there camped in the fields to the south of the castle. But an entire garrison had moved inside, and they were camped in the courtyard. The drawbridge was up, both sets of gates were closed, and soldiers lined the ramparts.

Landing in the rear of the courtyard, Khaldun and Mira went inside, and found Jezebel in the keep's private hall with Allure. The sorcerer greeted them, hugging them each in turn.

"Semblant and I just arrived a few minutes ago," she told them.

The four of them sat down at the head table, and the staff served them wine. Jezebel had already been updated on the day's events, but Allure, Khaldun, and Mira spent several minutes providing her with a more detailed account.

"Your Highness, today, we faced Xythor, Metamorph, and Artifice in Wayland. Gnasher and Howler were in Franconia, and the water mage must have been Hydra," said Allure. "Semblant, Sage, and I believe the elves are probably regrouping in preparation for an assault on Castle Barclay. We can expect to face all six of them here.

"Typhoon, Scream, and Comet participated in the attack on Keepstone today," she continued. "But that leaves Reaper, Blaze, and Plague unaccounted for. We fear they could show up here."

"Wait, they attacked Keepstone today, too?" said Mira.

"Yes, and Leto's forces suffered losses similar to ours," said Jezebel. "But they held strong, and the elves failed to win the day. Has the elvish army there disappeared, too?"

"No," said Allure. "Battleaxe reports that they're camped about a mile out from the battlefield."

"I'm not familiar with Scream, Comet, or Plague," said Khaldun.

Allure took a deep breath. "Scream is able to use her voice to affect people's minds. She can render soldiers unconscious, or make them turn against their commanders."

"Similar to Siren, then," he said.

"Yes, only stronger. Luckily, Legion was ready for her, and was able to cancel her spells before she inflicted too much damage. Comet can fly short distances—she streaks across the sky like a fireball when she does it, thus her name."

"They could use her to get inside the castle," Mira said.

"Indeed they could," Allure said, "but they haven't yet. Plague possesses a kind of magic I've never heard of anywhere else. He can inflict an enemy force with illness that spreads very quickly. It's magical, so it can be canceled, but if you don't treat every infected person, it starts spreading again."

"I wonder if Reaper's still able to control demons from inside an elvish body," said Khaldun.

"Assuming he *is* in a body," said Allure, "I'd tend to doubt it. I'm guessing he might have chosen to remain in demon form. He'd probably be more effective against humans that way—more powerful than any demon we've encountered before."

A chill ran down Mira's spine.

"Right after killing his body, Allison banished Gnasher," said Khaldun. "But he reformed almost instantly and reanimated another elf body. It seems like they're impossible to kill, now."

"His demon reformed *immediately*?" asked Allure.

"Yes," said Mira. "It turned to smoke when she banished it, but then retook solid shape."

Allure frowned. "That shouldn't be possible. When a demon is bound, that can happen. That's one of the main advantages of becoming a necromancer. If Allison or I summon a demon, someone who knows the spells can banish it, sending it back to the spectral plane. We can summon another one, of course, but that takes time. And there would be no reason for the first one to return."

"A necromancer can stop the banished demon from returning to the spectral plane?" Khaldun asked.

"Yes," said Allure, "any demon the necromancer binds acts as an extension of his or her will, so it can reform almost instantly."

"Then this makes no sense," said Mira, shaking her head. "Nyro's a demon, too. She can't possibly have bound the other demons to her, could she?"

"No," Allure said with a frown. "I'm afraid I don't understand it either. Even if she's taken an elvish body like the members of her Sacred Circle, she still wouldn't be able to bind them like a necromancer. That's not possible for elves."

"I banished Xythor's demon after Semblant killed his body, and he *didn't* reform. I'd expect him to return eventually, because the demons of the circle have a vested interest in helping Nyro return to power. But Gnasher's immediate return means there's something else going on here. Nyro must have found a way to reestablish her bond with them, though I cannot comprehend how."

"Do you have any idea where the missing armies might have gone?" Jezebel asked.

"If Nyro showed up with her pyramid, she could have used it to open a portal for them," said Khaldun. "That would enable her to send the armies anywhere she wants."

"Surely they'd be here by now if that were the case," said Jezebel.

"Yes, the move would be instantaneous," said Khaldun. "Of course, it's possible they've gone somewhere else, and will show up here the same way once they're ready to attack."

"Giving us little to no warning," Jezebel said with a sigh.

"True, but opening a portal takes a tremendous amount of energy," said Allure. "I doubt even Nyro could sustain it long enough for more than a few people to pass through, never mind thousands."

"How did their armies disappear, then?" asked Khaldun.

"One or more of their mages could have tucked them into the void," said Allure.

"An entire army?" Khaldun said skeptically. "I didn't think that was possible."

"It wouldn't be for us. But the Sacred Circle are much more powerful. One of them might have pulled it off. The mages would have a much easier time traveling without being detected. And then they could release their army at a time and place of their choosing."

"Once again, with little to no warning," said Jezebel.

"Yes. However, they wouldn't be able to make the journey here much faster than our troops," said Allure.

"Could Nyro's mages use this against our troops in battle?" Jezebel asked. "Tuck thousands of them into the void?"

"I suppose so," Allure said with a shrug. "But it wouldn't do them much good. We could free them again immediately."

"Ah, of course," Jezebel said with a nod.

"What if *Nyro* tucked the armies into the void?" Khaldun asked. "Then they could move through the portal with her, without taking any extra time."

Allure shook her head. "Not possible. Nothing in the void can move through such a portal."

"What would happen if she tried?" Jezebel asked.

"Anything in the void would be stripped away from her and left behind," said Allure.

"I'm sorry, but how do you know this?" Khaldun asked.

Allure took a deep breath. "I'm not at liberty to say. But rest assured, I have this on the highest authority."

Mira thought of Shadow, the mysterious entity who resided in the seven-sided tower at the university, and figured she had to be the source of Allure's information.

"That explains why Nyro needed ships to get her armies to Anoria," said Jezebel. "If she could have sent them here through the portal, I'm sure she would have."

"So we must assume members of the Sacred Circle have tucked their armies into the void, and are on their way here with them," said Khaldun. "It's a three days' march for our people from either Wayland or Franconia. Their mages could keep going day and night, and they left during dinner this evening."

"Given their greater speed, that could put them here as soon as tomorrow night," said Jezebel, heaving a long sigh. "We could be in trouble. There are currently only five thousand troops stationed here. And roughly eight thousand elves survived each battle?"

"That's our best estimate, Your Highness," said Allure.

"Meaning we'll be outnumbered three to one."

"The rest of the sorcerers and I should start transporting our armies here immediately," said Khaldun. "With each of us tucking a hundred of them into the void on each trip, we could get them all here by morning."

"Yes," Allure said, getting to her feet. "I'll alert the others."

"We shouldn't leave the castle unprotected," said Jezebel.

"I'll remain here," said Mira. "I won't be any help in this process anyway. But my null should protect us from any thaumaturgic attack while the rest of you are away."

"Agreed," said Jezebel. "Let's do this. Good luck, all of you."

Mira held Khaldun tight for a minute. She kissed him, then he hurried outside with Allure. Mira accompanied Jezebel to the top of the mage's tower. She opened her channels of power, expanding her null to its full size, encompassing the entire castle and half of the city to the north, as well as their army camped to the south.

"Thank the stars you're here," said Jezebel. "I honestly don't know what we would do without you."

Mira squeezed her hand. "It's my honor, Your Highness."

Allison arrived a little later, landing out beyond the army camp, and outside Mira's null. Eight soldiers had ridden with her on the carpet. She held out one hand, and a hundred more appeared on the field. They started making camp, and the princess took off again.

Only a few minutes later, Sage arrived, dropping off a hundred more soldiers. Allure and Semblant showed up next, followed by Khaldun. It took the whole night, but the sorcerers managed to get both armies to Castle Barclay. And still, there was no sign of the elvish forces.

Jezebel and Mira went inside to meet the others. Allison embraced Jezebel, kissing her deeply, and Khaldun hugged and kissed Mira. They all sat down in the private hall for breakfast.

"You should get some rest after this, Your Highness," Mira said to Jezebel. "You were up all night."

"So were all of you," she said. "I'll be all right."

"Sorcerers can stay awake for several days straight, Your Highness," said Sage. "Lady Mira is right. You should get some sleep. You'll need to be at your best when this battle starts."

Just then, Mira heard horns blowing somewhere outside.

"What the hell was that?" Jezebel said.

The doors flew open, and Imani strode into the hall. "Your Highness, the elvish armies have arrived."

"That's impossible," said Khaldun as they all got to their feet. "How could they have gotten here so quickly?"

"That I can't say, my lord, but they are here," said Imani. "They showed up out of nowhere, first one army, then the other, in the fields east of the castle. They're forming ranks now. General Amari has our forces moving into position to engage them."

Mira got to her feet with the others, and they followed Imani up to the east-side ramparts. The soldiers there cleared a space for them along the wall. Far across the moat, the elvish armies were forming ranks. Their own forces were moving in a steady stream from the fields south of the castle to take position on the battlefield.

"Our people will be facing directly into the morning sun," Imani observed. "This will give the enemy an advantage."

"I'm sure that's why they chose to attack from this direction," Jezebel said.

"We should do what we can to create some chaos in their lines," Allure suggested.

Jezebel nodded. One by one, Allure, Semblant, and Sage mounted their carpets and took off. Allison embraced Jezebel before flying after them.

"Be safe," Mira said, kissing Khaldun before he took off after the others.

The sorcerers went invisible. Only Mira and Jezebel could follow their progress using their carpets' beacon spells, but these provided no way to tell them apart from each other. Once they'd moved out of range, Mira opened her channels of power, extending her null to protect the castle and their troops.

Mira spotted Semblant going visible when he landed out beyond the elvish lines. His carpet vanished as he transformed into the giant bear and stomped through the formations, leaving a trail of devastation in his wake. Two ghouls erupted into existence at the other end of the battlefield, adding to the carnage. Mira knew Allure and Allison had to be responsible for these. Fire orbs started appearing in random places, turning every soldier within to ash; this had to be Sage's work. And the individual elves being incinerated from within must be Khaldun's doing.

Strangely, the elvish mages did nothing to combat the sorcerers, and their magic produced the desired effect: it kept the elvish forces in disarray long enough for Spanbrook's armies to take the field.

"Where is the Sacred Circle?" Jezebel wondered out loud.

As if in answer to her question, someone banished the ghouls, but two more appeared moments later, continuing their predecessors' path of destruction. Despite the chaos, the elvish horns sounded, and their armies advanced. They reached Spanbrook's forces, and the battle was joined. Battle cries and the crash of weapons against armor drifted up to their position on the ramparts.

The battle raged for an hour, and their sorcerers continued to do their work unhindered by the elvish mages. Mira didn't understand where they could have gone. But suddenly, she spotted objects dropping out of the sky from multiple starting points, landing on the ground and shattering among their troops. They looked like pots or jars.

"What the hell are those?" Jezebel asked.

"Some sort of thaumaturgic attack, I'd wager," said Imani. "But they won't do any good inside Mira's null."

"They're coming from high above my null, whatever they are," said Mira. "I don't understand how."

Some of their soldiers started screaming. Mira spotted a few of them running into the moat.

"NO!" Jezebel screamed. "The demon fish will poison them!"

"The ones running were near those falling objects," Imani said. "Look!"

Looking closer, Mira noticed holes in their armor, exposing burning flesh within. More jars fell from the sky, and she realized they were splashing their contents all over nearby soldiers as they shattered. She pointed this out to Jezebel and Imani.

"It's some kind of magic," said Imani.

"Impossible inside my null," said Mira.

"They might have used magic to concoct a potion that burns through anything it touches," Jezebel suggested. "The spell wouldn't be active now."

"Can we cancel the potion's effects?" Mira asked.

"Perhaps," Jezebel said. "You'll have to extinguish your null first."

"Wait," said Imani, gripping Mira's arm. "Why wouldn't her null have already canceled it?"

"My null only cancels active magic," said Mira. "Like any mage, I can cancel fire even if it was created by normal means, but not with my null."

"It's like canceling the air beneath a dragon," Jezebel said. "The air wasn't created magically, but you can still cancel it to rob the beast of its lift."

"Yes, exactly," said Mira. "But my null won't cancel it."

"All right," Imani said skeptically, releasing Mira's arm.

Mira closed her channels of power, eliminating her null, then nodded to Jezebel. The two of them went to work, trying to cancel the potion's fire. This seemed to work. The soldiers they hit with their spells stopped screaming, and didn't try jumping in the moat. It wasn't enough, though. The pots kept falling, hitting more and more soldiers.

"This isn't working," Jezebel said in frustration as she waved her wand. "We've got to figure out how they're doing this and stop it."

"I have a bad feeling I know exactly what they're doing," Mira said. Gazing skyward, she focused on one of the pots' points of origin, and reached out with her power to cancel invisibility. Sure enough, she'd revealed a carpet, drifting slowly over their troops.

"I'll be damned," said Jezebel. "How did they get carpets?"

"Nyro's had fifteen years to ponder the magic that makes them work," said Imani. "Is it any surprise that she figured it out?"

Mira used cancellation spells to uncover two more carpets. They were too high to see who was riding them, but Jezebel pointed her wand and canceled the air beneath one of them, and it plummeted earthward. As it dropped, several riders moved into view. It looked like two elvish mages—one controlling the carpet, and a second standing amidst three soldiers sitting by the edges. The soldiers must have been dropping the pots, but where were they coming from? Mira couldn't see any on the carpet.

The mage managed to regain control of the carpet right before it hit the ground. As he swooped over the battle, his partner pulled a jar out of the void, handing it to one of the soldiers. Jezebel tried canceling the air beneath them again, but one of the mages blocked her cancellation spell.

"Quickly, reestablish your null," Jezebel said.

Mira opened her channels of power, and her null exploded to its full size. The carpet fell like a stone, crashing into the earth. A cheer went up from Spanbrook's soldiers. Mira extinguished her null, and Jezebel called fire, incinerating the carpet.

The other two carpets had stayed high above Mira's null, and restored their invisibility spells. They continued dropping potion jars on their troops. Jezebel made them visible, then she and Mira canceled the air providing their lift. Both carpets crashed, and Jezebel called fire to destroy them. Mira expanded her null again.

Spanbrook's troops moved to surround the elvish mages. They closed in, attacking them with sword and spear. Naked, unarmed, injured from their falls, and bereft of their magic, the elves put up little resistance. The Spanbrookers slew them, leaving their corpses to rot.

The battle raged on, the casualties mounting on both sides. With their mages meeting no thaumaturgic resistance, Spanbrook seemed to be winning, the enemy's losses outpacing their own.

But before long, six elves emerged from the fighting, moving out beyond their lines and incinerating their clothing. The six Sacred

Circle members had taken new bodies and rejoined the fray. They banished Allure and Allison's ghouls, and focused on Semblant, trying to ignite him from within. The giant bear reared on his hind legs, screaming to the sky. Fires erupted in his fur, burning into his flesh. Someone, probably Allure, canceled the spells, and Semblant went back to killing.

The elves moved several companies to the bridge crossing the moat. Sage concentrated her efforts there, hitting them with fire orbs. The elves sent reinforcements to replace the slain.

"What are they doing over there?" Jezebel said. "With the drawbridge up, they have no chance of getting inside that way."

"They don't have any siege engines, either," said Imani.

Returning her attention to the battlefield, Mira realized she'd lost track of some of the elf mages; only three of them remained out beyond their lines. Only minutes later, she spotted something streaking across the sky toward them, and pointed it out to Jezebel and Imani.

"What the hell is that?" Imani asked.

As it moved closer, Mira realized it was an enormous winged serpent. It flew directly over their heads, landing in the courtyard near the gates. Dozens of soldiers scampered off its back, hurrying over to the gatehouse.

"Shit," Jezebel muttered.

"I'd better get down there—with your leave, Your Highness?" Imani said.

Jezebel nodded, and Imani hurried off, running down the steps to the courtyard and firing off orders to her people. The soldiers defending the gatehouse held the elves off, but the serpent was making it impossible for any others to assist them. It kept snapping people in half with its jaws and thrashing them with its tail.

"That must be Metamorph," said Jezebel.

"Yes," Mira agreed. "She transformed before entering my null, so she needs no active magic to retain this form."

"You'd better extinguish your null. We're going to need the sorcerers to combat this thing. If they get the drawbridge down…"

Mira nodded. She closed her channels of power, and Jezebel pulled out her mirror to alert the others to their situation. Allison, Khaldun, and Sage landed on the ramparts moments later.

"Holy shit," Sage muttered.

The three of them went to work. Sage tried hitting the serpent with fire orbs. Though the monster screamed, they didn't slow it down. Allison summoned a ghoul, and it wrestled the beast away from the gates. Khaldun incinerated several of the elves by the gatehouse from within as more soldiers rushed around the serpent to join the fight, Imani in the lead.

The Shifari woman moved through the enemy like a whirlwind, cutting down one elf after another. But suddenly, one of the elves screamed, her illusion of clothing disappearing as she encased Imani in a glowing sheet of energy, binding her limbs together. Waving one hand before her, she released two hundred more elvish troops from the void.

The newcomers rushed the Spanbrookers defending the gatehouse, quickly overwhelming them. One of the sorcerers freed Imani, and she charged the elvish mage, swinging her sword. But the elf vanished, and her blade sliced through empty air.

In only minutes, the elves got the gates open and lowered the drawbridge. The companies waiting on the outer bridge hurried inside, swamping the courtyard and overcoming the castle's defenders. Sage, Khaldun, and Allison kept bombarding the serpent, and took out dozens of elvish soldiers. But more troops kept pouring in through the gates. The elves had moved several regiments to block the Spanbrookers from sending reinforcements to the castle.

"You should take out the drawbridge, Your Highness," said Mira.

Jezebel met her gaze for a moment and nodded. The two of them hurried around the battlements to the front of the castle. Jezebel waved her wand, calling fire, and the bridge went up in flames. Allure must have realized what she was doing, because she added her own spell, and the bridge turned to ash moments later, cutting off the fresh supply of elvish troops.

At that moment, Imani came running up the steps. "Your Highness, we must evacuate you and your people immediately."

"Forfeit Castle Barclay?" Jezebel said, her expression aghast.

"Your Highness, the castle is already lost."

Mira took in the situation in the courtyard. Despite the sorcerers' efforts, the elvish soldiers outnumbered their own, and were cutting down more every second. And one of the enemy mages had banished Allison's ghoul, leaving the serpent free to add to the carnage. The tide had turned out on the battlefield, where the elves were rallying, driving Spanbrook's forces away from the now-useless castle entry.

Allison landed on the ramparts. "We need to get out of here," she told Jezebel, taking her hand. Jezebel gazed around the courtyard, horror in her eyes. "We knew this day could come, and we've prepared for this. It's time to put our contingency plan into motion."

"We're losing everything we've built," Jezebel said, her voice catching in her throat. "Our entire heritage."

"Not everything," Allison said. "Remember what you told me. We'll sacrifice anything else, but *not our family*. Alanna and Leda need us. It's time to go."

Taking a deep, steadying breath, Jezebel nodded, and ordered the retreat.

CHAPTER TWENTY-ONE
RESTORATION

yllith struggled against her bonds, trying once again to tip her chair over, but it was no use. She tried using her magic, and managed to conjure a tiny flame, but couldn't get it to last more than a second. It wasn't enough to ignite the ropes tied around her.

She sat there in silence, trying to figure out how she could escape. They'd have to untie her to move her to the ship, and that would probably be her only chance. If she could overpower one of them, she might be able to run for it. Of course, this was assuming they didn't knock her out before removing her bonds.

"*Shit!*" she screamed. For a minute, she thrashed about, swearing at the top of her lungs in her rage. But she accomplished nothing but giving herself rope burn.

She calmed down finally and sat in silence for a long time. Although she didn't remember falling asleep, she started awake at a loud noise. Listening intently, she heard screams, then footsteps running toward her. Someone ran into view carrying a torch, and she realized it was Krigo. His mage, Yulong, appeared moments later, brandishing his wand at something she couldn't see. Suddenly, the wizard went up in flames, screaming for a moment before the fire consumed him.

"P-please," Krigo stammered, dropping to his knees. "M-maybe we could be partners, eh? I'll cut you in for half—"

"Half?" a voice repeated as Ming strode into view, wielding her staff. "Forget it, Krigo. You're done." She called fire and the man screamed as she incinerated him from within. His charred corpse hit the floor and Ming hurried over to Syllith.

"How did you know where to find me?"

"I have people watching all of his hideouts," she explained as she untied her.

Syllith tried getting to her feet, but her muscles were stiff and sore, and she had to cling to the post to stay upright.

Ming held out her staff, removing a bundle of cloth and a pack from the void. "Get dressed. I've provided mage's robes along with a tent and bedroll." She took a heavy money purse out of the void next, setting it down on the chair with a jingling sound. "One hundred forty gold coins."

"What about your take?" Syllith asked as she dressed.

"My take is Krigo's entire business. With him out of the way, I'm taking over. Don't worry, I'll make much more this way. I never could have gotten away with it if he hadn't taken you, so I figure I owe you."

"Who would have stopped you before?" Syllith asked.

"Everyone else," Ming said with a sigh. "Outside of my building, you would have been fair game. But moving in on a rival's home turf is against the rules."

"Honor among thieves?" Syllith asked with a grin.

"Something like that," Ming muttered. "And in any event, my negligence caused you harm, so you deserve the full payment for all of your clients."

"Your negligence?" Syllith repeated. She stuffed the money purse into the pack.

"One of my mages guards the entry to my office at all times, and casts a spell to cancel illusion whenever I get a visitor," she explained. "So when Zhi showed up to inquire about you, I took it for granted that it was her. But Krigo had paid off my guard. I've disposed of him accordingly.

"I believe Yulong lowered you out the window into the alley," Ming continued. "Otherwise he would have had to sneak you past several other guards on the way out."

Haitao arrived a moment later. "Everything is ready, my lady," he said.

"Excellent. Let's go," she said, leading the way out of the warehouse.

"Where are we going?" Syllith asked, hoisting the pack over her shoulder and following them out.

"You'll see," Ming told her as they headed to the end of the alley and turned onto the main street.

They walked along the river for a few minutes, until they reached the docks. Ming took them to one of the biggest merchant ships in the harbor. They met two men waiting at the bottom of the gangplank.

"This is Captain Sun and his first mate, Han," Ming said. Syllith shook their hands. "I've booked your passage to Northcoast. They're going to set sail right away, just in case one of Krigo's lackeys catches wind of this and tries to claim you for their own. Haitao will be accompanying you to make sure you have a safe voyage. From there, you should have enough money to get yourself to the university, I believe."

Syllith could hardly believe her ears. "This is very kind of you. I'm not sure if I should trust this."

"Like I said, because of you, I've added Krigo's business to my own. I'm going to be very rich, thanks to you. This is the least I could do. Now, please, get word to the governors before it's too late, all right?"

"Thank you," Syllith said, embracing her. "I will."

"Oh, one last thing before I forget," Ming said, holding up her staff. "I'm going to cast an illusion to make you look like a Kongese noblewoman. This should help you avoid attention." She performed her magic, and Syllith held out her hands. Her skin tone had reverted to a normal human's. "And take this," Ming added, taking something out of the void and handing it to her. Syllith took it from her, and realized it was a longsword and belt. "Without your magic, you're going to need some way to defend yourself."

"Again, thank you."

Ming bade her farewell, and Syllith boarded the ship with Haitao and the two sailors. The first mate escorted them below deck to a lavish cabin at the rear of the ship. Syllith watched out the window as they left the harbor and sailed out to sea.

"You should get some sleep," Haitao suggested. "I'll stand guard, but I'll need you to keep watch during the day so I can rest."

Syllith nodded. Setting her pack down, she climbed into the bed without undressing as Haitao sat in the chair across from her. She hadn't realized how exhausted she was, and drifted off almost immediately.

They had an uneventful voyage, and a few days later, docked in Northcoast late in the afternoon. Ming had booked Haitao's return voyage, but the ship wasn't departing until the following morning. Syllith invited him to stay at an inn with her that night, and he agreed.

Disembarking, they found a seaside inn nearby. Syllith booked them two rooms, then they went to the common room for dinner. They ate a hearty meal, and sat up late drinking beer. Haitao told her he'd trained at the university many years earlier, and remembered seeing her.

Syllith tried to get news from some of the other patrons, but nobody had heard anything about an invasion in Maeda or Dorshire. One couple laughed at her when she suggested an elvish army was sure to be on its way, and she refrained from offering information to anyone else. She kept her eyes and ears open, though, and neither saw nor heard any evidence that an elvish invasion had begun. She started to get her hopes up that maybe she wasn't too late, after all.

Haitao and Syllith went up to their rooms, and Syllith got a good night's sleep. Early the next morning, she ate breakfast with the wizard, and accompanied him to his ship. Then she said farewell, and went to find a horse. Someone in the market outside the castle told her where to find a breeder outside of town. So, she walked there, met the owner, and purchased a young mare.

Once they'd tacked her up, Syllith shouldered her pack and mounted the horse. She stopped at the market to stock up on food for her and the animal, then set out for the university. She stuck to the road, and made good time. Come nightfall, she found a clearing by a stream a little way into the trees, and made camp. She fed the horse, and let her drink from the stream, then sat down to eat. Once it was fully dark, she climbed into her tent and went to sleep.

It took Syllith twelve days to reach the university's lands. She passed many other travelers coming and going along her way, and she asked them all if they'd heard any news of an elvish invasion. None had. Of course, it would take a long time for news to reach this area if they'd landed on the coast of Dorshire, southern Maeda, or Shifar.

Regardless, it was imperative for her to keep her identity a secret. If the elves had landed, they could have spies everywhere by now. She could not afford for them to learn who she truly was. This wasn't something she'd thought about in Kong. It just didn't seem likely that Nyro would bother spying on traders and gang leaders. But now that she was in Maeda, it was a huge concern. She sent a silent *thank-you* to Ming for casting this illusion spell to provide her a disguise.

It was conceivable that Nyro had already learned of her escape from Reaper. And if that were the case, they'd certainly be on the lookout for her. Nyro could invoke her true name even from afar, but Syllith doubted she would do that. Doing so would cause her to lose control of her Sacred Circle. And of course, if Nyro had learned about her escape, she could liberate one of her demons from its body, and it could travel to her through the spectral plane almost instantly. The fact that that hadn't happened almost certainly meant Nyro was still in the dark.

She crossed the bridge over the River Mayne and rode up to the barrier. But without her magic, she had no way to go any farther. Even if her powers had come back, she was sure they would have changed the spells in her absence. There was nothing to do but wait.

About an hour later, a group of young mages approached, probably students returning from Arthos. Syllith greeted them, explaining that she needed to see the governors.

"I'm sorry, we're not allowed to let anyone inside with us," one of the witches said apologetically.

"I understand, but the situation is grave. The elves are preparing to invade Anoria, and I have to warn the governors before it's too late."

"The invasion has already begun," a wizard said. "How do we know you're not here to help them take the university?" he added, pointing his wand at her.

"I have lived through hell to get here. Please, I must see the governors."

"We will let them know you're here," the witch said. "But we cannot grant you passage."

"All right, fine," Syllith said. "But please, hurry!"

The witch cast the spell to open a portal in the barrier, while the wizard guarded her, not lowering his wand. Once the others had moved through, he followed, closing the barrier behind him.

Syllith dismounted and waited. In much less time than she thought possible, a witch rode into view, with a dozen armed soldiers riding in her wake. They stopped at the barrier and the witch stared at her for a moment. "I am Governor Amelia." Syllith had never heard of her, but it had been a long time. "Some students have informed me that you have important news for us. Who are you?"

Syllith eyed the soldiers. "An ally. But I cannot afford to reveal my identity to anyone but you."

The witch regarded her for a moment in silence. "We'll escort you to the administrative building, and you can make a report to the full council."

"No—only you."

"All right. But I'm keeping my wand on you the whole way, and you'll need to turn over your sword. Try anything, and I'll order them to strike you down." Syllith nodded, and the witch opened a portal in the barrier. Syllith led her horse through by the reins, and the witch closed the barrier behind her. Syllith removed her sword belt, handing it to one of the soldiers, then mounted her horse.

When they reached the university, Syllith's eyes welled up. She never thought she'd see this place again. Amelia and Syllith dismounted, tying their horses to the post in front of the administrative building. Amelia asked the guards to wait for them, and led her inside, keeping her wand trained on her the whole time. They went into the council chamber, and sat down at the table.

"Let's hear it," Amelia said.

"First, I need you to put the spells in place to ensure no one else can listen in on this conversation, magically or otherwise."

Amelia did as she asked.

Syllith knew she couldn't possibly tell her story without revealing her identity. She didn't know if she could trust this woman, but she had no choice but to take that risk. "Now, please cast the spell to cancel illusion."

"Excuse me?"

"This is not my true appearance."

Amelia got to her feet, backing away from her. Syllith remained seated. Amelia canceled the illusion, her eyes going wide when she saw her. "*You…* but you're a necromancer?"

"Yes, but I'm no traitor—"

"I know. Sage told us all the truth about Nyro embedding a fragment of her soul inside of you."

"Good, then you must hear me out," Syllith pleaded, worried she'd run for the guards. "Nyro has held me in captivity for fifteen years, and stopped my powers from returning. I have information I must get to those fighting her. But *no one* can learn of my presence here."

"All right, I'll listen."

Syllith told her the whole story, unable to contain her emotions when she recounted the abuse she'd endured at Nyro's hands, and then Reaper's. She had to fight back sobs for many parts of the account. At one point, Amelia went outside to dismiss the guards, returning with Syllith's sword, and finally retaking her seat. Syllith finished, doing her best to keep her composure. It had grown dark outside by the time she was done.

Amelia took a deep breath. "This is dire news. I'm sorry to inform you that the invasion has already started. Nyro has not turned up yet, but members of her Sacred Circle are leading her armies. They've destroyed Rockport, Blacksand, and Oldport, and defeated the forces in Keepstone and Spanbrook.

"We dispatched all of our sorcerers to provide assistance to those last two, but it wasn't enough. Prince Leto, Princess Jezebel, and their remaining troops are falling back to Stoutwall as we speak. I think that is where you must go."

"Yes, I agree," Syllith said with a sigh. Dread knotted her stomach at the thought of Nyro's forces conquering Anoria. She was too late. But there was still much she could do.

"I can alert Prince Augustine to expect your arrival," Amelia said.

"*No*! No one can learn of my presence in Anoria until I reach Stoutwall!" She told her about her plan. "But if Nyro catches wind of this, she will devote all of her resources to recapturing me, and we'll lose this opportunity."

"That is incredibly brave," Amelia said, sadness in her eyes.

"You must not tell *anyone* about me—not even the other governors can know. Nyro could have spies all over the continent by now."

"Your secret is safe with me, you have my word."

Syllith nodded. She still didn't know if she could trust her, but without her magic, she had no choice. "Thank you. If you don't mind, I will make camp here for the night and set out in the morning."

"No need to camp," Amelia said with a smile. "You are welcome to stay with me, Governor Syllith."

It was heartening to hear the witch address her that way, even though the title was no longer hers. She hadn't known if her arrival would be met with acceptance or scorn, and was relieved that it was the former.

"But first," Amelia continued, "I'm pretty sure I can restore your magic."

"What? How?" Syllith said, taken aback. "Nyro did something to stop it from coming back. I don't think there's anything you can do."

"We'll see," she said with a sly smile, getting to her feet. "Come with me."

Syllith grabbed her sword belt and followed her out of the room, and they went down to the basement. Amelia called a small flame to light their way. The area was cluttered with boxes and crates. The witch retrieved a long crate from the rear corner, setting it down on the floor. She opened it, reached inside, and withdrew a staff, handing it to Syllith.

As she took it from her, she gasped. "This was mine!" It had been fifteen years, but this had been her sole instrument from the time her magic first revealed itself when she was only a girl. She'd recognize it anywhere; the feel of the wood was so familiar in her hands. "Where did you find this?"

"Lord Khaldun recovered it after you disappeared," she explained. "He brought it here, and we've kept it in storage ever since."

"You're going to transfer its power back to me," Syllith said. "I don't know if this will work."

"I have a feeling it will," she said with a smile. "You'll need to—"

"Disrobe," she said with a nod. "I know."

Syllith took off her clothes. Grabbing her staff, she held it tight against her, and said, "I'm ready."

Amelia held out her arms, pointing her wand at Syllith and reciting a string of spells, finally speaking the word of command. After a bright flash of light, Syllith's staff started to glow. Its brightness continued to increase, and she felt it growing hot against her flesh. She cried out as the pain became almost unbearable, and she had to shut her eyes against the light. Syllith felt herself growing woozy, and didn't know how much longer she could hold on. But then there was a tearing sound, and her staff disappeared.

Opening her eyes, she found her vision going dark around the edges. She stumbled forward, placing her hands on a giant crate for support. Amelia helped ease her onto the floor, and after a couple of minutes, Syllith recovered.

"I've performed that spell for others," she said, taking a deep breath. "I never appreciated how painful it was."

"You did great," said Amelia. "Most people pass out. Try some magic."

Syllith held out one hand and called fire. A small flame appeared in her palm. Canceling that, she got to her feet and made herself invisible.

"It would seem we were successful," Amelia said, her eyes failing to find Syllith.

Syllith canceled her spell and got dressed, fastening her sword belt around her waist. "Thank you for this."

"Well, I don't know about you, but I'm starving," Amelia said. "Why don't we head over to my house?"

Syllith nodded. "It would be best to restore the illusion I wore when I arrived. If anyone saw us entering the building, it would look strange if someone else left with you. But I'm afraid I never got a look at myself in a mirror."

"I can take care of that," Amelia said. She pointed her wand, calling the magical force. Syllith saw her hands change color. "That should be close enough."

They headed outside, and Syllith untied her horse, leading her by the reins. The soldiers had already taken the governor's horse to be stabled. Amelia took her across the grounds to the governors' mansions. Syllith noted with satisfaction that they'd constructed these new dwellings from brick and stone. She tied her horse, and followed Amelia into her house.

The governor's staff was already preparing dinner, so she let them know she'd brought a guest. They sat down at her dining room table, and one of her staff poured them wine. Dinner was served a few minutes later.

"So, which sorcerer is bound to you?" Syllith asked, taking a sip of wine.

Amelia said nothing for a minute. "Things have changed in your absence. You saw the soldiers, for example? Conjurnors no longer serve as governors. After what Dredmort did, we've put precautions in place to make sure no one else can compromise our security the way he did. I have no idea who any of the conjurnors are."

"A wise precaution."

They ate in silence, and Syllith considered her situation. So far, Amelia was the only one who knew about her presence in Anoria. She needed to keep it that way. The woman had restored her powers, which made her feel like she was probably trustworthy. But there was still the possibility that someone else had seen them. If Nyro had a spy here, they would probably take steps to interrogate the governor.

This left Syllith with few options. She didn't want to kill her. But if she invited her to accompany her to Stoutwall, and she refused, then what? She could abduct her. Tuck her into the void and take her along.

After dinner, Syllith told Amelia she needed to discuss something with her in private. They retired to her library, and Syllith cast the spells to prevent anyone else from hearing them. She explained her dilemma.

"I'll go with you to Stoutwall," Amelia said without hesitation. "Let's set out tonight. We can wait until the staff has departed, then slip out quietly. Put some distance behind us and camp somewhere in the forest. That way, if Nyro does have a spy here, they won't realize we've left. We can cross the barrier in the morning, and be long gone by the time anyone realizes we're missing."

Syllith breathed a sigh of relief. She'd decided she would kill the governor if necessary, but wasn't looking forward to it. "Perfect."

They returned to the dining room. Amelia let the staff know they'd be up late, and that it wasn't necessary for them to stay. The two of them shared another bottle of wine, and once the others had left for the night, Amelia put out the oil lamps.

Syllith made them invisible, and they slipped out through a rear entrance. Moving to the front of the house, she untied her horse, expanding her spell to include her. The two of them mounted, and Syllith took them out to the stables. Amelia took one of the university's horses, and they set out. Syllith expanded her invisibility spell again to include the governor.

After a couple of hours, they found a clearing in the woods and stopped for the night. Syllith made camp, and took the first watch while Amelia got some sleep inside the tent.

Syllith woke her sometime after midnight, taking her place in the bedroll. She still didn't feel certain about this woman, so she remained awake to see what she would do. If she were a spy, or in league with one, she would certainly contact someone by mirror once she thought Syllith was asleep. But the governor did no such thing. She sat quietly outside the tent, her wand at the ready, and roused Syllith at dawn.

They broke camp and continued on their way. When they reached the barrier, Amelia cast the spell to open a portal, closing it again once they'd passed through. Turning onto the south road that would take them to Stoutwall, Syllith decided she could trust this woman. For the first time, she felt like her goal was within reach.

CHAPTER TWENTY-TWO
CASTLE MONROE

mani led the way along the ramparts, hurrying to the castle's southeast tower. Mira and Jezebel followed, Allison bringing up the rear. The other sorcerers were still fighting, so Allison used her mirror to contact them and Amari, and let them know Jezebel had ordered the retreat. She told them to get clear of the castle and meet them at the rendezvous point.

Once inside the tower, Allison stuffed the mirror inside her suit, and retrieved one of her swords from the void, then asked Mira to extend her null. Allison hated being inside of it—she felt naked without her magic. But it would be best to make sure none of the elvish mages could destroy the castle around them as they made their way down to the escape tunnels.

They hurried down the spiral staircase, passing the main level, and emerging into the undercroft. Running across the main chamber, they reached the entrance to one of the secret tunnels. Imani pressed the stone that activated the mechanism, and a section of the stone wall receded, revealing a hidden chamber within. Once they'd all moved inside, Allison pushed the wall back into place, engulfing them in total darkness. Clinking noises let her know the latches had engaged.

Mira extinguished her null, and Jezebel called a flame to light their way. Imani led the way down another staircase, and once they had all started down, Allison lowered the wooden lever in the wall. This released a ten-foot-thick stone wall that fell from the ceiling, crashing into place and sealing off the entrance to the stairway. She hurried after the others.

At the bottom of the steps, they emerged into an enormous chamber. Allison lit the torches lining the walls with a thought, then pulled another lever, sending a second stone wall slamming into place at the bottom of the steps.

They'd built this chamber to provide a space where Jezebel and the children could survive for weeks should an enemy force occupy the entire area surrounding the city. The space was stocked with dried fruits and raw oats, an underground stream provided a fresh water supply, and the area included separate sleeping quarters.

But they wouldn't need this space today. Imani led the way into a tunnel that passed beneath the castle's eastern walls and beyond the moat. Once the others had entered the tunnel, Allison worked the lever to lower the final wall into place.

The tunnel was narrow and dank, and only tall enough for the Spanbrookers—Imani had to stay crouched to avoid hitting her head. They kept up their single-file march in silence, finally reaching the end of the passage two hours later. Allison used her mirror to contact Khaldun; he reported that the coast was clear. Imani climbed the ladder, throwing open the hatch in the ceiling.

They emerged into the big barn on the Barclay farm. Outside, they found Khaldun waiting for them as the remains of their army passed by on the road. He grabbed Mira, hugging her tight.

"Where do we stand?" Jezebel asked him.

"We took heavy losses, Your Highness," Khaldun told her. "Allure estimates that fifteen thousand troops survived out of the twenty-one thousand that entered the battle. General Amari is leading them to Castle Monroe, as you can see. The elves are not pursuing. They've taken the castle, and stationed several regiments outside the city's eastern walls. The rest have made camp in the fields around the castle."

"Why take Castle Barclay?" Jezebel asked. "They've destroyed all the others."

"Including Keepstone," Khaldun told her. "I heard from Battleaxe. The elvish mages there used fire to weaken the castle walls, then called earth to knock it down. Leto's forces are retreating as well, and they will meet us in Stoutwall."

"Nyro grew up in Spanbrook," said Allison. "Perhaps she sees it as some kind of symbolic victory. It's also the most heavily fortified castle in all of Dorshire, and she needs a base of operations somewhere if she's planning to take the entire continent."

"That's true," said Khaldun. "Looking at it that way, I can think of nowhere better."

Jezebel sighed. "The thought of that monster sleeping in our bed and eating in our hall…" She trailed off with a shiver.

"I know," Allison said, taking her hand.

"We'll regroup in Monroe," Jezebel said. "There's not much point flying everyone there, as it would take nearly as long as letting everyone walk. Once we've arrived, we can decide the best way to proceed. If the elves give chase, we'll need to establish a position there. Otherwise, we can continue our march, and start ferrying people to Stoutwall."

"In the meantime, Khaldun and I had better establish an air patrol around the city," Allison said. "We can keep an eye on the enemy and make sure there are no surprise attacks."

"Agreed," said Jezebel. "If their army were suddenly to disappear, then they'd probably be on their way here. We can have the university mages fly patrol around our people as we march. For now, Lady Mira, let's go without your null. We should have ample warning if a threat arises."

"Yes, Your Highness," said Mira.

Allison took the first patrol. Pulling her carpet out of the void, she sat in the center and shot into the sky, making herself invisible as she flew. Passing directly over the city, she could see the regiments stationed outside the wall, and the rest of the army camped in the fields. There was no sign of anyone preparing to pursue them.

She flew around Castle Barclay, her blood boiling as she watched the elves moving about on the ramparts and in the courtyard. As she moved northward, she spotted someone standing on the top of the old castle's tallest tower. Flying in closer, she could see it was a female elf, wearing no clothing. This had to be one of their mages. There were no other signs of life in the castle, making Allison suspect this elf was the only one here. For a moment, she seemed to look directly at Allison, and she noticed a scar running down the left side of her face. This didn't look like any of the other mages they'd encountered.

Allison shot out of range as the elf held out one hand, casting a spell to cancel invisibility. "Shit," she muttered—the mage *had* sensed her. She'd have to be more careful.

She circled the area slowly, curious to see what the elf was doing here. For a few minutes, she gazed out across the city, still as stone. But finally, she withdrew a carpet from the void, flying off the tower to a position out in front of the castle. Standing straight, she held her arms out to her sides, and Allison could feel the power emanating from her. The castle's walls glowed, and sections started to melt.

There was a sound like thunder, and the entire city began to shake. Allison heard screams coming from the surrounding buildings, and a few moments later, Castle Spanbrook collapsed. Allison gasped as an enormous dust cloud billowed across the city.

She couldn't believe the power this must have taken. Her understanding was that Xythor was the only member of the circle strong enough to generate an earthquake. He'd certainly been present in the battle that morning, and although there was no way to tell which elf-mage was which after they'd taken their new bodies, this elf didn't resemble any of them.

Allison realized with a start there was only one person this could be.

The mage flew away from the city, and Allison followed. She landed outside the army camp south of Castle Barclay, tucking her carpet into the void and striding toward one of the larger tents. The other six mages emerged, taking a knee before the newcomer. Their deference confirmed Allison's suspicion: this had to be Nyro.

After Nyro had spoken to them for a minute, the other mages rose. She took one of the males by the hand as the others returned to their tent. Pulling her carpet out of the void, she flew the two of them to Castle Barclay, landing on the balcony to the master suite—Allison and Jezebel's chambers.

A crowd had gathered in the courtyard, and they cheered when they saw the two mages. Nyro tucked her carpet into the void, and addressed her people. She spoke elvish, and Allison wished she could understand what she was saying. The speech lasted only a couple of minutes, then the audience cheered again.

Nyro and the other elf moved inside, and Allison lost sight of them. Flying in closer, she hovered by the balcony's edge, her heart pounding. Through the open doorway, she could see the two kissing. Nyro pushed the male onto the bed, climbed on top, and started making love to him.

Allison had seen enough. She took off, circling the city, but keeping her distance. Sure enough, Nyro had taken their castle for her own. The thought infuriated her, and she considered waiting until Nyro was alone, then trying to assassinate her.

That was crazy, though. Allison's power had grown tremendously over the years, but she knew she wasn't yet strong enough to face Nyro alone. She didn't know if she'd *ever* possess that kind of power. It was tempting to try it anyway—if she could catch her by surprise, she might have a shot. But she'd promised Jezebel she wouldn't take this kind of risk again. And thinking of Leda and Alanna strengthened her resolve. Her primary duty was to protect *them*, and she couldn't very well do that if she were dead.

Khaldun arrived at sunset to relieve her. They flew side-by-side while Allison updated him.

"You're sure it was Nyro?" he asked.

"Certain. No one else could have commanded that much power. And the other mages would have shown such deference only to her."

Khaldun whistled through his teeth. "All right. Thanks for the warning."

Allison flew back to their army. They were making camp in a field by the roadside, so she landed nearby and went to find Jezebel. She told her everything she'd seen.

"That bitch," Jezebel muttered, shaking with fury as she embraced her. "I don't know when or how, but mark my words, one day, we will take our home back from her."

"My home is wherever you are," Allison said, kissing her. "But I agree. We will find a way to retake Castle Barclay."

"Did you see any other carpets?"

"Only the one. But we have spares, so you can count on the elves having them, too."

Jezebel nodded. "If they had carpets, why did they come to Anoria by ship? They could have tucked their armies into the void and flown them here."

"That's too great a distance to travel by carpet, even for Nyro, and there's nothing but ocean between here and there."

"No islands they could use to stop and rest?" asked Jezebel.

"None that anyone's ever charted," said Allison. "And the fact that Nyro *didn't* bring her armies here that way proves that she doesn't know of any, either."

The two of them chose a company at random and sat down to eat dinner with them. Allison could have flown Jezebel ahead to Monroe, but she insisted on traveling with the troops. After their defeat in Spanbrook, she felt it would be best for morale if their leaders stayed with them.

Once they'd eaten, Allison and Jezebel retired to their tent. Two soldiers stood guard as they went inside. Jezebel lay quietly in Allison's arms for a minute.

"I considered trying to kill Nyro when I saw her in our chambers," Allison told her. Jezebel stared at her, hurt in her eyes as she opened her mouth to reply, but Allison pressed a finger to her lips. "But I thought better of it. I know I'm not strong enough, and I won't risk losing what we have. With or without a castle, you, Alanna, and Leda are the loves of my life."

"You mustn't risk yourself that way again," said Jezebel. "We promised each other we'd sacrifice anything else to defend Anoria and put Nyro down, *but not our family*. Not either one of us. After what you did with Gnasher, I still worry about the choices you make. You could have saved Khaldun without fighting him."

"I wouldn't have done it if I weren't confident of the outcome. I know my limits. But I couldn't squander that opportunity to get the measure of my own power against one of the circle. Now we know for sure I can stand against them if necessary. But Nyro… she's on a level all her own. I *would* have taken my chances if it weren't for you and the girls. But I gave you my word I wouldn't take that kind of risk, and that's why I backed off."

Jezebel kissed her, and the two of them made love. They did their best to stay quiet, but Allison was pretty sure the guards must have heard them. Jezebel drifted off after that, but Allison's mind wouldn't stop racing, and sleep eluded her.

Khaldun came to get her in the middle of the night. He reported no developments in Spanbrook. Allison took off on her carpet, and flew her patrol around the city. There was no light inside her former chambers, and even from the balcony, she could see no activity inside. The bed looked empty, but she supposed that made sense. Nyro was unlikely to sleep where she'd make such an easy target.

The rest of the night was uneventful, and Allison returned to their army at dawn. Their people broke camp and continued their march to Monroe. Allison walked with Jezebel and Mira in the center of their line. Allure, Semblant, and Sage took turns flying patrol, taking the lead or rear guard positions when they weren't in the air.

Khaldun caught up to them at midday, brimming with excitement. "I've heard from Chieftain Lavinia of the dragon lords," he told them. "She's requested that I bring Mira there immediately."

"Did she tell you why?" asked Mira. "Will she and her dragons finally join the fight?"

"She said only that they're having a problem with their dragons that only you can solve," he told her with a grin.

Mira frowned, shaking her head. "What help can I possibly provide with *their* dragons?"

"You need to find out," said Jezebel. "Whatever the reason for this invitation, it gives you another chance to persuade her to join us. The dragons could very well change the outcome in Stoutwall. Without them, I'm afraid the odds are stacked against us."

"Yes, Your Highness," said Mira. "I will do everything I can."

"We'll leave right away and contact you by mirror as soon as we know anything," said Khaldun. He went to fetch food, camping gear, and furs for the two of them. Once he'd returned, he pulled his carpet out of the void, lying it on the ground, and tucked the rest into oblivion.

"Fly safe, both of you," Jezebel said, hugging them each in turn. Allison embraced them, too, and then they took their seats on the carpet. Mira strapped herself in, and they took off.

Allison left a few minutes later to fly patrol around Spanbrook. Jezebel asked Allure to switch off with her that night, while Sage and Semblant maintained the air patrol over the army.

They continued their march the next day, finally reaching Castle Monroe a little after sunset. Alanna and Leda came running outside to meet them, and Allison felt tears welling up in her eyes as she hugged them. They told Allison and Jezebel all about their stay here as the four of them went inside.

"Emma has finally agreed to marry Arthur Asterly!" said Alanna.

"She decided since we've been forced to flee the castle, it hardly matters where they live anymore," Leda added.

"And with the whole world practically collapsing around us, she realized how short and precious life is, and she doesn't want to waste another minute of it," Alanna said.

"You've been spying on her again!" Jezebel said.

"Maybe…" Leda said. "But it was Alanna's idea!"

"You agreed to it!"

"Incorrigible," Allison muttered, failing to suppress a grin.

The provincial minister greeted them in the courtyard, and escorted them into the great hall for dinner. They sat down at the head table with the minister and his family, Carlo, and Yolanda. Susan and James from Rockport sat next to Alanna and Leda. James seemed more comfortable than he had been in Spanbrook, talking and laughing with the others. Allison suspected their girls had had something to do with this, Alanna in particular.

After dinner, the minister's steward showed Allison and Jezebel to their chambers. Alanna and Leda had an adjoining room, so they spent a few hours catching up with them before turning in for the night.

Allure came to wake Allison in the middle of the night; it was Allison's turn to fly patrol around Spanbrook. Allison put on her leather armor, but when she slipped out of their chambers, closing the door behind her, Allure said, "Your Highness, I'd like to discuss something with you before you go."

"Of course," she said. "But *please*, don't call me that. My name is Allison."

Allure nodded, flashing her a smile. "As you wish."

"Let's go downstairs, though. I don't want to wake Jezebel or the girls."

The two of them went to the great hall.

"It will take us at least thirteen days to get everyone to Stoutwall on foot," Allure began. "We can do what we did to transport Blacksand's troops to Spanbrook, but with fifteen thousand people this time, it wouldn't be much quicker than walking."

"It would stagger their arrival over those thirteen days, though," said Allison, "instead of having nobody there until the last day."

"Yes, but that's not good enough—the elves could have their entire army there in a day. But there may be a way we can transport *thousands* of people per trip instead of hundreds."

"How?" Allison said.

"By combining our power," said Allure. "After seeing Dredmort's wraiths hide an entire army with an invisibility spell fifteen years ago, we tried it at the university. Not with an army, but four of us working together managed to cover a field large enough for one with our spell. It would be completely different doing it with void magic, but I think I may be able to adapt the spells."

"We'll have to try it at some point," Allison said.

"How about now?" Allure said. "Semblant and Sage are nearby— they're taking care of the air patrol around the castle—and most of the troops are sound asleep. It'll only take a few minutes, and none of them will ever know."

Allison nodded. "Why not?"

Allure led her outside. They found Semblant and Sage, and headed out to the field where the army was camped. Allure told them what she was thinking.

"That's smart," Sage said. "I doubt we'll be able to do it with all fifteen thousand of them at once, though."

"So do I, but it's worth a shot," Allure said.

Allure let the soldiers on watch know what they were planning. Then the sorcerers spread out, taking positions at the four corners surrounding the army, keeping in touch with Allure by mirror. Once they were ready, Allure started her spell. It involved drawing power from the other three, so they had to open their channels of power and allow her to siphon it from them. Allison could feel her magic flowing into Allure, but sure enough, it wasn't enough for so many people.

Once they'd repositioned themselves around only two-thirds of the troops, Allure tried again. But this also proved to be too much. They tried again with five thousand, and this time it worked. Allison felt an enormous surge of power, and suddenly, their section of the camp vanished with an earsplitting pop. Allure gathered her strength for a moment, then reversed the spell to bring them back.

"I'm impressed," said Sage once they'd returned to the castle. "I'd never considered trying this with void magic."

"I tethered them to myself, but all four of us would have to fly together for this to work," she explained. "It would take the same amount of power to release them from the void."

"That would mean leaving the rest of the army unprotected from thaumaturgic attack," said Allison. "But you wouldn't need the *same* four sorcerers to release them, would you?"

"No, I wouldn't," she confirmed. "As long as Shatter's there when we arrive, he could help, allowing one of us to stay behind."

"If the three of us fly on the same carpet, we could get there much faster, too," said Sage. "It should be about a six-hour trip each way for one of us, but we could probably cut that in half with three of us calling air."

"With three trips, we'll be looking at about eighteen hours total," said Allure. "A lot better than ten days."

"I'll present this idea to Her Highness in the morning," said Allison, "but I'm sure she'll approve."

Allison flew back to Spanbrook to maintain the air patrol. She found the enemy army exactly where it had been before. Nothing had changed by morning, and Allison returned to the castle.

She woke Jezebel, and told her about their little experiment during the night. Jezebel approved the plan wholeheartedly. "We'll have to ask Imani and Amari to alert the troops. I'm sure the vast majority of them have never moved into the void before—that could be quite alarming without the proper notice."

"No doubt."

Allison contacted Prince Augustine's steward, explained what they were planning to do, and that they'd need Shatter's help once they arrived there each time. He assured her he would present the idea to the prince and convey his response as quickly as possible.

Jezebel heard from Khaldun a few minutes later. He reported that they'd reached their destination safely, but were still working on the chieftain. She told him about their plan to fly everyone to Stoutwall. Right after that, Augustine's steward contacted them to say that Shatter would be ready and waiting to assist.

Allison contacted Battleaxe next, and told her what they were planning. She could do the same thing with Cyclone, Mist, and Legion, then leave Legion behind while the other three flew to Stoutwall. Unsurprisingly, Battleaxe loved the idea, and told her she knew the spells Allure had used to combine their power.

After breakfast, Jezebel held a privy council meeting in the great hall. In addition to the two princesses, Imani and Amari were present, as well as Emma, the local minister, the delegates, Camilla and Gregor, Sage, Prince Carlo, and Princess Yolanda.

"Good morning, everyone," Jezebel said, gazing around at them. "As you all know by now, Nyro herself has taken Castle Barclay. Their army has shown no sign of pursuing us. Despite our offer to bring her here, Princess Jelena has insisted upon remaining in Rockport, and she reports no unusual activity there. The elves' occupying force remains, but no additional ships have arrived."

"Is that something we're expecting?" Camilla asked.

"It's nothing more than a hunch," said Jezebel. "I am surprised that the elves have not pursued us thus far, and we've tried to imagine a reason for it. They must know we're making for Stoutwall—us and Keepstone's people. It's our next logical course of action, and on top of that, we have reason to believe that they've replaced the carpets we destroyed."

"Meaning they probably have someone flying an air patrol to keep track of our movements," said Sage.

"Yes, and Keepstone's," said Jezebel. "They will face the armies of Blacksand, Spanbrook, Keepstone, and the Bastion in addition to Augustine's forces in Stoutwall. We have fifteen thousand troops who survived Spanbrook, plus the remaining five thousand from our southern provinces, for a total of twenty thousand. Together, Keepstone and the Bastion will bring another ten thousand. And Stoutwall has a standing army of twenty thousand, giving us a total of fifty thousand soldiers, a third of them completely fresh."

"Meanwhile, the elves will have roughly fourteen thousand from Spanbrook," said Allison, "and about half of that from Keepstone, for a total of twenty-one thousand."

"They must be waiting for additional troops to arrive," said Gregor. "That's the reason for the delay. We might have lost the battles, but we hurt them worse than they expected, and they're bringing in reinforcements."

"That's what we believe," said Allison. "And at this point, it would make the most sense for them to land in Northcoast. That would provide the best launching point for an army headed to Stoutwall."

"We have been in touch with Northcoast, and so far, no ships have arrived," said Emma. "So we should be able to beat them to Stoutwall."

"Right now, our forces outnumber theirs more than two to one," said Jezebel. "But we have no way of knowing how many troops they might be bringing. It could be a force large enough to match ours."

"We will also have eleven sorcerers fighting for us," said Allison. "The three of us from Spanbrook, the six from the university, plus

Legion and Shatter. Not to mention at least as many normal mages. We have not seen all of the Sacred Circle yet, but we have to expect that all twelve of them will participate in Stoutwall."

"This will give us roughly equal numbers," said Jezebel. "Every elf on the battlefield can wield basic magic, but all of our troops will be wearing enchanted armor, and we've already shown that neutralizes their advantage. The elvish mages are much more powerful than our sorcerers, but our people held their own in Spanbrook and Keepstone."

"The problem is that it's a thirteen days' march from here to Stoutwall, at least," said Prince Carlo. "And with this many people, I'm not sure transporting five hundred at a time will get us all there much faster than that. Meanwhile, the elves can be there in a day."

"We've found a solution for that," said Jezebel. "Working together, our sorcerers will be able to transport everyone—all fifteen thousand of us—in three trips. It will take about eighteen hours altogether."

Several people expressed surprise or disbelief at this news.

"I'm sorry, Your Highness," said Yolanda, "but we've lost every battle. Perhaps not as convincingly as we might have, but we've still lost our princedoms. They've destroyed our castles, and slaughtered twice as many of our people as we have theirs. And on top of that, we haven't encountered Nyro in battle yet. If this war is to be decided in Stoutwall, as you seem to be suggesting, then we can count on her making an appearance there. Even if we can get everyone there as quickly as you say, I'm not convinced it will be enough."

Allison desperately wanted to tell them about the dragons, but she'd discussed this with Jezebel, and they'd decided to keep that to themselves. For one thing, it was far from certain that they could count on the dragon lords' help, and they didn't want to get anyone's hopes up. But more than that, they wanted to make sure word of the dragons didn't make its way back to Nyro. The beasts were impervious to magic, and just four of them had nearly cost them their victory in Highgate fifteen years ago. Heaven knew what kind of damage an entire crash could inflict on an enemy.

"We are waiting to see if we're right about more ships arriving," said Jezebel. "If they do, Princess Salerna is prepared to send her army to Stoutwall, along with Azure. That would provide us with an additional twenty-five thousand troops. And if we lose in Stoutwall, we can still fall back to Highgate."

"It will not come to that," said Allison. "I am confident we will prevail in Stoutwall. We know what to expect now. These initial battles have exposed their strengths and weaknesses—as well as our own. And while I am not at liberty to reveal anything more, we may well have a few additional tricks up our sleeve this time." Jezebel squeezed her hand, giving her a warning glance. "That's all I'll say, I promise," she added, and the others chuckled.

"Today we will fly to Stoutwall," Jezebel said. "Our sorcerers will begin transporting our people using their carpets and void magic this morning. And in Stoutwall, we will claim victory!"

CHAPTER TWENTY-THREE
MAGNA

haldun and Mira flew all day, landing in the forest somewhere between the rivers Torsa and Mayne to camp the first night. The next day, they continued their flight, reaching the dragon lords' aeries just after nightfall. They'd encountered a few dragons in the mountains, and they escorted them to the castle. Landing in the courtyard, they found the young dragon rider, Kashi, waiting for them.

"Greetings, my friends," he said, "and thank you for coming. Please, come inside."

Khaldun tucked his carpet into the void, and they followed the man into the great hall. He invited them to sit at the head table, then lit a few torches in their sconces on the walls and hurried off.

"What's going on?" Mira whispered.

Khaldun only shrugged.

Kashi returned a minute later with a carafe of wine and three glasses, setting them on the table. "Chieftain Lavinia will be with you shortly," he said, before leaving again.

Khaldun and Mira sat quietly. A few minutes later, Lavinia arrived, sitting down at the head table and pouring them each a glass of wine. She sat back in her chair, taking a few sips, regarding them in silence.

Khaldun cleared his throat. "My lady, you said you were having a problem with your dragons?"

Lavinia finished her wine and poured herself more. "They refuse to take a rider. Every last one of them. For several days now. The rest of the clans have demanded that I bring Lady Mira here to see if she can resolve our little issue."

"I'm sorry, but I don't understand," said Mira. "Why would they want me here?"

Lavinia took a long drink of wine. "Magna has shown me a vision of you. It's exactly as my father described his dream."

"Do you think your father shared that with Magna?" Khaldun asked.

"No. I'm beginning to suspect my father never had that dream in the first place."

"You think he made it all up?" Mira asked, confused.

"I think *Magna* was the one who had the prophetic dream," said Lavinia. "And he shared it with my father, not the other way around. He's also shown me the vision of Anoria burning and all the princedoms falling."

"Your father's second prophetic dream?" Mira asked.

"*Magna's*, if I'm right," Lavinia said, taking a deep breath. "And the dragon has shown me more visions. The first depicted all of our people and dragons lying dead in our aeries." Lavinia shook her head. "Including me and Magna. The final one showed me Magna leading our entire crash into battle... with *you* on his back," she added, locking eyes with Mira.

"I've never heard of dragons having prophetic visions," Khaldun said with a frown.

Lavinia laughed, but it was short and harsh and expressed no joy. "No, neither have I. And I chose to ignore it at first. Dragons feel emotions at least as deeply as we do. Magna's upset about my father's passing—which is to be expected. The two were inseparable for his entire life. Losing him has unsettled him, I figured, nothing more.

"Only then, the other dragons started showing their riders the same visions. It seems when Magna failed to get through to me, he shared his dreams with the others. The riders came to me, asking what it all meant. I encouraged them to ignore the visions, too.

"But after that, the dragons started refusing to take a rider. Every last one of them. And whenever we try to ride them, they keep showing us their visions, over and over again. Finally, my people demanded that I bring you here."

"What can I do?" Mira asked.

Lavinia laughed again. "Try communicating with Magna, I suppose. See if you can talk some sense into him."

"My lady, the invasion of Anoria *has* begun, and it is going poorly," Mira told her. "The elves have destroyed Rockport, Blacksand, Oldport, and Keepstone, and captured Castle Barclay in Spanbrook. We are falling back to Stoutwall to join with Prince Augustine's forces and make what may prove to be our final stand."

"The end of the world is upon us," Khaldun muttered.

"Your dragons could help us turn this around," Mira said.

Lavinia finished her wine. "As I've told the others, it's nothing but sadness on Magna's part. He longs for the connection he shared with my father, but understands he's gone. Meeting you brought this on. He had some dream about a wayfarer woman years ago, and now he thinks that you could be his new rider. That he could find the same connection with you he shared with my father."

"That doesn't explain how he foresaw the downfall of Anoria," Khaldun said.

"I will *not* lead our dragons into war," Lavinia said, suddenly standing up. "Nor will I allow anyone else to do so. This is the only remaining crash on the entire continent. Leading them is my birthright, and I will *not* see them go extinct."

"They are impervious to magic," Mira said. "And our weapons cannot hurt them. I doubt a single one of them would die in battle. But they could change the outcome of this war."

Lavinia opened her mouth to reply, but stopped, shaking her head again. "Come with me."

She strode out of the hall, and Khaldun and Mira followed her. Outside the castle, visible in the moonlight, Mira spotted dozens of her people perched around the building's perimeter—apparently, they'd been listening in on their conversation.

Lavinia led them down the steep path to the basin, and the others followed, more emerging from their caverns along the way. By the time they reached the plateau overlooking the giant bowl in the rock, an entire crowd had gathered.

Khaldun waited with the others as Lavinia led Mira down the steps to the basin's floor. There were no dragons this time, and Mira wasn't sure why they'd come down here. Lavinia cupped her hands to her mouth and made a trilling sound that echoed off the mountainside. A moment later, a dragon's roar answered her call.

Magna flew into view, soaring once around the basin before landing only yards away. He took a few steps toward them, lowering his head. Lavinia patted him on the snout.

"Here she is, you old codger," she said.

Magna sniffed Mira, nudging her with his nose. Mira reached out and stroked him, still not comfortable being this close to the mighty beast. Magna made a low purring noise that she felt more than heard.

Suddenly, Mira saw a vision of her riding the dragon, the others flying in formation behind them. The power of it felt like a knife stabbing her in the head, and she cried out in pain.

"Mira!" Khaldun called out.

"I'm all right," she replied.

"He's communicating with you?" Lavinia asked.

"Yes," Mira said, and Lavinia sighed.

Focusing on the dragon, Mira formed an image in her mind of the battle in Spanbrook, the elves driving their forces away. After a moment, Magna fed the same vision back to her, this time with her on his back flying high above the battle, and him raining fire down on the elves.

"Magna wants to fight for us in this war," Mira told Lavinia. "He's shown me as much."

"Aye, he's shown me, too, but I will *not* allow it."

Magna reared, startling Mira, raised his head to the sky, and roared. Dozens of dragons answered his call. Mira spotted a few of them circling the basin high above. One of them swooped in, perching on the stone wall along the basin's perimeter. Another landed across from him, and within minutes, a dozen of the beasts formed a ring around them.

Magna roared again, and this time it sounded almost like a wolf's howl. One by one, the others joined him, raising their heads to the stars and adding their voices to his. The entire mountainside rang with their song.

Lavinia gazed around at them, shaking her head in disbelief. "They're declaring you their leader."

"That cannot be," said Mira. "I'm no dragon lord! I've never even ridden one. We came to ask for your help, not to replace you, you have my word!"

The dragons stopped their song as one. Magna lowered his head in front of Mira until his lower jaw was touching the ground. He dropped one wing and shoulder, too, and Lavinia said, "He wants you to ride him."

Mira's heart jumped into her throat. "I-I can't," she stammered. "What if I fall off?" She thought of the straps she used on Khaldun's carpet, and realized she had no idea how dragon riders managed to stay on their mounts. The one they'd seen in Highgate hadn't had any kind of saddle or anything.

"He won't let you fall, my lady," Lavinia assured her. "They have the balance of a cat, and adjust their flight to ensure their riders are safe."

"All right," Mira said, taking a steadying breath. She couldn't believe she was about to do this.

"Hold onto this spine here," Lavinia told her, "and place one foot right there in the wing joint." Mira did as she said, and the chieftain gave her a boost. "Now reach up to the next row of spines and haul yourself onto his back, right between the shoulder blades."

Mira clambered up, finding it easier than she thought it would be. She settled herself where Lavinia had indicated, finding a ridge running down his middle, with a little hollow in that area that felt almost like a saddle. Magna raised his head and roared, and Mira held onto his spines for dear life.

Magna took a few steps, beating his enormous wings, and the next thing she knew, Mira was soaring over the valley far below. She rose and fell with his wingbeats, feeling weightless for a moment each time he reached for his next stroke. They climbed higher and soared through the mountains. There was no shield spell to block the wind the way there was on a carpet, but the air flowed around the beast's neck in a way that kept it out of her face.

Mira heard other dragons roaring. Peering over one shoulder, she realized a dozen more riders had followed them. Magna caught an updraft, suspending them in place with his wings fully extended. The others flew around him, their riders whooping victoriously.

It would seem Mira had solved their problem, after all.

Magna went into a dive, his wings folded at his sides, and Mira screamed. She was completely weightless, and it felt like she might go tumbling right over his head. But Magna showed her a vision of her using her legs to hold herself in place. Mira squeezed her thighs against his back and screamed again, but didn't fall.

After a few minutes, Magna brought them back to the aeries, landing in the basin. Someone was there waiting for them, but it wasn't Lavinia—the chieftain was nowhere to be seen. Magna lowered his head and wing, and Mira climbed off, feeling a little unsteady on her feet when she landed. The other dragons dropped off their riders, and perched once again along the basin's rim, their wings extended.

"That was incredible," Kashi said, rushing over to her. "I've never heard of a dragon sire taking a new rider after a leader's death!"

"Where did Lavinia go?" Mira asked, afraid of the answer.

Kashi's expression grew serious. "This is a lot for her to take in. She grew up expecting Uriah to become chieftain one day."

"Her brother?"

Kashi nodded. "After his death, it took her a long time to accept the idea that she would become leader. Yet now, with her father's passing, it seems she may not, after all. And seeing Magna take another rider…" He shrugged, taking a deep breath. "She will come around. Give her some time."

"Listen, I truly do not intend to take Lavinia's place," said Mira. "I can't. I have a family and a home, and it's not here. We've got to find a way to win this war and reclaim what is ours. You and your dragons can help us do that, but then, that's it. I won't stay here."

"You must, Lady Mira," he said. "From this day forth, *you* are our chieftain. The dragons have made their wishes clear."

Kashi showed Khaldun and Mira up to the same cavern where they'd stayed last time. He started a fire while she set up their tent, then they sat together, eating from the provisions they'd brought.

"This situation is impossible," Mira said with a sigh. "I'm no dragon lord, and I can't be their chieftain."

Khaldun shrugged. "I don't see how you can avoid it. The dragons chose you."

"But we're going to return to Spanbrook when this is done. I can't stay here!"

"The dragons can come with us."

"That's not funny," she said, rolling her eyes.

"I'm serious. You and I could live in the estate in the northern hills. That area would be perfect for them."

Mira tried to imagine the chaos it would cause with Spanbrook's major landowners to have dragons flying about, feeding on their livestock.

"It's late now, but we'll have to check in with Jezebel in the morning and let her know what's going on here," he said.

"Don't tell her anything yet," said Mira. "Lavinia hasn't agreed to anything. I've got to find a way to convince Magna to help us without making me their leader. Once he accepts that, then we should be able to convince Lavinia. I'm sure she'll be glad to assist in exchange for remaining chieftain."

"I've got to let Jezebel know we made it safely, at least," said Khaldun.

"Yes, yes, of course. Tell her that their dragons have refused to take a rider, but don't say anything about them making *me* their leader. Just say that we're still trying to convince Lavinia to help us." Khaldun raised his eyebrows at her. "What? That's the truth!"

"Very well, my lady," he said.

"Oh, it's 'my lady,' is it?" she said, giving him a little push. "Fine, my lord." Khaldun chuckled. "It is interesting that Magna was the one who had the prophetic vision about me, not Vano."

"It does explain a lot," he said with a nod. "He was foreseeing his connection to you. So it was sympathetic magic echoing through time, not thaumaturgic."

"That makes sense," said Mira. "I'm invisible to thaumaturgic prophecy, so I didn't understand how Vano could have seen me that way."

"We should tell Sage about this when we see her again. I wouldn't be surprised if this is the first case of a dragon prophecy in recorded history."

The next morning, Khaldun and Mira ate breakfast with Lavinia and the other clan leaders in the great hall. The chieftain said nothing to them during the meal, but when they were done, invited Khaldun and Mira to stay behind.

Once the others had left, she said, "I have considered the situation, and I cannot allow you to take the mantle of leadership from me. My family has led the dragon lords for generations, and there is no reason to break that tradition now. Magna is going through some sort of crisis, and I'm sure he'll get over it in time."

"Chieftain Lavinia, let me assure you again that I have no intention of supplanting you," said Mira. "If I can convince Magna that I cannot join your people, and he accepts you as the leader, what would happen to him?"

"My dragon would become sire," said Lavinia. "And Magna would occupy a place of honor among our people and in his crash for the rest of his days."

"If I can get him to agree to that, would you consider coming to our aid?"

Lavinia took a deep breath. "It is clear my father intended to do so," she muttered. "Yes. My people and our dragons will help you save the continent. But only with me as their leader."

Mira left the castle with Khaldun, and they found Kashi waiting outside for them. "How did that go?" Mira described her exchange with Lavinia. He sighed.

"Can you teach me how to call Magna?" she asked.

"Yes, of course."

Kashi led them up to a plateau overlooking the castle. He brought his hands to his lips, making a sound similar to the one Lavinia had used to call Magna. Moments later, a dragon swooped into view. "See? Here's Darkwing. I've let her know I was only showing you how to make the call." The dragon flew away again. "Most of us can call only our own dragon. They respond to the sound of our voices. But I summoned her with my thoughts as well. As chieftain, Lavinia can call the entire crash if she wants. And because the dragons have chosen you as their leader, you possess that ability as well."

"Lavinia was still able to call Magna last night, though," Mira said.

"Yes. The dragons understand that she has not conceded the mantle of leadership to you yet. They will continue to answer her call as well as yours."

"I don't want to summon the entire crash," said Mira. "How do I call Magna by himself?"

"Make the call, and focus only on him," said Kashi. "Keep the call short, too. A longer one would be used to summon the entire crash."

Mira tried it, and sure enough, Magna flew into view a minute later. He showed her a vision of her riding him across the valley, but Mira didn't want to fly right now. She imagined him landing next to them on the plateau. Moments later, the dragon did just that. He lowered his head and sniffed her.

"I need to talk to you," Mira said out loud, stroking his snout. In her mind, she formed an image of Lavinia riding her dragon, leading the entire crash into battle in Stoutwall. The dragon squawked. He sent the same picture back to her, but with Mira riding him in the lead position.

Mira sighed. She tried several more times to convince him to accept *her* version of the image, but he refused. Next, she showed him an image of her with Khaldun, Jezebel, Allison, and their daughters at Castle Barclay. Magna modified that vision to include him and the rest of the dragons soaring high above Spanbrook.

"I don't seem to be getting anywhere," Mira said to Khaldun and Kashi. "He will accept only his version of coming events."

"Dragons are even more stubborn than chieftains," Kashi said with a knowing smile. "I have spoken to the other clan leaders, and they are unanimous in their support for you. But they will not take any action until Lavinia agrees to step down."

"Which means we're stuck here," said Khaldun. "Neither the chieftain nor the sire will budge."

"Give Lavinia a little more time," said Kashi. "Everyone else realizes the outcome here is inevitable. We must come to your aid to save ourselves. Lavinia doesn't want the dragons to die out, and deep inside, she must already realize there is only one path that leads to their salvation. Her mind will catch up with her heart eventually."

Mira heaved a sigh. "If that doesn't happen soon, there won't be much left to save."

CHAPTER TWENTY-FOUR
STOUTWALL

ezebel wanted to leave someone behind with a mirror in Spanbrook so they could keep an eye on the elvish army there. Camilla volunteered. She already had a mirror connected to Allison's and Jezebel's, so Allison flew her to the Barclay farm. The witch knew the area well enough to find vantage points where she could monitor the enemy while staying hidden. Allison embraced her and wished her luck, then returned to Monroe.

The combined armies of Spanbrook and Blacksand prepared to depart. General Amari separated them into three groups. Allure, Semblant, Sage, and Allison took their positions around the first group, and Allure cast her spell. Drawing power from the other three, she tucked the entire group into the void.

Allison was staying behind to guard the remaining troops, and Jezebel was going to take Alanna, Leda, Susan, and James with the others to Stoutwall. So Allison embraced Jezebel and the girls, and wished them a safe flight. Allure sat down in the middle of her carpet's front edge, while Semblant and Sage took the rear corners. The others took their seats among them, and they took off, shooting into the sky.

Allison conferred with Amari for a moment. He was going to have the rest of their people move out and start marching for Stoutwall to cut the travel time of the next carpet trip as much as possible. Pulling her own carpet out of the void, Allison sat down and launched into the air.

The others returned only a little over five hours later. Allure explained that in addition to the three sorcerers, Jezebel, Alanna, and Leda had called air, too, making the flight that much faster.

Allison landed to rest for a little while as they prepared the next group. Once the other sorcerers had taken off again, she returned to the sky, flying circles around their people on the ground. At one point, she flew over to Spanbrook and back, but the elvish forces there were maintaining their position.

The other sorcerers returned again, and the third group got ready to depart. Allison tucked her own carpet into the void, then boarded Allure's once everyone was ready. They shot into the sky, and with the four of them calling air, made it to Stoutwall only a few hours after nightfall.

Allison had never been here before, and found the view of the giant waterfall spilling into Rhun Lake in the light of the twin moons breathtaking.

Augustine had built his palace on the lake, right behind his castle. Allison spotted him on the patio at the rear of the palace, recognizing him only by his crown. Standing nearby was the largest sorcerer she'd ever seen. This had to be Shatter. Allure set them down in the meadow behind the palace, and Augustine came to meet them, Shatter right behind him.

"Princess Allison," he said, taking her hand and kissing the back of it. "It is such a pleasure to finally meet you."

"Likewise, Your Highness," she said. She wanted to berate him for addressing her that way, but held her tongue.

He introduced Shatter, but the sorcerer only nodded, without saying a word.

Much of the area surrounding the palace and castle was crowded with the people from their first two trips, as well as the troops from Keepstone. Allison wondered where Stoutwall's army was camped, and guessed they must be out beyond the castle.

"Give us a moment, and then you can release your passengers from the void," said Augustine.

"Of course," said Allison.

Shatter turned, walking away a few steps. He held his arms out to his sides, and his hands began to glow. Allison wasn't sure what he was doing, but suddenly, there was a popping sound, deafeningly loud, and the palace vanished. Shatter had tucked the entire building into the void. Allison had never seen anyone do this with a structure so large. Its absence left only bare earth. Combined with the meadow, there was now more than enough space for the rest of their people.

Drawing power from Allison, Semblant, and Sage, Allure cast the spell to release their people from the void. There was a tremendous popping sound, and five thousand people appeared, nearly filling the remaining space.

Augustine invited the sorcerers to join them in the castle, and headed off with Shatter. Allison followed them with the other three, but grasped Allure by the arm and held her back. "How was Shatter able to tuck that entire monstrosity of a palace into the void on his own?"

"He tethered it in place rather than to himself," said Allure. "That doesn't take nearly as much power. You could have done it, too."

Allison nodded. Though her power had grown by leaps and bounds over the years, she'd used void magic primarily to conceal her weapons. She hadn't spent much time trying to use it on larger objects.

Though she'd never been here, Allison was intimately familiar with the castle. Augustine had provided them its plans when they were designing Castle Barclay. They crossed the bridge over the moat, moving through the gates into the courtyard. Augustine escorted them into the keep.

Shatter left, but the prince led them into the great hall. Jezebel, Alanna, and Leda came running when they spotted Allison. She hugged them tight, tears of joy slipping down her cheeks.

Augustine had had his people prepare a hot meal for the new arrivals, so they sat down to eat. The prince didn't stay long, instead saying goodnight and retiring to his chambers.

"Where are Battleaxe and the others from Keepstone?" Allison asked Jezebel.

"You just missed them. They dropped off their second group and took off again maybe a half hour ago. Keepstone is half again as far from here as Spanbrook."

Once she'd eaten, Jezebel and the girls showed Allison up to their chambers. They had adjoining rooms, Alanna and Leda in one, and Allison and Jezebel in the other. Allison was exhausted, and fell asleep right away. But noises drifting in through the window awakened her in the morning. It looked like it was only a little after dawn. Gazing out the windows, she saw that the sorcerers from Keepstone had arrived with their final group.

Alanna and Leda were still sound asleep, so Jezebel and Allison got dressed quietly and headed downstairs to greet the newcomers. Battleaxe, Mist, Cyclone, and Legion were just entering the keep when they reached the entry hall. Allison and Jezebel welcomed them, then Battleaxe said, "Is dinner ready? I'm starving!"

"Dinner?" Allison said with a chuckle. "Breakfast perhaps."

"Dinner for us," Battleaxe retorted. "We're behind a few meals."

They moved into the great hall, where they found Prince Augustine, Prince Leto, Commandant Bishop, Prince Carlo, and Princess Yolanda seated at the head table with their respective mages. Legion went to join them, but Jezebel and Allison sat down at one of the other tables with the three university sorcerers. Allure and Sage walked in and joined them moments later.

"I know Semblant's not exactly a social being," said Battleaxe, "but where are Khaldun and Mira?"

Allison caught Jezebel's gaze, and she nodded. "They've gone to see the dragon lords, trying once again to enlist them in this fight."

"We sure could use a few dragons, knowing what's coming," Mist muttered.

"What was it like fighting alongside Legion?" Allison asked. "I've heard they're formidable."

"The stories are true," said Battleaxe. "I've never seen anything like it."

"Let's just say they're worth five or six sorcerers in battle," Cyclone said.

The staff served their meal, and brought ale for the three sorcerers who'd arrived from Keepstone.

"Alcohol with breakfast," Allison said with a shiver. "The thought alone makes me ill."

"Dinner, Your Highness," Battleaxe said with a grin, taking a swig. Allison bristled at the honorific, but forced herself to take a deep breath.

They ate in silence, then exchanged stories about the battles they'd fought so far.

"They didn't use pots of fire in Keepstone," Cyclone said. "Scream tried getting our soldiers to turn on each other, but Legion did a great job of canceling her spells. Of course, Battleaxe tried to kill me before I canceled Scream's magic."

"Did not," said Battleaxe. "I was only trying to scare you."

"It worked," Cyclone muttered.

"Typhoon was the most effective one we faced," said Mist. "Once she figured out that her twisters wouldn't affect the troops, she brought in hail the size of melons. Crushed people's skulls right through their helmets with that."

"What about Comet?" asked Jezebel.

"She didn't do anything special," said Cyclone. "I'm sure she would have if their goal had been to take the castle like it was in Spanbrook. It would have been easy for her to get inside."

"We didn't manage to kill a single one of those bastards," Battleaxe said with a frown. "Wasn't from a lack of trying, though."

"It wouldn't have mattered if you did," said Allure. "They just reanimate another body."

"You killed one?" Mist said.

"Semblant tore Xythor's head off," Allure told her. "And Allison cut Gnasher's throat in single combat."

"You're joking," said Battleaxe.

"No, it's true," said Allison. "I was pretty confident I could do it. Now we know for sure."

"Damn," Battleaxe said, gulping the rest of her ale. "I went against Typhoon and lost. Twice. Khaldun saved me the first time back in

Oldport, and this one got my ass out of there the second time outside of Keepstone," she said, bumping her shoulder against Cyclone. "I don't think I'll be trying it again."

"Jezebel and Mira killed all six of the Sacred Circle members in Spanbrook," Allure said. Allison felt pride swelling within her.

"How?" Mist said, her eyes wide.

"Our soldiers delivered the death blows," said Jezebel. "But Mira and I brought down their carpets when they were dropping those pots."

"Xythor disappeared when I banished him," said Allure, "but Gnasher reformed immediately and took another body. That shouldn't be possible, but it must mean Nyro's found a way to bind them to her."

"How?" said Cyclone. "She's a demon herself, now. Even from inside an elvish body, that shouldn't work, should it?"

"No," Allure agreed. "Elves can't perform necromancy or interact with demons. We don't understand how she's doing it."

After breakfast, the staff cleared the tables, and Augustine used the great hall for their council meeting. With all the visiting royals and their advisers, he explained there was no room in the council chambers. The prince started by inviting Jezebel and Leto to provide his people with accounts of the battles in their princedoms.

Shatter had sat to the prince's left, and Allison caught him staring at her several times, and not only when Jezebel was speaking. She wasn't sure why. He was an ugly man. But if the stories were true, he could crush an enemy's skull with one fist. She'd be happy to have him by her side in battle.

"Our lookouts in Keepstone and Spanbrook report that the elves are still there," Augustine said when they were done. "However, we now know that they can transport entire armies by carpet. They could arrive in Stoutwall with only a few hours' warning.

"We believe they are waiting for additional forces to arrive on the continent before attacking here. Their most likely landing point would be Northcoast, but our contact there has yet to see any ships.

"Highgate has a standing army of twenty-five thousand. Princess Salerna will keep five thousand there regardless, but twenty thousand could come to our aid. However, the princess is understandably reluctant to send them until we know for sure where any additional elvish forces are headed. Which we won't until they get where they're going. It's possible they could go to Highgate."

"And if they do come here, it would then take all of our sorcerers three hours to transport ten thousand troops from Highgate here, if they work in two teams, transporting five thousand each," said Jezebel. "Then they'd have to make a second trip for the rest."

"Battleaxe and I can teach two of the others the necessary spells," said Allure. "It would take some time, but we could start as soon as we're done here. Then if the four of us each transport five thousand, and travel together, we could get all twenty thousand here in one trip."

"That would also eliminate the need to remove more than four sorcerers from Stoutwall," said Battleaxe. "And if the four of us were to fly to Highgate ahead of time, and wait there to see where the elvish reinforcements go, we could get Salerna's people here in ninety minutes or so."

"That is certainly more feasible," said Augustine. "Let's plan on doing it your way. Do we know how our people are doing with their, ah, special mission?" he asked Jezebel.

"We do not have a final answer, Your Highness," she said. "But they believe they are making progress."

"Very well," Augustine said with a nod. "Once Lady Mira does arrive, we'll want her to refrain from using her null around the castle. Regrettably, the battle in Spanbrook has shown us how easily the enemy can get their forces inside our walls. I have asked Shatter to put a shield spell in place to protect against a similar attack here. That should keep shapeshifters out as well as carpets, projectiles, and thaumaturgic attacks."

"With all due respect, Your Highness," said Battleaxe, "we're going to want Shatter in the field. With the possible exception of Princess Allison, he is the most powerful sorcerer among us."

"I agree, my lady," said Augustine. "Shatter assures me our other mages will be able to keep the barrier in place once he has initiated it. With this many sorcerers participating in the battle, I believe we can spare them for this purpose."

"With deference to Lord Shatter, he has yet to face the Sacred Circle," said Allure. "I do not believe your mages will be strong enough to maintain the shield spell against their magic. We'll need to have a sorcerer assist them."

"I can do it," said Cyclone. "I'll need a position on the battlements to work my spells anyway. I can help keep the shield in place at the same time."

Augustine glanced at Shatter; he nodded. "We agree," the prince said. "That should conclude our business this morning. Let's make the necessary preparations, and then there will be nothing left to do but wait."

The meeting adjourned, and Allison headed outside with Allure, Battleaxe, and Semblant. Allure explained that Semblant insisted on going with her to Highgate, so he'd have to be the one to learn the new spells in addition to Allison. Once they'd crossed the moat, they headed out to Spanbrook's camp. Allure took care of Semblant while Battleaxe taught Allison what to do.

Allison had no trouble channeling Battleaxe's power into her void magic. It took Semblant a little longer to acquire the skill, but once he did, Allure let the army commanders know what they were planning so they could alert the troops. Once they'd had a chance to spread the word, Semblant proceeded to channel energy from the other sorcerers and tuck five thousand troops into the void. He released them, and then Allison took a turn. It proved to be much easier than she'd imagined.

She heard clapping behind her and turned to see Jezebel watching her progress with Alanna and Leda. "Where would I be without my admirers?" she said, embracing them.

"We'll miss you while you're gone," said Jezebel. "Please, be safe."

"I will," said Allison, "I promise. Let me know the moment you hear anything from Camilla, Keepstone, or Northcoast. Or from Khaldun and Mira, for that matter."

Allison took off with Allure, Battleaxe, and Semblant on Allure's carpet. With the four of them calling air, they made it to Highgate in no time. The army was camped on the plain below the city, and Azure was waiting for them on the keep roof. He escorted them inside, and took them to meet with Princess Salerna. They updated her on the plans in Stoutwall, and then Azure showed them to their chambers. Allison had a room with a view of the courtyard and the city beyond.

She spent most of the day in her chambers, checking in with Jezebel repeatedly. But the day wore on, and there had been no word from any of their lookouts. Just before sunset, there was a knock at her door. It was Battleaxe, inviting her to go find dinner somewhere in the city. Allison agreed; she was getting much too restless waiting in the castle.

Battleaxe told her she'd invited Allure and Semblant, too, but Semblant didn't want to leave the castle. He despised cities, and there was nowhere to go outside Highgate's walls, so he and Allure would be taking their meal in their chambers.

There was a tavern in the lower section of the city Battleaxe had come to favor during her last stay in Highgate, so they went there. The food was delicious, and they ended up staying quite late drinking.

Allison hadn't checked in with Jezebel once from the tavern, so she contacted her the moment she'd reached her chambers. But there was still no news.

In the middle of the night, something roused her from a deep sleep. Opening her eyes, she realized it was her mirror. She lit the oil lamp with a thought, and grabbed the mirror to find Jezebel staring back at her.

"We've heard from Northcoast finally," she said, fear in her eyes. "*Hundreds* of ships have been spotted. We don't know for sure yet, but there could be as many as fifty thousand additional elvish warriors. The first ships are docking now, so we should know more soon."

"It'll take the better part of a day to get that many ships unloaded," said Allison. "What about the armies in Spanbrook and Keepstone?"

"They're breaking camp. We expect they'll depart any time now."

Allison was too nervous to go back to sleep. She went up to the keep roof and sat down, gazing out at the city. *This is it*, she thought, taking a deep breath. Anoria's fate could be decided in the coming days.

She met Battleaxe, Allure, and Semblant in the great hall for breakfast, and gave them the news. After the meal, Jezebel contacted her again to report that the armies in Spanbrook and Keepstone had vanished. The ships in Northcoast continued to unload, and the elves had sent a regiment to destroy the palace. The prince had evacuated the moment the ships were spotted, so there were no casualties. But they had no army, only the prince's guard, and they had gone with the royal family to their country estate.

"Now we wait," said Allure.

Several more hours went by, and Jezebel reported that the armies from Spanbrook and Keepstone had arrived in Stoutwall, up the river from the castle. Their contact in Northcoast had stayed in the city in order to continue providing them with updates, but so far, their ships were still unloading.

Allison was preparing to venture out into the city for dinner with Battleaxe when she heard from Jezebel again. The ships in Northcoast had finally finished unloading. Their contact had given a final estimate of sixty thousand troops. They had disappeared, twenty thousand at a time.

"Mother of God," Battleaxe muttered. "If they all go to Stoutwall, we'll be facing eighty thousand elves."

They reached the tavern, but Allison had lost her appetite. She and Battleaxe drank heavily instead. There was no way she'd be able to sleep, and Battleaxe felt the same, so the two of them went up to the roof to keep an eye on the plain below.

A few hours later, Jezebel contacted Allison to report that twenty thousand additional elvish troops had shown up in Stoutwall. Twenty minutes later, she told her that a second group of twenty thousand had arrived.

Allison had to remind herself to breathe as they waited to see where the final group would appear. Yet after an hour, it hadn't turned up *anywhere*.

"I don't like this," said Battleaxe. "They could have gone somewhere else."

"To what end?" asked Allison.

"Who knows? Maybe they're going to station them somewhere to block our retreat."

"We can fly our forces here if it comes to that," said Allison.

Jezebel finally reported that a third group had appeared in Stoutwall, but they estimated that there were only ten thousand this time.

"Where did the rest go?" asked Battleaxe.

Before Allison could reply, she spotted something in the distance, out beyond Highgate's army. "I think they're here."

Allison pulled her carpet out of the void, unfurling it on the roof. The two of them sat down on it and took off. Allison made them invisible as they soared over the city. She took them in low over the plain, shooting over Highgate's camp. Sure enough, it was an elvish army that had appeared beyond them. She estimated there were about ten thousand of them.

After circling their camp a couple of times, they were unable to locate any of the Sacred Circle. They could be invisible, but Allison didn't sense any active spells, either.

They returned to the castle and went to wake Princess Salerna. Ten minutes later, they accompanied her to her conference room, where they met Azure, Allure, Semblant, and the rest of Salerna's advisers. Allison gave the others the news.

"Ten thousand troops and no one from the Sacred Circle?" said Azure. "I doubt they intend to attack here. They've brought only enough troops to ensure we don't send any to Stoutwall."

"I agree," said Salerna, taking a deep breath. "I'm afraid we won't be able to provide reinforcements, after all."

"We understand completely, Your Highness," said Allure. "Perhaps one of us should remain here, in case they do decide to attack. They may have some regular mages."

"I appreciate the offer, but that won't be necessary," the princess replied. "You're going to need everyone in Stoutwall. With none of the Sacred Circle present, Azure and the rest of our mages will have no trouble here."

Salerna adjourned the meeting. She bade them farewell, wishing them luck. Azure escorted them up to the roof. Allison boarded Allure's carpet with the other three, and they shot into the sky, heading back to Stoutwall.

CHAPTER TWENTY-FIVE
THE BATTLE OF SIX ARMIES

llison reached Stoutwall with Allure, Semblant, and Battleaxe as the sun cracked the eastern horizon. The combined armies of Spanbrook, Blacksand, Keepstone, the Bastion, and Stoutwall had already formed ranks in the fields to the north of the castle. Beyond them, the elvish armies stretched as far as the eye could see. They'd started forming their lines, but didn't seem to be in any hurry. Allison felt hollow inside, icy fingers of dread creeping up her abdomen.

Allure landed in the courtyard, and Allison got to her feet, running toward the keep to go find Jezebel. But she nearly crashed into her before she reached the doors. Jezebel grabbed her by the arms, gazing into her eyes for a moment, then kissed her.

"Where are the girls?" Allison asked.

"In our chambers," Jezebel told her. "I've got Emma watching them, and she knows she's not to leave her post for any reason. Should it become necessary, she's ready to evacuate them with Augustine's family."

"Perfect," Allison said, kissing her again. "I want to go see them before this starts."

The two of them ran inside, up to their third-floor chambers. Alanna and Leda were sitting by the window, staring out at what would soon be a battlefield. Allison hurried across the room, hugging them both.

"You will stay here, and do whatever Emma tells you to do, am I clear?"

"Yes, mother," said Alanna, rolling her eyes. "We've already promised."

"We did," Leda said, nodding earnestly. "Three times already."

"Augustine's steward even showed us the way to the escape tunnel, just in case we have to evacuate," Alanna said.

"It leads to a cave hidden inside a ridge in the forest," Leda said.

Allison chuckled. "Very good. See that you keep your promise." She hugged them once more, then departed with Jezebel.

They left the keep, crossed the courtyard, and made their way up the steps to the ramparts. Shatter was there with Cyclone and one of the court wizards. Allison spotted another wizard and two witches evenly spaced around the courtyard.

"We'll be putting the shield in place in a few minutes," Cyclone told them. "You can fly through it when you leave, but you won't be able to get back in after that."

"Thank you," Allison said with a nod. Gazing out at the battlefield, her heart turned to ice. There were *so many* elves arrayed against them. With their numbers and greater physical size, their own force of fifty thousand looked small by comparison.

Jezebel squeezed her hand. "Don't lose hope, my love. We may yet prevail."

Allison sighed. "I wish I could see how."

"I heard from Khaldun and Mira." Allison snapped her gaze to hers. Jezebel was smiling from ear to ear.

"What did they say?"

"They left the dragon lords' aeries a couple of hours ago," she said, "heading here. With an entire crash of dragons."

Allison screamed, bursting with joy. "That's exactly what I needed to hear," she said, kissing her. "As long as we can hold out until they arrive, we may have a chance. How many dragons are in the crash?"

"Mira said they have about a hundred in total," Jezebel said, and Allison's heart soared. "But don't get too excited—about twenty are hatchlings, and too young to fly this far, let alone fight. They need to leave some of the mothers behind to look after them. And another dozen or so are too old to make the trip. But almost four dozen are coming here."

Allison hugged her, tears of joy streaming down her cheeks.

Shatter and Cyclone put their shield spell into place. The other mages added their own power to it, and Cyclone took over from Shatter. His greater power made the spell stronger than it would have been without him, but Cyclone was strong enough to maintain it at that level in his absence.

Shatter pulled his carpet out of the void and took off. Allison had to laugh; he was so big, the carpet looked more like a towel.

"I'd better get out there," Allison said, kissing Jezebel once more. "I love you. Stay safe."

"You too," Jezebel said, squeezing her shoulder.

Allison stepped into an embrasure and dove off the wall as she removed her carpet from the void. Landing on it, she shot into the sky, making herself invisible. The sorcerers had linked their carpets, so she could see the others' beacons zipping around over the battlefield. Only minutes later, horns sounded from the elvish formations, and drumbeats joined them. Their forward lines advanced.

There was a roar, and a giant bear charged into the elvish lines before they'd even reached the human armies. Semblant smashed soldiers beneath his paws, grabbing others in his jaws and tossing them across the field. A ghoul formed at the other end of the lines, stomping through their midst, incinerating individual elves as it went. Allison summoned a ghoul of her own, and sent it charging right up the middle of their formations, striking from the rear.

Despite all the chaos, the elves pressed ahead, engaging the humans moments later. The sound of metal against metal filled the air, along with the combatants' grunts and battle cries.

Allison started throwing fire orbs, consuming a dozen elves at a time. Someone else joined her in the effort, and she knew it had to be either Sage or Shatter. Cyclone hurled fire tornadoes from her position on the ramparts, and they carved paths of destruction through the enemy lines.

A dense fog rolled onto the field, engulfing the forward formations. Lightning bolts started hitting random targets, cutting off the victims' screams as they died. Someone started incinerating individual elves as they escaped Mist, and Allison figured that was probably Battleaxe.

Additional regiments moved into position behind the elves' forward lines. One of the other sorcerers started hitting them with a spell Allison had never seen before. It seemed to liquify bone, causing its victims to turn into blobs of jelly covered in elvish skin. She had a feeling Shatter had to be behind this; it seemed like something he would do. Allison flew in closer, opening her senses to the magic. Once she had it, she tried the spell herself, and succeeded in turning a dozen elves into wobbling masses.

Behind her, dozens of elves screamed. Allison turned to see a pack of giant wolves charging through their lines. Where the hell had they come from? Though many elves had fled out of their way, Allison realized they were illusions.

Allison circled high above the battlefield. Despite their barrage of thaumaturgic attacks, the elves kept coming like a tidal wave. There were so many of them, the sorcerers had barely made a dent.

Swooping in lower, Allison summoned another ghoul, sending it through the elves already blinded by Mist's fog. But then the elvish mages took the field. Allison couldn't see them, but first, a stiff wind started blowing across the battlefield, knocking her carpet off course. She had to put all of her power into her air spells to avoid being blown away.

The wind pushed Mist over the lake, turned their ghouls to smoke, and canceled all the rest of their spells. A massive fire tornado formed, filling the entire airspace above the battle, without touching the ground. It was too much for Allison to overcome, and she found herself flying high above the lake, along with half of their other carpets.

A high-pitched sound filled the air, and Allison felt a powerful urge to hit her fellow sorcerers with fire orbs. Fighting the impulse, she realized this had to be Scream's work, and canceled the spell. It felt like a physical weight had been lifted from her body.

Allison flew back to the battlefield to find a giant wolf and an enormous, three-headed lion rampaging through the human armies. Howler and Metamorph. She summoned a ghoul and sent it after the wolf. It wrestled the beast to the ground, igniting its fur, but then the ghoul went up in smoke.

A giant octopus came out of nowhere, slamming into Metamorph and enclosing her in its tentacles. This was Semblant, for sure. He ripped off one forepaw, and then another, and the lion monster collapsed on its chest. But the lion quickly regrew its missing limbs, and attacked the octopus, each head ripping off a tentacle.

Suddenly, the entire area around the castle turned into a nightmarish hellscape, with volcanoes spewing lava toward the human formations. The sky turned black, and enormous fissures opened in the earth, jets of fire erupting through their openings. Allison could tell the landscape and half of the fissures were merely illusions—Artifice's work, no doubt. But the soldiers had no way to tell the difference, and many fell to their doom in the real fissures.

One of the enemy mages started hitting the shield spell protecting the castle, and it rang like a giant bell, over and over again. But Cyclone and the other mages managed to keep it in place.

Allison spotted one of their carpets streaking across the sky over the battlefield, a tail of fire trailing off of it. The rider's invisibility spell had collapsed, and she realized it was Shatter. His carpet hit the ground behind the enemy lines, but he'd called air to soften the impact. The elves saw him and charged. Shatter pulled a weapon out of the void—a long-handled sword with a wicked blade on one end and a spike on the other. As the first elves reached him, Shatter swept the blade around in a giant circle, cutting off their legs, then with his free hand, punching them in the head. His fist went right through their helmets, and bits of brain and gore splattered their shoulders as he crushed their skulls.

In no time, an entire regiment of elves had surrounded the giant sorcerer, but he'd gone into a battle trance, wielding his weapon so fast it was a blur. Some fell when he slashed off their head or legs, others when he impaled them in the chest with the spike. But none were able to touch him.

Allison swooped around the enemy forces, throwing fire orbs and casting the spell to melt bones. She left dozens of dead elves in her wake.

Across the battlefield, another one of their carpets went up in flames, and Allison realized it was Battleaxe. She crashed amidst the elvish troops, calling air to control her landing. Rolling once, she sprang to her feet, pulling her axes out of the void. The elves attacked her, but she cut through them like a small tornado. She had a severe disadvantage in height and reach, but this didn't seem to slow her down.

But then Allison spotted one of the enemy mages striding toward Battleaxe, her naked body gleaming in the light of Artifice's fires. The elves cleared a pathway for her, and she engaged Battleaxe with her giant sword. The sorcerer blocked her first swing with her weapons, but the force of the blow sent her flying. Landing flat on her back, she recovered quickly, charging toward her enemy. The mage swung her blade again; Battleaxe managed to parry it with one axe, embedding the other in her chest.

The mage raised her head to the sky and roared, ripping the weapon out of her torso and flinging it across the battlefield. She unleashed a frenzied assault, swinging and thrusting her sword, trying to deliver a death blow. Battleaxe managed to fend off her attack, but she was in trouble. After parrying one of her thrusts, the mage kicked her in the ribs, launching her through the air again. Crashing into the earth, she lost her second axe.

Allison raced in to assist. Leaping off her carpet, she tucked it into the void as she withdrew her swords. She landed right in front of Battleaxe as the mage lunged in for the kill, deflecting her swing with one blade and stabbing her in the ribs with the other.

The mage retreated, screaming in fury. Battleaxe got to her feet, withdrawing a second set of axes from the void. Allison charged, falling into her battle trance and pressing her attack, overwhelming the elvish mage with her ferocity. She disarmed the elf, lunging in to stab her in the heart. The mage's face registered surprise for a moment, then Allison freed her blade, spinning around and decapitating her with the other. The headless corpse hit the ground, and its demon rose from the earth, towering over her. Allison banished the monster, and it turned to smoke, the wind blowing its tatters across the battlefield.

"Damn," said Battleaxe. Allison had forgotten she was standing there. "Thanks for that."

"Don't thank me yet," Allison said as the surrounding elves formed a circle around them. She and Battleaxe stood back-to-back, and in moments, their enemies attacked. Allison fell back into her battle trance, cutting down elves with both swords as Battleaxe fought behind her.

Allison parried, slashed, and stabbed, her conscious mind taking no part in this fight. Instinct and reflexes, conditioned in hundreds of hours of training kicked in, and she meted out death to all comers. Minutes or hours might have passed, she had no way to know.

The next thing she knew, the attacks stopped. She was standing next to Battleaxe, covered in sweat and blood, gazing back at the trail of elvish bodies they'd left behind as the two drifted across the battlefield. They'd moved beyond its outer edge by the lake, and none of the others looked interested in engaging them.

At that moment, an earsplitting thunderclap shook the ground, and a bolt of lightning hit the shield spell protecting the castle. It had struck right where Cyclone was standing. The shield was intact, but a dozen more lightning bolts hit the same spot, and the spell gave way. One bolt after another hit Cyclone, and she fell from the ramparts.

"NO!" Battleaxe screamed. Pulling her spare carpet out of the void, she jumped onto it, Allison right next to her, and flew over the battle, landing by the castle wall. Cyclone had landed on the thin strip of land between the wall and the moat. Battleaxe knelt beside her, stroking her hair. "Where's Allure?" she asked, searching the area. "She might be able to save her."

Nothing but a blackened hole remained where Cyclone's heart should have been. "She's gone," Allison said, grasping Battleaxe's arm. "There's nothing Allure can do."

Battleaxe met her gaze for a moment, her expression defiant, but then she stared at Cyclone and nodded. "You're right. Dammit."

A roaring scream filled the air. Staring at the sky, Allison spotted an enormous winged serpent flying toward the castle. Pulling her carpet out of the void, she shot into the sky, calling fire and hitting the beast with multiple lightning bolts. It screamed, but kept flying. Allison hit the serpent with fire orbs next, as she soared above it. The spells didn't seem to affect it, but they obliterated the soldiers riding on its back.

Shatter streaked in from high above, landing on the ramparts and reforming the shield spell only moments before the serpent reached the castle. The monster shrieked in rage, and Allison hit it with more fire orbs, incinerating the remaining elves on its back.

Allison swooped around the battlefield. It was hard to tell precisely, but it looked like they'd lost almost half of their troops already. The elves kept advancing with more and more fresh regiments from what seemed like an endless supply. She'd lost track of time fighting alongside Battleaxe, but the sun was still fairly high in the sky. At this rate, they might not make it through the day.

A giant roar distracted her, and Allison spotted Semblant, in bear form, stomping through the lines of the latest elvish reinforcements. Another cry answered his call as the flying serpent swooped out of the sky, breathing fire on the sorcerer. He screamed as his fur went up in flames. Allison hit the beast with lightning, fire orbs, and the spell to melt bone, but none of these seemed to affect it.

The serpent circled around, hitting Semblant with another blast of fire. He screamed as the flames engulfed his bare flesh. Another carpet swooped in, its rider hitting the serpent with a barrage of fire tornadoes, trying to blow it off course. The monster screamed, but made a third pass, hitting Semblant with yet more fire.

This time, the sorcerer fell and did not move. Allison summoned a ghoul, and it caught the serpent in its hands, wrestling it to the ground. Another ghoul appeared, helping the first, and Allison realized the other rider had to be Allure. The two ghouls kept the serpent busy while Allison landed near Semblant, Allure right behind her. The sorcerer had transformed into his human shape, lying unconscious on the ground.

"*NO!*" Allure cried, kneeling beside him and stroking what remained of his face. The serpent's fire had melted much of his flesh, exposing the bone in some places. Allure held her hand against his chest, and it began to glow, but nothing happened. She sobbed, falling on top of her lover's corpse.

Allison's heart froze in her chest. She couldn't believe Semblant was gone.

The surrounding elves were closing in. Allison tucked her carpet into the void, withdrawing her swords. Returning to her battle trance, she attacked, unleashing her rage on the enemy soldiers. They retreated, trying to escape her fury, but she continued to advance, cutting them down, one after another, until her rage was spent.

Finally, she relented, taking a moment to catch her breath as the nearby elves fled. Swapping her weapons for her carpet, Allison took to the sky. She couldn't see Semblant or Allure anywhere—she must have removed his body from the battlefield. The sun was much lower in the sky now, and their forces had continued to dwindle. They'd lost two sorcerers now, with no way to destroy the enemy mages. And the elves showed no signs of letting up.

Despair threatened to swallow her. She refused to succumb, but no longer could she see a path to victory. Then she heard a roar, followed by dozens of others. Climbing higher, she searched for the source of the noise. That's when she spotted the dragons—dozens of them, emerging from the hills to the northeast. Pulling out her mirror, she reached out to the other sorcerers, warning them to fly clear of the battle.

Mira clung to Magna's back as Stoutwall came into view in the light of the westering sun. Catching sight of the battle, the dragon roared, and several of the others answered his call. Lavinia had kept up her stubborn refusal to help until the previous night. She'd woken up from a deep sleep to find Magna perched on a broken section of castle wall outside her window. The dragon had had another vision, this time of flying into battle with Mira on his back and half the crash behind him, going to defend a castle by a lake. The chieftain had tried to ignore him, but Magna wouldn't stop flooding her brain with the vision, and finally, she'd relented.

Lavinia had come to wake Khaldun and Mira, and within a couple of hours, they'd left the aeries with a dozen other riders, and four times as many dragons. Khaldun had flown alongside Magna on his carpet. They'd stopped once to rest and eat, then pressed ahead, finally reaching Stoutwall.

Khaldun went invisible, and Mira could see him swoop into the battle only by the light of his beacon spell. The scene below was horrifying. It had to be an illusion, but all was scorched earth, with rivers of lava flowing across the battlefield, pouring into giant fissures in the ground. At least a couple of those were real, though. The human army seemed small compared to the elvish forces. Mira knew the numbers hadn't been *this* uneven at the beginning, and despaired when she spotted their fallen soldiers, far outnumbering the living ones.

Magna dove, raining fire down on the elvish troops. The other dragons followed, breathing jets of flame on the enemy. The elves' screams drifted up to her, and she spotted several running toward the lake like living torches.

The elvish mages unleashed their magic, hitting the dragons with all variety of spells, but the beasts' hides protected them. The mages tried hitting the riders, but their mounts turned and twisted in the air to protect them. They started canceling the air giving the dragons their lift, and several tumbled from the sky, roaring in fury.

One elf got lucky, hitting a rider with lightning, and he fell from his dragon. The animal roared, breathing fire at the source of the spell. It didn't affect the mage, but exposed the sphere of his shield spell. Mira expanded her null, revealing all of the elf-mages on their carpets and undoing their magic—their shield spells as well as the ones keeping them airborne. She closed her channels of power again as they fell from the sky, and the dragons incinerated several of them with their fire. Their demons rose from the corpses before disappearing.

The dragons continued unleashing their fury, inflicting levels of carnage Anoria had not seen in centuries. Elves perished by the hundreds, and soon, their numbers diminished almost as much as the humans'.

But then, as the sun reached the western horizon, there was an ear-splitting thunderclap. A blinding light pierced the sky, emanating from across the lake, by the top of the waterfall. Shielding her eyes with one hand and trying to get a closer look, Mira realized the light was coming from a portal that had opened in thin air, Castle Barclay visible beyond it.

Two elves stepped through the portal, one male and one female, both naked, and the portal vanished behind them. The female held out both arms, her hands glowing. The demons of the fallen elf mages gathered around her, and within the next several moments, the remaining mages landed near her on their carpets. She pulled a giant sword out of the void, and as the remaining mages approached her, she decapitated them, releasing their demons, leaving only the one who'd arrived with her in a living body.

The surviving female had to be Nyro. Mira suspected her companion had to be Blaze, Reaper, or Plague, the only members of the Sacred Circle who'd yet to make an appearance. Lined up on either side of them were the remaining circle members in demon form, nine in total.

Nyro pointed one arm toward the battle, and the demons swarmed, heading directly toward Mira. The demons couldn't affect her, but she had no idea what they could do to dragons. She opened her channels of power, expanding her null. But it was too late.

Each of the demons had slammed into a dragon, disappearing inside its body. The affected beasts' eyes began to glow red, and they went berserk, roaring and flailing around in the air. Mira didn't think possessing the dragons had gone the way the demons might have hoped.

Mira's null prevented them from breathing fire, but they used their jaws, biting down on the necks of their brothers and sisters. But then one of them attacked another *possessed* dragon. Mira didn't understand why they would do that. Perhaps possessing them enraged the beasts without giving the demons the same level of control they'd have over a human.

Magna bellowed in rage as several dragons died, their corpses falling to the earth. Mira wept, screaming in desperate fury, trying to figure out how to repel the demons. As long as they were inside her null, they couldn't leave the dragons they'd possessed, and none of the sorcerers could banish them. So she led Magna toward the castle, showing him an image of the rest of the crash joining them. Her null had no effect on the sympathetic magic required to communicate with the dragons.

Magna relayed her vision to the others, and he landed on the castle's tallest tower, roaring at the sky. The other dragons landed on the ramparts, and Mira closed her channels of power, extinguishing her null.

The possessed dragons circled above, and one of them dove, heading straight for her. But at that moment something happened that Mira could not explain. The demons rose from the beasts as one, floating above them and not moving. The dragons they'd possessed landed on the ramparts. One or more of the human mages must have banished the demons, because they all turned to smoke, blowing away on the wind.

Mira opened her channels of power again, expanding her null to protect the dragons and the castle. At that moment, there was another ear-splitting thunderclap, and a blinding light emanated from the top of the waterfall again, as if the sun had landed on the earth. Shielding her eyes, Mira saw that another portal had formed, but this time, she didn't recognize the area that lay beyond. It was a castle on an island. Nyro mounted a carpet, flying through the portal and leaving her male companion behind. The portal closed behind her.

Silence filled the battlefield as the sun finally set. The elves retreated, moving away from the castle. A commotion below caught Mira's attention, and she spotted a group of soldiers escorting two women toward the castle gate. Someone inside lowered the drawbridge and opened the gate, and the guards led the women inside. The drawbridge rose again behind them.

Mira climbed off of Magna, and hurried across the ramparts. She ran into Khaldun, who'd landed before she expanded her null, and the two of them ran down the steps to the courtyard. They reached the gates in time to see the two women moving inside. The gates clanged shut behind them. Mira could tell by her golden skin that one of the women was a sorcerer, and as they drew closer, she recognized her.

"*Syllith!*" said Khaldun.

CHAPTER TWENTY-SIX
SYLLITH'S RETURN

y lady," Augustine said to Syllith, his expression one of surprise. "We never thought we'd see you again. What are you doing here?"

Mira spotted her eyes. "You're a necromancer," she said before Syllith could reply.

"Yes," she said. "And I have a way to destroy Nyro's Sacred Circle."

"Wait," said Augustine, raising one hand as if to say "Stop." "Let us meet in the hall. There are others who must hear your story."

Mira and Khaldun followed Syllith and her companion and the prince into the keep. Over the next several minutes, Jezebel, Allison, Prince Leto and Legion, Commandant Bishop, Prince Carlo and Princess Yolanda, Allure, Sage, Battleaxe, Mist, Shatter, and the rest of Augustine's advisers all gathered in the great hall.

Once everyone was seated, Syllith introduced her companion as Governor Amelia, and told them her story, from the time Nyro first possessed her and took her through the portal to the elven continent, until her recent departure from the university. The others listened with rapt attention. Mira had to fight back tears when she described what had befallen Gemma.

"We reached Castle Stoutwall in time to see the dragons arrive," the necromancer said. "And we watched in horror as the demons possessed some of them, turning them against the others. As long as they were inside Lady Mira's null, there was nothing I could do. But as soon as she closed her channels of power, I was able to use my connection to the demons to force them out of the dragons.

They would have overpowered me immediately, but then one of you banished them."

"Two of us, actually," said Allure. "Allison and I."

Syllith nodded. At that moment, the doors flew open, and one of Augustine's guards rushed into the room.

"My apologies, Your Highness," he said with a bow, "but that portal by the waterfall opened again. The elf lady returned, another naked male with her."

"Thank you," Augustine said, and the guard left, closing the doors behind him.

"Nyro knows I'm the only one who could control her demons like that," said Syllith. "She must have returned to her island in Drengrvollr to find out how I escaped. The elf she brought here has to be Reaper."

"Who was the elf she brought with her the first time?" Allison asked. "Blaze or Plague?"

"It must be Plague," said Syllith. "Blaze never returned. I asked Nyro about her, but the question enraged her, and she told me never to speak of that one again."

"You said you have a way to destroy the Sacred Circle?" Augustine said.

"Yes," Syllith said, taking a deep breath. "Nyro bound me to her as a sorcerer. She forced me to bind her demons, meaning my soul has merged with them. If one of the sorcerers here can reassign my bond to another conjurnor, that person can invoke my true name. I have fasted for seven days, so there's no reason to delay."

"You would die," said Augustine.

"Yes. And my soul would be destroyed—taking the demons with me."

"Are we sure about that?" Yolanda asked, her tone skeptical.

"Yes," said Allure. "When you invoke a sorcerer's true name, it erases them from existence, soul and all, ensuring they cannot return as a demon. When you do it to a necromancer, it also eliminates their demons. As Syllith explained, the rite a sorcerer uses to become a necromancer merges her soul with the demon's."

"We can't ask you to do this," Khaldun said, tears in his eyes. Though they hadn't had a chance to discuss it yet, Mira knew how much her return meant to him. She'd been his mentor, and they'd been through a lot together prior to her disappearance.

"It's the only way," said Syllith. "Only invoking a necromancer's true name can destroy her demons. If you banish them, they'll just keep coming back."

"Syllith's right," said Allison. "We've killed some of the Sacred Circle, but they've returned every time, sometimes immediately."

"When the demon in Spanbrook was haunting Allison, you gave us a spike we used to trap it," Khaldun said. "Why can't we do that now?"

Syllith shook her head. "That method works only in controlled situations against lesser demons. The ones who are crazed with desire for the pleasures of the flesh, and lose themselves to it. Like Nyro, the members of the Sacred Circle all took steps in life to retain their faculties after death. On top of which, they've already had time to sate their carnal desires in their elven bodies. Luring them into a sorcerer's body that way will be difficult if not impossible.

"And on top of that, there are far too many of you here. When I employed that method with Enigma, he was the only sorcerer for hundreds of miles, so getting our target to possess him was easy. And in Allison's case, the demon was fixated on her, and you were the only sorcerer available.

"In this situation, we would be extremely lucky to destroy a single demon that way, never mind eleven of them."

"Shit," Khaldun muttered.

"So, Nyro realized Syllith was here when she forced the demons to leave the dragons," said Jezebel. "And she won't invoke Syllith's true name because she's hoping to save her demons."

"Meaning she's going to be looking for a way to get inside the castle to retake Syllith," said Allison. "We must act quickly."

"We cannot do the rite of binding here," said Allure. "Mira would have to drop her null, and the moment she does, the demons will attack Syllith."

"Not only that, Nyro could use her pyramid to open a portal into the castle," said Allison.

"I've had some time to think about this," said Syllith. "One of you will have to tuck me into the void and take me somewhere else to perform the rite."

"We'd have to implement the void magic the moment Mira extinguishes her null," said Allison. "The timing is critical—the demons are sure to surround us the instant the null comes down. But demons can't enter the void, so Syllith should be safe at that point."

"Yes, but the trouble is that no matter where we take her, Syllith's bond to the demons will enable them to locate her," said Allure. "Moving through the spectral plane, they can arrive there instantly."

"Can you perform the rite of binding inside the void?" asked Mira.

"No," said Sage. "The moment Syllith's soul separates from her body, it would be ejected from the void. We'd lose her, without ever getting the opportunity to invoke her true name."

"Nyro would lose control of the Sacred Circle at that point," said Allure, "but she would only have to take another mage, trigger their transformation into a sorcerer, and force them to bind her demons again. As she did with Syllith."

"There is but one place we could perform the rite," said Sage.

Allure met her gaze. "Yes. We'll need to take Syllith to the university."

"Why the university?" said Khaldun, visibly confused. "The barrier surrounding it doesn't keep demons out."

"No, but the seven-sided tower does," said Sage. "We can perform the rite there, without any interference from the demons."

"Are we finally going to learn about the entity who lives in the tower?" Allison said.

"No," said Allure. "Soon, I suspect. But not today."

"I'm sorry, what entity?" said Augustine. "And what tower? I'm afraid you've lost me."

"Apologies, Your Highness," said Sage. "There is an ancient tower on the university grounds, and while its original purpose remains a closely guarded secret, powerful enchantments protect it from denizens of the spectral plane, including demons. Once inside the tower, we'll be able to reassign Syllith's bond, and her new conjurnor can invoke her true name."

"Thereby destroying the entire Sacred Circle?" said Augustine.

"Yes," Sage confirmed.

"Even with Syllith tucked into the void, the demons are sure to pursue you," said Allison. "They may not be able to reach her, but they can possess whoever is flying the carpet."

"I don't think so," said Allure. "Nyro's demons know they don't have to chase us, because normally, they could simply wait until Syllith emerges from the void, and then appear instantly at her location by moving through the spectral plane. However, neither Nyro nor the Circle knows anything about the tower. Its builder took steps to ensure they could never find it. And when Syllith emerges from the void *inside the tower*, it will prevent them from locating her."

"They won't know where she's gone once she's moved into the void," said Sage. "To them, it will be as if she vanished from existence. They'll still feel their bond to her, so they'll know she lives. But when our carpet takes off, they won't be able to tell if she's tethered to one of us or someone here in the castle."

"It's possible they'll believe the carpet to be nothing but a ruse," said Augustine.

"Yes, exactly," said Allure. "That being said, Allison and I should both fly on the carpet, just in case. If the demons do attack, we should be able to keep banishing them until we reach our destination."

"And I should remain here," said Mira. "The demons are sure to infiltrate the castle to search for Syllith as soon as you leave."

"Or Nyro herself," said Allison. "Your null can keep the demons out and prevent Nyro from using her portal to get inside."

"Very well," said Augustine. "Lady Syllith, I will approve this plan so long as you declare to us that you undertake it of your own free will. I will not force you to do this, nor will I allow anyone else to do so."

"Yes, Your Highness," said Syllith. "I do appreciate having control of my own fate. And this is my decision. I will execute this plan of my own free will."

Suddenly, Mira felt a powerful spell slam into her null. It was unlike anything she'd felt before, as if someone were trying to open a rift inside of it. "Your Highness, I believe Nyro just tried to penetrate the castle using a portal."

"Understood," the prince said, getting to his feet. "We'd better get to work." The others rose as well, but then Augustine added, "Lady Syllith, on behalf of the people of Stoutwall—indeed, the people of Anoria—we thank you for your sacrifice. Because of you, we may yet prevail against this foe. We will ensure that you are forever remembered as a hero."

"Thank you, Y-your Highness," Syllith said, her words catching in her throat, and her eyes welling up with tears. "As always, it is an honor to serve."

Mira hurried out of the keep with everyone else. She gathered in the courtyard with Allure, Sage, Allison, and Syllith. The dragons stood sentinel, still occupying their perches along the battlements.

"I'll tuck you into the void the moment Mira's null comes down," Sage said to Syllith. "Allure will remove her carpet from the void at the same time. Lady Mira, the instant we're done, you should reestablish your null."

"How will you fly?" Mira said.

"We'll leave the castle before we take off," said Sage. "Is everyone ready?"

"Yes," said Mira. Allure and Syllith nodded.

"Now, my lady," Sage said to Mira.

Mira closed her channels of power, nervous that Nyro would take advantage of this opportunity to infiltrate the castle. But Sage tucked Syllith into the void, Allure withdrew her carpet, and Mira opened her channels of power again, her null erupting into existence, and nothing else happened. Mira breathed a sigh of relief.

"Governor Allure, I'd like to go with you to the university," Jezebel said.

"Of course, Your Highness," she said. "We'll need a non-sorcerer to become Syllith's new conjurnor."

"Jezebel, *no*," said Allison. "Alanna and Leda are here. Stay here and look after them. I'll return soon, I promise."

"Emma is looking after them," Jezebel replied. "I can't bear to remain behind while you fly off into danger again. Please, let me accompany you."

Allison shook her head. "Danger could find you here, too. The girls need you. *Please.*"

Jezebel nodded, tears streaming down her cheeks as she embraced Allison. They kissed, and then Allison said, "We should get underway."

"We will need someone to serve as Syllith's new conjurnor," Allure said. "If Princess Jezebel stays behind, she won't be able to invoke Syllith's true name from inside the null."

"We can send Gregor," said Jezebel. "The last I knew, he was up on the top of the northwest tower."

Augustine sent a messenger, and he returned with Gregor a minute later. Jezebel explained what was happening, and he nodded gravely.

Augustine ordered the gates opened and the drawbridge lowered. Allison, Allure, Sage, and Gregor headed out, and they closed the entrance again behind them. Mira hurried up to the battlements with Jezebel and Khaldun. They watched the four mages hurry across the grounds, boarding Allure's carpet once they'd left Mira's null, and shooting into the sky.

"I hope this works," said Mira.

"It saddens me that Syllith has to sacrifice herself like this," Khaldun said with a sigh. "When I saw her walk into the courtyard, I thought she was back. For good, I mean."

Mira hugged him, rubbing his back. "I'm so sorry."

Down in the courtyard, a guard ran out of the keep. "Your Highness! The elves have infiltrated the castle! They must have come in through one of the escape tunnels!"

"Oh, no," Jezebel muttered as she ran down the steps, Khaldun and Mira right behind her. Alanna and Leda were inside the keep.

CHAPTER TWENTY-SEVEN
AVENGED

ezebel, Khaldun, and Mira reached the courtyard as an elvish warrior burst out of the keep right behind the guard, stabbing him in the back with his sword. The guard looked down in surprise at the blade protruding from his chest. The elf withdrew his sword, and the guard dropped.

Three more elves emerged from the keep, and the four of them stood aside, one of them holding the door open. A naked female elf walked out. Mira noted a scar running down one side of her face.

"Where is she?" the elf called out, her voice booming. Mira knew this must be Nyro.

"You're looking for Lady Syllith?" Augustine replied from across the courtyard. "I'm afraid she's not here. Now, take your people and leave my castle immediately!"

"You're telling the truth," Nyro said, staring at Augustine. "A hidden building at the university? My demons will find it."

Mira had to stifle a gasp. How had Nyro figured that out? She must have used sympathetic magic to read Augustine's thoughts.

Nyro swept the area with her gaze, finally locking eyes with Mira. "You're the null," she said with a smile.

Mira gasped, backing up a step as her heart pounded in her chest. Khaldun stepped in front of her.

"Come with me, and you shall become an honored member of my Sacred Circle," Nyro said. "We could accomplish much together."

"His Highness gave you an order," a voice said, deeper than any other Mira had ever heard. Mira realized it was Shatter, as he strode toward Nyro in his full plate, grasping his peculiar weapon in one hand.

Nyro turned her attention to the sorcerer. Taking a sword from one of the elves, she strode forward. "You're the one they call Shatter. I've been looking forward to this."

Shatter raised his weapon. Nyro charged, unleashing a barrage of thrusts and slices, her sword moving too fast for Mira's eyes to track. She heard the clash of steel on steel as Shatter blocked and evaded every shot. Nyro kept up her onslaught, driving the sorcerer back.

Finally, Shatter went on offense, driving the spike of his weapon toward Nyro's chest. She evaded the strike at the last moment, stabbing him in the armpit through the tiny gap in his armor. Shatter hardly seemed to notice; Mira suspected he had to be wearing chain mail beneath his plate armor. He continued the attack, alternately slashing with his blade, and stabbing with the spike.

The sorcerer lunged in with an overhead blow, shattering Nyro's blade when she tried to block it. Pressing his advantage, he followed up with several more blows.

Nyro retreated, evading his every shot. He backed her all the way to the keep wall, moving in with a killing blow with the spike of his weapon. Nyro sidestepped, and Shatter's weapon struck the wall, blowing a hole in the stone and spraying him with debris.

One of the other elves tossed Nyro his sword. She caught it as she kicked out the back of Shatter's leg. He dropped, his knee smashing into the ground. Nyro moved in before he could regain his feet, thrusting her blade through his helmet's eye slit.

Shatter cried out, rolling away from the attack and landing flat on his back. Nyro moved in, kicking him in the head and knocking his helmet off. She was blocking Mira's view of the sorcerer, so she couldn't see what kind of damage she'd done to his head.

"Yield," Nyro said, pointing the tip of her sword at his face, "and I will allow you to join me."

"Lady Mira," a low male voice said in her ear, startling her. She turned to find Legion standing there—she hadn't noticed where they'd come from. "You must extinguish your null."

"What? No—that's *Nyro*," she hissed.

"She's going to kill Shatter if we don't act. We can stop her." Mira stared at them in disbelief a moment longer, and they added, *"Please."*

Mira complied. She closed her channels of power, shutting down her null—but remained ready to expand it again in an instant.

"Nyro!" Legion called out in their low voice, striding across the courtyard.

She turned as a simulacrum of the sorcerer appeared, approaching from the opposite direction. Nyro faced the newcomer, and a third appeared, between the other two. After a couple of seconds, there were six instances of Legion marching toward her.

The Legion that had been standing next to Mira threw out one hand, calling fire and hitting Nyro with bolts of lightning. The others attacked at the same time, each using a different spell—a small tornado, a fire orb, the spell to melt bone, a sheet of energy, and an earth spell.

Nyro canceled them all. Forming a shield spell around herself, she hurled the same spells back at each of the Legions. The spell to melt bones met its target, and that sorcerer collapsed, no more than a blob. The others managed to cancel the spells or form shields of their own.

Shatter dragged himself away as Nyro unleashed a barrage of magic more ferocious than anything Mira had ever seen. One spell after another hit each of the Legions in rapid succession. Mira opened her channels of power, and her null exploded into being.

It was too late for most of the Legions. One had been incinerated from within, lightning had struck down two others, and a fourth had exploded, spraying blood and gore all over the ground. Nyro had hit the last one with an unknown spell, and they'd fallen to their knees, crying in pain with the voice of an old woman.

Nyro threw her sword, impaling the final Legion in the face. The weapon embedded itself right up to the hilt, the blade protruding from the back of their head. The dead body fell over.

Augustine ordered his soldiers to move. There were several dozen of them in the courtyard, and they advanced, forming a semicircle around Nyro. She swept them with her gaze, but at that moment, another elf emerged from the keep, saying something to her in elvish. Nyro shot Mira one glance, then departed with her people, vanishing inside the castle.

The soldiers hurried after her, running inside. Mira, Khaldun, and Jezebel followed them in, and Jezebel led the way up to her chambers. They reached the third-floor corridor to find Alanna and Leda running toward them.

"They've taken Emma!" Alanna cried, tears streaming down her cheeks. Leda sobbed as Alanna held out a staff.

"*What?*" Jezebel said, taking it from her. "This is Emma's. Who took her and where did they go?"

"The elves," Leda said between sobs. "They ran down the stairs."

"We tried to stop them—all three of us," said Alanna, "but our magic wouldn't work in the null."

"Shit," Jezebel muttered, dropping the staff and hurrying back the way they'd come.

Khaldun and Mira followed, Alanna and Leda right behind them. They ran into Augustine on the main level. Shatter was lying on the ground, and the court healer was tending to his wound. It looked like the blade had missed his eye, but it had torn open an ugly gash along the side of his head.

"Where did the elves go?" Jezebel demanded.

"They left through the same escape tunnel they used to get inside," Augustine said with a sigh. "My people pursued them, but once Nyro had made it out of Lady Mira's null, she collapsed the tunnel."

"We've got to get Emma back before it's too late," said Jezebel. "Besides the fact that she's family, Nyro could use her the same way she did Syllith."

Khaldun nodded. He led the way out to the courtyard, Jezebel and Mira on his heels. Alanna and Leda had followed them, too.

"You two get back inside to our chambers," Jezebel told them. "Bar the door and remain there until I come for you."

"We want to help!" Alanna said. "Why can't we come, too?"

"We'll do everything in our power to get her back. Now, *do as I say!*"

Alanna still appeared defiant, but Leda dragged her away, back inside the keep.

"Chieftain Mira," a voice said. She turned to see Kashi hurrying over to her. "My apologies, but I released the dragons so they could hunt. They can become rather, ah, testy when hungry."

"Yes, of course," Mira said, gazing up at the battlements and realizing only now that the dragons were gone. "Thank you," she added, gripping his arm. "But please, don't call me chieftain. Lavinia is your leader."

"The dragons have decided otherwise," he said with a grin.

Mira let it go. She'd have to address this issue eventually, but there was no time right now. She eliminated her null and Khaldun removed his carpet from the void. The two of them and Jezebel shot into the sky moments later.

A dragon swooped in from above, roaring at them. It was Magna. He showed Mira an image of her riding him while he breathed fire on the elvish camp.

"Magna, no," she said out loud. She formed a vision of him hunting elk and deer.

The dragon roared again, soaring off in the other direction.

Khaldun made them invisible and flew over the enemy camp. They searched for any sign of Nyro or Emma's whereabouts, but couldn't find them anywhere.

"Look!" Jezebel said suddenly, pointing toward the waterfall.

Mira turned, and was almost blinded. Another portal had formed, the brilliant light turning night into day. Khaldun shot toward it, and they spotted Nyro moving through it, someone floating along in front of her. On the other side, Mira could see the same island and castle that had been visible before.

The portal closed before Khaldun could reach it.

"*Damn!*" Jezebel shouted.

Nyro had taken Emma to the elven continent.

Allison flew northeast with Sage, Allure, and Gregor, all four of them calling air to speed their journey. She kept alert, ready to banish any demons that might show up, but none did.

They slowed down when they reached the university, and Allure opened a portal in the barrier, closing it again behind them. As they approached the central quad, Allison spotted a shadow racing across their path. She pointed it out to Sage, who changed course, shooting higher into the sky. From this vantage point, Allison realized at least seven or eight demons were swirling around and around the buildings.

"How did they find us?" asked Sage.

"I don't know, but I think they're looking for the tower," said Allure. "It's invisible to them, but they're sure to notice us when we get closer."

"We've got no choice," said Sage. "That's the only place this will work."

Allure closed her eyes for a moment. When she opened them, she said, "Take us in fast."

"All right," Sage said skeptically.

"Be ready," Allure said, catching Allison's gaze.

They shot earthward and headed for the tower. A demon appeared right in front of them, but Allison banished it, turning it to smoke. Another erupted out of the earth when they landed, but Allure took care of that one. The others closed in, but at that moment, a ring of fire formed around them and the tower. The demons tried to move through it, but it repelled them.

"Quickly," said Allure. "This won't work for long."

"Your doing?" Sage asked as she tucked her carpet into the void.

Allure shook her head.

Sage raised both arms and spoke an incantation. Allison and Gregor followed Allure through the building's brick wall, Sage right behind them.

A chill ran down Allison's spine. The shadowy interior seemed to extend forever in all directions, only the stone floor visible.

Sage released Syllith from the void. "We're in the seven-sided tower?" she asked. Sage nodded. "I always wondered what it looked like in here. Now I wish I didn't know."

"Are you ready?" Allure asked.

"As much as I'll ever be," Syllith muttered. She undressed, dropping her robes, and lay down on the floor. "Let's get this over with."

Allure had everyone back away. Then, she held out one hand, and shackles of stone grew out of the floor, pinning Syllith's wrists and ankles. She tested her bonds for a moment, but then fell unconscious. Allure began uttering a long string of incantations.

Allison had never witnessed the rite of binding. She'd been present for her own, of course, but remembered nothing about it.

Syllith cried out in pain, thrashing against her bonds, but then went still again. A golden glow emanated from her. Green flames engulfed her body, but didn't burn her, despite their intense heat.

Allure recited a series of spells, her voice loud and clear. Waves of power radiated from her, and Allison found herself growing woozy. After several more minutes, Allure produced a silver dagger, dropping to one knee and plunging it into Syllith's heart.

Withdrawing the dagger and setting it aside on the stone, Allure moved to Syllith's head, placing her hands on her temples and closing her eyes. After several more minutes, she got to her feet, holding her arms to her sides and chanting in some foreign tongue. Allison didn't recognize the words, but heard Gregor's name among them.

Flames erupted again, this time coming from inside Syllith's body. They were blue, and emitted no heat, nor did they burn her flesh. Finally, the flames receded, and Allure said, "It is done."

The stone shackles disappeared into the floor. Syllith moaned, her eyes fluttering open. "I feel awful." Sage helped her to her feet, and Allure put her robes on her. Syllith seemed a little unsteady on her feet, holding onto Sage for balance. "It worked?"

Gregor nodded. "Yes, my lady. I know your true name."

Syllith nodded. "We'd better get on with it," she said, taking a deep breath. "There is a place Enigma and I used to go. A little waterfall on the stream north of the quad. Could we go there for the final step?"

"I'm sorry, but it wouldn't be safe," Allure said, her eyes welling up. She swept one arm in a giant arc, and their surroundings vanished, revealing the area outside the tower. The demons were racing around them, trying to get in. "They'll find you the moment we leave this building."

"I know the place," Sage said with a sniffle. Allison realized she was crying. She held out one hand, casting an illusion. Half of the surrounding area turned into forest, overlooking a stream with a small waterfall. The university was still visible the other way, the demons swirling round and round.

"Yes," Syllith said with a gasp. "This is it." With Allure's help, she moved toward the water, sitting down on the bank.

Sage wiggled her fingers, and a perfect simulacrum of Enigma appeared, sitting next to Syllith. He put his arm around her, and she leaned into him. Allure sobbed, and Allison had to wipe the tears from her eyes.

"My love," said Syllith.

They stood still for a few moments, the gurgling of the waterfall and the chirping of birds the only sounds. Then Syllith held Enigma tight and said, "Do it now, before I change my mind."

Gregor took a deep breath. "Syllith Fierceheart... I name thee!"

Syllith held onto Enigma without flinching or crying out. Flame consumed her, and it was done. A brief roaring sound reached their ears from outside the tower before the demons turned to smoke and did not return. Sage canceled her illusion. Enigma disappeared, and darkness surrounded them once again.

CHAPTER TWENTY-EIGHT
THE ROAD AHEAD

haldun and Mira woke at dawn and headed down to the great hall for breakfast. They'd stayed up late the night before, only getting a few hours of sleep. Allison, Allure, Sage, and Gregor had returned after midnight to report that they'd been successful. Nyro's demons were gone. Mira knew how close Khaldun had been to Syllith, and her sacrifice, however necessary, came as a major blow.

Not long after the mages' return, the elvish armies had disappeared. Their entire camp vanished without a trace. The sorcerers believed Nyro had tucked her people into the void single-handedly, and flown away on her carpet.

After breakfast, Stoutwall's people cleared the tables, and rearranged them for a privy council meeting. Prince Augustine presided. Also present were Princes Leto and Carlo, Commandant Bishop, Princesses Jezebel, Allison, and Yolanda, Shatter, Sage, Allure, Battleaxe, Mist, Gregor, and Governor Amelia, along with Augustine's mages and advisers.

"We need to decide how to proceed," Augustine said, once his steward had called the meeting to order. "My understanding is that Nyro has taken Princess Jezebel's steward, Emma, who is also a witch. She can trigger her transformation into a sorcerer, bind her, and force her to bind demons, becoming a necromancer. And using her connection to Emma, she can control those demons. It seems we're right back in the same situation we were before."

"With all due respect, Your Highness," said Allure, "it's not the same at all. Because of Syllith's sacrifice, we have destroyed the Sacred Circle. In life, they were the most powerful necromancers in the history of Anoria. In death, they were the strongest demons ever created. Yes, Nyro can repeat what she did with Syllith, but the demons she controls this time will not be nearly as strong.

"Moreover, the members of the Sacred Circle were fiercely loyal to her in life. We have no reason to believe the same wasn't true in death. However, any new crop of demons she enlists will almost certainly not share their loyalty. She'll have to force them into service. And I daresay they will not be as dedicated to her cause as the last group."

"Thank you," said Augustine with a nod.

"Is there no way we can rescue Emma?" said Jezebel. "She's not only my steward, Your Highness, she's also my s-sister," she added, her bottom lip trembling.

"She took her to the elven continent," said Sage. "It would take many weeks to get there by ship. By then, it will be too late—Nyro has probably already started the process of transforming Emma and binding new demons."

"There is a way we might get there faster," Allure said pensively. "But not yet."

"What?" said Khaldun. "How? The only faster way I can think of would be opening a portal like Nyro did. Unfortunately, we have no way to do that."

"As a matter of fact, we do," said Allure, taking a deep breath.

"We do?" said Governor Amelia, looking confused.

"Enigma never destroyed the artifact you took from Dredmort," Allure said to Khaldun. "However, the problem is that none of us are powerful enough to use it that way. Yet."

"Yet?" asked Jezebel. "How can we get one of you to that point? My sister is probably being tortured as we speak, just like Syllith was."

"One of us would have to become a necromancer," said Allure.

"I'll do it," said Khaldun. "We all knew this day might come. And if this is the only way to rescue Emma, it'll be well worth it."

"No, you don't understand," said Allure, locking eyes with Allison. "Only *one* of us would become strong enough to create a portal."

"What, me?" said Allison, sounding shocked.

"You and I are the only ones with a strong enough affinity for the spirit world," said Allure. "And I lack the raw power."

Allison took a deep breath, letting it out in a long sigh. "All right. Then I'll do it." She squeezed Jezebel's hand. "I'll get Emma back."

Allure shook her head. "You'd also have to bind a particularly strong demon. We know of only one that would be suitable. But she's not ready, and you're not yet strong enough to control her, even if she were."

"I'm sorry, but how do you know all of this?" Yolanda asked incredulously. "This sounds rather hypothetical."

"It's the entity from the tower, isn't it?" said Khaldun. "She's a demon."

Allure took a deep breath, turning to catch Sage's gaze. Sage nodded. "Yes. She took Allison's measure when we were there last night."

"Who is she?" Jezebel asked. "Or who was she in life?"

"We are not at liberty to say," Allure replied. "Her name is Shadow. That is as much as I can reveal at this time."

"Why?" asked Augustine.

"Shadow has been the university's true leader for centuries," said Sage.

"She has?" said Governor Amelia. "Why have I never heard of her?"

"Shadow has revealed herself only to select sorcerers over the years," said Allure.

"I only learned of her existence after Henry's downfall fifteen years ago," said Sage. "And only because we lost Enigma."

"What we can tell you now is that Shadow will be joining this fight," said Allure, "when the time is right."

"And when will that be?" said Jezebel. "My sister is suffering *right now.*"

"I'm sorry for putting it this way, but time is *not* of the essence where Emma is concerned," said Sage. "Nyro is certain to have triggered her transformation and bound her by now. Emma will be safe because Nyro *needs* her to control her new demons. As an elf—or as a demon for that matter—doing so would be impossible. Even for her."

"None of us have ever been to the elven continent," said Khaldun. "We wouldn't even know where to find her."

"That may not be true," said Amelia. She waved her wand, and a book appeared on the table. "Nyro made Syllith record her rise to power on the elven continent. Those records were left behind when Syllith returned to Anoria. But on her way from Hido to the university, she wrote everything down again. From memory, but her recall was quite good.

"In these pages, you will find the details of her captivity. Where they held her, Nyro's other holdings under her elven name, Estrid, as well as details about the mage who rescued her. Once you are ready to go there, this information should help you find Emma."

"Thank you, Governor Amelia," said Jezebel.

"Yes, thank you," said Augustine. "That will be a tremendous help in the future. But now, we must decide what to do in the present. Of the fifty thousand troops who entered the battle here, only a little over twenty thousand have survived. The surviving elves disappeared, and we don't know where they went. And there is still a force of ten thousand outside of Highgate City."

"Your Highness, I spoke with our witch, Camilla, right before we started," said Jezebel. "She reports that Nyro and her remaining army have returned to Spanbrook. By her estimate, their force numbers close to fifty thousand.

"Also, Princess Salerna reports that the elvish army has disappeared from her doorstep as well. That group has not yet shown up in Spanbrook, but my guess is that is where they are headed."

"That would be my guess as well," said Augustine. "We have dealt Nyro what I am sure was an unexpected blow. She is probably regrouping to give herself time to assemble a new cadre of demon mages. How much time, we cannot say. But we have to assume it won't be long.

"Between our remaining forces here and Highgate's army, we have the only remaining soldiers in Dorshire and northern Maeda. We must convince Princess Miranda of Bayfast to come to our aid. As well as Prince Kamari of Okset, and Princess Zuri of Horn. The Shifari armies are quite formidable. Uniting the continent may be the only way we can defeat Nyro."

"We can contact Princess Miranda's sorcerer by mirror," said Khaldun. "And my mirror is connected to that of Prince Kamari's sorcerer in Okset. But we'll need to send an emissary to Horn. They've refused to establish communications with us in the past."

"Your Highness, we can count on the dragon lords in any future battles as well," said Mira.

"Yes, please tell us about your relationship with them," said Augustine. "We all noticed that it was you riding the lead dragon."

Mira sighed. "The dragons have insisted upon making *me* the chieftain. Which is obviously absurd. I'd never even seen a dragon up close before this, never mind ridden one. Members of Chieftain Lavinia's family have led the dragon lords for generations.

"However, she and the other riders have agreed to support us for the duration of this conflict. The dragons follow their sire, Magna, and at this point, Magna has bonded with me. I'm not sure that I can command him, per se, but so far, he has, ah, agreed with my suggestions."

Some of the others chuckled.

"You are, of course, free to handle the dragon lords as you see fit," said Augustine. "However, it would be quite helpful for our cause if you were to accept your position as their chieftain, at least until we have defeated Nyro."

"Yes, Your Highness."

The meeting adjourned, and Mira left the hall with Khaldun, Jezebel, and Allison.

"Thank you both for volunteering to rescue Emma," Jezebel said to Khaldun and Allison. "I can't begin to imagine the hell she must be enduring."

"Of course, Your Highness," Khaldun said.

"We know for sure Nyro will keep her alive," said Allison. "Once I'm able, we *will* get her back."

Jezebel nodded. "Well, we had better go spend some time with Alanna and Leda."

"How are they doing?" Mira asked. "They had quite the ordeal last night."

"They're blaming themselves for Emma's abduction," Allison said with a sigh.

"Oh, no," said Mira. "There's nothing they could have done."

"Try telling them that," Jezebel said. "It's a good thing your null was in place. If they'd hit those elves with a couple of simple spells, the elves probably would have killed them."

"I can try talking to them, too, if you'd like," said Mira.

"Thank you," Jezebel said.

"Princess Allison," a deep voice said, and the four of them turned. Shatter had just emerged from the hall. "You fought with courage yesterday. I saw you save Battleaxe from the elvish mage."

"Thank you," Allison said, sounding surprised. "She would have done the same for me."

"Of course," Shatter replied with a nod. "I would be honored if you would consider training with me during your stay. It has been many years since I've had a worthy sparring partner."

"I look forward to it," she said with a smile.

Shatter headed up the stairs, and Allison turned to the others, her eyes and mouth wide open in shock. "*Shatter* wants *me* as a sparring partner?"

"Better you than me," Khaldun said with a chuckle.

"You'd better wear an extra helmet," said Jezebel.

"I'm not sure it'll help," said Allison. "He punched right through the ones the elves were wearing."

The princesses headed up to their chambers, and Mira left the keep with Khaldun. They ran into Battleaxe and Imani out in the courtyard. The two of them were laughing about something.

"There you are," said Battleaxe. "Imani, Mist, and I are heading into the city tonight to find a decent tavern. I'd say we all deserve to get good and drunk. Would the two of you care to join us?"

"I'm pretty sure we would," Mira said, looking up at Khaldun. "Right, my lord?"

"Yes, indeed," he replied with a grin. "Her ladyship and I would love to accompany you."

"We'll see you tonight, then," said Battleaxe.

Khaldun and Mira spent some time with Allure later that day—he'd hoped she might be able to help him with his transformations. He explained that he could change his hair, eye, or skin color—or others'—but nothing else.

"That's how it started for Semblant," she said. "He could alter little details in his appearance, or in objects he touched, but nothing more. But you're able to create lasting changes in others? Their appearance doesn't revert to normal once you've broken contact?"

"No, it stays the same," he said with a shrug.

"Can you show me?"

Khaldun focused for a moment and turned Allure's hair pink.

"Without physical contact," Allure said, sounding impressed as she ran her hands through her mane.

They spent almost an hour working on it, and despite Allure's best efforts, Khaldun made no progress. Finally, she took his head in her hands and closed her eyes. "I do sense latent powers within you. In time, you could become a shapeshifter… and I believe shifting others may be possible for you, too."

"Meaning I could turn someone into a dragon?" he asked skeptically.

Allure shook her head slowly, her eyes shut tight. "It's hard to say. That ability seems less certain." She opened her eyes, withdrawing her hands. "I've never heard of anyone doing that before. But Semblant was the first one to change objects, so who knows?"

Khaldun nodded. "Thank you. I have new motivation to practice."

"Now, can you change my hair back, please?" Allure said.

Khaldun chuckled, but Mira ran her fingers through Allure's hair, saying, "I don't know… I kind of like it." Her heart fluttered as Allure gave her a sultry smile. But Allure insisted, so Khaldun restored her normal appearance.

That night, Khaldun, Mira, and Allison headed off to Stoutwall City with Imani, Battleaxe, and Mist. Unlike Spanbrook and many of the other princedoms' capitals, it was a few miles away from the castle. The city was quiet—most of the citizens had evacuated ahead of the invasion—but they found an open tavern. They took a large table in the back corner, and a man hurried out moments later to serve them ale.

"Where's Princess Jezebel?" Battleaxe asked before taking a swig of her drink.

"In the castle, keeping an eye on our two mischief-makers," Allison said with a grin.

"Speaking of mischief," said Mist, "one of them might have told us that Princess Jezebel is pregnant?"

"She is," Allison said with a nod.

"And the father might be a wayfarer?" Battleaxe said. "Sounds like that was a good time, eh?"

"Alanna's going to pay for this," Allison said, turning a deeper shade of gold as she drank her ale. "Yes, one of the wayfarers is the father."

Mira felt bad for Allison and decided to save her any further embarrassment by changing the subject. She told the others about the reading Allure performed for Khaldun.

"You'd better get to work on that," said Battleaxe. "After losing Semblant, we could use a new shapeshifter."

"I agree, my lord," said Imani. "You could transform an entire regiment into giant bears. Combined with the dragons, they could decimate Nyro's entire army."

"I'll see what I can do," Khaldun said.

Their food arrived a minute later, and they grew quiet as they ate. They drank more and chatted late into the evening, until finally, Imani raised her glass and said, "To reuniting with old friends."

Battleaxe lifted her glass and said, "And to our fallen comrades, Semblant and Cyclone."

"And Legion," Mist added, "though I hardly knew them."

"And Gemma," said Mira, her eyes welling up with tears as she lifted her glass.

Khaldun gazed around at them for a moment, before finally lifting his glass and saying, "And Syllith."

"Syllith most of all," Allison said.

They clinked their glasses and drank.

After breakfast the next morning, Khaldun and Mira headed out of the castle to take a walk around the grounds, hand in hand. They made their way up to the river, and sat on the bench looking out over the top of the waterfall.

"This is the same place we sat last time we were here together," said Mira. "When we were discussing my return to Graystone, remember?"

"I do. These are darker days, by far, but I must say, I'm much happier this time," he said, putting his arm around her and holding her tight.

"Me, too," she said, leaning into him. "The days ahead will get darker still, I'm sure. I'm glad I don't have to face them alone."

They sat quietly for a few minutes, enjoying the view, until an ear-splitting roar shattered the quiet, startling both of them. Jumping to her feet, Mira turned to see Magna standing behind them, lowering his head toward her.

Caressing his snout, she said, "You frightened us!"

The dragon purred, sending her a vision of her flying over the lake on his back. Mira returned the same image, but with one addition. The dragon purred louder.

"Magna has extended his permission for you to go for a ride with us," she told Khaldun with a grin. "Are you feeling up to it?"

"Me?" he said, fear in his eyes. "Riding a dragon?"

"And why not? I've been a passenger on your carpet for the last fifteen years. It's your turn!"

"All right," he said, "let's do it!"

Magna lowered his head and one wing, and Mira showed him how to climb onto his back. Once the two of them were seated, Mira in front, and Khaldun holding onto her for dear life, Magna took off, beating his mighty wings. They soared over the waterfall, and then the lake, far below, and Khaldun whooped for joy.

Mira didn't know what the future might hold, but at that moment, she felt like she could take on the world.

To be continued...

www.ingramcontent.com/pod-product-compliance
Lightning Source LLC
Chambersburg PA
CBHW051322190726
48290CB00001B/268